T0366160

Reunion

A Self-Contained Trilogy

George D. Schultz

Order this book online at www.trafford.com
or email orders@trafford.com

Most Trafford titles are also available at major online book retailers.

Printed in the United States of America.

ISBN: 978-1-4907-4362-2 (sc)
ISBN: 978-1-4907-4361-5 (e)

Trafford rev. 01/15/2015

www.trafford.com

North America & international
toll-free: 1 888 232 4444 (USA & Canada)
fax: 812 355 4082

PREFACE

HAVE YOU EVER WONDERED -- what it would be like, should your path cross, with a significant (or, maybe not all *that* significant) other, from *way* out of your past?

After all those years -- *decades*, maybe -- would some almost-long-forgotten romance be, magically, reignited? Would this be an answer to some conscious (or subconscious) lifelong prayer? Would you -- *could* you -- recapture some (or all) of the, real-or-imagined, "magic", that had once sprung (whether in your imagination -- or otherwise) from the relationship?

This is *not* to advise you (or admonish you) to "be careful what you wish for". Far *from* it! The adventure *might* turn out to be every bit as rewarding -- as you might have imagined. Or even hoped for. It may jolly well *surprise* you. (*Shock* you, even.)

In this celebrated tome, we bring you the stories -- of three such, by chance, reunions. Three such monumental discoveries.

But, we also ask the question -- whether time and space could/does *ever* "cooperate", with the many situations, that the expectant mind, the uninhibited imagination, the possibly-needful psyche, might have come to expect.

Can anyone really divine such things?

As that famed philosopher, of Upper Montclair, NJ, -- Lawrence Peter Berra (aka Yogi) -- once said: "I can sum it up in two words ... Ya Never Know".

THE BOOK OF GORDON

ONE

The year: 1965. The month: September. The place: A large, rather- opulent, hotel -- close by O'Hare International Airport, in Chicago, Illinois.

I'd just shown up -- blown into the, unexpectedly-large, unquestionably-lavish, hospitality room. This, after having, hurriedly, unpacked my few travel belongings, while initially ensconced -- in my, not-quite-so-overwhelming, (relatively-cheap) quarters, located two floors above.

I was trying to size up -- my many fellow writers. This was the first time I'd ever attended the renowned *ChicagoLand Writers Conference*! Listen, this gathering was (Huzzah!) one of the most prestigious writers conferences, in the known, civilized, world. In point of fact, after the, world-famous, *Maui Writers Conference* -- which had always taken place, in Hawaii, shortly before Labor Day, (for decades) -- this one, in Illinois, had always been the second-most-sought-after gathering, of us, "ink-stained", writer-type stiffs.

I'd called myself knowing a goodly number of authors -- mostly fellow fiction-creating wretches. To get someone -- to publish a non-fiction "masterpiece" -- you most usually have to be someone incredibly famous. Or incredibly infamous. At least, that's the way it's always seemed to work.

Obviously, no one, apparently, would care about -- what I'd ever thought of "The Presidencity". Or of our sainted Congress. (And don't get me started, on them!) But, I'm positive that -- were my name (say) Barak Obama -- there would, undoubtedly, be a large potential audience, for such an "informed" tome. Merely a fact of life. (Well, a writer's life, anyway.)

Looking around the room, there were only two people, whom I'd semi-recognized. Both were black men -- from Rochester, New York. I'd once traveled the 50 miles -- from my apartment, in Buffalo, to attend their august group! There had been seven people in attendance, on that occasion. All black men. I'd been the only Caucasian, and -- by far -- the youngest man there. I was 31- or 32-years-old, at the time. It seemed forever ago!

At thirty-five, I'd appeared to have aged, substantially, more than they had.

There was, however, a pretty fair racial mixture, in attendance, in Chicago. A few more whites-- than blacks. And ten or twelve more women -- than men! Always a nice mix -- albeit a bit of a surprise. On the other hand, I seemed to not recognize any of them. Any of the women. Or, really, any of the white guys. At least, at first -- that appeared, to be the case. Not even close!

Hold on! Wait a minute! That one lady! The one -- seated, with four other women, on the large, really-fancy, white-leather, rounded, couch, in the far corner! I could swear that our paths had crossed before. Somewhere! Once -- at the very least. Probably more often than that! I was an-inch-shy -- of being absolutely positive -- but, I felt that she was not a writer! At least, not at whatever time I might've known her. If I'd known her, at all. Well, I didn't believe -- that she'd been involved, in the "writer's craft", at any rate. Not "back then" -- whenever then might have been.

Who is she? Who could she possibly be? More importantly, what do I do ... to meet her? Re-meet her? Greet her? What can I do, to -- one way, or another -- get to make contact with her?

In the past, I'd attended two other such "intellectual" gatherings -- in, home-town, Buffalo -- plus one, in Cleveland. The first one -- in my own stomping grounds -- had consisted of many easy-to-approach people; no matter the race, age, or gender. The second, of those two, seemed to have been attended -- almost exclusively -- by a snobbish bunch of, totally-unapproachable, cretins. The get-together, in Ohio, had fallen somewhere in between.

So, how to act -- here, in Chicago? Apparently, never my strong suit. Obviously, never my strong suit! Well, I'd not had all that much experience, at the noble trait. Even at my age. Just ask Carole -- my former wife.

This woman, though -- the one in Chicago -- who'd appeared to be (roughly) my age, was conversing (quite animatedly) with two, other ladies. On that dazzling (to me) rounded couch!

Listen, I've never been comfortable -- when it came to interrupting people! Anyone! No matter where! And (again, to my way of thinking) "horning in" is a blatant form, of -- unforgivable -- interruption! Still, I've never been considered an introvert. It's just that -- in that particular area, of conduct -- color me "a shivering coward". Or -- as I've always liked to think of it -- I'm merely "overly courteous".

A man, my age -- and "culture" -- should never be nearly so hung-up. on the, well-known, horns of such a dilemma. Maybe, in this situation, it was simply the, more-intimidating-than-I-could-ever-have-imagined, surrounding environment. But, I was drawn -- overwhelmingly -- to the feminine quartette. So, I (casually, mind you) "sauntered" over, in their direction.

I narrowed my gaze -- «lowered my sights» -- upon my unsuspecting quarry! Except she was not that "unsuspecting"! Not after she'd looked away, from the elderly lady -- with whom she'd seemed to be engaged, in deep conversation! It was then -- that she saw me!

"Gordon!" she'd half-shouted. "Gordon Bloodworth! Gordon! How nice! How nice ... to see you! How gloriously nice it is ... to see you! To see you, again!"

"Dahse? That's you? That's really you? Dahse?"

Actually, her name was Doris. Doris Clayton! But, from the time she was a little girl, her father had always called her "Dahse"! (Rhymes -- loosely -- with words like "possibility" or "hostile" or "fossil". Very loosely! Best I can do. It's the "ah" sound, that does it.)

Until I'd met her -- in early-1951 -- her "Daddy" was the only person, in the entire universe, to have ever called her that. Ever! But, I'd moved into his world! His monopoly! Almost immediately! She'd -- thankfully -- always seemed to have liked the "intrusion". Had advised me -- on many occasions -- that she'd out and out welcomed it! Most gratifying for me!

Her husband was named Eddie. He and I had served, in the Navy, together. I'd always called him "Dad". That was a, kind-of-slang, word -- very popular, back then. Largely kicked around -- in the early-fifties -- by a whole lot of comedians. Most notably, by Phil Harris -- and his radio show "second-banana", Elliot Lewis. Bob Hope, occasionally, had referred to Bing Crosby -- as "Dad".

So, from the start, the Clayton couple had always been -- to me, anyway -- "Dad and Dahse"! It all had simply seemed to have fit. That might appear to be a bit, of a stretch -- but, it actually did work!

At the time, Eddie and I had both been assigned to *The Fleet Aviation Accounting Office* -- located on the huge *Naval Air Station,* in Norfolk, Virginia.

He had spent most of the previous three years, aboard the aircraft carrier *USS, Kearsarge.* I'd put in less than a year, aboard the carrier, *USS Franklin D. Roosevelt* -- then, had done three months, at *Aviation Storekeeper School,* on the *Naval Air Station,* in Millington, Tennessee. Just outside Memphis. Then, it was on to *FAAO,* in Norfolk!

Eddie had always been one rate (rank) ahead of me. He'd made petty officer 2nd class -- at the same time that I'd become petty officer 3rd class. Then, a year later, we'd both moved up -- to first-class, and second-class. By then, we'd become really-fast friends.

He'd headed up the section, to which I'd been assigned -- for 15 months. And he'd been positively thrilled, for me -- when I'd gotten to head up my own section. We'd become, at that point -- I'd always thought -- really close buddies. Close enough -- that one of the less-popular members, of the office, did his best to start some really distasteful, sexual, rumors about us! He'd even expanded the slanderous, unforgiveable, campaign -- to include "Dahse"! Until Eddie and I confronted him -- in no uncertain terms -- in the men's "head"! (The "head" is the naval term -- for the bathroom.)

Eddie had married Doris -- that pretty girl, from his native Baltimore -- shortly after having been assigned to *FAAO.* I'd gotten to meet his new bride, about a month-and-a-half, after the nuptials -- once they'd taken a once-upon-a-time, attic, apartment, in Norfolk.

The place wasn't much. But, you see? Korea had just broken out -- less than a year previously -- and the "Police Action" (which still, legally, exists) had, immediately, caused a, more-than-fair-sized, almost-critical, housing-shortage, throughout the entire Tidewater Area!

The happy couple's "apartment" had taken up the entire attic area -- of a rather-old, otherwise-two-story (plus attic), home. The Clayton's "facility" was made up -- of only one room! But, a quite-large one. The homey expanse extended the entire length-and-breadth -- of the house. But, the tenants (all of them) had to use the one available john. And that necessary convenience, had been graciously provided -- on the second floor. So, it was a bit of a "journey" -- when one had to "go"!

The house, itself, had originally sported four bedrooms. All, on that same second floor. Presumably, these rooms had all been, similarly, "converted" -- into, apparently-one-room, "apartments". (Somehow or another.) I was given to understand that they'd all been afforded kitchen utilities! How? The mind boggles! I cannot imagine such a, tiny, torturously-unusual, unit! Especially -- times four! And all on that one floor!

If the Claytons' relationship -- that, between husband and wife -- had ever seen "one bug in the ointment" (and it was so unlike "imperceptive little old me" to have recognized such a problem) that uneasy quotient was the fact that the marriage had, forever, seemed so, totally, "one-way". At least, it had always appeared that way -- to me. She was so wrapped up in him! Totally taken -- with every aspect, of her husband!

But, regrettably, there had been so many times -- even in front of me (maybe especially in front of me) -- where he had seemed, well, completely unresponsive, toward her! I mean totally unresponsive! Unresponsive -- to a fault! In my eyes, anyway! I simply couldn't imagine -- the, seemingly-constant, degree of coldness, in his manner.

She was always wanting to hold his hand -- or even "smooch" a little -- and he just seemed to always ignore her "advances". At least, when I was around. In their own private world? Who knew? But, to me, the implication was never good! Still, the marriage was working! Or, at least, it seemed to be!

Probably once-a-month -- or, maybe, every six weeks -- they'd take me, up to Baltimore, with them, for an entire weekend. That was always great! I'd always appreciated these little get-aways! It was extremely nice of them. And -- without fail -- I'd, forever, looked forward to those welcomed weekend "respites".

Their parents had, really-neat, homes! Those glorious old, narrow, two-story, row-houses (with traditional skylights -- and equally-traditional, ivory stoops-and-steps). These picturesque, parental, domiciles were located -- merely a half-block apart. Both in the, equally-picturesque, Glenmont area -- of the Maryland city. "Dad" and "Dahse" had, pretty well, grown up together. Chums from the third -- or fourth -- grades on.

And, it had always seemed -- to me, anyway -- that Doris' parents had held the same troubling opinion of their relationship, as I'd had. That the young Claytons' partnership <u>had</u> been -- overwhelmingly -- "one-way". And her folks -- the O'Banions -- seemed to be not totally happy about the situation. (Especially, Norman -- the "daddy", of "Dahse"!) Well, they always did their best -- to disguise the unease. Around me, anyway. But, still, you could tell. It was <u>there</u>!

I remember this one time -- a week or so before Christmas, of 1952, in Norfolk -- when the three of us had just finished trimming a small tree, situated atop their table-model, *Admiral*, black-and-white, TV. Doris and I had decided that the project -- had needed substantially more icicles. So, we'd walked down, to the drugstore -- two blocks away, on Newport, at 35th Street -- and had picked up a box, of the tinsel dandies. When we'd gotten back, from that critical errand -- Eddie had fallen asleep, in his overstuffed chair.

"Aw look, Gord," his wife had gushed. "Isn't he cute?"

"Yeah, 'Dahse'," I'd grunted. "He's cute."

But, I remember thinking: Please, Lord! Whoever I may wind up marrying ... please let her be *even close*, to being that taken, with me!

Doris was only "slightly pregnant" at that point. By the time that I was discharged -- in April, of 1953 -- she was "showing" -- flagrantly! "Standing out" -- pretty good!

In 1953, I'd gone ahead, and had moved back to Buffalo -- once I'd been "discombobulated". from "This Man's Navy". Had begun my glorious "civilian life" -- at age 23 -- by moving in, to my mother's apartment. She'd long-since divorced my father -- who I'd seldom seen, since I was seven or eight. She was living, in a small flat -- in suburban Depew -- with my sister (who was seven years my junior).

I'd wound up working, at a whole bunch of low-paying -- and highly-frustrating -- jobs. A total, unproductive, series of them! Often, as a hotel clerk. Working midnights, most usually. Although I did do a round or two as a (blatantly-unsuccessful) vacuum cleaner salesman. I'd also met with an, equally-lacking-in-positive-results, career -- attempting to sell such items, as encyclopedias, waterless cookware, as well as, horribly-overpriced, cutlery sets. There was also a so-so endeavor -- in the Wonderful World of Bartending. (They're now known as "mixologists", Dahling. My own, personal, universe was not nearly as "sophisticated" -- nor as satisfying, nor as stimulating -- as that term would seem to indicate.)

This all could've been avoided -- had I wanted to "follow Mother's direction"! Had I obeyed her, oft-repeated, edict -- and had gone on, to attend Accounting School. Heavy emphasis -- on the word "direction"! The (ah) "suggestion" had always seemed more akin -- to a Gestapo command. Mother was never the epitome, of diplomacy! She was, undoubtedly, correct -- in her, summing-up, analytical, evaluation, of my employment prospects! I probably -- I undoubtedly -- should have heeded her "advice". But -- stubborn old me -- I did not! I'm sure there was a moral in there -- somewhere! Could it have been her "presentation"? A little -- on the aggressive side! Continually!

Listen, for all my entire life, I'd always hated school! Always! Any school! At any time! At any location! At any age! Hate, hate -- hate! Had, as a matter of fact, dropped out -- halfway through the 11th grade! To join the Navy! "See the world" -- as they'd always promised/advertised! To be stationed, on an aircraft carrier -- as the Buffalo recruiter had promised! That coveted assignment -- had, thankfully, been realized! I'd loved that ship!

The glorious duty -- as a "plane pusher", on the flight deck -- had lasted eight or nine, most-fulfilling, months! Then, sadly, the ship was put, into dry-dock! And I was sent off -- to Tennessee! To school! Org!

Let me tell you: While I'd been a good bit more successful -- throughout my Naval Accounting career -- than for which I'd ever given myself credit, I was not thrilled, with the accounting field, itself! So, subsequent accounting school was out!

Besides, as a civilian, I was going to make a fortune -- selling those, remarkable, encyclopedias! And those, very-finest, "dirt suckers"! And/or a whole lot of other goods and "services"! If not them, then I was advised that I was "home free" -- in that "always-dependable", honorable, field -- the used-car universe! Actually, that statement -- fortunately -- turned out to be, at least, "semi-true", for me. At least somewhat! I'd -- finally -- found a, semi-comfortable, niche, in the "pre-owned" vehicle mart!

Eventually, the constant, never-ending -- day in/ day out -- maternal-"advisory", conflict got to be way too much! Was constantly "in the way" -- in my wondrous home life. The proverbial 600-pound elephant (or whatever) in the room!

This all came to a head -- about a-quarter-of-the-way through my first year, of my floundering, in the, diverse, "enterprising" career path(s), that I'd chosen! Especially did the ever-present thunderhead really begin to bloom -- once I'd begun dating! Seeing a woman -- named Carole. She was from Cheektowaga -- another Buffalo suburb.

I'd wound up moving into a "posh", basic-needs, single, $10.00-a-weel, room -- upstairs, over a neighborhood bar, in Cheektowaga. Only three blocks, from the parents' home -- of "The Love Of My Life"!

It was shortly before I'd "declared my independence" -- from all this inspired, hardening-by-the-minute, maternal "guidance" -- when I'd gotten a letter, from Eddie, stating that his wife had miscarried, some months previously. That missive -- the sad news, of it -- would be the last correspondence that, I'd believed, I would ever hear, from my former "shipmate". But, who could know? Who could tell?

Carole and I had gone ahead, and "tied the knot" -- in September, of 1954. The non-lavish ceremony -- held, at *Resurrection Catholic Church,* in Cheektowaga -- was (loudly) "boycotted" by my mother! This -- despite the fact that my bride was kind (and thoughtful) enough, to have asked my sister, Anne, to be her Maiden of Honor. (My sibling was, of course, honored -- to be so designated. And she had -- throwing off her own ration, of uncalled-for, maternal, hostility -- hastily, accepted the honor!

She was, of course, magnificent -- in the "role". Well, she figured to be!)

Mother'd had no problem -- that my wife-to-be was to be Carole. That -- the identity of the bride -- was not the problem! Far from it! The woman involved -- Carole, or anyone else -- mattered not at all! The "travesty" -- was that I was being wed, in the first place! That I'd had "the temerity" -- of taking on that manner, of "sacred responsibility" -- while my "professional career" had continued to be such "a stupid, damn, mish-mosh". (Guess who that comment had come from.)

I could have married Elizabeth Taylor -- or Princess Elizabeth -- and the bride's identity would not have made any difference, maternal boycott-wise! (The Princess, of course, had married Prince Phillip -- a couple years previously. And I've never been able -- to keep up with Miss Taylor's multi-marriage format. Probably just as well.)

Alas, my ill-fated marriage lasted "only" eight years. Eight childless years! Although extensive medical tests were made, doctors were never able to establish whose "fault" the fallow condition could be attributed to.

We'd run into other problems, of course. My "skid-more" career was not the least of them. (Logically or not -- those, employment-caused, doldrums were thought, perhaps, to be at the very bottom of our "barren" path, in the childbirth area! By more than a few people. Medical -- and non-medical.)

Seriously, behind it all, we'd never been possessed of the proverbial "two nickels ... to rub together" -- financially! Nothing close! To me, that had been the center -- around which all our other problems had orbited! We were always broke! Always! Mother was proving to be damnably correct -- dammit! At least, in that critical area! (Damnably correct!)

I'd usually managed to arrange to take Carole and me, to a movie -- virtually every Friday evening. We even used to eat -- at a wonderful fish-and-chips joint, after the outing, despite a constant challenge to our, forever-precarious, financial condition. But, it was never enough! (How could it be? How could it ever be? I mean, that -- pretty much --had been it! A two-and-a-half- or three-hour "frolic" -- on Friday nights! Period!)

In addition to my, never-ending, employment difficulties, I was (and still am) a total "music nut"! Had been, for -- literally -- all my life! (Another "sore point between Mother and me!)

At the height of Carole's-and-my fiscal difficulties -- 1958, it was -- my *Columbia 360* "Hi-Fi" record-player gave up the ghost! (This was the machine, which I'd so proudly bought -- and had paid for, with a goodly portion, of my Navy separation money. That "stupid-assed" transaction had brought about -- yet another mother/son "difficulty"!) And then -- In '58 -- my one, cannot-do-without-it possession, had, regrettably, sounded its death knell! After a long -- and, highly-distinguished -- career!

And I simply could not face the future! Not without a quality instrument -- for playing my many, cherished, almost-worshipped, LP albums. (Those records, themselves -- the number, and cost of them -- had also presented a serious number of problems, throughout the marriage.) Obviously, my spouse had never been, the least-bit, thrilled with "schmaltz". Of course, I'd retained my, life-long, rapturous, need for it! And my collection, of all those LPs simply -- overwhelmingly -- reeked of that, to-me-vital, even-critical, need Practically a "life-support", "absolutely-necessary", requirement!

A few years later, I would relate it -- to a line that Lee Remick had spoken, in the movie, *Days Of Wine And Roses.* Her character -- and that, of her costar (Jack Lemmon) -- had become an alcoholic. And, toward the end of the flick, she'd uttered the statement, "I couldn't face life ... without being able to have another drink"!

It was the same with me! I'd have been unable to face life ... without being able to listen to my cherished records! Truly -- a "schmaltzaholic"! A serious one!

So, when I'd gone ahead -- and violated all laws of reasonableness -- had bought a, brand new, floor-model, marked-way-down-in-price, demo-unit, *Olympic* hi-fidelity player -- Carole had threatened to <u>divorce</u> me! On the <u>spot</u>! Then and <u>there</u>! Had <u>seriously</u> threatened -- dissolving the marriage! It was the better part of a week -- before she'd even <u>speak</u> to me!

"I need you to go to the store ... and get a quart of milk, and a large onion", was the memorable, to-be-etched-in-stone-for-all-the-ages, statement -- that she'd ultimately spoken! That classic utterance -- had, at long last, ended "The Great Silence"!

After that, earth-shaking, shocking, <u>declaration</u>, of course, I don't know -- for sure -- but, <u>this</u> could've been the, well-known, "Beginning of The End"! Maybe it <u>was</u>! <u>Probably</u> it was! Actually, who <u>knows</u>? (I certainly don't!)

The situation simply went (or, most likely, <u>continued</u>) downhill -- from there! And at break-neck speed, most of the time! Then,, in 1962, we decided to "shoot the rapids", of New York State's -- ultra-convoluted, your-guess-is-as-good-as-mine, -- "enlightened" divorce laws! Ultimately, we managed to (in a fairly-civilized manner) disentangle ourselves, from one another! A situation which was to leave me completely <u>rattled</u> -- for the longest time! This -- despite the fact that our precarious matrimonial condition had been in-the-making! For, literally, <u>years</u>!

Two months later, Carole upped -- and <u>married</u> a college professor! A very well-off gentleman -- from *State University, at Buffalo.* As far as I know, they're still fanny-deep, in wedded bliss. I sincerely hope so. She was a nice lady! Still is -- as far as I know! So, I wish her the best! Sincerely!

❖

From a, very-fortunate, practicable, standpoint (a very strange, virtually-unknown, perch for me), I'd wound up, under no financial (or any other) obligation -- vis-a-vis our "failed marriage"! My mother kept preaching, "Thank God ... for that!" (Yeah -- I s'pose! Another correct maternal pronouncement! One which she'd never let me forget! One of many!)

I'd continued to drift -- from job to job. Had been fortunate enough, however, to have been able to rent a, rather-nice (if smallish), two-room, apartment, in Williamsville, a rather opulent community, just north of Buffalo. This "happening" took place, one month before the divorce had actually labored its way through "the system" -- and had become final.

Fortunately for me, there had existed, at that time, a fairly-long string, of 12, moderate-sized, stores -- located on Main Street. They had, strangely enough, featured a generous number, of "efficiency" (read cheap) apartments, taking up the large amount of floor space, on their second floor. My, filled-the-bill-nicely, living quarters were located, only six blocks from the wonderful *Lincoln-Mercury* dealer -- for which I'd begun toiling.

I'd started, at this nifty dealership -- as a "treasured" member, of the "clean-up" team: Eight people, who'd devoted all their illustrious, "professional", careers -- to making-ready every one, of the new, and used, cars -- for delivery to our sainted buyers. From the very start, these were fine -- extremely thoughtful (and generous) -- people, for whom to work. I was very fortunate -- to have been able "catch on", with them! Most fortunate!

A few months, into my tenure, with the dealership -- and given the promise, of "making thousands of dollars every month" -- I took a different, more-challenging, "position". I'd become a sales representative -- working out of the used car office. My course had (moderately) progressed -- to meet, with mixed results. The "promised" thousands never did come. Not all at one time, anyway. But, thankfully, the position did provide me -- with a treasured company car! Any non-Lincoln (or non-Cadillac) on the lot! A not-insignificant "fringe".

So, that was where I'd remained -- "gainfully employed" -- up to (and including) the time, of the aforementioned, highly-looked-forward-to, breathlessly-anticipated, Chicago writers gig!

I'd been -- thankfully -- able to begin to devote a fairly-sufficient amount of time, to pursuing my, newly-discovered, writer's "calling"! And to even be authorized, by my generous employers -- to tool my company car out of town, on occasion, to attend such venues, as the writers gatherings. (Was able to snarf a year-old, full-sized, Mercury -- for most of those voyages. However, for the venture, out to Illinois, I managed to purloin a, more-economical, compact, two-year-old, Plymouth Valiant.)

Probably, I was making more money there -- at the car lot -- than, at any other employment venue, in my civilian life. It just didn't seem that way! (It had never seemed to be that way! Story of my life, don'tcha know.)

In the celebrated hospitality room, of the O'Hare-area hotel, I'd been floored -- by the fact that Doris Clayton had actually recognized me! And by the fact that the woman had even been Doris Clayton! ("Dahse"!)

She'd even hastened to break away -- from her feminine counterparts! It must have taken her all of 15 seconds! Incredible! This was -- to me -- mind-boggling! Immediately -- arms extended -- she'd arisen, from the couch, and had (hurriedly) headed, straight toward me!

She enveloped those welcomed arms, around me! And I'd responded, in kind! I had, of course, embraced -- had even kissed -- this lovely woman before! Many times! But, there had always been an understood, unspoken, brother/sister "flavor" -- to whatever affection may have ever passed between us! From the moment, that we'd first *met*! *This* exchange, though -- the one, in Chicago -- was *far*, from a brother/sister exchange! (*Far* from such a display! Even *I* could figure that out! *Recognized* it -- right from the git-go!)

She was -- firmly -- pressing her lower body, up against mine! More tightly -- than *any* woman had *ever* "embraced" me, there! Including *Carole*! *Ever*! Then, Doris *kissed* me! *Deeply*! *Passionately*! "Soul-to-soul" -- as they used to say! *Imagine*!

"Dahse," I managed to rasp (at long *last*), "what ... what brings *you* here?"

"Apparently, the same thing as *you*!" Her voice was -- substantially -- stronger than *mine*, at that point! "I'm a *writer*, now, y'know! Wrote ... and I just got *published*! Published ... would you believe? ... a *romance* novel! About seven or eight months ago, actually! Just submitted my second one ... well, my *agent* did ... just this last Wednesday!"

She, more-or-less, pushed me back -- to arms length, but kept her hands upon my shoulders. Then, she smiled, broadly, and said, "It's so *good* ... so good, to *see* you, Gordon!"

She "reeled me back in" -- and kissed me again! *Deeply*! Even *more* deeply! Definitely more *passionately*! *Definitely*! Something I'd thought to be *impossible*!

I was totally *withered* -- reduced to being almost completely lifeless -- by then! Simply stood there -- my arms somehow entwined with hers! But, they'd become completely limp! They were becoming even more devoid of life -- the more overwhelmed, that I was becoming! And that fact was firming up -- as an ongoing process! Dazzlingly ongoing! Dazzlingly an ongoing -- continuing -- process!

She then led me -- as one would lead some brand-new, tongue-out, panting, slobbering, puppy -- to a small, white-metal, two-fannies, loveseat, located directly across the room, from where she'd been, so recently, seated.

"Now," she half-sighed, "tell me all about it, Gordon! Tell me ... all about you! All about yourself!"

"I ... uh .... I really don't know where to begin! Married, y'know. Well, I was. Was married, y'know. Married ... and now, I'm divorced! No kids! No money! No really-wonderful job! No nothin'! Just, really, a schlepper, y'know! A ne'er-do-well! Seemingly, been that way ... for all of my life! Simply trying to break in, y'know. Trying to shoehorn myself ... into the writer's thing! Congratulations ... by the way! Congrats ... on your success! I'm green ... all over ... with envy!"

"Well," she responded -- in a much-lower, more-reserved, tone, "don't be. It's not really that big a thing! Not that hard! I'm not Louisa May Alcott. It's, actually, not anywhere near that difficult. The romance game, I mean. Not that hard ... to break into. Although ... God knows ... it has been a bit of a struggle, for me. I just discovered ... not all that long ago ... that the easiest way, for a new writer, to break out, is to be writing this stuff. The romance novel. There's simply such an overwhelming market for them, y'know! For these books! An overwhelming market! They're all over the place ... these books! Those books! Look in just about any store! And, listen! There are so many genres, y'know. And so many subgenres!"

"That sounds positively frightening! To me, anyway."

"Naw. Far from it! You just have to be able ... to pick the right one! The genre ... that fits your own talent! Fits your interest! Maybe your interests! Complies ... directly ... with your own hang-ups, if you will! Even your secret hang-ups, maybe! You gotta have an interest, though ... a helluva big interest ... in what it is, that you're doing! A real intense interest! Don't try and write ... about stuff, that you're not totally passionate about. Then, you don't wanna let your family ... or your friends ... read your stuff! They'll learn all about your private passions! And your, really-personal, hang-ups! Then ... if you can get onto the right agent ... voila! You're in! That's really all it takes!"

"All? That's all?"

"Yep! Not nearly as complicated ... as they always make it sound. As I probably make it sound ... even as we speak."

"Geez, Dahse! I ... I can't believe you're ... that you're here! Really here! Here ... in Chicago, for heaven sakes!"

"I can't believe that you even recognized me, Gord! I'd put on a lot of ... a lot of weight ... y'know! A lot, of weight! A helluva lot, of suet! Over a hundred pounds, I'd gained ... at one time! Have managed ... thank God ... to take most of it off! Dropped a goodly amount, of it! But, listen! I've got a long way ... a helluva long way ... to go! Trust me! A really long way!"

"You've never looked better ... or prettier ... to me! Listen, are you ... you and Eddie ... are you still ... ah ... still together? Still happily married?"

"Him? Eddie? Hah! Are you kidding? Hell no! We broke up! Long ago! And it was about damn time! I guess it's been about ten years, or so, now! Maybe a little longer! Listen, it was too just much, Gordie. Just too much! Way too much! For me, anyway! Too damn much! I mean, I just kept giving! Giving, giving, giving! And all he was doing ... was he just kept taking! Damn taking! And taking! All the time! Just simply kept taking!"

"I'd kind of thought that might be the situation," I mused. "Eventually, anyway. Had thought that ... for years, actually. Felt that was the case. Right from the git-go. But, I never ..."

"I know you never! You simply never! Maybe you should have! No! That wouldn't have been you! Not the Gordon ... the one, I always knew! And loved! It probably wouldn't even have been right! Probably wrong ... for you, to have shown any kind of emotion, in that direction! Undoubtedly, it wouldn't have been ... ah ... what would be considered to be correct! But, there were times, y'know, Gord! Times ... many of them ... when I'd wished that things would've been different! Could've been different! Could've turned out, y'know, really different! So damn different!"

"What kind of different, Dahse? I mean, I couldn't very well ..."

"I know," she rasped -- more wistfully, than I could've imagined. "Gord? Gordie, you used to, always, go on ... dreaming about some kind of perfect woman. For as long as I ever knew you ... you'd always dreamed up this woman! An imaginary woman! Some perfect woman, she was. Who'd lived ... in your dreams! Even in your ... probably in your ... well, in your fantasies! Probably only in your fantasies! I remember ... you'd get yourself, all wrapped up! Wrapped up ... in some, really-sentimental, lyric! A really, tear-filled, lyric! In some schmaltzy love song! And, I could tell! You'd be dreaming of some perfect ... some saintly perfect ... lady. Did you ever find her, Gord? Did you ever ... ?"

"No," I'd responded -- way too quickly. And way too emphatically! "Naw," I lamented. "Not even close! I don't know ... that she even exists! That she could exist. Could ever have existed. In ... or out ... of my fantasies, as you'd, so-ably, put it."

"I'm sorry, Gord. Truly sorry! I mean that! Sincerely!"

"Well, it's not that I've been all that experienced, you know. I've only been with ... been with, y'know ... been with, just one woman. Just one! In my whole, entire, life! That's been the extent of it! One woman! And I went and married her! Wound up ... marrying her, y'know! She was far ... from being that 'perfect girl'! The one, that ... you're right ... the one, that I'd always envisioned! For one thing, she could never get 'in' ... to all these schmaltzy lyrics. To any of those schmaltzy lyrics. The beautiful music ... all, of that beautiful music ... that I'd always had stored up, in my alleged mind. My, fantasy-filled, mind! She just never cared for it! Nowhere nearly as deeply ... as I'd always been! As in ever! That was so ... well, it was so damn frustrating!"

"I can imagine. Well, maybe I can't!"

"But ... let me tell you ... I was no bargain either. We were always broke! So damn broke! Always! Desperate ... for money! Continually! At all times! Our natural damn state! She finally divorced me ... as she ought to have done. Probably, long before she did! Now? Now, she lives a nice, really-comfy, life ... on some stupid-assed college campus, in Buffalo."

"And you had no place to go? Nowhere to go? With your ... quote/unquote ... 'stupid-assed' lyrics?"

"No, dammit," I muttered. "Never have! Problem is ... I've never thought they were all that stupid-assed. Still don't! Whatever sense that may ... or may not ... make!"

"Well, you know, they weren't! They aren't! Stupid-assed, I mean! They've never been stupid-assed! I remember ... when I was pretty damn pregnant ... and you took me to the *Newport*. To the *Newport Theater.* When we were in Norfolk. While Eddie went around the corner ... to that other movie theater ... and he watched some really stupid-assed swashbuckler flick. We ... on the other hand ... we got to see *April In Paris.* Remember? Remember that?"

"How well I remember!" I positively glowed, as the. warm-all-over, memory returned -- in glorious *Technicolor.* And *CinemaScope.* "How could I forget that?"

"And," she continued, "when Doris Day sang that song ... the title song, y'know ... I really couldn't take my eyes off you! Really couldn't! Wished that it could've been ... could've been Eddie sitting there. Him, sitting there. And him being all wrapped up ... in that lyric. Hung up! Like you were. Maybe even him crooning it, to me. Like ... in my ear. With his hands ... you know where! At least, one of 'em! One of his hands!"

"Dahse! I never had any idea that ..."

"Yeah," she groused. "Of course you didn't! That was the general idea! You weren't supposed ... to be having any idea! I *was* married, you know! To *Eddie*! Remember? Was even carrying his *baby* ... don'tcha know,"

"Oh, Dahse" I chirped. "I'm *sorry* ... *really* sorry ... about that. About you miscarrying, and all!"

"It was *worse* than that, The baby ... well, it was a ... it was a still-born situation. *Much* worse! Dear *God*! *Horrible*! Absolutely *ghastly*! But, that's all ... all in the *past*! Thank *God*! Things *did*, though, work *out* for me. *Eventually*! Really worked out really *well*! A little more than a year later ... I had a little *girl*! *Cathy*, her name is! *Easy* pregnancy! *Way* easy! *Much* easier ... than I'd feared! She's almost eleven now! *Beautiful* little girl! Well, she's not so *little* anymore!"

"I was going to say, 'I can *imagine*'. But, I *can't*! Not *really*! After all these *years* ... and not *knowing* you, over those years ... I can't *picture* you, with a little girl. A little *girl*, for heaven's sakes!"

"One who's not so little, anymore" she responded, laughing heartily.

"So! So, you're ... ah ... *divorced*? Single ... these days?"

"Yeah. Single. But, *that's* not the entire story."

"*Uh*-oh! What do you mean? What does *that* mean? Did I just ... ?"

"No. You're fine. I'd gotten remarried, you see! Got myself hitched ... for a *second* time! Listen, I just managed ... to get myself legally disentangled from *him*! Well, it was a few months ago! *That* ... that,

God-awful, marriage ... that brought on the weight thing! All that weight that I put on! It devastated me! The horrendous time! The crappy time ... when I'd gone, and gained all my weight! Packed on all those horrible pounds. Like I said, I have managed to drop a goodly amount ... most of all that crappy-looking suet ... over the last little-while. The last five or six months."

"Same situation ... as with Eddie? Was that it? You giving? Him taking? Your second husband, I mean."

"No. Not really. He was ... in a manner of speaking ... a good man. To an extent, anyway. Well, he was ... maybe ... too good. He was ... highly religious! Although I did use to worry ... about the way he'd, sometimes, look at Cathy. I guess he might've been ... just exactly what I'd needed, back then. I really don't know. For one thing, I couldn't find a job, at the time. And I had this little girl ... depending on me. I was living ... with my parents. Well, I still do. They were always very generous, with me. And with Cathy! Indulged me! Indulged us ... all over the place. Always! Especially Daddy. Now, here I was! The one ... doing all the taking! All the damn taking!"

"Aw, Dahse. I'm sure that ..."

"Oh, believe me ... they were pleased to do it. But, along came this man ... this Leon .. who was always wrapped up in some kind, of righteous, impressive, campaign or another. All, undeniably, admirable!

Feeding the indigent, y'know! Clothing the poor! Chasing all the volunteer fire trucks ... to help out! To offer assistance ... of any kind! Whatever it took! Whenever it was needed! No matter the time of day! Or night!"

"Sounds pretty worthwhile to me."

"Yeah," she sighed. "They were! It was! I guess! But, it ... the whole thing, y'know ... it just, flat-out, just-plainly, wore me down! Wore me down ... to a nub! Wore me out! We lived, then, in a little town ... just west of Baltimore."

"Oh? Away from your folks?"

"Yeah," she nodded. "And everybody there ... in the whole damn new town ... they knew us! All of 'em! Put the arm, on us ... always! Came to us ... for money, mostly! And there were so many of them, who ... well, they didn't deserve it! Didn't deserve a penny of it! Never got off their fannies ... to help themselves! Ever! Plus, the damn fire alarm! It would go off ... in the middle of the damn night! Just down the block ... from where we were living! Startled the ... you should excuse the expression ... the shit out of me! Every time! We'd always have to get out,,, get up ... and go, to the stupid fire! See what we could do there! To help out! It was ..."

"I ... I can't really imagine ..."

"I finally took a job! Got a job! Low-paying son-of-a-gun! To help out, you know! Leon? He was working fifty ... sometimes sixty ... hours, a week! Every week!

Every day! And he was ... was giving it all away! I was just reaching a point ... where I got tired, of working my fanny off! Working it off! And for nothing! Plus ... it was affecting my daughter! Affecting her, y'know! Big time!"

"Geez! Something else I can't imagine!"

"In addition ... it was, well, his own personal habits! He almost never took a bath! We didn't have a shower! And .. dear Lord ... his religion! His religion! It called for him, to tell anyone ... everyone he'd ever meet ... about every sin, he'd ever committed! Ever! In his life! His entire life, for God's sake! I'm not particularly proud of this ... but, I just simply couldn't take it! Not anymore! Just could not hack it! Not anymore! Not one day more!"

"That," I muttered, "I can understand! I don't know how many years you could've ..."

"Well, it was a little over three. Three God-awful, stupid-damn, years!"

"Well, then you're a better man than I, Gunga Din."

"I don't know about that! Finally, I moved back. Back with my parents. Daddy had ... back after you'd gotten discharged ... he'd built an apartment, for us. For Eddie and me."

"An apartment?"

"Yeah. Little one. Dinky one. On the second floor ... of their house, on Mathews Street. They still live there, by the bye. And the apartment ... it still exists! That's where Cathy and I now reside. Eddie? he would never live there! Period! Paragraph! Simply refused ... to even consider it! The whole thing broke Daddy's heart! He'd put in a nice little kitchen ... and everything else. Well, except a second bathroom. Eddie, flat-out, insisted ... once the Navy was behind us ... insisted, on buying a house! A new house! Way ... on the other side, of Baltimore! That's where we lived ... when all hell broke loose."

"So, now you're back ... living with your parents? On Mathews Street?"

"Yes!" She was back to being enthused. "And Aunt Agnes ... and Uncle Albert ... they still live next door!"

Aunt Agnes and Uncle Albert! (Yes -- Uncle Albert.) They'd let me stay -- in their home -- on our, early-fifties, trips up to Baltimore. That was the softest -- most restful -- mattress, on which I've ever lain. To this day.

It was at that moment, that the group -- which was going to attend the symposium on Romance Novel Writing -- was to assemble, in a room, down the hall. I'd intended to attend the one -- devoted to Character Development -- which was to begin, in another half-hour!

But, I'd suddenly decided -- instead -- to further my knowledge (which, to then, had been absolutely zilch) in the, apparently-filled-with-publishing-potential, field of writing "romance classics"

TWO

It had been a worthwhile, highly -informative, symposium! Conducted, with great aplomb, by a prestigious editor, from *Silhouette* -- a publishing entity which, along with *Harlequin*, has been, over the years, the largest, and most-influential, generator, of boodles, of all types, of romance novels.

I'd wound up learning a lot, Mostly, though, it was simply a massive -- a thorough, and a highly-illuminating -- expansion of the few things that Dahse had already expounded upon, ever so briefly, in our first, all-too-brief, conversation. Our first -- highly-enriching -- exchange, in about 13 long years.

There were, I was to learn, a goodly number of, carved-in-stone, "rules of the road" -- which held true, in virtually every genre, and subgenre, of the entire romance "industry". For instance: A woman -- the heroine and (always) the main character, in such novels -- had (always) to be an exceptionally <u>strong</u> woman. Except in a very limited -- <u>very</u> limited -- number, of subgenres. None of which held much interest for me.

The heroine/protagonist is <u>required</u> to battle all manner -- of, seemingly-unconquerable, odds. She would go on to accomplish some major, all-but-impossible-but-well-worthwhile, always-unselfish, unquestionably-highly-principled, undertaking! And/or she would resolve some, perceived-to-be-"impossible", conflict. Under most genres, she cannot be afforded the merest amount of help. Especially -- from a man. Any man. (In most cases, he should be the one -- who represents the unrelenting, seemingly-unconquerable, odds.)

While a goodly number of the titles, of these tomes, turn out to be quite lurid, most genres require a rigid, usually-subject-to-assault, highly-moral, pathway -- for the dedicated, determined, undeterred, protagonist. At least, those had been the, carved-in-stone, criteria -- in the mid-sixties.

There did, however, have (always and ever) to be "sexual tension" -- present, in virtually every genre, and subgenre. (I guess literally every genre and subgenre.) In some of the, "more-relaxed", categories, some sexual conduct may be permitted, But, usually not until "the last chapter or two". And then, it should not be vividly described. (Since then, some of those. rather-restrictive, rules have been "relaxed". Substantially "relaxed" -- in a number of the newer, good-deal-more-permissive, current, criteria.)

The editor/speaker delved, further, into some of the more-popular genres -- all of which featured their own special, finely-tuned, needs, and restrictions.

But, the overall, ever-popular, field -- basically operated, pretty much, as described above.

I'd been working in a number of different, diverse, all-over-the-field, areas -- in the novel-writing persuasion. But, not in the romance portion. Had recently completed a time-travel novel -- of which I was fairly proud. Had submitted the "classic" -- to a number of agents, and a few publishers. So far, I had met with a spectacular lack of success. (Spectacular!)

At that moment, I'd been in the midst of authoring a crime/police/detective "classic". After having attended the Romance Seminar, however, I'd become absolutely convinced -- that I'd stand a far better chance, of ever getting myself published, by concentrating my efforts, in that, richly-popular, specialized, broadly-targeted, species, of fiction writing!

An important bonus: I'd been visibly encouraged -- all during the, informative, fast-moving, 90-minute, gathering -- by Doris. Every time the editor would uncover yet another "rallying point", my long-lost associate would gush, in my ear, "Yes! Yes, yes ... yes! Listen to him! It's true!"

After that, highly-informative, first get-together, Dahse and I attended a second, illuminating, symposium -- which pertained to making your characters' dialogue believable.

The, printed word, exchanges -- in conversation -- should seem natural. Not stilted -- most writers' main difficulty, in this area. Nor, necessarily, does it have to be grammatically correct. No one speaks faultless English. Well, not all the time. I was able to learn a great deal, from the gathering -- although I'd always considered dialogue to be my "strong suit". (If I, indeed, had actually possessed any such "strength".)

My old friend and I wound up -- down, in the hotel's coffee shop (as opposed to their fency-schmency restaurant) -- at a-little-after-six, on that special evening. Neither one of us was all that "flush". So, it was nice of her -- to suggest that we "go Dutch", for din.

The food-serving establishment had been -- thankfully -- playing a variety, of soft, "schmaltzy", music -- in the background. Such "fluff" had always been right up my alley -- although I'd not been paying all that much attention, to that particular assortment, of such "corny" instrumental, mostly-strings-in-the-forefront, selections. Not until Doris came up -- with a rather surprising comment:

"You hear that, Gord? It's *Because You're Mine.* They're playing *Because You're Mine.*"

"Yeah," I'd muttered. "That's right. Great song. Always been one of my faves ... although, God knows, I haven't heard it. Not in ages."

"I remember," she said, wistfully -- closing her eyes, "I remember the last Christmas ... the one, when you were in the Navy. The one you spent with us ... in Norfolk. And then, up in Baltimore. Nineteen-and-fifty-two, it was."

"Uh huh. Yeah. So do I. It was great!"

"You remember? Do you remember ... that you bought Eddie, and me, that forty-five rpm phonograph? Got it for us ... for Christmas ... that year?"

"Yeah. I remember. Of course I remember. I also remember that ... after I'd bought it ... I'd wondered, if that was really a good move. How it would go over ... with your husband. At the office, he never really seemed all that interested ... not wrapped up, in schmaltz ... of any kind. I used to play my own record player, y'know. Pretty often. Sometimes ... during our lunch break. He didn't seem to be, at all, moved by the music. Not all that much, anyway. Near as I could tell."

"Well, he really wasn't. Part of our problem, stemmed from the fact that ... when you weren't around ... I'd want to, you know, play the phonograph. Play some of those records ... those wonderful records ... that you gave us. But, he ... all that he wanted to do ... was he'd always wanted to watch tee vee. And, hell ... Norfolk only had that one stupid channel, back then, you know. And so, the whole thing ... became a bit of a sore point. So, there was, you see ..."

"I'm sorry. I sure didn't mean for it to become any sort of ..."

"No! It was fine! The record player ... it was a great gift! For me, anyway! The last couple or three weeks, of my pregnancy ... when I really couldn't work anymore ... I was always home. Home alone. All day. And, actually many nights! Eddie, you see ... well, he'd gone, and gotten himself entangled. Entangled ... with this one nurse! A Wave! Nurse ... on the Base! So, the machine ... your machine ... turned out to be a real God-send! I listened to it ... all the time! All the time! Really ... all the time!"

"Well, I'm glad that it worked out." I let go a massive sigh. "At least for you. At least ... that part, of the gift. At least ... for that part, of the time. The obviously difficult time."

"It worked out ... eventually ... for practically all of the time. After awhile, anyway. But, that song. The one, that was just playing ... *Because You're Mine* ... brought back, one of the most wonderful things, that you did. That you went and did."

"Oh? That I did? I went ... and did? What was that?"

"Well, you'd given us that whole passel of records ... along with the phonograph. And one of them, if you remember, was *Because You're Mine* ... by Mario Lanza."

"Yeah. I remember."

"Well, I wound up ... telling you that I'd rather have had Nat Cole's recording, of the song."

"Yeah? So?"

"So you went ... and you took the Lanza one back. And brought us ... brought *me* ... the one, by Nat Cole."

"So?"

"So ... I thought that was so *nice* of you. I *never* should've ..."

"It was no big deal. I liked both recordings. I just think that I'd always liked Mario's a little bit better ... mainly because, of the orchestration. I'd always liked Ray Sinatra's arrangement ... a little better than Nelson Riddle's, for Nat. Well, Lanza's record also had a chorus ... backing him up. Wasn't any biggie."

"Well ... to me ... it *was* a biggie. A *real* biggie. And ... over the years ... I've *agreed* with you. Mario Lanza's recording *was* the better one. Probably *because* of the arrangement. And, of course, the chorus."

"Aw c'mon, Dahse. T'weren't nothin'."

"Yes it *was*! *T'were*! And ... stupid as it may sound ... that was one reason, why I've always *missed* you! Really *missed* you, Gord! You were always so ... well, so ... so *nice*! So *caring*! About ... well, about *everything*! So, I really don't know ..."

"Yeah," I muttered. "You probably *don't* know. Ask one woman ... the former Carole Bloodworth! Ask *her* ... how loving and caring I was."

"I don't know about her! But ... and I've thought this, many times ... Gordon! Thought of this ... often: Listen! Listen to me! If we'd have married, Gord ... if we had married ... we'd have made it work! We would have ... you and me! I know that! I believe it! Really have believed it! Deeply! Known it! Known it ... for years! Sure of it! Positive! With all my heart!"

"You ... you've thought that? Thought those thoughts? Actually, thought them? Many times?"

"Yes! Many times! A whole lot of times! And that's why ... after having also given this lot's of thought ... I'm inviting you, up to my room! An honest ... open ... invitation! With all ... that it would suggest! Lots of thought ... I've given this! Lots! You can't know how much! Or in how much detail! How much graphic detail!"

"Dahse! Look ... I don't know if ..."

"Listen, Gord. You listen! I've lived a rather disjointed life ... since Eddie and I separated. Hell, even before we ever separated! For one thing, when we parted ... Eddie and I ... I was devastated! Flat-out devastated! I really 'fell off the wagon'.

"Off the wagon? You fell off ... off the wagon?"

"Yes! The wagon of ... of virtue, I'm talking about! I'd never cheated on Eddie! Ever! Was a stupid-assed virgin ... when we got married. But, in my mind, he'd gone, and thrown me ... thrown me, onto the damn garbage dump! Right on the old dung heap! And ... as it turned out ... that's where I threw myself!

Wound up throwing *myself*! Right onto the damn *dung* heap!"

"Threw *yourself*?"

"*Yes*," she answered, nodding firmly. "Look ... I started sleeping *around*, for one thing! *Sleeping* around! Big *time*! *Big* time! *Cheapened* myself ... to the point, that my *parents* even threatened to take *Cathy*! My *parents* ... for God's sake! Take her *away* from me! My own *daughter*! And it was my own *father* ... who was gonna *do* it! My *Daddy*! I had always been 'his little *girl*', for heaven's sake! 'His little *girl*'! And, now ... here he *was* ..."

"Doris? Doris, I don't think ..."

"No! Let me *go*! Go *on*! Let me *continue*! Let me *unload*! *Really* unload! This has all been ... been really building *up*! Building *up*, in me ... *inside* me ... for the longest damn *time*! A *helluva* long time! I *finally* ... at long last ... I finally got myself, to where I'm feeling ... well ... feeling '*right*' again. *Almost* right, anyway! Listen, it was about damn *time*! It was *then*, that ... God help me ... that I wound up *marrying* Leon. Marrying *Leon*!"

"The ... uh ... religious one? The ultra-moral guy? *Him*?"

"Yeah! When I'd started going with him, my parents started to ... ah ... 'welcome me back'. Well, Daddy had never *actually* thrown me out! Not out of the *house*! I don't think ... he could *ever* bring himself, to do *that*!"

"I wouldn't *think* so."

"I was still allowed," she continued, her emotions accelerating, "to live ... in my own little apartment. The one Daddy built ... upstairs. But, I couldn't keep *Cathy*! Was *alone*! All the damn *time*! *Always*! Could not hardly even *associate* with her! With my own *daughter*! They ... Mom and Daddy ... they moved *her* next door. She lived, over there ... with Aunt Agnes and Uncle Albert. I couldn't hardly even *see* her! Not even at meals! Or, practically, any *other* time! You can't *imagine* ... you can't *possibly* imagine ... the ..."

"Dear Lord! *That* must've been absolutely *devastating*! *Had* to have been God-awful *devastating*! I mean, to not be able to see ..."

"I guess that may have been one of the reasons ... that I'd started going, with Leon. Started really going to church ... with him! To *his* church! Three ... and four and five times ... a week. Mom and Daddy ... they let me have *Cathy* back! Let me take her back, again ... *after* I'd started going, with Leon. The marriage? Well, *that* just seemed to come ... more or less ... come naturally. A natural *progression*, y'know."

"But, *that* didn't turn out? Not the way you'd wanted? Obviously, it *didn't*!"

"Well, actually, I guess it *did*. In a way, anyway. It *was* seeming to work. At *first*, anyway."

"Maybe *that* was simply ... because you got your *daughter* back? I know that, if I ..."

"Quite possibly. Hell, probably! I really don't know! Not for sure! You see, Gordie? You have a way of ... of, well ... of organizing things. Sifting through ... sifting through, all the crap!"

"There's a whole regiment of people, out there, who'd dispute that whole observation! About how well organized I am! Can you say 'half-assed'?"

"No! For as long as I've ever known you, you've been the one solid fortress. At least, to me! The only one ... that I've ever met. Ever! Outside of Daddy, maybe. But ... always ... you have been ..."

"Look, Dahse! I've not been that one solid fortress! Nothing even close!"

"Well, in my eyes ... you always were, you know! When I was in the process, of disentangling myself from ... getting away from ... Leon, I even tried to find you. Tried to locate you ... up in Buffalo, y'know. Couldn't! Could not find you. And ... God knows ... I tried!"

"That's not a surprise. Lived with my mother, I did ... for a good while. Then, I'd flopped, in a cheap room ... upstairs, over a bar. And ... even after I'd married Carole ... I really couldn't hold a job. Not a halfway-lucrative one, anyway. And, most always, the phone was ... generally ... disconnected. What else?"

"Listen, Gord! From the time ... practically, from the time, that you got out of the Navy ... I've thought about you! Thought and thought ... and thought!

And ... I have to admit ... sometimes in the most *intimate* of ways! *Really* intimate! *Some* of the things I'd imagined ... well, you don't wanna *know*! You ... *spectacularly* ... do *not* want to know!"

"Well, now you're ... you're really *embarrassing* me!"

"I don't *mean* to. Well, hell ... maybe I *do*! While Daddy would *never* think of most of those thoughts ... think of them, as being, anywhere-near-wholesome, y'know ... *I'd* never had any *problem* with 'em. With *any* of 'em! Listen! *Listen* to me! I have a pretty *vivid* imagination, y'know! Pretty damn *vivid*! You'd be *surprised*!"

"Doris, look! This all, maybe, ... well, maybe ... it's just a little too ..."

"Does my being so ... well, so openly *aggressive*, so *forward* ... does *that* scare you? *Frighten* you? It's really not *like* me ... my public persona ... y'know."

"I *know* ... and, I guess, it *does* make me a little bit uncomfortable. Hell, in a way, it *does* scare me! More than a *little* bit!"

"Gordie, *you* may not know it. Probably *don't*. But, what I feel for you is ... well, it's so ... so *right*! So *definitely* right! It's ... these feelings ... the whole deal, is something, about which I've *thought*! *Pondered*! *Meditated* on! Sometimes ... hell, most of the time ... it's all been *intentional*! Intentional as *hell*! And, *many* times, those images ... those, really-far-out, *fantasies* ... would come roaring in! Even when

I'd thought ... that I was thinking, of something else! For the longest time ... I've thought them! Imagined them! Welcomed them! Yearned for them! Flat-out longed for ..."

"Geez, Dahse. I don't know! Look, it's such a hackneyed old saw ... but, this is so sudden! Really! I mean ... all my life ... I guess, maybe, I might've thought, of this sort of thing. Some of this sort of thing. But ..."

"This sort of thing? Being seduced? Being flagrantly, shamelessly, propositioned? Having some sex-crazed bimbo ... throw herself, at you? Flagrantly throw herself at you? After only a couple, or three, hours? It's a wonder ... that I haven't taken my damn clothes off! Maybe taken yours off!, too! Right here ... and now!"

"Naw! C'mon! It's not that! I mean ..."

"If it's not that ... not having some lady, of obviously-questionable moral turpitude, throw herself, at you ... then, what is it? What else could it be?"

"For one thing, through the years, I've had a problem with ... a problem with ... well, with ... with you-know-what."

"You mean ... getting an erection?"

(You have to remember, dear reader: This was all taking place -- in the mid-sixties! Well before there had been so many, pervasive, "discussions" about "E.D." And a multitude of drugs -- to "cure" it! At the time, I -- myself -- probably would've thought that the initials would've pertained to some board of education, or something.)

If *Viagra* had been around, back then, I'd certainly never heard of it. So, Doris' stark reaction -- her using that word -- had been enough to complete the total-unraveling process, of/for yours truly!)

"Listen, Gordie! Do you remember that last Halloween night? Your last one ... in the Navy? When we ... us two girls ... when we dressed you three guys up? When we dolled you up? Dressed you ... all three of you ... as women? As young girls? Remember that?"

"How could I forget? Ever forget that?"

"Did it ... did that excite you?"

"Uh ... well, yeah! I guess it did! Well, I don't have to guess! It did! It did ... give me a bit of a rush! Hell, I haven't thought about that! Not in years!"

She was speaking about another coupe -- Lou Lindquist, and his wife. Lou was in the Navy, back then -- along with Eddie and me. Everyone called the couple "Lou and Lou". I'd not been going with anyone, in Norfolk -- where men outnumbered women, about ten-trillion-to-one. So, as always, I was ever-present "The Fifth Wheel On The Cart".

We'd all had dinner -- at Eddie's and Doris' one-room, attic, apartment, in Norfolk. Suddenly, someone (I think it was "Dahse") got this "bright idea" -- to dress the three guys! Dress us -- as women!

The plan was -- that we would then go, and visit Mr. Finch, at his residence. Walter Finch -- a chief warrant officer -- was Assistant Officer In Charge, at our office. The man was -- had always been -- a saint!

Lou, Eddie and I were all pretty much the same age -- and size. Doris was positive, that she'd had sufficient clothing -- in appropriate sizes -- to outfit all of us guys! The problem was -- we were located in, as previously noted, a one-room apartment! Look Ma -- no walls!

Our hostess had proceeded to lay out our feminine frippery, on the bed -- at one end, of the large room. The girls, then, retreated to the dinette table -- at the other end, of the joint. They'd given us their "sacred promise" -- that they would cover their eyes, when us guys were about to get down to our skivvies.

But, "The Secret Ingredient" (well-known advertising ploy/word, at the time) in the whole "unusual" operation -- was that Doris had laid out ladies underpants! One lacy, silky, pair -- for each of us. Us guys -- each of us -- had looked (kind of uncomfortably) at one another. But -- once we'd each gotten down to our undershorts -- we'd slipped into our bras (thoughtfully stuffed, with six pairs of Eddie's, rolled-up, socks). Then, we'd donned our skirts and blouses. (Well, in my case, it was a, one-piece, full-skirted, dress.)

None of us had positioned ourselves -- in any special direction! We were covered -- by our skirts -- anyway. We'd, each, simply slipped -- out of our drivvies! And in to our panties!

The girls, then, made all of us up! My first bout -- with feminine cosmetics! Then, we each applied a, provided-for, babushka. And we were ready to go. I suppose that we were -- all three of us -- breaking the *Unified Code Of Military Justice*, for dressing in the garb of "the opposite gender"! And Mr. Finch was a commissioned military officer. But -- he was also a complete and utter saint! On the other hand, we did surprise him! And caused Mrs. Finch -- to break up, in gale upon gale, of hysterical laughter! (She was also pretty saintly.)

One thing we'd not counted on: That would be Mr. Finch's, seventy-something, father -- who lived with them! The old man -- genuinely -- thought we were the real thing! Actual young ladies! And he'd "put a move" on me! On me!

"Then," this was, present-day, Doris talking -- and the sound seemed to be coming, from some subterranean cave, or something. It had been an exciting memory -- that I'd been, excitingly, reliving. "Then," she pressed on, "you do remember? Remember ... wearing my panties?"

"Uh ... well, yeah." I lowered my eyes -- and murmured, "Yeah, I ... I remember."

"I've always held those panties ... as special," she responded -- smiling broadly! "I only wore them, y'know ... on special occasions! Like whenever ...

when *you'd* come to visit. I don't know ... if Eddie ever *noticed* that, or not. I think that ... by then ... he didn't much give a damn. Couldn't care less ... one way or another. But, how ... oh *how* ... how I'd always *wished*, that I could've found a *way*! A way ... to let *you* know!"

"You *did*?" I was becoming less and less capable -- of dealing with the direction, in which the dialogue was going! "Uh, I never would've ... never would've *dreamed* ..."

"We were both *peeking*, y'know. Both Lou's wife ... and me! When I *finally* got a chance to *see*, what you *had* ... under that *uniform* ... I just about ..."

"I ... look, Doris. I don't know! I mean, I can't ..."

"Whatever happened to *Dahse*?"

"You ... you don't *seem* to be ... well, ah ... there's been a *change*! Maybe not a God-awful *change*! But, a *change* ... nevertheless. You don't *seem* like ... well, like the same *Dahse*! The one I used to *love*!"

"*Used* to? You *used* to ... used to *love* me? And *now*? Now, you *don't* love me?"

This whole, entire conversation was getting *away* from me!

"Of *course*," I finally replied. "You were always ... always, just like my *sister*! *Remember*? Like my own *sister*!"

"Well, of course, I'd always *tried*, you know, to *be* that! To actually *be* your sister! *Think* like that! *Think* that way! Think ... in those *terms*, y'know!

But ... and this took me *years* to come to grips with ... I'm pretty *sure* that I'd always thought of myself, as *more* than just a *sister*, for you! *Especially* as Eddie was getting less and less ... ah ... attentive! *Especially* on Halloween night! *Seeing* you unclothed! Well, more or *less* unclothed! As much as I ever could've *hoped* ... to be able to see! More than I was afraid ... that I'd *ever* see!"

"*Listen*, Doris! *Listen* to me! I've only been with ... been, with one *woman*! In my whole *life*! My *wife* ... my *former* wife ... Carole! Only *her*! And ... too many times ... I really couldn't *perform*! Could *not* perform! Couldn't even come *close*, half the time! You know what I *mean*! What I'm *referring* to!"

"Did you ever stop to think that ... this might've been *her* fault? Maybe *she* just, simply, couldn't ... ah ... she, maybe, couldn't turn you *on*! Maybe she just *wouldn't* turn you on! Women ... some of them, maybe a *lot* of them ... they have their own spooky reasons, for that, don'tcha know."

"*No*! *Listen*! I'm *sure* that ..."

"You were *also* sure that you did, just-an-ordinary, job ... when you were in the Navy. Eddie ... while he didn't say you were *spectacular* ... he told me. that you *always* did your job. Did it ... extremely *well*. Especially, when anyone ever considered the guy ... and then the Wave ... who'd ultimately *replaced* you. And *Eddie* was not ... was *definitely* not ... the type, to go handing out compliments. Listen, Gordie!

You were only the second *friend*! Only the *second* friend ... that Eddie had ever *had*. In the whole everlovin' *world*! In his whole *life*!"

"*Really*?"

"*Really*! His first, was this guy, from high school ... Arthur Lawrence. I knew him ... just a little bit. He lived, maybe, three or four blocks over. He and Eddie ... they'd gone, and joined the Navy. Joined it ... together."

That's funny. I don't remember Eddie ever *speaking* of him. Of Arthur."

"That's because they both got assigned, to that same aircraft carrier ... the Kearsarge ... together. Right out of boot camp. They'd *figured* ... at the time ... they'd *figured*, that they'd been very *lucky*! *Truly* lucky! I mean ... to be able, to be *together*!"

"Yeah? *Weren't* they?"

"Not really! On their first cruise out ... Arthur was *killed*! Got blown, into a whirling propeller ... as I understand it! Got 'chopped *up*'! That was *Eddie's* term."

"Dear *Lord*!"

"You see? Listen, I always gave Eddie ... a goodly amount of *slack*! A *goodly* amount! Let me *tell* you something: Listen to *this*! When Eddie was about eleven or twelve ... just barely old enough to understand such things ... his mother *told* him! Told him ... that she'd done everything she could *think* of! Everything she could possibly think of ... to get *rid* of him! To not have him! As soon as she'd found out she was pregnant with him!"

"Dear Lord! I can't imagine!"

"I don't know ... if that involved the old coat-hanger trick," she rasped. "Don't want to know! Don't know anything about ... what it may have involved!" The, obviously-rattled, woman shivered -- from head to toe! "But," she continued, in barely-above-a-whisper, "that had to have been one of the reasons! One of the reasons ... why he couldn't get close to anyone! Well, not hardly anyone! Had to be!"

"Good Lord! And then? With that guy ... on the ship?"

"Right! His friend! His only friend! And he was ... was killed! Was taken from him! You were ... were the only other one! His only other real friend! The only one ... that he'd ever had! Which is another reason ... that I'd always found myself really drawn. Drawn so close to you! And so quickly! And so ... ah ... permanently! And ... eventually ... so X-rated! Two ... or three ... Xs! Maybe more! In my warped mind, anyway!"

"Well, wouldn't that be ... his mother telling him that ... wouldn't that be a pretty good reason? A helluva reason ... for his being rather unresponsive? To your displays ... of affection? I've always noted how affectionate you are. Always been aware of that. How could I miss? How could anyone miss that?"

"You've noticed that?" she responded -- laughing heartily.

"Who could help ... but notice? I remember that one night ... in Baltimore, just before Christmas, of fifty-two ... when we were at that nightclub. At *The Patrician* ... with all those friends of yours."

"You remember that?"

"Of course! Of course I do! Of course I would! That was the first ... the first ... 'non-sisterly' kiss, that you'd ever given me. Well, really the only one! The one and only one!"

"I did that ... I guess ... because I knew that you were leaving. Leaving ... the service. Leaving ... in all too short a time. That's what I kept telling myself ... at the time ... anyway."

"There was a guy there. I think his name was Woody."

"Think? You know damn well ... that his name was Woody. I'd attended high school with him. Had even dated him ... a good many times. In fact, he and I had become a thing, y'know. Albeit a non-sexual thing. Were a thing, there ... for a few months! In eleventh grade, it was."

"Well, I did notice ... that he was, forever, patting you, on the fanny! Kept patting you ... right on the old bum! A goodly number of times! A goodly number of times!"

"That's the only time you'd met him! Just like I believe that Halloween night ... was the only time you'd ever met Lou, and his wife. But, this was far from the only time ... that Woody's ever patted me, on my fanny! He's always patted me, there! Look, I enjoy ... having my bottom patted. Something you might very well take note of. Eddie never seemed to mind Woody ... and his displays of affection. Which always tended to piss me off! Eddie's not caring, I mean. I loved the pats."

"Eddie's lack of reaction? That was what pissed you off?"

"Certainly! Like I said ... it was not the pats! It was never the pats! Trust me! As I've told you before, I always went out of my way ... to indulge Eddie. And his ... ah ... hang-ups."

"'His hang-ups'? What do ya mean by that? By 'his hang-ups'?"

"Well, like I've always liked being patted, on the bottom ... by Woody ... Eddie had always enjoyed wearing ladies panties. I never knew that ... till that Halloween. But, he always wore them ... and nothing else ... around the house. Used, even, to wear them ... on the base! Beneath his uniform!"

Her mood deepened! It almost darkened! And I can't describe her facial expression! Can't even come close! It was not a scowl. Not nearly. But, I really cannot think, of another word! One -- that even comes close. And the almost-contortion seemed destined -- to remain!

"All right," she said, at long last -- sighing deeply. "I'll come off ... all the intimate stuff! Despite what you're probably thinking ... what you're *undoubtedly* thinking ... I don't *need*, to get *laid*! Not so desperately ... that I'm going to continue propositioning you! Not gonna *continue* ... throwing myself at you! Although, it *is* tempting! But, listen. There's *one* thing ... that I *do* want you to know! One thing ... about which you don't have a *clue*! You have not ... the faintest idea about this."

"And what might *that* be ... oh, Seer Of The Truth?"

"That you've got a inferiority *complex*! One of the all-time *biggies* ... in that area, That *I've* ever seen, anyway."

"My shrink says, 'That's no *complex*! You *are* inferior'!"

"You can joke around ... all you damn please! But ... hopefully ... sooner or later, you're going to realize that you're *not* inferior! Not at *all*! In fact, you're one of the *great* men, in my life! You're a *great* man, Gordie!"

"*Me*? No one's ever *said* that to me before! *Ever*! Nothing *close*! *Ever*!"

"Well, they damn well *ought* to! They *should* have! A whole *outhouse*-full of people! They should *all* have told you so! Should've ... everyone ... should've *told* you that!"

It was close to midnight -- and, ensconced in my room -- I'd just turned off the TV. I'd been watching some supposed "blockbuster", of a movie. I have no idea what it was. Or what it might've been about. (Probably starred Theda Bera -- or "The Ever-popular May Bush" -- or someone.)

I'd spent most of the evening worried -- substantially worried -- about Doris. (I was having a bit of a problem, at that point, referring to her, as "Dahse".)

My, rather-intense, concern about the situation? Well, it didn't lessen -- once I'd learned that her room was merely across the hall -- and down three doors -- from my own little assigned bailiwick!

But -- so far, anyway -- she'd been a "good girl". I'd had not the foggiest idea -- how "saintly" she might've been, in the privacy of her own inner sanctum. But, at least, she'd stayed out of mine! Till then, anyway!

Then, of course, came that "fateful" -- you might say panic-filled -- rapid-fire rapping! An out and out pounding -- on my door!

I hurried to the entrance! Don't ask me why!

"Gordie!" It was her! (Who else?) "Let me in, Gordie," she was shouting. "Let me in ... now! Right now! Come on! I'm naked! I don't have any clothes on, Gordie!"

"Naked? You're ... you're naked?" That has to rank with one of the most stupid responses -- in the history of mankind! Till this one followed: "What're ... what're you doing ... doing naked?"

"Trying to get you to ... for God's sakes ... to let me the hell in! Now, hurry!"

"Doris! You shouldn't be out there! Certainly not naked!"

"You're telling me? You ... are telling me? Now ... dammit ... let me in!"

Of course, I did let her in! And -- true to her word -- she was unclothed! Totally! Not a stitch! First time -- in my entire life -- I'd ever seen her, in the buff! Never before -- had I ever come close!

"Doris! You can't ..."

Well, of course, she could! In fact, she did! She had! Big time! Immediately, she stifled my protest! Shut it down -- altogether! By welding her lips -- securely -- to mine! And by keeping them -- solidly -- pressed! I never realized how vital your nose is -- to your breathing apparatus! Not advisable -- to have the inhaling/exhaling process cut off! Even in this manner!

Plus, her hands and fingers -- and who-knew-what-else -- was/were all over me! All over me! Instantly! "Working their magic"! She was -- without a doubt -- "having her way" with me! It was as though I'd collided with a tidal wave! A tsunami -- of, frighteningly-unbridled, passion!

True! I -- no doubt -- could have mounted a much-more-rigorous defense! I cannot tell you when my defenses totally (and completely) broke down! But the, fast-folding-up, procedure certainly didn't take long!

Something else is lacking from this "report": That being the, shorter-than-it-should-have-been, amount of time, that the unfolding event, ultimately, took me -- to divest myself, of all my troublesome clothing! (My "authentic" comment can only be this: It sure didn't take long!)

"Afterward" -- as they used, always, to say -- we'd simply lain there (sans our clothing, of course). It took, probably, ten minutes -- after I'd rolled over, onto my back -- before I became aware of the fact, that nobody had bothered to close the door, to the room. The portal was left -- three-quarters of the way -- open! I, finally, arose -- to remedy the "untimely" situation!

The bed was not -- directly -- where we could, easily, have been seen, from the hallway. And the hour -- was late! But, still! Actually, as near as I could tell, we'd not drawn any kind of audience! (Anyone who would have owned the popcorn concession, for the "festival" -- would've been greatly disappointed!)

I'd always made light -- of all of the, totally-non-spectacular, disgustingly-basic, sexual carryings-on -- that, to that point, I'd experienced, in my "vanilla" life. If there's a shrink in the crowd, he or she would, undoubtedly, be aware of the logical, explainable, reasons -- for such things. But, based on that night's, out-of-this-world, performance, he or she might -- positively -- rid him/herself of the fact that I actually was inferior! At least, in that aspect, of my life! At least, for that "one shining moment"!

As I'd schlepped back to where Dahse (yes, she was back -- to being Dahse) was awaiting me -- with (literally) open arms -- the seriousness, of the, fraught-with-problems, situation, was beginning to overtake me! Consume me! Big time!

"Dahse," I muttered, (half under my breath). "This has ... this whole thing has me ... has me scared! Scared as hell!"

"You scared? You think I'm not? Listen! Who just ... a very few minutes ago ... hollered, 'Let me in ... I'm naked'? Shouted it out! For all the world to jolly well hear! In case you don't remember, it was me! And I was! Was naked! Naked as hell! I still am ... in case you've not noticed. You think that's not scary, for moi?"

"Why? Why'd you do that? Why in the hell would you ... ?"

"I really don't know, Gord! Well, I guess ... that maybe I do! I wanted ... did want ... wanted this!" She lifted herself, onto her left elbow -- and made an expansive sweep (of the entire bed area) with her right arm. "I wanted this! Wanted this! Wanted for this ... to happen! Just what we did! I don't know why; but, I figured that I'd have to take off all my clothes ... to make it happen. Then, again ... maybe I do know why! I guess that, maybe, I do! It took some kind of moxie, though ... for me to go running, through the halls, like that! Being ... you know ... being, bare-assed, naked!"

"You've got that right," I muttered. "It took a lot of moxie! A helluva lot of moxie! I probably should've ... should really have spanked your bum, for you! Should've gone ahead ... and done that! Right from the top!"

"I might even have enjoyed that!"

"Doris!" She was back to being Doris, again. "I don't ... I don't believe this! Any of this!"

"Well, believe it, Kiddo! Bee-damn-leeve it! You just made love to me! Or else ... you just screwed me! How-ever-way, you want to think of it! And it was wonderful! Either way! And it was ... was my idea! Right from the top!"

"I ... well ... we made love," I managed to stammer. "We did make love! I could never think of it ... in any other terms! Especially not ... in the one that you just offered."

"Then, what's to worry? Accept it! Accept it ... for what it is! For what it was! For what it'll always be! To my way of thinking, anyway! We made love! Period! Paragraph!"

"Yeah," I grumped. "Well there's more to it! More than that! Much more!"

"Like what? Like I might be trying to get myself pregnant? So that I can trap you? Trap unsuspecting little old you? Trick you ... into marrying me? Well, you can relieve yourself ... of that thought! I'd never do that! Like ever! Don't get me wrong! I'd not even thought of such a, bastardly-evil, thing! But, if I was to have become pregnant ... from our little doo-rah here ... I'd treasure it! Would actually welcome such a thing!"

"Listen, Doris. This isn't ..."

"I'd most certainly ... bring the baby to term," she continued on -- undeterred. "Most certainly! But, I'd never blackmail you ... into marrying me! Not after two previous marriages! Both of which left a helluva lot to be desired! Look, Gord. Listen. I've really treasured this moment! What we just did! And I'd certainly treasure any result from it! Any result! But, believe me, I'd never even think of ..."

"It's not just that," I groused. "That's not what I was speaking of! Or even thinking of, actually. I've told you ... that I've only been with one woman: Carole! My wife! Well, my former wife! Past tense! But, to do ... to do, what we just did ... requires a commitment! No matter what you might think! Requires a firm commitment! At least, in my alleged mind, it does. You don't just go ahead, and ..."

"Do you think I even considered this, to be a ... be a one-night stand? Simply ... a roll in the hay? Simply ... getting laid? Gordon? Gordon, listen to me! I've been thinking, of this ... of what we just did! Thinking about it ... for a good long time! For years! Literally!"

"Oh, that's patently ridiculous!"

"No! No it's not! I can't really say that I'd gone ahead ... gone ahead, and planned it this way! For one thing ... I never dreamed I'd ever see you again! So, this was no, meticulously-laid-out, grand seduction scheme! I was just following my ... my natural instincts! How-ever-warped they might be!

I was at a loss for a response! This was all happening -- far too fast!

She made another sweeping gesture -- encompassing her entire, uncovered, body. "I just didn't expect my clothing state, to be quite this ... ah ... quite this natural! Listen, Gord! If you want to spank me ... why, then go ahead! You can do anything you want ... with me! Anything you want ... to me! It wouldn't matter! I don't care! This ... is what I wanted! Pure and simple! What I've dreamed of! Dreamed of ... for years! For ... probably ... decades, for heaven's sake! And it has come true! So, I'm good!"

"There's a line," I rasped. "A line ... from Frank Loesser's *Guys And Dolls*. A line ... from a song called *I've Never Been In Love Before*. And this one line ... well, it says, 'But this is wine ... that's all too strange and strong'."

"Yes! And the next line says, 'I'm full of foolish song ... and out my song must pour.' This was simply ... well, maybe not so simply ... my song! Pouring out! Foolish song ... or not!"

"You knew that? You knew that line? From that song? From that show? That, fifteen- or sixteen-year-old, song? You actually knew that?" I was incredulous!

"Of course I knew it! I knew that *Guys And Dolls* was one of your favorite shows. Have known that ... all along. If you ever knew ... knew, of all the damn trouble! The trouble I'd had to go to ... to ever find a copy of Fran Warren's recording of *I'll Know* ... you'd kiss me! Right on my fanny! Maybe you ought to, anyway! Instead of doing ... doing the other!"

"You found that record? You must've moved heaven and earth! I've always loved that recording. Best record ... she ever made. I once met her, y'know! Met Fran Warren!"

"I know! In her dressing room! You never let us forget it! Eddie ... or me!"

"And you went to all kinds of trouble ... to get that record? That particular record?"

"Yep! And all in memory ... of you!"

"Turn over! Roll over ... onto your tummy!"

"On my tummy? What're you gonna do?"

She'd wound up -- with the most confused look on her face. But, she complied -- albeit somewhat reluctantly! I leaned over -- and kissed her! With a goodly amount of out and out tenderness! Right on her behind! Both sides!

"Whew!" she sighed -- heavily! "That was a relief! I thought you were gonna do something else!"

After that particular, in-her-mind, "escape", Doris/Dahse sat up, reached down -- and pulled the bedclothes up around us. Then, she snuggled herself up -- against me. In about ten seconds, she was fast asleep. It took me -- at least -- an additional 25 or 30 seconds, to follow suit.

At six-fifteen -- the following morning -- we made love again. It may not have been initiated by me. Not totally, anyway. The emotion had come naturally! Much less out-of-the blue -- than had been the case, the night before. The "encore performance" probably should have raised as many question marks -- as had been the case, on the "unusual" night before. I don't know about my newly-minted lover -- but, at that point, I (for one) was all "question marked out"!

As we'd lain there -- side-by-each, once again -- my guest set about launching a campaign; the sum total of which was to reassure me that any worries, that I might have harbored -- no matter, for how long -- about "being unable to perform" were groundless! Totally without merit! I still wasn't that convinced -- but, the declaration was, most assuredly, nice to hear! Definitely, a step -- in the right direction!

And so far -- so good!

We finally rolled out -- at a little after eight. I lent her a shirt -- to cover her Lady Godiva mode, for her voyage back to her room!

We went to breakfast -- at about 8:45AM -- and attended three more symposiums that day. They'd had mostly to do with identifying your market -- no matter which field of endeavor you might have chosen for your writing profession. Well that -- and finding an agent. Oh -- and proper length, of manuscripts. A little dry -- in some instances -- but, the total, beneficial, guidance, that the gatherings had provided, was more than useful.

We parted -- Doris and I! Promising to meet again -- soon. We'd exchanged addresses. (I did not have a telephone.) But -- surprisingly or not -- we'd made no specific commitment, to meet again. (Soon -- or otherwise.) Imagine!

Her plane left, on Saturday evening. I drove home to Buffalo. It took me all night! I didn't really need the "deadhead" drive time -- to be forced into thinking! Into pondering the weekend's events -- erotic, and otherwise. But, that was the way everything had turned out!

Was this to have been a "weekend to forget"? One to always remember -- forever? Well, it could be anything! Anything -- but, easy to forget! Was there a commitment? Of any sort? From either one of us?

And -- on the sexual side? She'd -- apparently -- "cured" me of my. overwhelming-impotence, questions! But, was that the only "benefit"? Had our uniting -- opened some kind of "Pandora's Box"? I'd never really enjoyed sex -- with Carole. Mostly, the, highly-frustrating, dissatisfaction had persisted -- I'd found myself always believing -- due to my consistent erectile dysfunction problems.

It took a real delayed action -- for me to have (finally) realized how much "satisfaction" I'd realized, from my, highly-exciting, sexual coupling(s) with Dahse! That realization -- the tardiness, of same -- would seem to be anything, but normal! Simply just another worry! Faced with an obviously-unknown future, there seemed to be no immediate answers! To any of those burning, real-or-imagined, questions!

In addition there was one additional -- overwhelming, mind-warping -- concern: Would Doris have wound up -- pregnant? From so few encounters? If so -- what then? Despite her constant, non-entrapment, declarations? Those assurances? If she turned up "with child", what should my response be?

THREE

Friday, December 24, 1965! Christmas Eve! And -- filled with some manner of, charitable, Christmas spirit (the non-alcoholic kind) -- I was paying a visit to my mother's apartment. T'was the season, don't you see.

I'd not been to that, always-tenuous, venue -- in, probably, close to a year. My sister, Anne, and I would run into one another -- every now and then -- at my favorite restaurant, on Transit Road, near Walden Avenue. But, not often enough. Not nearly. A couple or three times, those meetings were, pretty much, semi-planned. But, fortunately, -- in truth -- there had been a semi-bountiful number of, pure-chance, path-crossings. I had always missed her. How could I not? Despite the, all-too-infrequent, meetings -- we were very close. Have remained so -- thank heavens -- over the years.

On the other hand, the thing -- my relationship (so called) with my mother -- was something else, altogether! We're talking -- pure chemistry, here! According to Anne, Mother had never stopped celebrating -- the "abject failure" of my marriage. I suppose that the only thing that would've repaired the, getting-wider-all-the-time, rift, between us -- would've been, for me to have enrolled, in that stupid accounting school. And -- as, stupidly-stubborn, as I've always been -- that was not "in the wood". Gordon -- ever the bullhead!

Fortunately, on this particular Christmas Eve, one of the, fast-rising, disc jockeys -- of the overwhelming roster, of rock (and not much else) stations, in town -- decided (shockingly, inexplicably) to play a number of actual, really-beautiful, carols! Yeah -- Christmas carols! A distinct upset! For some reason or another, the bonus ration, of the glorious, seasonal, music, really "got to" me. And so, I paid a surprise visit -- in Depew. At a little-after-six.

Anne, of course, was glad to see me. Mother? Not so much! And the heart-warming Christmas spirit was -- ever so quickly -- beginning to dissipate! Big time -- after a few minutes! The music, after all, could go only so far!

At about 6:55PM, I'd finally realized -- had come to know -- that I was licked. I'd just stood up -- to, sensibly, leave. It was then -- that the phone rang! Anne answered.

"Hello? Who? Yes ... he's right here, as a matter of fact! Yes! Yes! Hold on! Please wait ... for just one minute!"

She handed the instrument to me! I couldn't imagine!

"Hello?"

"Merry Christmas!"

"Dahse? Doris? Is that you?"

"It ain't your Aunt Fanny!"

It had been far too long -- far too long -- since I'd heard from her. Too damn long! Once we'd left Chicago, we'd begun exchanging letters -- "early and often", as they say. In fact, over the ensuing months, she'd given me a couple of ripe plot ideas -- for my projected romance novel. The "masterpiece" that she had continued to encourage me to write. She'd even offered to put me in contact -- with her agent.

As time had gone by, however, the letters -- the number and personal content (which had grown, to where they'd become just this side of semi-intimate) -- seemed to have, for some reason, diminished. Ever so gradually -- but, the decline was, most definitely, there. It was unmistakable! And unforgivable!

I was as guilty as she was. Probably guiltier. And I'll have to admit: I'd not thought all that much, about the troubling situation, until -- on the way to my mother's place -- that rock station had "slipped", and had played Fred Waring's recording of *Oh, Holy Night*. My, all-time, favorite carol! All time!

This remarkable arranger/conductor/composer, Mr. Waring, had recorded that beautiful carol -- sometime, back in the forties. Maybe even the late-thirties. My parents had bought the album -- in which that rendition had been included. Had cherished it -- on those clunky old 78rpm records -- when I was a kid.

Mr. Waring had, just recently, re-recorded it -- same arrangement -- in high-fidelity, and stereo. On a *Decca* LP. I have no idea -- as to the identity, of the soprano -- on the original recording. But, on the "new and improved" one, the soloist was a young woman, named Patti Beams! She'd had a remarkable voice! An incredible talent, she was! And -- together with the, genius-like, arrangement (and Miss Beems' ultra-talented voice) -- the, most-recent, recording had "set me off", with all these feelings, of good will.

It had, sadly, been a long while -- since I'd been nearly so moved, by a recording. And, with it being Christmas Eve, and all, I was, just-this-side, of being -- well -- overcome! Engulfed in some kind of emotion! A whole host of emotions, actually! Most of which I couldn't identify! Well, maybe I didn't want to even attempt to sort them out. Any of them!

Of course, when I'd arrived at Mother's, she was, already a good-bit "on the muscle" -- which was not helping! So, Doris' call could not have come at a more opportune time. Hopefully, at the most fortunate of times! To say that I'd been dazzled -- by the prospect, of talking with her -- would be putting it mildly!

"How," I finally asked, "how did you find my mother's number? How did you know ... that I'd even be here?"

"Well, you did ... truth in advertising ... tell me her name. Once or twice. Even told me ... what street she lives on. She's listed ... in the phone book ... y'know. There was only one Judith Bloodworth, showing ... in Depew."

"The phone book? They still have phone books ... actual phone books ... available?"

"Yeah. Hard to come by, these days. Vanishing breed, don'tcha know. But, I'm the proud possessor ... of one, of the very rare survivors. I just simply took a chance ... a wild chance, y'know ... that you'd actually be there. But, I figured, 'what the hell?' ... and took the shot."

"I ... I can't believe this! That you'd actually go to all the trouble to ..."

"I didn't do bad ... did I? I mean, you're not upset ... are you? I mean, it sounds like ..."

"NO! Hell no! No ... of course not! You've just brightened my whole ... my whole entire ... day! My day ... and night! Well, my evening! My entire Christmas season ... what little there was, of it!"

An interruption: Big time! "Who is that?" My mother's voice would've shattered glass! "Who the hell is that? Who's he talking to?"

"I think it's that lady from Baltimore," answered Anne. "I think her name is Doris. I believe it's her."

"You knew that?" Mother was incredulous. "How could you know that?"

"Gord's spoken of her! Often! Really often! To me, anyway."

"Did I just stir up a hornet's nest?" came the voice, from over the phone.

"No! Well, no more than usual," I responded. "Dahse! Listen! I'm so glad ... to hear from you! To hear from you! To hear your voice!"

"Dahse?" Mother was far from being through. "Dahse?"

"His name for her," furnished my sister.

"Look, Dahse," I said -- trying to cover the mouthpiece. On the other hand, my voice was as strong -- as it had ever been. Stronger, maybe. "I can't believe my good fortune ... in being able to talk to you! To hear your voice. Especially tonight! Especially ... on Christmas Eve!"

"I can tell," she replied. "Am I wrong ... in guessing things haven't been going well, for you? Is it the season? Or could it be, that you seem to be in a ... well, in a ... in a hostile environment? Trapped, maybe? In a hostile environment?"

"A little of ... well, hell ... all of the above! For one thing, I just found out, this morning ... they closed the dealership, at noon today ... that I'm gonna be out of a job! Again! Soon! My natural state!"

Both Doris -- and Judith Bloodworth -- exclaimed (at the same time -- and, in total unison) "WHAT?"

My sister -- as struck, by the news, as were the other two respondees -- managed to (in some way) shush my mother. Doris, on the other hand, blurted. "You ... you just lost your *job*?"

"Yeah. Well, I *will*! *Will* be losing it! Come the end of December! They told me, about it! Told me ... just this morning. They'd signed some kind of a damn contract ... effective the first of the year ... with some new-fangled sort, of management outfit. With all *kinds* of radical ideas! Radical ... to *me*, anyway! Big *shake* up, coming! *Huge* reorganization! They're letting *everybody* go! I mean *everybody*! Sales manager ... for the entire dealership! Used car manager ... *my* boss! Guy in charge, of new car sales! The comptroller ... *he's* gone too! Even all six new car ... and us three used car ... salesmen! One of whom, of course, is *me*! *Gone*! All *gone*! *All* of us! Complete *revamp*, over there! Helluva Christmas bonus!"

"Oh, *Gordie*," came the mostly-sigh, from over the phone. "Gordie ... I'm so *sorry*!"

"Yeah," I groused. "So am *I*!"

"What're you gonna ... gonna do *now*?"

"*Cry* a lot," was my stupid retort. Then, I -- finally -- wised up. "Damned if I *know*, Dahse. I'm sure that *something'll* open up. I've, actually, been *fairly* successful, though ... at selling the damn used cars. *Fairly* successful!"

I found myself *hoping* that the caller had not heard the extra-loud "HAH!" that had poured forth -- from my mother's sainted lips! But, in point of fact, I knew that the, high-decibel, screech, had burst forth, in unrestrictive fashion! Landing on the ears -- of "The Immediate World".

"I'm sure," I continued, "that there must gonna be some opening come up ... somewhere!"

Another -- top-of-her-lungs -- "HAH!" from dear old Madre!

"Listen, Gord." Doris seemed not to have heard the most recent, zoo-like, exclamation. "Why don't you consider ... at least consider ... moving to Baltimore? Moving down here?"

"Moving? Me? Moving to ... to Baltimore?"

"Why not? Is there someone there ... right there, in Buffalo? Someone, to whom you're so close ... that you'd not be able to leave? Really attached to ... to some person? Someone you feel ... well, you feel ... that you'd be deserting? From what little I know of you ... there doesn't seem to be someone, who'd fit that description."

"Well," I grumped, "only Anne. Only my sister."

"Do you think that she'd stand between you ... and, hopefully, happiness? Some degree of happiness, anyway? Some sort of potential ... for happiness? If she met, and married, someone ... and she'd decided to move, with him, to California ... would you stand in her way? Besides, it's not as though you'd never see her again."

"Hmmm, Baltimore. Baltimore!"

"Ball-ta-goddam-more?" Mother's robust echo, of my, almost-whispered, musing, must've deafened every dog, in the neighborhood!

"Would you need some help?" came the voice from over the phone. "Some help ... financially? Like, in maybe ... the plane fare? The bus fare?"

"No," I muttered. "I don't think so. I'll get my final paycheck ... on the thirty-first, y'know. On New Year's Eve. And, hell, I really haven't dazzled anyone ... with my sales figures. Not this month, anyway."

"Wonder why that is," continued my female parent. "Why that could be."

"Sales have been weak," I hastened to explain. "For the entire dealership. Especially over the past week ... or ten days. Christmas season does that. But, for the first half, of the month, I did pretty well! Surprisingly ... I guess. They've got me, on a base-plus-commission thing ... which, as I understand it, they're gonna change, in sixty-six. Radically change! I'll get my commission ... for the entire month ... at the end of the month."

"So," she reasoned, "you think you'd be able to fly out? Fly out here? Or, maybe, even take the bus? Or do the dog-paddle? Whatever?"

"Yeah. Hell, I may even be able to drive!"

"You don't have a car." It was my mother, and sister -- in unison (albeit in much different tones, and loudness, of voice).

"Do you *have* a car?" The almost-echo was the voice, from Baltimore.

"No," I answered. "I'd really not thought, much, about getting one. Hoped to score another job, you know ... with another car dealer. They'll usually *provide* you ... with a company unit, to drive. That was how I got to Chicago. *Company* car!"

"Chicago," she echoed -- wistfully. "That seems like such a long *time* ago!"

"Yeah. To me too. *Too* long ... probably. Too damn *long*! Listen, there's a car ... a nineteen-fifty-nine Dodge ... that we took in, on trade, for a new Lincoln! This was some time ago. Couple months ago. The guy ... when he'd brought it in ... he *said* he hated to part with it."

"That's what they *all* say," was Judith's contribution to the uplifting conversation. "What would you *expect* the guy to say?"

"I've driven it ... a number of times," I said, into the mouthpiece -- ignoring you-know-who. "I *love* the car! Two-door hardtop! It's gold-and-white, y'know! *Beautiful* car! *Looks* ... almost ... like the fifty-seven and fifty-eight. Except, they really went ahead ... and *refined* it, with the fins ... in fifty-nine. I've been in *love* with that car ... for the entire time, that it's been on the lot. I'm probably the only one, though ... in the entire known universe ... who's turned on, by fifty-nine, full-sized, Dodges. I *think* they'd let me *have* it ... the powers that be will ... for, maybe two-hundred bucks! The dealership would cut me some kind of deal. At least, I think so. Maybe two-fifty. They can't have much more than that ... tied up in it. And it's been, on the lot ... since forever. The son, of the dealership's owner ... the guy who'd actually tied the can to me ... he told me, that they'd sell me any car. Any car ... on the lot ... for what they have in it. So, there's an avenue, y'know. An avenue ... there! Hopefully, a pretty good one."

"Well, if you could get that car ... without, you know, getting hurt, financially ... that sounds like it might be the way to go!"

At the same time that the above rejoinder was emanating, from the phone, my mother was observing, "That's the dumbest ... most stupid ... damn thing, that I've ever heard! You? Your own car? You? One that's not ... some goddam, rusted-out, old rattletrap?"

"I'm pretty sure ... I can pull the deal off," I assured Doris. "I just ... I don't know what I can do ... about finding a place to live, down there. All I'd need would be a small apartment. Or, hell. even a single room ... up over a bar, or something. I've done that before. For a good while."

"Oh ... I'm certain that you could bunk in, with Aunt Agnes and Uncle Albert. At least temporarily. That room, y'know ... the one, with the mattress that you've always loved ... well, it's still available."

"Really? You really think that? That they'd ..."

"Virtually certain of it! Literally certain of it!"

"Dahse! That'd be great! I'll be ... are you sure, now? Are you sure you actually want me, down there? That your parents ... that they'll have me? Will want me ... so close by? And Aunt Agnes ... ?"

"Do I want you? Did I want you? Only bad enough ... to stand out, in the stupid hall! Stand out there ... stark, bare-assed, naked! Or have you forgotten?"

"Who could forget? But ... but, that was long ago! So damn long ago!"

"Too damn long ago ... I think I heard someone say!"

"What about your daughter? Cathy? What about her?"

"She's ... she's had an ... an unusual childhood. Her biggest problem ... her biggest disappointment ... has always been her father! With Eddie! With his ... so unexpectedly ... turning his back on her. Once we'd separated ... why, he never would come by. She'd, pretty well, accepted Leon, I guess ... and even his religious leanings. Some might call it ... his religious zealotry! I don't think it ... ever ... went quite that far. Close, sometimes! But, I have to tell you: Our life ... our life with Leon ... was, most assuredly, unusual! Highly unusual! I think she was a little uncomfortable ... Cathy was! With the way he'd looked at her ... from time to time! But, listen! She's a wonderful kid! She really is!! A very remarkable kid!

And she wants me, to be ... wants me, to be happy! And so do my folks! So does Aunt Agnes. And, probably, even Uncle Albert."

"And my being there? That ... do you think ... that would make you happy? Make you happy?""

"Oh, please!" This came from the, always-in-good-taste. lady of the house -- emitting that, pause-that-refreshed, reaction. "I could frigging puke!"

"Of course it would make me happy," came the, hoped-for, reply! The one I was waiting for! Hoping for! Wanting to hear! "It would," Doris proclaimed, "make me incredibly happy!"

And so it was decreed! That I would pull up "the old tent stakes" -- and move to Baltimore! At the end of the month/year!

The moment after I'd hung up the phone, Anne came over -- and plopped herself into my lap! The perfect response -- from a wonderful young lady! Tears were streaming down her cheeks! They fell -- moist, as could be -- on the top of my head, and onto my forehead, as she kissed the crown, of the old pate!

Don't ask me when -- but, I'd begun to pat her, on her bottom! Until I'd heard my mother (loudly) grunt her displeasure -- at such a "disgusting" display, of "out and out perversion"!

"Are you sure?" my sister asked, at length. "Are you positive, Gord? That you really want to go?

That it's the ... the answer? That you actually want to relocate? To Baltimore ... of all places? It's a big move ... a really big move ... y'know."

"Yeah. And it's a little scary! Well, it's a lot scary. But, if you only knew Dahse. Knew Doris. If you knew her ... like I do! You'd see ..."

"I know of her, Back from the time you were, in the Navy. I know that you've both been kind of working ... collaborating, I guess, on a book. How's that coming, by the way?"

Another emphatic grunt -- from the mother figure.

"Well," I'd answered, "we really weren't collaborating. She's been very encouraging, for me. To me. With me. Suggested a few plotlines, y'know. I've sent her a few samples ... of some of my writing. She's usually sent it back ... with a goodly bit of 'corrective encouragement'. Sometimes, a lot ... a whole lot ... of 'corrective encouragement'! There were a few times ... when all that 'encouragement', got to be a little discouraging! But, she's always had my best interests, at heart. Of that, I'm lead-pipe sure. Certain. Absolutely positive."

"Do you think you'll be able to get along ... with her folks? And her daughter?" asked my sibling. "I mean ... you're walking into, a whole, entire, new world! A whole helluva lot of ... of out and out unknowns there!"

"You're telling me? The 'knowns' ... here ... aren't all that encouraging! I have no idea, though ... how

I'll get along, with anyone, down there! Her folks ... and her aunt and uncle ... they'd all seemed, to have accepted me. But, that was twelve and thirteen ... maybe, fourteen ... years ago. Who knows ... what they'll be thinking now! And ... as to her daughter ... that's really scary! Scary ... as hell!"

Anne kissed me! Flush on the lips! And insisted: "Gordie? If it doesn't work out, please don't be afraid ... don't be too proud ... to come back! To come home! Don't let your pride ..."

"I won't! I'll come back ... if it doesn't work out. I promise."

I'd gone ahead -- and repeated the shaky pledge. More in response. to my mother's, much-too-loud, highly-emphatic, statement! Her one-word answer -- in reaction to that promise -- more than anything else! (i.e. "Bullshit!")

But, in reality, I'd lied! To a point, anyway! I'd had not the foggiest notion -- as to how anything might actually work out! (Including whether or not I'd be able to become owner, of that gorgeous Dodge.) I'd found myself wishing that I'd not made such a big deal -- over the car -- to Doris. Or anyone else! Not being able to negotiate the purchase of that auto -- would simply represent (yet and still) another failure. One that the sainted Judith Bloodworth would never let me forget!

I kept trying -- to reassure myself: Nothing ventured, nothing gained ... and all that, I kept telling myself. Some of that "brave" statement was true, I'd supposed. But, most was probably simply talking! Pure blathering! Well maybe a little smidgeon of it was beginning to "take" -- in my heart of hearts. But -- for sure -- nothing close to all of my bloviating content, was registering as "positive"! Not to me, anyway!

Well -- hoo-HAH -- I was able to get my precious Dodge! (YAY!) The son, of the owner, advised me -- that the dealership had $335.00 invested, in the "market-stodgy" model. The, higher-than-expected, balance took me a little aback! Well, a lot aback! But, he -- quickly -- promised to sell me the car! For (can you believe this?) fifty bucks! "As Is ... Junk"! FIFTY bucks! That particular sales category -- while, quite-probably, offensive, in sight and sound -- simply means that the car is all mine! Period! Paragraph! The dealership is relieved -- of any and all responsibility. Of any sort. This was extremely nice of them! Extremely nice! Of him!

Looking at that beautiful two-door hardtop -- and thinking of it as "junk"? A shattering emotional experience! Really! Despite the, rock-bottom, price! I still find it offensive! To look at -- to gaze upon -- that golden top, and those beautiful golden fins (which

Chrysler had "modified", to include a little additional chrome) on that, pure-white, body was (to me, anyway) an enriching, highly-satisfying, journey, into complete, and utter, satisfaction!

And those extended, long, tubular, chrome-wrapped, taillights! Well, those red beauties just simply completed the "Work Of Art" motif! (Who else -- besides me -- do you know, who could get so emotionally involved? Over stupid taillights?) Obviously, I'd sprung -- for the half-a-hundred! On the spot! Quick! Before he could change his mind! (He didn't! As nice a man, as he was -- he wouldn't!)

When I'd received my final paycheck -- December 31, 1965 -- they'd included a $50.00 bonus! Those nifty people, at that wonderful dealership, had always -- I mean always -- been really good to me. The finest group -- for whom I'd ever worked. I still hold that opinion -- despite a couple of confrontational years, of "spirited" maternal arguments, to the contrary. I'd found myself, sincerely, wishing them the best of luck -- embarking on the new (rather radical) path, that they were fixing to follow. It was filled with potential minefields! (Years later, I was to learn -- sadly -- that it didn't work out, for them. What had been an institution -- in Buffalo, New York -- had gone out of business! So sad! So incredibly sad! At one point -- in the forties, and into the fifties -- they'd been the largest-selling Lincoln-Mercury dealership, in New York State! Tragic!)

❖

Tuesday -- January 4, 1966! I found myself in Baltimore, Maryland! (Also YAY!) I'd left early, on Sunday morning -- 24 hours, after New Year's Day had presented itself. I left then -- to avoid any potential roadwork delays. The drive itself, though, took a good deal longer than I'd anticipated. Arrived in town -- late Monday evening!

Was too tired -- at that point -- to go looking, for Mathews Street. Checked in to a fleabag hotel. And -- despite the fact that I'd not eaten all day (after an early three cups of coffee, and a sweet roll, somewhere in Pennsylvania) -- I fell right asleep! Immediately -- almost upon entering the, rather-drab, room.

Slept -- deeply -- till after-ten, Tuesday morning! Might still be asleep there -- had the room clerk not called, to inquire as to whether I was going to stay another night, ensconced in their particular species of "splendor". (Not hardly! I'd been surprised that the joint had even provided a phone!)

Most of me attributed the, in-excess-of-twelve-hour, "nap" -- more, as a means of escapism! Rather than to actual body-fatigue! Here I was! Opening a brand new -- completely unpredictable (and scary as hell) -- chapter, in my illustrious life! Pretty damn scary!

I'd had all these goofy, mental, pictures -- of my having "dug a hole", in that rather-lumpy mattress, the night before! And had "pulled it in, after me"! Escapism, it had been! Pure and simple!

I phoned Doris -- once I'd began to operate, as a bona fide human being. (In theory, anyway!)

I'd neglected to get her phone number -- on that memorable Christmas Eve. But, thoughtfully, she'd sent me a telegram (remember them?) which had included the number -- as well as the Mathews Street address -- on the 26th. I'd wired her back -- on Sunday morning. Just before I'd left Buffalo. Advised her -- that (ta-DAH!) I was on my way! Then, I spent most, of the trip -- wondering if that had been the right thing to have done.

Back to my initial Baltimore phone call: Mrs. O'Banion, as it happened, had answered my call. She'd sounded glad to hear from me. (Sounded glad.) Immediately, she put her daughter on! Of course, the older woman and I had always seemed to have been fairly close. But, again, that had been years before. And I really couldn't have been absolutely positive she'd truly remembered me. But, seemingly, she had! Great!

"Hello?" It was Doris -- at last. "Gordie? Is that you? Are you here? Here ... in Baltimore?"

"Yep."

"I'm so relieved! I was so afraid ... that this'd be you! And you'd be telling me ... that you'd gone, and changed your *mind*. That you were still ... still up in ... up there, in *Buffalo*! That you weren't ... weren't actually *coming*!"

Her response kind of startled me. It was *flattering* that she'd be so excited. Thrilled -- by my being in town. But, the fact that she seemed so inclined to think that I'd back out -- on, what to me, had been a solemn promise -- was just the least bit troubling.

"Well ... ta-DAH ... I'm *here*," I finally responded.

I gave her the name -- and approximate location -- of the "palatial" motel, which I'd been gracing, with my presence. She gave me explicit directions -- to get, directly, to her parents' home. The instructions were much less complicated, than I could've expected. And they were, as indicated, extremely accurate. Less than 20 minutes later, I found myself pulling up -- across the street, from the O'Banion residence! *Amazing*!

3005 Mathews Street. (3007 -- next door -- was where Aunt Agnes and Uncle Albert lived! Along with that remarkable mattress!) And *both* those domiciles had never looked *better* to me!

Mrs. O'Banion answered the door! And -- *immediately* -- gave me a rib-crushing hug! She actually *did* remember me! Big *time*! Right behind her mother -- was *Doris*! A new -- and, surprisingly-slender -- Doris! What few of my personal muscles, tissues, ventricles, etc. -- that had been left partially intact by her mother's, grizzly-like, hug -- found themselves under intense pressure, once more! From that, follow-up, "sincere", embrace!

Directly behind Doris -- was Aunt Agnes! How about that? Her "harness hold" wasn't quite so life-threatening, as that, air-extinguishing, first pair had been. But, she was glad to see me! I could tell! Was this great -- or what?

The overwhelming display, of affection, was -- well -- overwhelming! But, the person that I beheld -- once that initial tsunami, of sincere emotion, had been, finally, exhausted -- was enough to leave me speechless!! It was Cathy!

This little girl! Well, she wasn't really all that little! Cathy! She was ten -- fixing to be eleven, in a few months. She'd outgrown the age -- where I think little girls are at their, absolutely-most-beautiful, best! They're always so fussy -- at five and six and seven and eight! Always such little busybodies, at that adorable stage of life!

Cathy was, maybe, a year or two beyond that. She was becoming a young lady! A young woman? And probably too quickly! But, she was the most beautiful young lady -- that I'd ever seen. And -- despite the fact that she'd hardly moved, since my celebrated entrance -- I could tell that she possessed a tremendous amount of, out and out, grace!

She was as unsure as I was, though -- as to what sort of greeting we should extend, to the other.

As it was, she simply extended her hand. I was puzzled, as to whether I should shake it -- or kiss it! I finally simply took it, in my right paw -- and covered it with my left. Then, patted it -- slightly. The "trick" seemed to work. Denks God!

"I'm glad to meet you, Cathy." My voice was, substantially, more raspy -- than I could ever have imagined. "I've heard so much about you."

"And I've heard so much about you, Mister Bloodworth."

"Please," I implored. "Call me Gord ... or Gordie. Mister Bloodworth ... he was my father."

As corny as the line was, it drew a broad smile from her! Encouraging as hell!

"As for what you may have heard about me," I'd continued, "lies! All lies! They can't prove a thing! Besides, I've reformed!"

That produced an out and out laugh! You've never seen someone -- in your entire life -- who was more relieved, by the reaction, than me!

Mr. O'Banion was not there. He was, of course, at work. I'd known that he'd owned his own business. But, I couldn't remember -- from that many years previous -- what manner, of enterprise, it had been. (His was an engineering/drafting entity.) Uncle Albert was also at work. He was an auto mechanic. Had worked -- at the local Chrysler/Plymouth dealership, for years. For decades, I'd guessed.

Aunt Ages went out of her way -- to assure me that "my billet" was still there. Still available. And that I was welcome to stay -- as long as I wished!

I'd never before -- in my entire life -- encountered such a dazzling, mind-boggling, display of out and out, genuine, affection! Never before! Ever! I couldn't even tell you what event would've been in second place! To say that I was completely overtaken -- with a boundless flood of emotion -- would be the understatement of the year! Akin to saying -- that "Marie Antoinette died ... from a sore throat".

Mrs. O'Banion had whomped up a, fit-for-a-king, breakfast. She'd just need to "put the finishing touches, on the eggs". We all found ourselves seated at their dining room table. During the elaborate repast, all I'd had to do -- was to keep my big mouth shut (an upset of immense proportions) and to listen! Simply listen!

Doris went out of her way to explain -- that she'd "dropped thirty-five pounds", in anticipation of my, highly-trumpeted, move to the Maryland city! She'd actually begun her rigorous diet regimen -- upon having returned, from Chicago!

Cathy said, "I understand ... that you used to work with my father. My biological father. Used to work with him."

Who said stuff -- like "biological" anything -- back, in the mid-sixties? Who? Especially "little girls"? But, this exceptional "little girl" did!

"That was so many years ago," interjected her mother -- a note of certain sadness, in her voice. "Many ... many ... years ago, Honey."

I finally spoke up -- enough to advise Mrs. O'Banion that I'd just partaken, of the finest breakfast, "since the last time, I was in Baltimore".

She accepted the compliment, with the expected grace -- and requested that I call her "Mom".

Doris had just completed -- and sold -- her second romance novel. It was, at that point. in the hands of the publisher -- "And I'm just waiting ... with great anticipation, y'know ... for the check".

"What are you going to do ... now that you're here, Gord?" inquired her mother. A question that was -- I was positive -- of more than passing interest, to my hostess!

"He's going to write a novel," answered Doris -- before the question had fully been asked. "Hopefully, a romance novel."

"Well," I answered, for myself, "I'm gonna need to find a real, bona fide, job here, first. But, I have been working on a couple plotlines, y'know. Brought the old Remington Noiseless ... the old typing machine ... with me. It's sitting, out in the car."

"Speaking of the car," interjected Doris, "I see that you got it! Your, gold-and-white, chariot! Congratulations! You were right! It is beautiful! Very beautiful!"

"Yes," added Cathy. "It is beautiful!"

"Why thank you, Ma'am," I responded, to the daughter.

"I think he's cute," she advised her mother. It reminded me, of Doris asking me -- so long ago -- if the, at-sleep, Eddie was "cute". Somehow or another, it was a little disquieting. I don't know why.

Once that initial, sumptuous, meal had been finished, Aunt Agnes accompanied me -- up to "my billet".

"You look like you're a little tired, Gord," she offered. "If you want to go ahead, and lie down for awhile ... take a little nap ... that'd be fine. We'd all understand."

Well, I couldn't understand why, but -- all of a sudden -- I'd become so terribly exhausted! I'd had a whole boodle of hours -- of sleep -- the night before.

I'd finally attributed the unmistakable -- the ultimate -- fatigue, to the emotional knot! The mind-warping, exceptionally-emotional, entanglement -- in which I'd been bound! Had been tied-up -- in all of the runaway unknowns -- for longer than I'd realized. Meeting -- and re-meeting -- all those people had, I'd finally realized, taken a substantial toll. And the troubling uncertainty -- the unbridled anxiety -- of this brand new (this frightening) future, that I was facing, was not helping! Definitely not helping!

Perhaps I was "digging, yet, another hole" in, yet, another pillow! (Or -- in this case -- in a soft, welcoming, feather-mattress)! Always a possibility!

I awoke three <u>hours</u> later.

When I walked downstairs, Aunt Agnes was not there. She was next door. And I joined the occupants -- at the O'Banion kitchen table. We wound up, spending a few hours, in small talk -- <u>none</u> of which was as threatening, as had been the, many-lengthy, exchanges at breakfast.

What <u>was</u> disquieting, however, was if (or how) I'd be accepted by Norman O'Banion -- and/or even Uncle Albert -- when they would return home, from their daily commercial pursuits.

As it happened, <u>both</u> seemed to be happy to see me. (Well, Uncle Albert <u>still</u> wasn't all that positive -- of who I actually <u>was</u>. But, Doris' father -- immediately -- bade me call him "Pop"!)

FOUR

And so began life, in Baltimore. On my second day, in my new city -- in my new home, and, now, with my new "family" -- I, immediately, embarked upon an extensive campaign, to find gainful employment. As quickly as possible. Highest priority!

First thing, I took hold of the want-ads, of course -- from the, evening-before's newspaper. The prospects, for employment, were (at least) half-again as encouraging -- as those, in Buffalo. There was even an ad -- for a used car salesguy. But, it was from Uncle Albert's dealership. I made the, distinctly-political, but-probably-intelligent, decision -- to stay away, from that particular "opportunity".

I'd thought that I'd had a pretty good shot -- at working, as a clerk, in a sporting goods store, once I'd embarked upon "making the rounds". But, that "opportunity" didn't work out. I'd also had a bona fide "opportunity" -- to work, at a coffee-and-donuts restaurant! But, after hearing the manager shout obscenities (continually) at his overwrought, harried, stressed-out, employees -- all during the entire, labored, interview -- I was convinced, that I should probably look elsewhere. Hopefully, this was not indicative, of the employers' typical "culture" -- in the Maryland city.

The people, at two, rather-questionable, "sales enterprises" wanted me to sign on -- immediately! In each case, to hawk their overpriced product -- on a commission-only basis, naturally. Not for me! Been there! Done that! (Although not particularly well!) Needed to do better -- in my new life!

I returned "home" that evening -- quite discouraged. But, I was -- uniformly -- encouraged! By all hands! Including Cathy! Obviously, that -- the latter's, unexpected, rather-enthusiastic, endorsement -- meant a great deal to me! A great deal! (Obviously!)

"I'm sure you'll find something soon ... Mister Gordie," she'd enthused. (Well, at least she, apparently, wasn't going to call me, "Mister Bloodworth", any longer! It was a step -- I'd supposed -- in the right direction.)

The following morning -- Thursday -- was Cathy's first day, back at school. After the long Christmas/ New Year's holiday break. (Yeah, they were still calling it -- gasp! -- "Christmas".)

It was also my second day out -- in search of a job. There'd been one ad, in Wednesday night's paper -- one that had not appeared, in Tuesday night's edition. I can't say that I was "inspired" to answer its calling.

But, I can't say that I was not. It was a cashier's position, at the giant *Food Fair* grocery market -- located only about a half-mile, from the two glorious residences, on Mathews Street.

The attention -- that I'd wound up giving the ad was ironic. In that, while I'd served in the Navy with him, Eddie had always spoken -- in almost rhapsodic terms -- about the place. He'd worked there (exact same branch) -- during most, of his high school days -- as a stock boy. "An overpaid ... under-performing ... stock boy", as he'd always described it.

That testimony thus inspiring me, I applied! First shot, out of the hopper! Was afforded a most courteous interview, by the manager -- who was, during it all; keeping numerous "duty balls" in the air. All at the same time. At first, he was the slightest bit disparaging -- due to my lack of experience, in trying to operate one of those fangled, rather-complicated, multi-keyed, cash registers, of the day.

Nowadays, we're all so used to (read spoiled by) those high-tech (a word I'd never heard, back then) grocery scanners, of today's market. Even us old folks -- tend to forget the complicated devices of (what we like to think of as) "not that long ago". But, those monsters had 38-million keys, to labor to punch. And everything -- every box of laundry soap, every ring of baloney, every roll of toilet paper, every *Tootsie Roll* -- had to be punched in! Separately!

Individually! Manually! (Using at least 1200, of that overwhelming plethora of punch-keys!)

Mr. Tontalo, fortunately, decided to (as he'd told it) "play a hunch" -- which more people seemed prone to do, in those, far-less-specialized, days. He actually hired me! Right there! Right then! On the spot! Can you imagine? (I couldn't! Especially -- as the interview had been laboring on!)

I'd work the 3:30PM-to-midnight (which is when they'd closed) shift. My days off -- would be Tuesdays and Wednesdays! I would be paid $150.00 a week -- which was a fairly-high stipend, in those days. (No wonder Eddie had always been so ecstatic, about the joint!) I would commence employment -- that very afternoon! I'd be expected to "pick up the routine" -- before my first shift would have ended! This was a warning! One which I'd found to be quite scary. But, I was thrilled -- to have gotten the chance, at least!

On Friday -- "if everything went all right" -- I'd be hailed, as a full-fledged cashier. The "threat", of course, was that -- if everything did not go all right, I'd rejoin the seemingly-massive ranks, of the unemployed, once again. But, I was pretty sure I could master that multi-keyed monster! I was afraid to even consider the alternative!

The interview had ended close to 10:30AM! So, I'd hurried back, to Mathews Street -- to shout, from the rooftops, of my good fortune!

Mrs. O'Banion -- "Mom" -- and Aunt Agnes, were happy to hear it! Doris was completely *overjoyed*!

Aunt Agnes suggested that I should probably go upstairs -- next door -- and take a quick nap. I, most assuredly, was not at the point of exhaustion -- but, the suggestion seemed to make a certain amount of sense, given the fact that my shift would keep me, at the store, till midnight.

So, I made my way -- up to "my billet", and that glorious mattress! Took great care to close the door. Had no idea -- as to what Aunt Agnes' daily schedule might've been. How many times she might be flitting past the old portal. Wanted to avoid any unnecessary, highly-embarrassing, moments.

I stripped down to my undershorts (boxers -- full disclosure) and piled into the feathers. Well, I didn't bother turning the blanket and/or sheets down. Just laid myself -- on top, of the bedclothes.

Surprisingly -- to *me*, anyway -- I began to fall asleep! Almost immediately! The sleep *must* have come from some -- overpowering -- sense of *relief*! Over the fact that I'd actually found a *job*! And *quickly* too! *Much* pressure -- especially after having permanently "renounced" my Buffalo life! And the stress -- all had *evaporated*, into thin air!

Just as I was teetering, on the welcomed edge of Morpheus, however, I heard the bedroom door open -- then, close! Fairly quietly! But, not *completely*! It was *Doris*!

"What ... what are you doing up here?"

"That should be fairly obvious," she answered -- as she began to unbutton her blouse. "Or, at least, it should be becoming fairly obvious!"

"But ... but, Aunt Agnes! Your mother! They could be ..."

"Oh, hush!" She was in the process of removing the, above-mentioned, blouse. "They both know that I'm here! And they know ... why I'm here."

"But ... but, but, but ..."

"Will you just hush up your mouth? You sound like an outboard motor!"

She began the process of pulling her skirt up over her head. (Remember -- before every female, on the planet, began wearing jeans and/or pants suits? Girls had to pull their, tight-waist, skirts/dresses -- up over their heads! Remember?)

She was wearing no slip or half-slip! Her diaphanous panties -- followed, immediately, by her lacy bra -- bit the carpeting! In a matter -- of seconds!

She was beautiful! Absolutely -- breathtakingly -- beautiful! The weight that she had dropped, she'd lost "in all the right places" -- as they say! The new form did much, to enhance her bust-line! That, exciting, pink-tipped, attribute! Complimented her beautiful bosom! Most especially! Most emphatically!

"Doris! Dahse! You ... you're beautiful!"

"I was <u>hoping</u> you'd think so. But, I probably would've settled for, 'Hey, Babe ... you ain't bad lookin;!"

"You ... you always <u>were</u> beautiful! Even going back to our salad days ... in Norfolk! But, now ... right <u>here</u>, right <u>now</u> ... you're absolutely abusing the privilege!"

She crawled up onto the bed -- and snuggled in, beside me. In a matter of seconds, she'd undone the three snaps -- at the waistband, of the aforementioned boxers! And, in an almost-unimaginable feat, of physical legerdemain, had those skivvies slithering (speedily) down -- past my, somewhat-shaking, knees!

"Do you know <u>what</u>?" she asked -- batting those entrancing eyelids, in feigned innocence.

"I haven't the slightest <u>idea</u>," I managed to rasp.

"When we were in Norfolk, you kept getting enraptured ... kept <u>being</u> enraptured ... in lyrics, of a gazillion of <u>songs</u>. I don't know <u>how</u> many times you'd told Eddie ... and/or me ... that your all-time favorite song, was *All The Things You Are*."

"Yes?"

"Well, this musical show ... came out, after you'd been discharged. But, there was a song, in there, that I was <u>sure</u> I'd hear some reference, from you ... once we'd met again, in Chicago. But, surprisingly, I never <u>did</u>!"

"Oh? And what song might <u>that</u> be?"

"Came from *Bells Are Ringing*. Broadway show. One that was especially written ... for Judy Holiday! Whole production showed off her talents ... to a tee."

"Yeah. I'm familiar with the show. Saw the movie ... a few years ago. When I was still married to Carole. She wasn't impressed. What song can you mean? I mean, *Just In Time* was a nice little tune, but ..."

"That's not the one?"

"What other one could it be? Surely, not the one where she sings about going back to work ... at the *Bonjour Tristesse Brassiere Company*."

"No, Silly. This one's called *Long Before I Knew You*."

"I've only heard that song ... just once or twice. Maybe a few more times than that. Are you sure that it's from *Bells Are Ringing*? They didn't include the number ... in the movie! And ... from what little I know of the song ... it's a very beautiful ballad! Very beautiful! I can't imagine them leaving something like that ... leaving it out, of the movie!"

"How many times have you bitched about ... all the beautiful stuff they'd left out of *Guys And Dolls*? When they made the movie? Or ... for that matter ... the same complaint, about *Damn Yankees*, when that flick came out?"

"Yeah," I muttered. "Bingo!"

"This lyric, is all about how the singer ... knew that he or she would meet the person, to whom he or she was singing it. Long before it ever happened! That's what it ... the song ... is all about. It has a beautiful line, at the very end."

At that point, she began -- to <u>fondle</u> my manhood. Causing an <u>immediate</u> response -- "down there"!

I was reacting, as referenced, to her manipulations! But, I'll go to my grave -- believing that I was more <u>touched</u>, by her recitation, of that, positively-gorgeous, lyric. The fact that she'd chosen, to memorize the work -- in its entirety, I was to later learn -- was simply dazzling, to me! And that she would choose that particular <u>moment</u> to relate it, to me was remarkable!

Of course, "one thing led to another" (as they say)! Afterward (as they <u>also</u> say) I found myself drifting off -- into the most blissful sleep, that I'd <u>ever</u> achieved! In my entire <u>lifetime</u>!

The next event -- of which I became aware -- was the rather-loud knocking, on my bedroom door! My <u>closed</u> bedroom door!

"Gordie!" It was Aunt Agnes. "It's almost two o'clock! Thought you might <u>need</u> a wake-up call."

Doris was, by then, conspicuous by her absence!

My very first day on the job! I found that Mr. Tontalo -- the manager -- was a very <u>patient</u> man. And the man -- Norman Brock -- who'd wound up instructing me, on the care and feeding of that monster, of a cash register -- was even more indulgent. Something I'd have thought impossible.

I made more than my share of mistakes -- "practicing" on a "dead machine", for the first hour, or so -- but, by the time when I was ready to "handle live customers" I'd found myself "doing pretty well". In fact, the speed was far from what I'd expected of myself, but I was, pretty much, holding my own. In fact, by closing time, I'd considered myself to actually be "holding my own" -- when compared, to the woman running the, equally-cumbersome, register, "next door".

As I'd dragged myself, to my beautiful Dodge, I was physically (as well as mentally and emotionally) exhausted. That nap had been a real help! (So had been "The Preliminary Engagement" -- starring one Doris Clayton!)

When I got back to Mathews Street, I found that, as promised, Aunt Agnes had left the porch light on, for me. She'd previously instructed me, to simply come in -- but, to be sure and lock the door. That accomplished, I could then proceed -- up to "My Billet".

I'd followed the orders -- to the letter. Only to find Doris -- who'd, thoughtfully, divested herself, of any bothersome clothing -- waiting for me!

My first weekend, in Baltimore found me, in a bit of confusion. Some things that I should've thought of -- but, hadn't -- began to make their presence felt. My days off -- at the *Food Fair* -- would not occur, till Tuesday and Wednesday -- my being the store's newest employee, and all.

It suddenly occurred to me -- as I arose at about seven-thirty, on Saturday morning, that there were so many things that I'd wanted to talk about! To so many people! Mostly to Cathy.

And, during those first few days, she'd been in school -- before I'd ever gotten up. And, of course, she was in bed -- well before I'd ever gotten home. ORG!

At breakfast -- that first Saturday morning -- there'd been a stirring amount of conversation, going on between all parties. Well, Aunt Agnes was there. But, Uncle Albert -- automobile mechanic, that he was -- had to be, at the dealership. Till shortly after noon.

I did get a few chances, however, to talk -- and rather extensively -- to Cathy! (Huzzah!) These, fairly-lengthy, exchanges were -- for the most part -- initiated by the young lady. She'd "pumped" me -- relentlessly -- about her father. Seemingly, to the, rather-slight, discomfort of her mother. And to the, much-more-obvious, unease -- of her grandfather.

"How well did you know my father, Mister Gordon?" she'd begun, toward the end of that first Saturday breakfast.

"Well, about as well as I'd gotten to know anyone ... anyone who I'd ever worked with. Worked closely with. Got to know him ... a good bit better ... when I'd visit your parents' apartment, in Norfolk. And, of course, they'd brought me on, up here ... on a goodly number of weekends. Actually, spent Christmas ... of 1952 ... up here."

"Was he a good man? My father? A good man?"

That question had brought on a half-cough/half-wheeze from Mr. O'Banion.

"Well," I answered, not really knowing how I should deal with it, "yeah. He was one of my very best friends. We did a lot of things together. He and I. He, your mother, sometimes ... and I. We all had a lot of really good times together. A lot of nifty times ... together. Nothing ... I don't believe ... that, you'd probably think, would be all that spectacular. Mostly, we simply sat around ... and talked. Nothing, I don't think, that you'd ever consider really adventurist. We seldom got up, off our fannies ... except that your mother whomped up more than a few sumptuous meals. But ... for the most part ... we all just simply sat around, and enjoyed one another's company."

"But, he was a nice man? My dad was?"

"Yes. Of course. I don't never hang out with anybody ... but, nice people."

The rest of that exchange seemed to serve to solidify virtually all of those "talking points". The ones that I'd begun with. Reinforced them -- from a large variety, of vantage points. But, the outcome was always the same: She'd wanted -- desperately, I'd gathered -- to be assured that her father, Eddie Clayton, was "a nice man". A "good man". Quite frankly, I didn't know how the conversation might have gone over -- with the rest of the adults, at the table. But, it had seemed -- to me, anyway -- to have been plainly satisfying to Cathy. That had been the most important ingredient! Again, to me, anyway!

Once that, initial-weekend, meal was over, Doris' father surprised -- not to say shocked -- me. He suggested that he and I walk over, to the barber shop -- two blocks away -- and get our hair cut.

That suggestion kind of set me back. I'd immediately recalled one, years-before, Saturday morning, in Baltimore -- when Eddie, his father, and I had all descended upon that same tonsorial parlor -- to have our locks trimmed.

To this day, I have no idea -- as to how rewarding that expedition might have been. To any of us! I'd not had much of a relationship -- with Mr. Clayton, the elder. And none -- absolutely zero -- with Eddie's mother. The barber shop trek had been "unusual"! To say the least! But, obviously, it had been more than slightly memorable. For me, at any rate. Every aspect of it seemed to come rushing back -- in a spectacular flood, of surprisingly-warm memories.

And now, here he was: Mr. O'Banion -- "Pop" O'Banion -- and me! Heading for that same establishment! What kind of situation -- is that going to present? What sort of memories?

On our way, we were passing -- directly across the street from -- Eddie's parents' home; a half-block from the O'Banion residence.

"Do they still live there?" I'd asked Doris' father. "Eddie's parents?"

"Yeah. I don't see them ... all that much. Not anymore. None of us do."

As it turned out, our tonsorial tour-d'force wound up being most satisfying! It occurred to me -- as we'd hiked, on, to our destination -- that I'd not had that much, of a relationship, with Dahse's father, either. That turned out, to be a bit of a surprise -- and a disappointment -- once I'd actually thought about it. Tried to analyze it.

"Pop" and I spent most of our time together -- while walking, and awaiting our turns, in the chair -- talking, basically, in generalities. Mostly sports -- along with some current events. A few politics. And -- surprisingly -- we were, pretty much, in agreement, about the political landscape.

When we got back, to Mathews Street, I was feeling pretty good. And a few pounds lighter! (I'd really needed to get my locks sheared!) Doris, though, was waiting for me! I'd had no idea -- as to what that might portend! (Why did everything seem like such a potential battle? Some kind of hurdle? A mystery -- at best?)

She "suggested" -- that we go up to her apartment, on the second floor. Her mother -- and Aunt Agnes -- were ensconced, in the kitchen. Pop had just plopped himself, in the living room, and had, immediately, turned on his *Sylvania* TV. Cathy was wrapped up, with her homework (I'd guessed) -- in the dining room. So, we'd be alone, upstairs. And I didn't want to even pretend to guess -- what that little adventure might hold in store!

The apartment was, in point of fact, two rooms: A rather-tiny kitchen/ante room, with a small table and two chairs -- along with a, moderate-sized, bedroom.

She guided me to the table. Once we'd seated ourselves, I was trying to steel myself -- for what I'd figured was some kind of oncoming "onslaught"! (Whatever that might pertain to!)

"I'm glad," she began, once we were seated, "that you talked kindly, of Eddie. Talked kindly, of Eddie. To Cathy. He and I ... obviously ... we'd had our problems. And she knows that. But, Daddy, you see? He was grossly upset ... with Eddie! Grossly upset! Well, I was always 'his little girl', y'know. We've always ... Daddy and me ... felt there was something special between daddies and daughters. Always! Goodness knows ... that's always been the case, between Daddy and me. Even ... strangely ... when he was taking my daughter away from me! And, as for Eddie? Well, for one thing, he'd gone, and screwed ... in, literally, a manner of speaking ... screwed his 'little girl'."

"I guess I can understand that," I'd muttered. "I guess."

"Mom?", Doris explained, "she was never, really, all that fond, of Eddie. Same went for Leon. Aunt Agnes ... she was really upset, with Leon. But, she kind of tolerated ... more or less ... Eddie. I don't know that Uncle Albert ever mentioned his name. Eddie, I'm talking about. Well, maybe not Leon, either. So, Cathy? She never heard much good stuff ... about her daddy. Not until ... well, until this morning. So, I'm most grateful ... for those things, you'd had to say, about him."

"You ... you're not upset? Not mad at me?"

"Of course not! Now, listen! I want you to go into the bedroom ... into my bedroom ... and take your clothes off."

"Look, Dahse. I don't know if ..."

"This'll be a surprise. Not what you're expecting! Go in there, take your clothes off ... and lie down! On your tummy!"

"On my ..."

"On your tummy!" It was almost a command! (Almost?)

I'd gone ahead, and complied -- still not having the remotest idea, as to what she'd had formulated, in her devious little mind!

A few minutes later, she'd entered the room -- holding a large container, of *Vaseline Intensive Care* lotion. She proceeded -- to rub me down. A very sensual massage! But, more than that, a very relaxing one! I sighed -- heavily -- and relaxed! Noticeably! And stayed that way!

She'd spent a goodly amount of time -- devoted to massaging my bottom! That little maneuver has always been something -- that I'd thoroughly enjoyed! Immensely! The same maneuver -- her rubbing me there -- had always been something, that had been a complete "turn-off", for Carole! Forever!

Doris spent so much time -- and devoted so much devotion to that admirable duty -- that I'd actually drifted-off, to sleep! A very deep sleep!

I was -- emphatically -- awakened, two hours later, by a "substantial" slap, on my still-exposed, well-massaged, behind!

"Rise and shine ... me fair beauty!" It was (thank heaven) Doris. "Time to get your, well-attended-to, fanny ... on off to work!"

It had been a most interesting morning, and early-afternoon! Most interesting!

I could never have imagined how busy the *Food Fair* store would've been -- on that Saturday! From the time that I'd arrived -- till I was able to take my hour's lunch break, at 7:00PM. By then, I was totally famished! That sumptuous repast, which had been breakfast, was -- by then -- long in the way-past.

There was a "mom-and-pop"-type restaurant -- directly across the street, from the store: *Pond's Cafe.* I'd headed -- with a surprising amount of energy (considering how pooped I'd been) -- for the. hope-filled, solace of the joint.

I took my place -- at the long counter. Their 15 or 16 booths were filled. Not that many diners, at the counter. A young -- rather heavy-set -- woman came up, from behind the counter, and proffered a gigantic, enclosed-in-clear-plastic, menu card.

"Hi," she greeted me. "I'm Lois. Lois Pond. What can I get for you?"

"Coffee! Badly needed coffee! And, also, probably a hamburger."

"Do you want onions? Onions on top? Raw onions? Or cooked onions? Or would you like them ... the onions, I'm talking about ... like them cooked right in? With the meat."

"You ... you cook the onions? Right in the burger? Inside the patty?"

"Yep. Specialty of the house. Only way my own father ... will even *eat* hamburgers."

That sounded great. When I was a kid -- "back in the day" -- my mother used to fry up *her* hamburgers that way! I *loved* it! Loved *them*!

Also -- over the years -- she'd made an abundance of delicious apple pies. And *always* -- as a glorious aside -- she'd whomp up a couple *large* "sides" of crust. About the size of manhole covers. And she'd top them -- liberally -- with cinnamon and sugar! *Surely* -- that had been a happier time! A *much* happier epoch! (*Surely*!) How times had *changed*! How -- and *why*? A cause -- for *much* pondering!

So, at *Pond's*, I'd ordered a burger, and coffee. The decision didn't take much pondering. Plus, it took only six or seven minutes -- despite the overwhelming number of hungry clientele, populating the joint -- and I'd had my *delicious* repast, set before me! It *tasted* as wonderful -- as it *smelled*!

I was about halfway through my relentless, buzz-saw-type, campaign to devour the delicacy -- when Lois sidled up, to stand directly across the counter from me.

"You're new ... around here ... aren't you?"

"Yeah."

"From around *here*?"

"Not hardly. Buffalo. Buffalo, New York."

"What's your name?"

"Gordon. Gordon Bloodworth."

The name seemed -- to strike some kind of inexplicable chord with her. For some reason, or another.

"What brings you to Baltimore, Gordon Bloodworth?" she queried.

"The quest for gainful employment ... for one thing. But, I've got some close friends down here."

"Uh huh. Close friends. Do those ... ah ... close friends include a lady?"

"Uh ... well ... yeah."

"Well, good luck ... with that! I mean that ... sincerely! And welcome ... to Baltimore."

With that, she'd walked away! The whole, entire, encounter left me with the damndest feeling! One -- which I'd found impossible to get a handle on! And the unease left me almost unable to enjoy the remainder, of my succulent hamburger. To enjoy it -- thoroughly -- anyway!

Sunday morning, after another all-universe breakfast -- prepared by "Mom", and Aunt Agnes -- we'd all filed off to church. I'd remembered -- from my old Norfolk days -- that the family had always attended church, on The Sabbath.

Eddie, Doris and I never did, however. Never had. We were -- always -- making ready, to begin our tidy schlep, back to Virginia. As soon -- naturally -- as the bountiful breakfast had finished. (Well, Dahse had usually helped, with the dishes -- then, we'd embarked on our trip home.)

The O'Banions (and Aunt Agnes) had been members of that same, small-but-now-bursting-at-the-seams, congregation -- for all those years. Uncle Albert did not attend. (Something that had escaped my notice -- in the fifties. But, had been brought to my attention -- quite emphatically -- once I'd entered my Baltimore reincarnation.)

The church building, itself, was very small. Pop O'Banion called it "downright tiny". At the, highly-inspirational, service, the pastor spoke -- briefly -- of the progress, in financing a new (and infinitely larger) facility. But, I think, that project -- the "New Church" -- had been "in process" for a good many years, at that point. It seemed to not be "here and now" stuff.

Doris and Cathy, of course, were a part of the ever-growing, crowding, congregation. Something -- a "happening" -- that was supremely satisfying to me: Cathy had wedged herself -- between her grandmother, and me! So, I'd found myself located -- two rows from the platform (the O'Banion's "regular pew") -- between Dahse, and her daughter. A most satisfying -- gratifying, as could be -- location! I was well pleased! And the two "girls" seemed equally as content.

There were a number of hymns -- sung by a small (but, very talented) choir. Religious music -- with which I'd never been familiar; growing up Catholic. One of these beautiful treasures, was *The Cornerstone* -- which, I was to learn, was the favorite of Doris. My own, newly-adopted, favorite was sung, by the soloist -- a beautiful, mid-forties, woman, named Arlene, who'd possessed a remarkable, crystal-clear, soprano voice. This turned out to be a most-inspiring hymn -- called *Majesty*. ("Worship His majesty".)

Doris had reached for my hand -- during the choir's rendition of *Cornerstone*. I'd devoted a copious amount of time to caressing hers -- while Arlene was favoring us, with *Majesty*.

It had been a most rewarding service. One that seemed to have especially moved Dahse! And her daughter! The net result, of which, had been really touching -- to moi!

Work wasn't nearly as stressful, on Sunday afternoon. Apparently, the "immediate city" did virtually all of their grocery shopping -- on Saturday. Very few people seemed to crowd the streets. I couldn't understand why "everybody" was staying home. The *NFL* season was over. The Green Bay Packers had defeated the Cleveland Browns -- 23-12 -- on January second. They'd won the *NFL* championship. This was, of course, pre-Super Bowl.

Came my "lunch time" -- which, of course, was 7:00PM -- I'd found myself headed, back across the street, to *Pond's Cafe*. I didn't know why. Well, not totally why. I was hungry, after all.

To my amazement, the joint was even more crowded! More densely populated -- than had been the case, on Saturday evening. Mostly, the place was overrun -- with "family units". Sunday night must be, I'd figured, the night when entire families all "went out to eat".

Still, despite the size of the current clientele, Lois greeted me. Like immediately! "Your special?" she'd asked. Then, when I'd nodded my head, in the affirmative, she swept away -- to the kitchen.

I didn't see her again, until -- twenty minutes later -- she reappeared with my "onions-in" burger, and coffee. I couldn't understand why -- but, I'd experienced a slight disappointment, at her absence! This was absolutely stupid! I was so happy -- being a, seemingly-significant, part of "The O'Banion Clan". And the experience -- at church, that morning, with Doris and Cathy -- had been so outstanding! So rewarding! So, why ... ?

Lois did stop back -- once I was about four-fifths of the way, through my sandwich. And she did make some small talk with me. (The subject of which -- to this day -- has long escaped me.) But, rather than our conversation taking place across the counter, she'd stood right beside me. Right next to me. Close beside me -- since I'd been seated, on the end stool. Hmmmm!

She'd found numerous occasions -- to tap me on the knee (and, eventually, close to the top of my thigh) -- which is, probably, one of the reasons, why I can't recall any of the topics we'd discussed. Whenever she'd have to leave -- to wait on a customer, or six -- she'd always managed to find a way to brush her bottom across my forearm. (Of course, after the first few times, I could have made the limb a little "less accessible". But, for some inexplicable reason, I did not! Full disclosure: Never came close!)

Walking back, across the street -- to the store -- I found myself wondering why! Why -- all of this? Lois' seeming "special attention" -- to me! But, I was also completely puzzled -- by the, absolutely-gnawing, question: "Why me, for heaven sakes? Me ... of all people?"

Surely, this could not be a case -- of everybody, in Baltimore, being nearly so dazzlingly friendly. Of course, on Sunday evening, I'd guessed that I'd probably been the only single guy, in the place.

But, on Saturday evening, it had been a vastly different crowd. There'd been numerous, seemingly-unattached, males floating about. And Lois had still devoted -- an inordinate amount of attention, to me. More so, possibly, than on The Sabbath -- only with her having been far less "aggressive" with her "touch"! A true "puzzlement"!

❖

On Monday, I'd decided that I'd needed to -- finally -- wash my prized Dodge. It had survived the long schlep from Upstate New York -- and a week of getting around the Maryland city.

Uncle Albert had advised me -- on two separate occasions -- how beautiful he'd thought my "chariot" was. That was, unheard-of, spoken volumes -- for him.

"I had a fifty-nine," he'd informed. "Just like yours. Two-door hardtop. Only mine was red-and-white. Got a four-door Polara now. Sixty-five. Blue one. Had that blue-vinyl top put on her. Gonna keep her. For a long while. Sixty-six ... it's the same damn car, as the sixty-five. Was considerin' a sixty-seven. But, hell. They went ... and screwed it up! Looks like crap! So, I'm gonna hold on to this one. Maybe for good and all ... now that I put the top, on her."

As I'd washed away an infinite amount, of dirt and grunge, a Sheriff's patrol car pulled up -- directly across the street -- and squealed to a stop! A uniformed officer stepped out! It was Eddie!

"Gord!" he enthused -- as he rushed up, to shake my hand. "You old son of a gun! I heard! Heard ... that you were here, in town!"

"Wow!" I responded -- pumping his hand (maybe a little too furiously). "Word sure gets around! How the hell are ya?"

"Great! You staying with the O'Banions, are you? With Doris?"

"Yeah! They've been *great*! Great to me! Been everything I could've ..."

"And *Doris*? How *is* the old girl? Wanna compare *notes*? How she is ... in *bed*? In the old sack-a-*roo*? How does she ... ?"

"Eddie ... come *on*!" My enthusiasm -- was taking a goodly hit. "That's not *like* you! Not like you ... at *all*! You're *better* ... a better man ... than that!"

"Yeah," he said, after (at least) 30-some seconds -- and sighing deeply. "*Thanks*! *Thank* you ... for that!" He shook his head -- sadly. "I don't know *what* gets into me! Gets *in* to me ... these days. Well, for too damn long. How *is* she? *Really*? How's she *doing*? *Actually*?"

"She's fine. *Seems* to be doing okay, anyway. Same for Cathy. Though, for a suggestion ... which is *spectacularly* none of my business ... you *might* want to see *her*, a little more often. Your *daughter*, I mean. *Cathy*. I *think* she misses you. Hell, I *know* she misses you! Always *asks* about you!"

"Not really." The look of sadness -- seemed to betray the slow shaking of his head. "Nah. Not really."

"Yes ... *really*! I think you might be *mistaken*! I've only been here a week, y'know ... but, I've gotten to where I think I *know* the little girl. Know her ... pretty well."

"That's *not* what Leon ... Doris' second husband ... not what *he* told me! What *he's* always said! Numerous times! And ... from time to time ... at the top, of his lungs! Listen ... of course, there's also Doris' parents! Especially her father! They've all got a real hard-on for me. A real hard-on!"

"I believe you're overstating it, Eddie! Badly overstating it. There's still, maybe, a few hard feelings. But, there's also your daughter. Your little girl! Listen, Eddie! There's always been something special ... between daddies and daughters! Something very special! Which probably would explain ... why Pop O'Banion is so pissed off, at you. Definitely pissed off! In his mind, you've not done right ... by his daughter!"

"'Pop'? 'Pop' O'Banion?" Obviously I'd upset Eddie! Upset him -- badly! "You ... you call him 'Pop'?"

"That's what he wants me to call him. I, certainly, didn't ask him."

"Naw." His mood seemed to soften -- significantly! In fact, he smiled. "I can see him ... doing that. I'll have think, though ... think seriously ... about this thing! The thing ... with Cathy. I mean, this clown ... this Leon! He let me know ... in no uncertain terms ... that Cathy was, as 'off-limits', as Doris was, when they were married. And he didn't hesitate ... to inform me! To clue me in ... of all her shortcomings! Doris' shortcomings! Things ... that were, to be desired! Desired ... don'tcha know ... required in bed! All disappointments! Big disappointments ... to him!"

"Well, he's out of the picture, now. Way out of the picture. Of that, I'm sure! Positive! No one ... no one in the entire family ... can stand him! Including your daughter! I think that everyone ... in the family ... considers him an asshole! Including Aunt Agnes. Well, she's never used that term, y'know. I don't know ... about Uncle Albert. Man of few words, you also know."

"Well, that's ... listen, that's encouraging ... to know. All these things. Look, Gord! I've gotta get going. Heard you were in town. Have driven by ... two or three times ... to see, if I could ever catch you. Get you ... by yourself. We gotta get together ... for lunch, or something ... sometime. You make a connection yet? For a job?"

"Yeah! Working at your alma mater! *Food Fair*! Same store, in fact."

"Really? That's great! Why don't we get together, sometime? At *Pond's* ... right across the street. Neat restaurant."

"I know where *Pond's* is."

"Oh? Then, you've ... undoubtedly ... met Lois!"

That remark was troubling! Again, I didn't know why! Maybe something in his tone of voice? Maybe it was his facial expression? I filled him in -- on my work schedule. Then, he took off! Rather speedily!

In reviewing the encounter -- while attempting to turn my attention, back to my beloved Dodge -- I'd considered that renewing acquaintances with Eddie, had been extremely satisfying! Yet, underlying the whole situation, was a whole, unknown, dimension. Some unidentifiable element -- an inexplicable element -- which was troubling! Deeply troubling!

FIVE

I'd walked back, into the house -- after having made my beautiful Dodge, even "beautifuller". Doris met me -- just inside the door. She was almost out of breath.

"Gord! I saw *Eddie*! *Saw* him ... out there! Saw you *talking* to him! What did he ... what did he *want*?"

"Wanted to just say hello. I *really* don't think he holds as much ... uh ... well, not as much *animosity* toward you, as you may think. Neither toward *you* ... nor your parents."

"*That's* a shock," she grumped. "You *might*, you know ... you might be *wrong* about that! What about *Cathy*? What about *her*? Did he even *mention* her? Even mention *Cathy*? His own *daughter*?"

"Yeah! A *lot*! And ... apparently ... so has *Leon*! So *had* Leon! *Leon's* been talking about her, also! *Often*! Always talking to *Eddie* ... about her! About *Cathy*! *Numerous* times!"

"*Leon*? *Him*? I'd had no *idea* that ..."

"On numerous *occasions*," I repeated. "Did his best ... as near as I can understand it ... to *convince* Eddie, that Cathy doesn't like him! That she *hates* him! Actually *hates* him! *Despises* him!"

"That's ... that's not true! It couldn't be true! Not true,,, at all!"

"Plainly! Look! You know it ... and I know it! But, Eddie? He doesn't know it. In spades! Hasn't the slightest handle ... on the situation! And I guess ... that Leon has crossed paths with Eddie, often enough ... that he'd, continually, warned Eddie, to stay away! Stay away ... from any, of you people! Any of you! From all you people! Apparently ... as I understand it ... he should especially stay away from Cathy! Eddie should! A deputy sheriff ... and he's afraid! Just plain frightened ... to come anywhere near you! Any of you! This Leon! He must've been quite a ... quite a ... quite a piece of work! I guess ... maybe ... he still might be!"

"You'd have to have known him."

"No thank you! By the bye, Eddie said that he'd like to have lunch with me sometime. Any problem there? It'd be on my lunch break ... at the store. And, also by the bye, he seemed thrilled ... that I was working, for *Food Fair*."

"That, I can believe. He loved that place. No, I really don't have a problem ... with you and him getting together, for lunch. As long as ... as it's not here! *Pond's*, maybe ... or someplace! Just not ... just not here! Not now, anyway. Not now!"

Doris, I knew, was trying to be nice. Well, she's always nice. But, I could tell -- that my encounter with Eddie -- well, it had been enormously disconcerting, to her. And, dammit, I'd had no inkling -- as to whether my hokey little play-by-play reconstruction, of the episode, had helped! Or had caused her even further discomfort! Could not tell!

❖

It was just before noon -- and, surprisingly, I'd worked up a bit of a sweat. Though it had been in a worthwhile cause -- that gorgeous Dodge, don't you see -- I did need to clean up.

Aunt Agnes and Uncle Albert did not provide a shower. Mainly, because their house didn't have one! But, they did see to it that there'd been a really nifty bathtub -- upstairs, between "my" bedroom and theirs. It was an old-fashioned tub -- set upon those short, fat, toenail-laden, dorky-looking, iron legs! And it was as comfortable, as it could be! In just the short week, that I'd been there, I'd already spent a goodly number of hours -- languishing, in the unending supply of, therapeutic, hot water!

And so it came to pass -- that I was, once again, relaxing in the healing (almost medicinal) waters -- of that glorious tub. About twenty minutes in to this beneficial tour of refurbishment -- in walked Doris! She was wearing a bathrobe!

But, not for long! Obviously, there'd been no clothing -- beneath that purple, woolen, dandy. She'd winced -- sighed, heavily -- at the water's temperature, once she'd crawled in! Crawled in -- and had lain atop me! Obviously, the tub was good for more than one application!

Afterward (again, that term) she'd remained "on top of things"! For an extended amount of time! Even -- most efficiently -- she'd maneuvered the Hot Water spigot (twice), to let even more of the therapeutic, healing, liquid in! Removing the drain plug -- we shouldn't flood the joint (any more than we already had, during those frantic first minutes) -- required a little more expertise! But, that phase -- of the, extremely-noble, undertaking -- was also accomplished! Deftly! With much, really-great, aplomb!

I could only assume that she'd not been that upset -- at my having crossed paths, with Eddie. Either that, or she'd needed the escape -- into the "relaxing" waters -- as much, as I had!

Tuesday and Wednesday! My days off! And -- strangely (or not) -- I'd not made any plans. On Monday night -- as I'd left the store -- I'd picked up five or six sacks of groceries, to present to Mom. As a partial -- a really partial -- payment, for all the magnificent meals, that she'd prepared.

Shortly after noon, on Tuesday, Dahse and I decided to walk the two blocks to a nice, moderate-sized, restaurant -- for lunch. The cafe was located, in the same concentrated, two-block, area -- as the fabled, storied, barber shop. The one that Pop and I had visited, three days previously.

A half-block -- up Mathews Street -- we'd been, of course, directly across from the, almost-brooding, Clayton home. It was, at that point, that Eddie's father had decided to step out, onto his white-marbled stoop. Apparently, he'd, just recently, begun his retirement, from whatever commercial field, in which he'd been involved, for -- I was sure -- a good many years.

I'd started to nudge Doris across -- to greet him! But, immediately, two things happened: My escort hesitated -- with great exuberance! She'd left no doubt -- as to her reluctance! And Mr. Clayton -- having spied us -- made his way, back inside! With great haste!

That whole exercise -- had come as a complete surprise to me! In both cases! Some things, I knew, I would never understand!

Out luncheon -- following which we'd taken in a movie at the next-door *Glenmont Theater* -- seemed a little on the labored side. I'm certain that the slight discomfort had come, for the most part, from the aborted attempted "greeting" -- on Mathews Street. And I still couldn't figure out why.

The supper, that evening, was particularly rewarding. Mainly because I was able to relate -- a little bit further -- with Cathy. Mostly about how she'd liked -- or disliked -- her school. (It was, primarily, the former.) We'd delved -- rather deeply -- into her curriculum, her schoolmates, etc. etc. etc. Very satisfying -- for the most part.

Noticeably absent from the conversation -- was any reference, to her father. I'd been positive that someone would've advised her -- of my having had my little encounter, with him. Another puzzlement!

The following Saturday, Eddie popped in -- at the food market -- at a few minutes before seven, and asked if I'd want to break bread with him, at *Pond's,* across the street. He was in uniform -- and seemed to know a lot of my fellow employees. At least, he'd interacted -- animatedly -- with almost all of them. Including Mr. Tontalo, the manager. Most especially -- with Mr. Tontalo.

I'd agreed to accompany my former "shipmate" -- across the street. Surprisingly -- to me, anyway -- Lois Pond seemed awfully glad to see him! (See him "again" -- as she'd, so gleefully, emoted!) Made me wonder -- even further -- about this woman. But, admittedly, there'd been nothing -- on which to "hang my hat". A larger question: Why was any of this even bothering me? In the first damn place?

As near as I could tell -- while the meal was progressing -- there'd been no dark, conspiratorial, reason, behind Eddie's wanting to get together. We'd spoken, mostly, of our naval careers. And had laughed (mostly) at some of the, semi-loony, incidents -- that the, memory-stirring, most-satisfying, conversation had dredged up.

Then, I kind of "snuck up" on him -- with a prospect, that had, admittedly, come out of the fabled, storied, well-known, "left field":

"Would you mind, Eddie ... if, sometime, we could get together, when I'm not working? And then, if I brought along ... Cathy?"

"Cath ... Cathy? Why ... why would you bring her up? Suggest bringing her, with you? I mean ..."

"She is your daughter, after all. And I know you well enough ... that I'm sure that you care! Care about her! You have ... to care about her!"

"I ... well, I ... uh ... sure. Yeah. I guess ... sure. What ... uh ... what about ... about Doris? About her? I mean, would she ... ?'

"I haven't the foggiest idea. I haven't come close ... to even broaching the subject to her. But, you know, it's something that ... well, something that ... that really should be addressed. One way ... or another."

"Yeah. I guess so." His tone of voice seemed to be coming from some sort of -- I dunno -- alter-ego, or something. It was as though I was talking, with someone else. Eddie was -- plainly -- less than enthused. Plainly!

"Well, give it some thought," I muttered. "And, perhaps, I'll bounce it off of ... off of Doris. And, maybe, Cathy ... herself. Perhaps."

"Yeah ... uh ... well. Okay ... I guess."

The whole prospect -- of a get-together with his daughter -- was something else! Another ball -- being juggled, precariously, aloft! Another one -- of my "deft" undertakings.

On Sunday, the following afternoon -- a couple of hours, after church -- Doris and I had wound up sitting, once more, in her tiny kitchen, upstairs.

She'd brewed me a cup of tea -- then, had stepped, into her bedroom. When she'd returned -- three or four minutes later -- she was wearing that same bathrobe. And, she saw to it -- that I'd recognized the fact, that there'd been nothing else -- under there!

"Look, Dahse," I began -- staring at her mostly-exposed bosom. "I had lunch with Eddie ... yesterday."

"You did?" The declaration had stopped her -- in her tracks. "Why? For heaven's sake ... why? Why would you do that?"

"Well, he suggested it. Popped in, y'know ... at the store. I'd run the idea before you! You don't remember that?"

The question brought absolutely no response. Not so you'd notice, anyway.

"Well then," she responded, at long last -- displaying, eventually, an iceberg tone of voice, I'd never heard, from her, before, "why don't you just go to bed ... with him?"

"Doris ... that's not fair! Not fair ... at all! He ... listen, he wanted to ... to go to lunch! You knew that! That's all! Just damn lunch! I simply agreed! We went to lunch ... for God's sakes! Was not a big deal! We, mostly, hashed over old times ... like I said. About when we were terrorizing the Naval Air Station, don'tcha know."

"Oh? And where did this nourishing discussion take place?"

"At *Pond's*. At *Pond's Cafe*. Across the street."

"And Lois Ponds? Was she there?"

"Yeah. I guess ... as I understand it ... I guess she's always there. At least, she has ... the few times, that I've ever been ..."

"Oh? And do you and she ... do you get along?" She was beginning to cover up as much cleavage, as possible. "Do you and she ... you and Lois ... do you really get along? Get along ... really well? Get along ... nicely?"

"Look! What the hell is all this? This stupid-assed inquisition? Some stupid-assed third degree? I went to lunch ... okay? Went to lunch ... with your former husband! As opposed to going to damn bed with him! I don't know where Lois was ... half the time."

"Listen, Gordie ..."

"Nor," I half-shouted, "did I damn well *care*! Nor *do* I care! *Look*! If this has all started a whole big *magilla* ... then, just put your clothes back on! In fact, it's probably well ... that you put your clothes back on, anyway! And let's just *drop* the whole damn thing! Let's go back downstairs! *Forget* it! Forget ... about the whole sexual *interlude*! I never thought I'd ever ... *ever* ... hear myself *say* this, to you! *Especially* not since Chicago! But, sex is *not* the damn answer! *Not* the answer, you know ... to *every*-damn-thing!"

"I'm sorry, Gord." She loosened her neckline again. With a good deal of vigor. "It's just that ..."

"*No*! I'm tired of walking on eggs, around here! If what I *do* ... if *everything* I do ... is gonna be subject, to the third damn *degree*, then, it's jolly well not *worth* it! If I have to move *out* ... then, by God, I will! Go put your *clothes* back on! Go get yourself *dressed*!"

She did -- exactly -- the *opposite*! She *removed* her robe! *Completely*! *Immediately*! Then, she seated herself -- totally unclothed -- across the table, from me!

"I'm *sorry*," she rasped. "I didn't mean to make you ... to make you ... make you *upset*! I just ..."

"Well, a good deal of all this ... may be, all in my *head*," I grumped. "Probably *is*! But, for one reason or another ... for *some* reason ... I've felt that every move I *make*, around here, is *weighed*! Every damn *move*! From three-weeks-till-*Tuesday*!"

"*Gord*! I had no *idea*!"

"And I, damn well, am getting tired of it!" For better -- or for worse -- there was no stopping me, by then. "And, for some reason or another, I have this feeling that ... as a, handy-dandy, remedy for all this ... we always wind up in bed! Or in the stupid bathtub! And, listen! While it's great ... it's always great ... it's not always the answer! Now, Eddie and I went to lunch! Went to lunch ... yesterday! And I have no idea ... where the hell Lois might've been! Or what she may have been doing! And, what's more, I asked him ... asked Eddie ... if he'd be interested in something really testy! Be interested ... in my bringing Cathy! Bringing her ... to have lunch with him. Sometime ... in the future!"

"You ... you did? You ... what'd he ... what did he say?"

"I dazzled him ... with the question! Brought it ... right out of the blue! He's ... well, he's ... he's not sure. Probably should have kept my big mouth shut! It was ... the whole thing was ... well, it was kind of left ... left, up in the air! Now, if he wants to ... are you gonna be ... gonna be the 'dog-in-the-manger'?"

"Dog-in-the ... ? Listen! I'd ... well, I'd have to think about it! Really think about it!"

"Then, dammit, think! Think! Clothed ... or unclothed! And ... while you're at it ... try and figure out what Cathy would want! It's really all about her, y'know."

With that, I got up -- and made my way downstairs.

Wound up playing six, or eight, games of Chinese Checkers! With Cathy! And I never brought it up! Never mentioned -- the subject of meeting, with her father -- with the neat kid!

❖

On Monday, when I'd pulled into the *Food Fair's* parking lot, I'd chanced to look across the street -- to the parking area, in front of *Pond's*. There was Uncle Albert's Dodge. Oh, there were, back then, a whole boodle of blue '65 Polaras. But, I'd never seen one -- with a full, dark-blue, vinyl roof! Not like Uncle Albert's! Not before! Not since!

Now what? Is HE mixed up with Lois ... too? Like everyone ELSE?

Things -- things, with this family -- were (to put it charitably) awfully damn strange! I was, by then, having serious thoughts -- about finding my own place. I ought to move, anyway! Under the best of circumstances, I couldn't, in good faith, continue -- to sponge off of them. They'd all been most unselfish -- really generous -- with me! Most unselfish and really generous! But, really, some of the O'Banion family! You had to wonder about them! Some of them, anyway. About what they might be thinking, beneath the surface! About what they might be planning! Surface -- or otherwise!

Monday night/Tuesday morning -- at about 12:25AM -- I pulled up to the twin residences, on Mathews Street! It seemed as though every light -- in both houses -- was blaring more illumination, than I could ever have imagined. And there three city police cruisers, parked in front -- as well as two, unmarked-but-equally-as-obvious, law-enforcement vehicles.

I rushed into the O'Banion's side -- and was greeted by Mom! I'd never seen her look so distraught! Or nearly so haggard!

"What the hell's going on?" I'd half-shouted.

"It's Cathy!" she'd responded -- in a tone, that dwarfed mine. "We think she's been ... that she's been ... been kidnapped!"

"Kidnapped? Cathy? She's been ... kidnapped? Kidnapped ... for God's sake?"

"We think so! She's never gotten home ... you know! Never did get home! Not from school!"

"From school? From school? She's been missing? Missing ... for all this time? For, like, eight hours?"

As Mom was nodding her affirmation, Doris came bursting out, from the dining room -- where all the other adults had gathered! Including two uniformed police officers -- along with three other law enforcement personnel, clad in plain clothes. The latter trio was comprised -- of two middle-aged men, and one late-twenties/early-thirties woman!

Everyone seemed to be talking -- all at once -- albeit in almost-hushed tones. Doris was -- by far -- the most distressed! Uncle Albert -- he, of the afternoon visit, to *Pond's* -- was seated, at the table, with most of the others. But, he looked to be almost-half-asleep. Was contributing nothing to the, rabid, vocal, goings-on. But, in a manner of speaking, he was taking nothing away.

Aunt Agnes was, far and away, the most animated! Until, at least, Doris had finished leading me back to the frenzied gathering. Then, the younger woman retook that role! She was -- by far -- the most frantic person, in the room! Perfectly understandable!

The police authority-in-charge was Lt. Daniel Meyer. The portly, mid-fifties, officer was -- at that point -- maintaining his assurance that, "everything that can be done ... is being done"!

A couple of minutes, after I'd joined the still-frantic group, Pop O'Banion introduced me -- to the lieutenant. The officer did his best -- to fill me in. But, there wasn't much to disclose! Cathy had, simply, not arrived home -- from school. The authorities had interviewed a number of people, from the facility -- and in the neighborhood. As near as could be determined, Cathy had left the building -- with absolutely no fanfare! As usual! No one had a clue -- as to what may have happened to her, after that!

"Have you tried," I'd finally wound up asking, "to get hold of her father?"

"Aren't you the father?" asked the lieutenant -- rather incredulously!

"No! He's ... the father is ... Eddie Clayton! He's the father! He's a deputy sheriff ... with the county. You didn't know that?"

"Hell no! Why the hell didn't someone tell me?"

Pop shrugged -- an overdone gesture -- and growled, "I guess it never occurred to us. To any of us."

"Yes," bellowed Aunt Agnes. "Why would it? We're all concerned ... about Cathy! About the little girl ... for heaven's sakes! We're not ..."

The policewoman -- Arlene Pruden -- immediately activated her radio set, and (I assumed) began trying to track down Eddie!

After that brief "gust", the lower-keyed "organized confusion" wound up being, troublingly, reinstalled! There were a few additional fillips! Mostly having to do with who -- among the family members -- had been responsible, for not informing the good lieutenant, as to the identity, of Cathy's biological father. But, not a whole lot was being accomplished.

Forty-five minutes later, Eddie burst in! He'd simply roared in -- through the front door! He was, of course, visibly upset -- to put it mildly! Almost as rattled, as his former wife!

Again, Lt. Meyer went over the particulars -- explained them, thoroughly -- with the newcomer! A whole raft of questions ensued! I was sure that -- having been in law enforcement, for a goodly number of years -- Eddie was able to have made a number of more intelligent inquiries, than the rest of us. But, seemingly, nothing would've moved us closer -- to any answers!

The following day was Tuesday. My day off! And, around the O'Banion household, very little got accomplished. Including the, usually-lavish, meals. The place was -- wall to wall and cover to cover -- atwitter. Even Pop O'Banion -- who'd taken the day off, from work -- was, continually, harping (or grousing) about something, or another. Uncle Albert, however, had gone off to work. With him, it seemed as though nothing out of the ordinary had taken place. What else was new?

My sole contribution had been -- that, maybe, the family could, at least, consider the fact that the person(s) responsible might, possibly, be either (or, possibly, both) of Eddie's parents. The girl's grandparents!

"They live ... just a half-a-block away," I'd suggested, more than once. "They've never been especially fond of Doris. Even Mrs. Clayton. Well, especially Mrs. Clayton."

That -- those suggestions -- had brought on a firestorm, of criticism! Surprisingly-bitter criticism! Toward yours truly!

"That's the most dumb-assed thing I ever heard," observed Pop. "I know Howard Clayton ... long enough, to know that he'd never hold still, for something like that! Let alone be behind such a rotten-assed, despicable, foul, deed! Her? I don't really know. But, he'd never permit it. Never allow it!"

"I know her ... a little better than most," added Aunt Agnes. "And ... whatever any of us may think ... she'd never stoop to something so low! As reprehensible ... as this! She'd be incapable ... of anything even close to something like this!"

"Yeah," insisted Doris. "We were never really close.. Not either one of them ... was ever particularly fond of me. Even before Eddie and I were married. And listen. Both of 'em could've shown a little more love ... a little more attention ... to their own granddaughter. But, neither of them would ... neither one of them could, I don't think ... stoop to anything like this!"

"What you're saying, Gordie," furnished Mom O'Banion, "is completely off the wall! Totally out of bounds!" That made everything unanimous!

So -- for once in my life -- I shut up! A distinct upset!

As the afternoon had dragged on, there weren't many of us -- saying much of anything! A frightenly-morbid, toxic, overwhelming, feeling -- of positive, undeniable, *doom* -- had, by then, pervaded the entire family unit! The pronounced, deadly-grim, portrait was fast becoming more and more pronounced -- as the afternoon was wearing on, and beginning to give way to early-evening! And *still* -- at that point -- not one *word*! From *anybody*! From *anything*!

Mom, naturally, had had her *Emerson,* portable, radio going -- in the kitchen -- all day! Tuned to a 24/7 news station! No *mention* -- not one *syllable* -- about the God-awful kidnapping!

Pop had had the TV blaring -- from the living room! *Also* all day! To one of the local channels. And *nothing* there! Nary a word -- coming over "The Tube"! *Nothing*!

The, pervasive, all-encompassing, down-in-the-mouth, wall-to-wall, *gloom* had infused every *inch* -- every *molecule* -- of every person, in the house. Including me.

Spirits were *not* lifted -- when Uncle Albert returned, from work and had, glumly, asked, "Not a goddam *word*?". He'd, of course, *known* the answer!

Then *HUZZAH*!

At slightly-before-seven o'clock -- Tuesday evening -- *guess* who showed up! It was *Cathy*! Along with her *father*!

Doris was practically, in *hysterics*! (*Practically*?)

"Cathy! Cathy ... baby!" She was communicating -- at the top of her lungs! "Are you ... are you all right?"

"She's fine!" assured Eddie. "Absolutely fine!"

"Did they ... did they ... did they hurt you?" Doris' voice had lowered -- considerably. An unmistakable -- overwhelming -- degree of fear had entered her tone! "Did they ... did they ... did they do anything? Do anything ... something, uh, bad ... to you?"

"Naw," answered the girl's father. "She's fine! Nothing happened! Nothing ... like what you're thinking!"

"How can you say that?" It was both Doris, and Pop -- in choral unison! "How can you possibly say that?" continued Pop. "How can you possibly ... say that? Know that?"

Because I damn well know it," answered the younger man.

"I am fine!" assured Cathy. It was the first time that she'd spoken. "I'm fine! Fine! Really!"

"They ... they didn't do anything?" Doris' voice was still overflowing -- with doubt! And out and out, sheer, fear! "They didn't ... uh ... they didn't ..."

"There was no 'they'," informed Eddie. "There was only one person involved! Nothing happened ... to Cathy! It was Leon! He took her!"

"Leon?" Every voice, in the room, echoed the word. "It was Leon?" asked Pop. "Him?"

That was all the response -- except for Uncle Albert! He'd grumped, "fucking Leon?"

For some reason, everything -- everybody -- in the room stopped! All eyes were zeroed in -- on Uncle Albert! Who'd then repeated the, two-word, question -- verbatim! But, in slightly higher volume.

"It ... it was ... was Leon?" asked Doris, at length -- while everyone waited for the smoke to clear away, from Uncle Albert's dual inquiry. "How could it be ... be Leon?

"Why not?" answered her former spouse. "To me ... it figured! Always figured! Right from the start! Logical ... as hell! Listen! Are you not 'living in sin'? 'Living in sin'? In a manner of religious speaking? With Gord?"

"Aw ... now wait a minute," protested Pop. "Just because ..."

"You have to remember," interrupted the deputy. "Pay attention ... to Leon's interpretation of ... of Christian morality! He simply ... in his way of thinking ... could not permit his, so-called, 'daughter', to be subjected, to such continued moral outrage! Could not allow it! He felt he had to act!"

"Damn," muttered Aunt Agnes. I'd never heard her use that word before. "He's right, you know," she expanded. "Eddie's right! We should've thought of that! All of us! We all should've thought of that. Of what Leon would think! How he'd react!"

"Since there seemed to have been no evidence of a struggle, at the school yard," explained the deputy, "I'd figured, that she'd ... that Cathy ... had simply been duped! Had simply been tricked! Tricked ... into getting into someone's car. With someone she knew!. I went on over to the school ... early this morning! Spent almost all day ... talking! Talking, with students! I have no idea ... as to how many! A lot, of 'em! A hell of a lot! I finally got this one little girl ... to tell me, that she thought that she saw Cathy get into a green sports car. A green foreign car. Well, Leon, y'know! He drives that, damn-fool, dark-green, Jaguar! That was enough! Enough ... for me! Enough for me ... to go ahead, and act!"

"Is ... is that true?" asked Doris -- of her daughter.

"Yes!" answered the young lady -- almost under her breath. "He told me, that you wanted him ... to pick me up!" Her tone of voice picked up a little -- in volume. "He said ... that you'd had something special going on! He just never told me ... what it was! So? So, I just got in! In the car ... with him! He took me to his ... to his apartment! I didn't even question it then! I expected ... when he'd opened the door, over there ... expected that all of you'd be there! At a party ... or something! There ... in his apartment! But, no one was! There wasn't anyone there! Just us! Me ... and him!"

The explanation was becoming more and more tension-filled. It was obvious that it would be difficult -- for her to continue! So, her father took up the narrative:

"He told her," he said. "Leon explained ... explained his 'reasoning' ... to her! His moral outrage ... at whatever might've been going on, between you, and Gord. Told her that ... as long as she'd behaved herself ... he'd not harm her. So, Cathy did ... what you'd expect her to do. What any girl ... with her head on her shoulders ... would've done! She behaved herself!"

"Yeah." The young lady was rallying. "I figured that ... at any moment ... someone would show up! To take me home! Would've promised Leon ... that Gordon ... that he would be moving out. Moving ... out of the house, or something. Whether that was gonna, y'know, be true ... or not!"

"Yep," renewed her father. "I really think that's all ... all that he'd really wanted to hear! Hopefully, he'd not been aiming to harm her ... at all! I don't believe he was gonna do her any harm!"

"That's right," affirmed Cathy. "He always let me go to the bathroom ... you know ... whenever I needed to go! Always let me close the door! He's only got one bedroom ... over there, where he's living now. And he let me use it! Could close the door, even! I did close the door! I never took off my clothes, though! Would never take my clothes off ... over there! I thought about sneaking out ... trying to sneak out ... in the middle of the night, you know! But, look! He was probably sleeping ... on the couch! And that's right inside the door ... in the front room! I didn't know what he'd do to me ... if I got caught! And, you know ... it was a 'so far, so good' thing, with me! So, I did what I could ... to just try, and get some sleep!"

"Not much?" I asked. "Not much sleep, Kid?"

"Nope," she answered with, what-you-could-call, a wry smile. "Not hardly any!"

"I managed to get there ... a couple hours ago," added Eddie.

"Surprised the bejeebers out of me," augmented his daughter. "Daddy ... he actually kicked in the front door! Kicked it right in! Scared the bejeebers out of me! Especially, when he came busting in ... with his gun drawn."

"Did Leon ... did he do anything?" I asked. "Do anything ... uh ... frightening? To protest? To resist?"

"Naw," responded my old naval buddy. "He damn well knew better! It wouldn't have taken much ... for him to have wound up, being awful sorry! Being damn sorry! To be damn sorry!"

"I was so glad ... so happy ... to see Daddy," exclaimed the young girl. "Gun drawn ... or no!"

She smiled up at him! There really is something special -- between daddies and daughters! Of that, I've always been sure! This was simply more proof! Documentable proof!

Eddie had gone on -- to explain that he'd taken his "little girl". (as well as the kidnapper) down to

Police Headquarters, and had spoken to "all the right people". He'd filled out all the "necessary forms" -- apparently, a paperwork avalanche! Then, he'd brought Cathy straight to the O'Banion house -- for the tear-filled reunion!

We'd all -- minutes later -- adjourned, to the most-expensive restaurant in town! Eddie included! To celebrate -- our good fortune! All except for Uncle Albert!

Leon, apparently, had had more than a few "connections", within his reach! At Police Headquarters, the Fire Department (and even City Hall)! Due to his always-seemingly-being-involved, when it came to a fire (major or minor) -- and even to a, surprisingly-significant, number of police standoffs/hostage situations.

As it turned out, he was out of Headquarters -- fully 45 minutes before Eddie and Cathy, had been turned loose.

SIX

On Wednesday -- also my day off -- I informed Doris, Aunt Agnes, Mom O'Banion, and also Cathy, that I thought it'd be best, for me, to look for quarters, "of my own".

I didn't really expect anyone to protest. Quite frankly, I didn't know what to expect. Certainly, no gnashing of teeth. Doris tried to hide her emotion -- but, there appeared to be the slightest (and briefest) expression of relief. Mom's reaction -- was no reaction! Not the slightest indication -- as to what she might be thinking. Aunt Agnes advised me -- that it had been a "pleasure" having me.

It was Cathy -- who'd moved me, emotionally! Had really jarred me: I guess it figured to be.

"I want to thank you, Gordon," she'd said, her eyes watering -- more than slightly. "Thank you ... for bringing my father and me together. The whole thing wasn't as spectacular ... not like me being kidnapped, or anything spooky as that. But ... right after you moved in here, you talked to me ... about Daddy. You were the one ... who talked to me, about him." She looked around the table -- flashing a look, that defies description. "And," she continued, "no one else, around here ... no one else ... would! No one else ever did!"

Something I would've thought impossible: The dazzling amount -- of pure, unadulterated, defiance -- she'd summoned, in her voice!

The statement, itself, could've (maybe should have) come from someone -- twice her age! Three -- or four times -- her age. I don't remember -- ever -- having been quite so moved! To the point, that -- no matter how hard I'd tried -- I'd come up, unable to muster a halfway-intelligent response. Totally tongue-tied! My only response -- was to do my best, to stifle the, more-than-few, tears, that had begun to stream down my own face.

My "Lucky Day" -- I guess. I was able to score a small, one-bedroom, furnished, apartment, three blocks, down the same street, from where the *Food Fair* was located.

In fact, Mr. Tontalo had put me onto the place. I'd indicated my intention, to him -- first thing, upon arriving, for my shift. He'd informed me -- that his sister-in-law was putting this particular place up for rent. But, it would not be available -- till Saturday. He then arranged, that I could go look, at the place -- on my lunch break.

It was just the thing! A small living/sleeping room -- and an even smaller kitchen/dinette.

The "larger" room featured a full-sized Murphy bed -- which pivoted, in and out of a surprisingly-vast closet. The only closet, in the joint. It was, obviously, sufficient, for my Spartan needs. Well, in addition, there was a, larger-than-imagined, set of, built-in, drawers -- located, in the bathroom. The, from-the-forties, gas range -- and the old-fashioned refrigerator -- were, I was assured, "in good working order". And listen! The $65.00-a-month rent was ideal -- "for the likes of me"!

I'd advised the denizens -- of Mathews Street -- on Friday, that I'd be vacating the premises, on Saturday.

Again, I'd met with "mixed results" -- to my announcement. Including the reaction of Cathy -- which was, more-than-a-little, disappointing. And unexplainable.

I was not aware of this, at the time, but a particular auto mechanic had left his place of employment -- a Dodge/Plymouth dealership -- had gotten into his blue Polara (with a full vinyl roof), and had driven, to a suburban apartment house; outside of which had sat a green Jaguar.

Once inside, he'd kicked in the door -- of one of the building's residents! The tenant's name was Leon! The intruder had -- immediately-and-efficiently -- strangled him! To death! With his bare hands! Then, the perpetrator had, calmly, made his way to *Pond's*

Cafe! Once he'd arrived, at the eatery, he'd -- equally as calmly -- had ordered one of their famous "onions inside" hamburgers. As well as a cup of coffee -- which, it appeared, was <u>not</u> a necessary, truly-needed, vital, ingredient for his mental/emotional wellbeing!

On Saturday, It had taken -- strangely enough -- all morning for me, to move my sparse amount of belongings, into my new abode. And -- by the time I'd finished buying the necessary foodstuffs, along with sheets, pillowcases, a blanket, a few towels and washcloths, plus a few dishes/coffee mugs/ silverware (the latter of these, I'd not <u>thought</u> of -- till the last minute) it was time to report for duty, at the store.

Not only was I virtually <u>broke</u>, I was <u>exhausted</u>! But, the physically (and emotionally) draining effort -- had been well <u>worth</u> the effort! As well as the expenses incurred. <u>Somehow</u>, I'd felt so -- so <u>free</u>! So much more independent -- and, certainly, a good deal more <u>confident</u> -- than anything I'd experienced, in <u>years</u>! In <u>decades</u>! In -- probably -- <u>forever</u>! Don't ask me why!

I'd not laid in a <u>phone</u>! I'd not felt the need for one -- for openers. Plus, till my next paycheck, I was -- literally -- a pauper! A "ne'er-do-well", if you will. Strangely -- or maybe not -- I'd felt no immediate duty, to call my former associates, on Mathews Street. If they'd have felt the need (or desire) to phone me -- they all knew that I was pretty well reachable. At the market.

As you may have guessed, none of them experienced the insatiable necessity -- to contact me. Troubling, in one manner of speaking. But, liberating -- in quite another.

As you can tell, I was having a goodly amount of difficulty -- dealing with the many, confusion-producing, emotions behind it all. A goodly amount of difficulty!

The absence of people -- ones close to me -- was having a definite effect! One that -- I was certain -- was not good! In my mind, I was, suddenly, in danger -- of becoming the next thing to a recluse. Seldom was I venturing forth -- from my, treasured, apartment. Except to go to work. A frightening prospect!

I continued taking in, my normal salary. Fortunately, there'd been very little, additional, outlay of cash, at that point. So, I bought an old, used -- "glorious"-black-and-white -- *Muntz TV* set. One -- with a 17-inch screen. And I was, for the most part, "held prisoner" to it. To the point, that I'd gone ahead -- eventually -- and invested, in a brand-new recliner chair. For my "viewing pleasure".

Except for an excessive amount of potato chips, popcorn -- and newly-discovered *Dr. Pepper* -- I wasn't spending an awful lot of my "wealth", on little luxuries, such as groceries. (Plus, I was getting a discount -- a substantial one -- on those.)

Oh, I was eating lunch -- two or three times a week -- at *Pond's*, across from the dealership. But, I'd felt, there was not really anything unusual about that. I was merely continuing a routine that had, basically, begun -- during my residence, on Mathews Street.

On the other hand, Lois and I were getting to be fairly-close friends. Closer than I'd imagined! Close enough -- that she felt no restraint, when it came to observing that I was "putting on a little weight". In fact, one evening -- when I'd ordered a piece of their delicious apple pie -- she'd refused to serve it, to me. Hmmmph!

To my way of thinking, though, there seemed to be nothing special going on with her. Still, we'd spent more and more time together -- as the days and weeks had gone by. Mostly chatting. By the time I would arrive, the dinnertime crowd was, usually, thinning out. Substantially, in some cases. So she'd had a few more minutes, to -- often -- spend with me. And, most often, she'd done just that!

On the other hand, I did find a small, fast-food, joint -- just around the corner, from the store -- that served the most magnificent-tasting hotdogs. I'd not struck up any new acquaintances there. In fact, employee-turnover, at the place, seemed to be "on the moon". Couldn't tell why. The environment, at the place, had always seemed docile enough.

These being my new "facts of life", I'd, eventually, settled in -- to a rather sedentary lifestyle. An existence -- without hardly any contact, with my immediate past. A hefty portion of me, however, was beginning, to miss the constant give-and-take -- at the twin houses, on Mathews Street.

I found myself especially regretting not hearing -- from Cathy! Being unable to talk to her! Those enriching, in-the-past, interchanges -- that I'd had with her -- had been few! Too few! Too damn few! But, they'd always been so enriching! So rewarding!

Then -- should I say "suddenly"? -- I was visited, at *Pond's*, by one Edward Clayton! My, seemingly-long-lost, Navy buddy! It was shortly after I'd arrived -- that he'd blown in!

Lois had rushed up to greet him! With a gigantic -- rib-crushing -- hug! That, off-the-seat-of-her-pants, maneuver, was causing a slight tug -- at the old heartstrings -- for me! Maybe not so slight a tug! Couldn't really understand why! Well, actually,

I guessed, I <u>could</u>! To a <u>point</u>, anyway! But, the display -- of pure, honest, affection -- should <u>never</u> have caused that <u>much</u>, of a, definitely-negative, reaction, on my part! <u>Should</u> it?

<u>Finally</u> Eddie seated himself, next to me -- at the counter. Ordered, merely, a cup of coffee. Then, reaching in -- to one of the breast-pockets, of his uniform shirt -- he proffered an official-looking document!

I was almost <u>afraid</u> -- to accept it! (<u>Almost</u>?) It turned out to be -- an <u>invitation</u>! A <u>wedding</u> invitation! An invite to <u>his</u> nuptials! His "hitching up" -- with <u>Doris'</u>! They were "getting back together"! In <u>spades</u>!

The nuptials were scheduled for ten-days hence. I <u>guess</u> I was not <u>shocked</u>! But, I <u>was</u> mildly surprised! When I'd attempted to <u>analyze</u> the union-to-be (numerous times) I'd found myself agreeing (with myself) -- that I'd <u>guessed</u> it made sense! Surely -- well, <u>seemingly</u> anyway -- it would, undoubtedly, make Cathy happy! To me, <u>that</u> would be the most <u>rewarding</u> -- the most <u>vital</u> -- aspect, of the whole, entire, highly-unusual, "reuniting"!

Two days later, Eddie phoned me -- at the store -- and asked me. to be his Best Man! <u>That</u> rattled me! <u>Really</u> jolted me! To the <u>bone</u>! Left me completely -- entirely -- <u>flummoxed</u>!

While I was still fighting "the good fight" -- how to, simply, react to the, out-of-left-field, request, my old "naval shipmate" assured me, "It's a totally-informal thing. All you need is a, halfway-decent-looking, dark-blue, suit. About the color of Uncle Albert's car. And, of course, a white shirt ... plus, a semi-presentable tie. Oh, and a passable pair of black shoes. They would help."

"I dunno, Ed. I mean, I have this feeling that I've been kind of persona-non-grata around there. Ever since ..."

"Nonsense! Everyone misses you! Everyone! They all love you! Including Doris! And Cathy? You're her hero! Her flat-out hero! She's thrilled ... at the thought, of you being included!"

"Oh, I doubt that. She's always been much more interested ... in you! You did save her, y 'know. And you are her papa."

"Yeah, maybe. But, you have no idea, how many times she's told me that you were the first one ... in the entire O'Banion household, including Doris ... who'd spoken well of me. Spoken really well of me. Which is why ... I want you, to be my Best Man! You had something nice to say about me. And you'd spoken up, to me! Set me straight ... when no one else would! When no one else did! When you were washing your car! Remember? Listen! You really straightened me out, that time! When I was blathering on ... about you and me comparing stupid notes, when it came to

Doris' performance, in bed! You told me ... that I was better than that. I wasn't, y'know! Not being ... better than that. Not at that point! I really needed my ass kicked! And you kicked it! You may believe this ... or not ... but, I'll always be grateful, for that. Gord? Gord look! I really want you to be my Best Man. Really!"

"Well, if you're sure ..."

"Gord ... I've never been more sure, in my life! Never more sure ... than realizing I've been a complete, and utter, horse's ass! A complete and utter horse's ass! In the way I treated Doris! And that I'd deserted my own daughter! My own little girl ... for God's sakes!"

"Oh, you didn't desert her!"

"That's where you're wrong! I did desert her! And let me tell you: The realization ... that I'd been such a total schmuck ... came, when I'd learned that you had moved in! Moved in ... to Doris' parents' house."

"Actually, I'd stayed with Aunt Agnes, and Uncle ..."

"Same thing! And I surprised myself! Shocked myself! I was jealous of you!" He took a deep slurp, on his coffee -- then, narrowed his penetrating gaze on me! "Jealous as hell," he muttered. "I found myself trying to think! Think, of how I could frame you ... for some damn thing, or another! Something really criminal! Set you up, you know! Then ... as a law officer ... I could run you in! But, your 'better than that' comment ... that took all the wind, out of those sails!"

"Eddie! I had no idea!"

"Look, Gord! Your coming here ... your coming to Baltimore ... it made me stop and think! Really think! Think ... about my whole attitude! About my whole, asshole, outlook, on life! On life ... and on everything else! You've got to accept, Gord! You've simply got to!"

Obviously, I'd accepted! I mean, how do you do otherwise?

It was a beautiful ceremony! Simple -- but, beautiful! In the church -- that the family had been attending, for all those many years.

Doris looked resplendent -- in her simple, powder-blue, suit! Eddie seemed to positively glow -- in, his somewhat-darker-blue, suit. Even Pop O'Banion -- who I'd always felt would look totally out of place, in any kind, of suit. He'd looked like some kind of fashion plate, in his, three-piece, medium-gray, business ensemble. Mom was wearing a dated, emerald-green, evening gown. And the frock -- it fitted right in! Really!

But, Cathy! She was, out-of-this-world, gorgeous! Resplendent -- in her brand-new, white-satin, gown. The outfit -- which her father had bought for her, for the occasion. They'd made a "special shopping expedition" -- just the two of them -- to Baltimore's finest fashion outlet, for that glorious purpose!

And -- most *importantly* -- the young lady kept *looking* at me! Looking at *me*! *Continued* looking at me! With so much *love*!

My life continued on! I'd remained, in the Maryland city -- over the ensuing years! My wife and I, only recently, celebrated our 37th wedding anniversary!

I have three *beautiful* daughters! *Three* of them! And do you know? The old saying/legend is *correct*! *Spectacularly* correct! There *is* something special -- something *extra* special -- between daddies, and daughters! A whole *lot* of special -- between daddies, and daughters!

And let me *tell* you, sometime *else*: Something -- a little more -- about my wonderful *wife*. My beautiful -- my extremely *loving* -- wife! Her name is (are you ready?) *Lois*!

Lois? *Lois*? How did that ever *happen*? How *could* that ever happen? I mean, she was, you know, very *friendly*. *Very* friendly. All the *time*! But, friendly -- with *everybody*! Well, seemingly, with all the *male* patrons, of the restaurant, anyway.

I wasn't recognizing it, at the time, but -- apparently -- she was showing me a little more attention! More -- than the others! I'd thought that her "attention" was all purely platonic! Even after she'd taken to patting me, on my bottom, from time to time. I'd always enjoyed it! But (duh!) never attached all that much significance to the welcomed actions!

Finally, after maybe three or four months, she'd, ultimately, asked me: "You don't remember me, do you? Don't really remember me. Do you?"

"I ... well, uh ... no. Should I?"

"There was one Halloween, you know ... back in the fifties," she'd immediately replied -- nodding, with a goodly amount of vigor. "In the early-fifties? In Norfolk? Remember? With my husband ... well, my husband, at the time? At Eddie and Doris' apartment? Do you remember? Remember any of that?"

"You mean you were ... ? I didn't remember you ... not as being called Lois, anyway. I hate to say it ... but, really don't remember much about you at all. I mean ... that was so many years ago, and ..."

That's because I was ... more or less ... going by the name of 'Lou'. Seldom referred to ... as Lois. My husband's name, if you recall, was Lou. And my name, Lois, was close enough ... that everyone just went ahead, and referred to the two of us, as 'Lou and Lou'."

"You're ... you were ... were Lou Lindquist's wife? His old lady? You're ... you were ... ? I just can't recall ..."

"Well, that's the only time ... that I'd ever *met* you. And you'd gotten yourself discharged ... pretty soon. Right after Lou came to FAAO. Well, shortly after. So, you wouldn't have ..."

"But, *you*? You *remembered* me? I mean ... after all these *years*?"

"Of *course* I did! Of course I *do*! I did *see* you ... see you *naked* ... after all, Well, you were pretty *well* naked, anyway. The *important* parts ... in any case."

"Yeah, but I couldn't *imagine* ..."

"Listen! My marriage to Lou ... was pretty well in the toilet, by then. And ... though seeing you, in the buff, from the waist down, was *more* than a little exciting ... I was, actually, more impressed, in the way you'd handled that old man. The warrant officer's father. When he'd tried ... to put the *make* on you."

"You ... you noticed *that* too?"

"Of *course*! How could I forget?" She smiled -- broadly -- and explained, "I remember talking, with Lou. Talking, with him ... on our way home, that night. Talking ... speaking at length, with him ... about how the old geezer was trying to lure you, into the sack! He said ... Lou said ... something about how it wouldn't *surprise* him! Wouldn't have *shocked* him ... if you'd have *let* him! Let him ... ah ... *have* you! In other words, he thought you might be *gay*!"

"*Gay*? Gay? *Me*? *Gay*? I had no idea that Lundquist ever *thought* ..."

"Oh, I don't know ... don't know, if Lou actually *thought* that. Probably, he *didn't*! This all came, y'know ... after I'd gone, and told him that I'd snuck a look at you! At the plumbing! Zeroed in ... on your you-know-*what*! Like I said, my marriage was ... pretty much ... shot in the fanny, anyway. I *think* I was just trying to *zing* him! Zing him ... a good one! Just, maybe, being a little bit *bitchy*! Maybe *more* than just a little *bit*! So, he was ... I'm sure ... just, simply, trying to zing me *back*! Get *back* at me, y'know!"

"This ... *all* of this ... it's all a big *surprise*! *Helluva* big surprise!"

"I shouldn't *wonder*! Truth to tell, I've always been a little disappointed ... that you *didn't* remember me! Ever since you first came in ... to the restaurant! Especially, with my knowledge ... that you were wearing ladies *panties*, at the time! Whether you even *knew*! Knew that I'd copped a *look* ... or not."

"Doris *also* snuck a look," I advised her.

"I didn't *know* that," responded Lois -- sighing heavily. "Don't hardly know her, at *all*. But, *that* little factoid comes as ... comes as no surprise."

"I ... I simply can't *believe* this! *Any* of this."

"Well, *I* can't believe that it ... that *none* of it ... had been the least bit *memorable* to you."

"Oh, it was *memorable*, all right. I just never really placed *you*, as being part of ... as part, of the Original Cast."

"Tell, me," she queried -- with the broadest of grins. "Did it excite you? Turn you on? Wearing female under-drawers?"

"Hmmmm! Doris asked me ... the same thing! Shortly after I'd renewed acquaintances with her! After not seeing her ... for over, literally, decades! One of the first things ... that she'd even asked me!"

"Were you?" The leer increased! "Are you?"

"Well ... uh ... yeah. A little. Maybe more than a little. I dunno. Either way, I've not indulged the interest ... the, I guess, slight interest ... since then."

"I'd had the inkling ... that it'd given you a slight jolt. Maybe not so slight! Same, you know, with Eddie ... I'd always thought."

I'd felt no inclination, to fill her in -- on Eddie's, more-than-casual, "interest".

"Look," expanded Lois, "I've already told you ... of how I was the slightest bit disappointed. Well, maybe more ... than just a little disappointed ... at your not remembering, how I'd been involved, in that whole little adventure."

"Well, I apologize. For not remembering. There's no logical reason. You are an exciting woman. Were ... I'm sure ... an exciting woman, back then. It's just that ... uh ... just that I ..."

I was stopped -- in mid-excuse -- by her kissing me! Kissing me -- deeply! Passionately! Right there! Right then! Right at the counter! In her parents' cafe! In front of God and everyone -- as they say.

❖

Well, one thing led to another! Right from -- later, that very night! I don't know how -- or from where -- she'd gotten my address! But -- as mentioned above -- on that very night, I heard a knock on my door! (Well, technically, it came at about one-thirty, the following morning!)

I let her in! And -- after another long, languid, kiss -- she'd headed straight for the, already-swiveled-in, Murphy bed!

From then on, it didn't take long -- before I'd "popped the question"! And was rewarded -- with an affirmative response!

I think (in my more honest moments) that the proposal probably came from out of the well-known blue! As a result of one of our, more-flagrant, exchanges.

From that very first "Murphy bed night", I'd spent -- literally -- every one of my lunch periods, at *Pond's.* (Natch!) And, on virtually every occasion. she'd inquire -- as to whether I was encased, in feminine underpants. And, always, I'd respond -- in the negative.

Then, about five or six weeks -- into this, highly-rewarding, dimension of our relationship -- I'd nodded my head, when she'd asked the question! I'd nodded -- enthusiastically! I cannot begin -- to describe the expression that had totally contorted her face!

When I got home -- that very night -- guess <u>who</u> was waiting for me to pull up!

It was during (well, shortly <u>after</u>) our, inevitable, frenzied lovemaking -- that the question of matrimony was <u>asked</u>! And, delightfully, <u>answered</u>!

The rest -- as the hackneyed old saying goes -- is <u>history</u>!

BOOK OF STEPHEN

ONE

I have the feeling that I should be opening some TV commercial -- or something -- when I say, "Hi ... I'm Stephen Jenkins".

Back in 1975, I was 43-years-old -- and managing a small, off-site, car-rental operation, just south of the immense Houston Intercontinental Airport (since to have been renamed, after President George H.W. Bush). We'd conducted our hokey little enterprise -- out of a, slightly-smaller-than-medium-sized, hotel, on John F. Kennedy Boulevard. I'd had a "gargantuan" staff of four, totally-dedicated, people -- two rental agents, and two service agents. It had turned out, to be a highly-gratifying situation. For me, anyway. Listen, back then, I was happy (maybe too well-satisfied) -- with my, uncomplicated, single-existence, life.

I'd been in the Houston area, for about 18 months -- having moved down from a suburb, of New Brunswick, in Central New Jersey. This move was made -- out of necessity, I'd felt -- shortly following a rather-acrimonious divorce. Very acrimonious, as a matter of fact!

My four children -- ages 14-to-21, at the time -- had, all, been pretty much grown (and, mostly, on their own) for a few years, when the separation had come to pass. Well, the youngest one had still been living, with her mother. But, she might as well have been on her own -- given that she'd always been (by far) the most independent, of the entire litter.

The split -- with my wife -- had been anything, but unexpected. Probably years -- in the making. Mostly, due to the fact, that we'd never had the proverbial "two nickels ... to rub together". Ever! We were always broke! (Always -- and completely!) Ultimately -- once the three oldest kids had been in high school (or close to it) -- I'd been forced to, flat-out, declare bankruptcy!

We'd wound up losing our only means of transportation (a four-year-old Ford Country Squire station wagon, with something like 80,000 miles on "the clock", in the, emotional, very-painful, action.

The children, thank God, had -- in each and every case -- turned out magnificently! The marriage's end just simply became a case -- of Margaret becoming (understandably) "sick and tired" of the, damnable, hand-to-mouth, day-to-day, existence.

The sordid, consistently-hopeless, financially-strapped, quagmire had (again, understandably) been the source, of the never-ending (and getting worse by the day) criticism (endlessly) flowing my way! Let me tell you: I was growing (understandably, or not) sick and tired, of that, without-end, situation! The constant harping was understandable! But, it was still becoming, more and more, unbearable!

Then, Margaret had found a guy! The "perfect partner"! A "savior" -- for whom, to "throw me over". (Again, understandably.) This, to-the-rescue, "prince" owned a chain of small restaurants -- throughout Central Jersey.

There was also this troubling rumor -- that he was Mafia-connected! But, no one really knew that! Not for a fact! Not for sure, anyway! I -- for one -- was never going to call the reputation -- of such a, pillar-of-the-community, "legend", into question. I'd enjoyed the "luxury" of being able to breathe, too much!

In any case, once Margaret got "entwined" with him, our marriage -- such as it had been -- wound up " so over" (as they say)!

Fortunately, the ending, of the relationship, worked out well! For both of us! The kids could -- after a few weeks -- see that I was still around! I'd not "abandoned" them -- a situation, upon which their mother had expounded! Numerous times! "Ad infinitum" (as they also say)! Stupid as it may sound, I'd seemed to have had more time, to spend with 'em (especially my young daughter) -- than when I'd actually lived with the offspring Amazing!

After five or six months, however, things were reaching a point -- where I'd seldom get to see them!

The three "boys" were always busy -- working at, really-serious, jobs, for the most part. The oldest two were, by then, partnering -- in an automotive repair facility. As of 1977, they'd opened their fourth such operation. Number-Three Son had, by then, become a regional manager -- for a substantial, East Coast, hamburger chain. (One totally separate from the domain -- of his newly-minted stepfather.)

At that point, I'd been working -- in New Brunswick -- at a local, one-office, highly-successful, finance company. I'd been there -- for several years, by then. (Seven or eight.) And then -- suddenly -- I'd gotten myself fired! This was at about the time my wife, Margaret, had met her new benefactor.

The office upheaval had, of course, occurred -- at the very height of all of our marital problems. (Didn't need that!) Three of the four kids were still (barely) living at home -- although Number-Two Son was a senior, in high school, and fixing to join with his brother, in the car-repair game.

I'd been hauling down a glorious $125.00 a week. Not a lot of money -- even for those "less sophisticated" years. This pronounced paucity of pay, I'm sure, comes as no shock to you, Dear Reader. Every now and then -- well, once or twice a week -- I'd go out, chasing delinquent debtors. Efforts to collect their past-due payments. Ones who'd -- most often -- not owned phones, (Or -- in so many instances -- had denied the presence of one.)

Every now and then, I'd collect a few bucks -- on, maybe, a Tuesday or Wednesday. And -- from time to time -- I'd "borrow" those funds. Use them -- for "little luxuries"! (Like, maybe, groceries!) But -- unfailingly -- I'd turn those payments in, on the following Friday! (Aka payday!)

But, inevitably, I did get caught! (As I should've known I would!)

Some lady -- sneaky devil, she -- one who did (after all) have a phone called. Talked to the manager. She wanted additional money. My boss advised her that more money was impossible -- unless/until she'd resolved her delinquency.

"Well," she told him, "I gave Mister Jenkins thirty-seven dollars ... on Tuesday night!" (It was true! She had!)

The manager -- Gerard Williams -- confronted me, with the accusation! I'd. of course, had to acknowledge the truthfulness, of the debtor's statement! This all took place -- just prior to lunchtime -- on a Friday! Before the "Care Packages (aka paychecks) had been handed out! Ergo, I'd not had the chance (read not the funds) to replace, what I had "misappropriated"! Ergo -- also -- I was fired! On the spot! (I'll go to my grave -- believing that they still owe me that final damn paycheck!) But, obviously, I was in no position -- to make any demands -- being "jail eligible", as I was!

To, then, have to go home -- and to be required to inform Margaret -- that (in addition to all our numerous other troubles) I'd just lost my "lofty" position, at the finance company!

That -- as you may have imagined -- turned out to be the *coup d'grace*! I don't know if that particular "event" had been the bona fide, the hated, "beginning of the end"! Lord knows, there'd been other "financially-challenged developments, over the years! Although they'd not been quite so earth-shaking! (At least, I'd not thought so!) But, my being "between jobs" (another "as they say") certainly "hurried things along" -- toward the eventual, the unavoidable, end!.

I'd really struggled -- to find work! With that obvious "black mark" hanging, over my head As you can well imagine! (Who would hire me? I'd just been fired! For theft!) We'd always been broke! Now, of course, we were, totally, out and out -- destitute! We'd been living (if you could call it that) -- in a positive, crappy, documentable, hovel! It was all I could afford! And the rent -- on that dump -- was coming due!

In the midst of all this -- about a week-and-a-half, after my termination, at the finance company -- my "luxurious" six-year-old Studebaker Lark station wagon's engine seized up! Locked itself up -- completely! So, now -- no car! The, getting-worse-by-the-day, situation left me with very limited choices -- when it came to means of transportation.

After nearly a *month* -- without wheels -- our "benefactor" (my marital replacement-to-be) bought (and gave to Margaret, *exclusively*) a, five-year-old, Ford Maverick!

I *was* -- forever -- most *grateful* for that. My wife even let me *drive* "The Gift From Heaven" -- from time to time.

Number-One Son -- thank God -- would contribute as much as *he* could! Whenever he could! But, he'd not yet gotten *his* financial well-being firmly established, at that time.

The *divorce* came -- understandably -- in the midst, of all this turbulence! The, always-devastating, totally-unsettling, mind-warping, action -- was, of course, financed by Margaret's husband-to-be.

Thankfully, he'd also provided, more-than-a-few, groceries. At one point, I'd sold a pint of my blood -- simply to put food, on the table. Only to find -- when I'd gotten home -- that *he'd* sprung, for a whole week's worth of food. I was *also* thankful -- *very* grateful -- for *that*! The bequest -- *had* been a true blessing! And I *did* appreciate the charitable act!

I'd finally *found* a job! Thank *God*! At the neighborhood hardware store! Just a block-and-a-half -- from our dandy little flea-trap, of a house. *That* employment only came about -- through the heroic, undying, efforts, of my next-door neighbor. Willard had worked at the store -- for 12 or 15 years. And, at long last, he'd persuaded the store's two partners to hire me! They turned out to be two of the nicest -- most caring -- men, that I've ever met.

They could not afford to pay me a great deal of money. But, given my lack of any sort of expertise -- in anything mechanical or electrical (to me, a rubber band is a "machine") -- I was thrilled to be earning the $100.00 a week!

The partners, the store manager -- and Willard -- always took over, when a customer had a question requiring advice in any sort of mechanical and/or electrical expertise. I was pretty good -- at selling Pyrex glassware, and paint, and grass seed, and stuff like that. So, I was liking to think that -- in some far-fetched way -- I was "pulling my weight". Even to this day, I'd like to think that this was true! In any case, the partners always seemed to be satisfied. Again, thank God!

After about six months -- and steeped in hardware lore -- I was beginning to find myself getting more and more frustrated. I'd gotten a $5.00-a-week raise -- which I'd, flat-out, cherished! But, my obvious mechanical/electrical limitations were becoming -- more and more -- a real hindrance, to me!

Plus, the divorce had ground its unrelenting, buzz-saw, swath through my life -- during my hokey little hardware career! More frustration!

I didn't have to move -- which might have laid me out completely! My wife's new husband moved Margaret, and my daughter, to "suitable" living quarters. To his "starter mansion" -- in Morristown (25 or 30 miles away).

Sum and substance was that -- once the move had been made -- I'd seldom gotten to see Jeanine, my daughter! This -- despite the fact I'd managed to scrape up enough money, to buy an eight-year-old Plymouth Savoy two-door (for the princely sum, of $95.00).

The store was open six days a week. And, by Sunday, it was becoming, more and more, a fact that -- my week, of toiling in such a, dead-end, employment environment, was leaving me physically, mentally, and emotionally, exhausted! (If there are any further ways to wind up totally pooped -- I would've been them, too!) And Margaret usually found some way to come up with a "social obligation" for Jeanine! On most Sundays, anyway! So, I seldom got a chance to see my daughter.

Number-One Son had gotten married, by then. And -- with his business expanding -- his life was becoming more and more complicated. He -- and the other two sons -- would "pop in" to the store, from time to time. But, out of necessity, they'd all been hurried exchanges.

So, I'd reached a point -- where I'd hated my life! Totally hated the fact -- that I could seldom interact, with my children. I'd always -- always -- hated the damnable "house", in which I was existing! I even hated my job -- although I loved the wonderful, generous, people, with whom I was associated, at the store. I'd gotten -- to where I'd even hated the store, itself.

So, I did a "patently stupid" thing -- according to the two partners, as well as the store manager, and Willard! I managed to put aside a little over $250.00 -- and resigned! Then, I headed my tired old Plymouth toward Houston!

I figured that if "My Old Friend" didn't make it, I'd try to carve me out a new life -- wherever it might be that she'd decide, to "give up the ghost". I'd leave it to fate -- or in God's hands! Or whatever!

Probably incredibly, the venerable automobile made it. Had a flat tire -- in Louisiana -- but, that had been it! Nice old girl! I love you, Savoy!

I'd arrived, in "The Bayou City", at about nine o'clock -- on a Thursday night. Checked into an economical little hotel, near the airport. I was asleep -- within five minutes, of hitting the sack! Slept for 11 hours!

On Friday, I went to breakfast -- at a *Denny's*, around the corner; back on the feeder road. Picked up a *Houston Chronicle* -- and, immediately, scanned the, fairly-voluminous, want-ads.

Fortunately, there were three or four, what-looked-like, promising ads, for employment -- at various finance companies. Right down my alley -- if I could "fudge" my corporate history, sufficiently. But, these opportunities were only available, at downtown locations. Well, one office was -- way over, on the south side of town. And I was barely within the northern city limit.

Listen! I was a new guy in town! And grateful -- plus being totally surprised -- to have gotten this far, at all! Thank you, Plymouth! I love you! (Or had I already said that?)

In contrast, I'd hated just the prospect -- of fighting my way through a totally-strange town! A big city! Fourth-largest, by then -- in the entire country!

So -- grabbing at wild ghosts, more than anything else -- I decided to answer an ad, for a rent-a-car manager! As mentioned, I was grasping at straws! But, I had worked at a car-rental operation, in Brooklyn, for almost two years. Of course, that had been about fifteen years before!

Those New York people -- a huge department store, trying to be a rent-a-car entity -- were the worst people, for whom I'd ever toiled. But, I had learned a good bit -- about the industry! It couldn't have changed, all that much, in just-shy-of-a-couple-decades! (Could it?)

I managed, with a good deal of difficulty, to find my way to that motel -- just south of the airport. Fortunately, I was able to catch the owner of the car-rental franchise -- just moments, after he'd arrived. A wholly unlikely -- and very fortunate -- prospect, as I would later find out..

He was an "unusual" sort. At least his business practices seemed rather odd. Certainly "unorthodox". At that point, he'd owned another franchise (same national corporation) -- with an off-airport operation, in Austin. Plus, a different franchise -- with a competing, nationwide, company -- in Lake Charles, Louisiana. And still another franchise -- with, yet, a third outfit, in western Arkansas. (How does one do that?)

He'd had a woman (well, he'd still had her) who'd pretty much run the day shift, in Houston. He'd offered her the manager-ship -- three days before, when his, then-current, manager had "blown out". That had, obviously, been the logical thing to have done. The woman simply did not want the job! Didn't want to "have to jack ... with the responsibility".

"When my shift is over," Evelyn had advised him, "I just want to be able ... to simply go home, and get into something comfy. Or nothing at all.. Don't need ... don't want ... the responsibility!"

So, this was the first day that this guy's ad had run! And I was (ta-DAH!) the first one to have answered!

We'd sat behind his moderate-sized counter -- in the, surprisingly-large, lobby, of the motel. More surprisingly (almost shockingly) -- he was asking me, simple, more or less primal/basic, totally-uncomplicated, questions, about the industry. Stuff I could've answered -- after having been, in the business, for only two weeks, or so. Evelyn, I'd noticed, must've actually rolled her eyes -- literally dozens of times -- as the, "in-depth", interview had gone on.

The outcome was, that -- incredibly -- he'd hired me! This guy offered me gainful employment! On the spot! (That brought a real eye-roll, from the day-shift lady!) Imagine! Me! Her new manager! I, also, never could've pictured -- such a, far-fetched, situation! Could never have imagined it! But, it was an answer -- to more than one fervent prayer!

I was -- instantly -- employed! How about that? I'm sure that the fact that I'd agreed -- to the extremely low-ball salary -- had been a most-significant factor! $800.00 a month! Peanuts! (Even back then!) Substantially less dinero -- I was to find -- than what Evelyn was making. But, the penurious stipend did include a company car! (So did that, of my employee. Well, so did the lady that toiled the 3:30PM-to-midnight shift. She -- her name was Maria -- also made more than me; albeit slightly.)

But, I'd needed the car! (Hell, I'd needed the damn job -- even more!) The venerable Plymouth, though, had served -- well above and beyond the call! So, I knew that it would be grossly unfair to expect a helluva lot more -- from "The Old Girl"! Plus, she was not insured! A not-insignificant factor!

So, I'd started -- immediately! And the owner? He blew out -- also immediately -- for Arkansas! Charitably, Evelyn was nice enough -- had enough class -- to guide me through the routine, of filling out the employment forms! Can you say "unusual"? That word -- summed up the whole, entire, out-of-focus, scenario! I was most grateful!

As the morning had worn on -- surprise! I was finding that things -- at least, in the mid-seventies -- hadn't changed, all that much. I was, fairly-well, picking up -- again, much to my surprise/amazement -- on the, amazingly-uncomplicated, routine. Much more quickly -- than I'd expected.

Evelyn -- ever the diplomat -- suggested "that I might want to" ride, with the service agent, who'd manned our airport pick up/drop off van. (Well, it was, actually, an Oldsmobile station-wagon.) We were always -- constantly -- transporting customers, to and from the airport. If I'd ride along, I could -- more quickly -- learn the locations (and the number) of terminals, at the gigantic facility.

The company's rental contracts were, of course, a little different -- than what I'd been used to. But, not *that* drastically. Basically, all such rental agreements were pretty much the same, back then. The variety of cars -- and the current prices -- had, obviously, changed. Substantially! This company featured a *lot* of Chevrolets. *No* Fords or Plymouths! That was due to the fact that our primary source was a *General Motors* dealership. We'd had a substantial number -- of Olds and Buicks. And *two* Cadillacs.

All things considered, there wasn't all *that* much difficulty -- in my adapting to those new factors.

By the time Evelyn had left -- and Maria had arrived -- I'd felt pretty good, about my "professional" condition. A *lot* more confident. A *whole* lot!

I'd had to leave at a few minutes after four -- to see what the apartment availability situation, in the area, might hold for unsuspecting little old me.

It was *not* good! At least, not at first. Eventually, though It took some *digging* ("research", as I'd considered it) I *did* locate a reasonable (read *cheap*) complex! One that didn't require, the traditional "arm and a leg", to move in. Of course, it was unfurnished. I'd have to sleep, on the floor, till my first paycheck would, thankfully, arrive. (And, of course, I'd be required -- to eat out, for the duration.)

Finally -- almost two weeks later -- my first, treasured, highly-anticipated, cherished, eagerly-looked-forward-to, glorious, paycheck arrived! I'd been filled with fear -- with out and out terror -- that I'd never receive it! The guy who'd hired me was so -- well, so weird -- that I'd been afraid (petrified, actually) that he'd have flat-out forgotten about ever hiring me! Might not have recalled that we'd even met! But -- denks God -- the stipend (such as it was) finally got there! Right on time, even! Hoo-HAH!

The only problem: I'd only gotten a third of the month's salary. We'd gotten paid twice monthly, and -- given the number of days I'd been employed, as well as when the pay period ended -- that was all that the company, legitimately, owed me, at that point, in my young life!

Didn't matter! I was guh-ladd to get it! I'd been just about reduced to eating "fish heads and rice". Couldn't afford to continue to eat out. So, after about eight, or ten, days, I'd bought one cheap aluminum kettle, one soup bowl (also cheap) and six or eight cans of *Campbell's* chicken noodle soup. (Had not figured -- on the need for a spoon. So, I stole one -- from (three guesses, pricewise -- cheap) restaurant I'd frequented, in those first few, "opulent", days. Had to stand, through all that "cuisine" -- bent over the sink's drain board. (Look, Ma! No table and/or chairs!)

Those "brilliant" financial maneuvers, however, helped see me through! (Thank God for the company car! And the free gas, company policy provided! For my trusted Plymouth -- had been running, on the proverbial fumes! From that first morning on!

Once I was flush, I let it all hang out! I went to one of those, vastly-overpriced, "Rent-To-Own" joints! And paid a vastly overpriced amount of future money, for an apartment-full, of "stylish" furniture -- including a 24" TV set (complete with stand), There was a sofa-and-chair combination. (Matching, yet.) Also included, was a, red-valor, recliner -- and a three-piece bedroom set. Even a deluxe mattress. Then, there was that "wood-grain", Formica-and-chrome, dinette table, and four matching chairs, I'd also laid in: A set of, well-overpriced, *Teflon* pots and pans, an electric percolator, a kitchen blender, a set of "service-for-four" dishes, four canisters (in which to hold sugar, flour, coffee, and tea), a collection of knives-and-forks (all matching -- a real upset, for me) and even some sheets and pillowcases. (As well as a couple of pillows -- and a blanket and spread.) Oh -- and a *General Electric* table-model radio! (With two speakers!)

Was I set -- or what? Well, yes! Except, I'd had to go, then, to *Kroger's* -- and cash out what amounted to "The War Debt" -- to buy sufficient amounts of groceries, to see me through what would, undoubtedly, be yet another, hand-to-mouth, half-month! But, at least, I'd be able to eat! (And to -- GASP! -- be allowed to, actually, sit down, while partaking of such "ambience"!) In addition, to be able sleep -- on (can you imagine?) an actual bed! That floor -- let me assure you -- was not soft! The carpeting did not offer all that much padding. Was no help -- at all.

Things, though, began to pick up! I was doing well, in actually running the car-rental operation! Depending (thank The Lord) -- less and less -- on the. more-than-wonderful, Evelyn (and on, equally-as-glorious, Maria). The two black, male, service agents -- were also nothing short of magnificent! Even the weekend crew -- was great! I was most fortunate! I could never have asked for more!

As the next few months had -- rather speedily -- rolled by, I'd gotten quite comfortable, in my new slot. This was -- by far -- the finest, most rewarding job (both professionally, and financially; although I'd not gotten a raise) that I'd ever had! As in my hardware store days, I was required to work six days -- but, I still looked forward to going to work! Every day! I was positively thrilled that I'd "taken that 'way-far-out' shot" -- at this nifty position! Positively thrilled!

Then, it happened! (HAH! Is that dramatic enough, for ya?)

I'd not noticed, actually, at first. But, the hotel's "limousine" (also an Oldsmobile station-wagon) had picked her up -- at the airport. And -- while she was checking in, across the lobby -- I'd been completely buried, in the month-to-date figures, relating to our own hokey little operation.

It wasn't until she'd inquired, of Evelyn, "Can I reserve a car ... for tomorrow morning? Will you have any Oldsmobiles available?" that I'd snapped to!

I'd thought I'd recognized the voice -- and looked up, as Evelyn was explaining, "Yes. We have many Oldsmobiles, in our fleet. Our biggest supplier is *Luke Clayborne Chevy/Olds,* on Interstate Forty-five. I'll put you down for one. Your name is ... ?"

"Janice?" That was me spouting -- just this side of a scream! "Janice? Is that you?"

"Yes! Janice Mayo." She was answering me! Well, me -- first. Then, Evelyn.

I got up, from my desk -- and hurried to the counter. "Janice! Janice! I can't believe it's you! That it's actually you!"

"Yeah, well it's me, all right, Stephen. How are you? I'm so glad to see you, again."

Janice had been in charge of the two other "front desk girls" -- who'd always answered the many phones, worked the counter, and did the bookkeeping/accounting -- at the finance company, in New Jersey. The one -- from which I'd been so, unceremoniously, fired!

Janice was one of the most beautiful women -- ever to walk the planet! I'd never met one "beautifuller". Had, actually, never met one -- nearly so gorgeous. And she'd never seemed -- to have been aware of it! Of any of it! Of her staggering beauty! The most down-to-earth woman -- you'd ever hope to meet!

Toward the end of my -- ah -- "tenure" there, she'd gotten married! Her engagement had lasted six or eight long months. And -- during that entire, quite-lengthy, time period -- she'd always been (continually) atwitter! Presumably 24/7! That seemed to be the situation, whenever I'd ever have had occasion to see her -- to behold her -- anyway.

In point of fact the, looked-forward-to, "beholding" didn't happen all that often! (Regrettably!) I'd been consigned, to a small work area -- in the "traditional" back room, of the joint. My job was to work the phones, back there, To constantly call delinquent debtors! Phone them, continually! All day! (All day! Every day!)

I'd sat -- between the company's two star skip-tracers! They were extremely expert -- at tracking down people who'd run out, on their obligation! And I do mean that they were stars! Both of them! I could never have done what they did -- daily! Hourly! Which was all -- patently -- against the law! Even in those, notably-less-stringent, much-less-regulated, times.

On my right -- sat one of the most-coarse, most-overbearing, ladies I've ever met. Her actual name was Alice. But, in her "professional mode", she was "Miss Drake". (She'd "borrowed" the name -- from a swanky hotel, in Chicago. Where -- according to Alice, herself, she'd spent "some of the most rewarding nights", of her "forty-something" life. (And, one guesses, some of the most erotic nights! You'd have to have known Alice!)

"Miss Drake" was working, she would advise relatives -- of those poor souls. that she was seeking to track down -- at *"The New Jersey State Employment Commission"*. And there was always "a problem" -- pertaining with the missing debtor's unemployment compensation claim! And it was critical -- that "Miss Drake" speak to the poor man (or lady)! Immediately! They needed "to get this thing straightened out ... quickly!" As you can imagine -- the "positive" results were absolutely amazing! (Absolutely amazing!)

On my left, sat "Sergeant Galante"! Of *"The New Jersey State Police"*. I don't remember this man's actual given name. He was always "Sgt. Galante"! (Always!) His, never-changing, "tale of woe" was, to inform the debtor's relative -- that "a three-year old license plate" ... which had been registered, to the debtor, had just turned up! In (no less) "a hit-and-run accident!"

Now, the good sergeant didn't think that the debtor was actually involved! But, it was critical -- that "Sgt. Galante (or was it "Sgt Valente? I couldn't remember!) speak with the debtor -- "to get this thing straightened out"! (Sound familiar?) His positive results were on a par -- with that of the celebrated "Miss Drake"! There was a fairly-popular song, back then, called *You're Gonna Hear From Me.* And whenever the hard-at-work "sergeant" would've scored a "find" (which was often) he'd belt out a basso-profundo rendition, of the ditty. (I think I'd learned the entire lyric, of the tune, back then -- by osmosis!)

What I had been doing was not nearly "at the edge of the law", but the powers that be, wanted me also to be as remote as possible -- from any "civilian" customers, who might be "out front". It was amazing -- that I'd ever accomplished anything! Given the fact -- that I was forever being bedazzled, by the "Drake/Sergeant" dynamic duo!

So, my "exposure" to the goings-on -- in the front portion of the industrious facility -- had been (always) extremely limited. Was not able to feast my eyes -- on the, mind-bogglingly, beautiful Janice -- all that often. To my eternal regret!

At the smallish Houston hotel, their new guest and I didn't have much time to exchange pleasantries. The "bellman" (hell, the bellhop -- I could never get used to the modern terminology) was waiting to accompany her (and her considerable amount of luggage) to her room.

But, in leaving the counter, she did say -- that we'd have to get together, for lunch, "sometime". That was encouraging! Well, semi-encouraging!

An hour-or-so later -- just before four o'clock, that afternoon -- she appeared, once more, at our counter. Maria -- not recognizing her -- offered to rent her a car. Oldsmobile -- or otherwise. But, she'd indicated that she'd wanted to speak to me! Like a panting puppy dog, I hurried up, to her presence!

"Can you get away?" she asked. "Maybe ... to the hotel restaurant?"

Having been to the hotel -- a number of times before -- she was familiar with the eatery. I'd become a regular lunchtime patron of the place. I'd found that I could afford their (cheap) burger-and-fries meal. To the point that I'd made friends with the two wisecracking waitresses -- who I'd come to call "Frick and Frack". I'd always ordered "a nude hamburger" -- one with absolutely no condiments! So, whenever I'd walk in, one of those, ultra-humorous, gals would holler out, "A nudie ... for Stephen!" -- which never failed to raise the eyebrows of, more than a few, diners.

But, when Janice and I walked in -- and seated ourselves -- it was as though neither, of these worthies, knew me. "What for you, Sir?" asked Frack. It had not occurred to me -- but, it seems that, it makes a big difference, if you're with a woman. I suppose that makes sense. But, I still don't understand it. Not totally, anyway.

We finally did settle in. Janice had ordered a T-bone steak -- and so I ordered the same. If that, radical, "non-nudie", choice had shocked Frack, she'd hid that reaction. Magnificently!

"Now," began my dinner partner, "tell me all about it! Tell me ... all about you! The last time we'd had any contact, your ... ah ... circumstances were not the best. Far from it!"

"Yeah," I groused. "Far from it!"

"I told Gerard ... told him, at the time ... that it was grossly the wrong thing to have done! To have gone ahead ... and fired you!"

"You ... you did?"

"Of course I did! Not only me ... but Joyce and Peggy too! Even Alice! Insensitive old Alice!" (Joyce and Peggy were the two other young women -- who'd worked with Janice.) "I do believe," she went on, "that Hal had something to say ... to Gerard." (Hal, it turns out, was "Sgt Galante". I could -- finally -- remember his "real" name.)

"Really? I'd never dreamed, that you guys would ever have ..."

"Listen," she interrupted, "everyone there ... they all loved you!"

"Really? They did? I never knew ... never thought that ..."

"You were always so damn cheerful, Stephen. Even with your hokey ... your corny ... jokes! We all loved ... even them! Loved you!"

"I ... I just never knew!"

"Well, you should have! We all knew that ... with all those kids, and in that crappy dung-hole you were living in ... you were having financial problems! Do you think that we all thought that, it was a damn coincidence, that ... on so many Fridays ... you'd always turn in a payment? After you'd had a chance ... to cash your check? Even Gerard had to have jolly well known!"

"Yeah," I grumped. "I guess I wasn't fooling all that many people."

"I don't know, if your wife ever told you, but ... Alice and I brought you a few dollars worth of groceries. About a week ... after Gerard let you go. You were out ... looking for work ... at the time. We just left it, and ..."

"Wait a minute! You? You ... and Alice? You brought us ... brought us ... groceries?"

"I'm assuming your wife never told you."

"No! No ... she never did! Not a damn word!"

"Well, we did! And ... looking back ... we should have done more! A helluva lot more! Joyce and I ... we'd talked about it. But ... damn us ... we simply never got around to it. I apologize!"

"Naw. You ... obviously ... did more than you'd ever needed to."

"What did you wind up doing? Up in Jersey? And how in thee hell ... did you ever find your way down here? To this place?"

I explained -- laid out, in great (maybe boring) detail -- the course of my life, since the sainted Gerard Williams had cut me loose. She *seemed* interested! *Intensely* (and, seemingly, *immensely*) wrapped up -- in what I was telling her. *That* was nice of her.

I'd just about finished my extensive "tour" of my life -- post-finance company -- when our steaks came! They were *remarkable*! Especially -- for such a, small-sized, facility! It had been a long *time* -- since I'd enjoyed *any* steak! In *any* venue! Under *any* circumstances!

While we were gnoshing down our, fit-for-a-king, meal, she'd advised me -- of the, highly-unexpected, somewhat-frightening, course -- that *her* life had taken:

"I'd stayed married to Borden ... for all of *five* months. A little *less* than five, anyway."

"*Really*? But, you were ... you were ... were so much ... so much ... in *love*! So *taken* ... with *Borden*! So in *love* with him! How did you ? How could it have ... ?"

"He was *not* the man ... not the one, I'd *thought* he was! *Not* the man I'd probably *invented* ... in my own, stupid, mind! In. probably, my heart-of-hearts! When he was *courting* me ... he was a, totally-different, *man*! *Totally* different! From when he got ... to where he felt that he *owned* me!"

"He ... he *owned* you? *Owned* you? How could he *possibly* own you?"

"Well, while we were going together ... during our engagement, and even before ... he couldn't do enough for me! A goddess ... I was! Worshipped ... I was! He positively worshipped me! He did! I knew ... back then ... that he was a real go-getter! Definitely, a rising young star ... at a commercial real estate-leasing operation, in Newark. And he was making good money! Really good money! That was important! More important ... than it, for sure, should've been! He took me, to all these ritzy ... these fancy, expensive ... restaurants, and clubs. In New York! In the heart of Manhattan! Broadway shows! Places ... where stars hung out! The best!"

"And that didn't ... it didn't last?"

"Nope! We had our wedding reception ... at *The Waldorf-Astoria,* dah-ling! The *Waldorf*! Nothing but the, damn-well, finest ... for this goddess! Then, when we got upstairs ... again, at *The Waldorf* ... we had sex! For the first time! First time ... in my life! You can believe this ... or not ... but, I was a virgin! Oh, we'd come close! On numerous occasions! But, gentleman that he always was ... gentleman that he'd always been ... he'd always backed off! Always stopped! Sometimes, barely in the ol' nick of time! But, he'd always stopped! Always!"

"And he didn't ... on that night? That's perfectly understandable! I'm sure you'd agree that he was ... ! Hell, I really don't know why we're having this conversation! I mean ..."

"Of course he didn't hold back! I never expected he would! And he didn't! And it was great!"

"Well then, I don't see how ..."

"After it was over ... after the most wonderful joyride, of my life ... he tied me up! Tied me down ... to the bed! To the other bed! We'd had two beds ... in the room!"

"Tied you? He tied you down? Tied you ... to the damn bed?"

"Yep! And he kept me there! Tied up ... and naked! The whole, entire, night! While he slept in the first bed ... the one, in which he'd deflowered me!"

"This is ... well, it's ... it's incredible! I mean ..."

"What was even more incredible ... was that we went 'home', the next day. To his luxury apartment ... in Rahway. He made me strip naked again! As soon as we were inside! Then, he locked up ... locked up ... took away, all my clothes! All of 'em! Locked 'em ... in a closet! One ... a closet ... with a huge iron bar, across the door! So, he'd had to have thought about this ... planned, extensively, for it ... ahead of time! Had a really big padlock, on it! So, I was ... effectively, and I do mean effectively ... naked! All the time! All the time!"

"That's ... why ... I can't believe this! Locking up ... locking up all your clothes!"

"Well, not all! There were three or four of my dresses ... mostly, with skirts far too short, or so he thought ... that he'd cut to ribbons! Well, one of them was not too short! He felt ... it was too tight. Showed my fanny too much! Well, 'puts your ass on display', as he'd called it."

"Incredible! But ... but, you're free now! Obviously! How long did all this crap last? How long did it go on? Could it go on?"

"Well, for only four days! But, it seemed like four damn years! The police, finally, raided the joint ... on that glorious fourth day!"

"The police? How'd that happen? How did they ... ?"

"Well, my loving husband really was a go-getter! He believed he'd gotten screwed! Only he'd used 'The F-Word'! But, royally shafted ... by this guy. He felt that this guy had really screwed him ... in a, really-big, lease deal! In Patterson! Turned out this guy ... he was part, of the Mafia! In, I think the same ... ah ... unit that Alice's fiancé ... that he belongs to."

"Alice? Her fiancé is in the ... with the ... the Mafia?"

"Yeah. I thought you knew! I thought that everybody knew! In fact, when she and I were on our way out, to bring those groceries to you ... to your house ... I tried to talk her into attempting to 'take you in'! Get her boyfriend ... to 'adopt' you! Make you some kind, of a low-level messenger ... or something. But, she refused! Wouldn't even consider it! Said you were 'too nice'!"

"Me? Too nice? Me?"

"Yeah. She said that there were no such things ... as simple 'messenger' jobs! That everything involved 'something unpleasant'! Really rotten! Bad! Bad ... as hell!"

"Her fiancé? In the Mafia? I'd never thought ..."

"Well, I really wouldn't call him her fiancé! He's never gonna marry her! The old thing ... about milk being so cheap, and all. Why buy the cow?"

"But ... but, how did this Mafia thing ... how did that wind up freeing you? Freeing you ... from your loving hubby?"

"Borden was going to kill him! Kill the Mafia, leasing, guy! Was gonna shoot him! I'd seen that rifle! Seen it ... in the trunk, of the car! Many times! That should've, I guess, told me something! He'd ... my husband ... he'd set himself up, in a vacant office building! Office building, across the street ... from the beer joint, where the Mafia guy had always hung out! It was a building he'd ... that my husband had ... controlled! Turned out ... he'd missed!"

"Missed? He actually fired at the guy? And he missed?"

"Well, he'd wound up ... grazing the guy! Bullet took out a chunk ... a small chunk, I guess ... of his fanny! Cops came and got Borden... my husband. I think the mob had a few cops ... on the pad, you know! So, they ... those cops ... were, apparently, close by!"

"On the pad? They didn't kill Borden?"

"No. I ... for one ... would've _expected_ them to! Don't know _why_ they _didn't_! I think there were, maybe, _others_ ... other officers, who'd got themselves involved! He ... Borden ... he finally wound up, in Newark! In jail!"

"Well, _that's_ a relief!"

"Yeah. I guess so. For one thing, the whole thing wound up ... being _awfully_ secretive."

"Secretive?"

"Yeah," she responded, nodding. "I was never _aware_ ... of _anything_ happening to him! To Borden. From a _legal_ standpoint! Mainly, I guess, because he'd tried to take out a, more-or-less, Mafia 'kingpin'. _No_ one really wanted to get too _deeply_ ... or, at least, _publicize_ a helluva lot ... about it the thing. I've _heard_ ... from a couple 'unofficial sources' ... that he's in _some_ prison! _Somewhere_ in the country! Under an assumed _name_! With a whole conviction record ... all phonied up!"

"That's ... why, it's almost ... it's _unbelievable_! Who ... finally ... set you _free_?"

"A couple Rahway cops! _Someone_ got them involved! They broke into the _apartment_! And there _I_ was! _Naked_! Naked ... and tied to the stupid damn _bed_!"

"Yeah," I muttered. "_That_ must've been a _million_ laughs!"

"Well, _that_ was only the _beginning_!"

"Only ... only the ... the beginning? Did he ... was he ... Borden always tied you to the bed? Even when he was ... when he was away?"

"No. He did allow me the run of the apartment. I just was not allowed to wear any clothes! I was naked! All the time! Whether he was home ... or not."

"But, on that day, he tied you up? Tied you down? Tied you to the bed? Why? Because he was gonna shoot ... kill the Mafia guy?"

"No. Borden had thought ... he was positive ... that I'd walked, in front of the windows! 'Paraded around' ... in front of them ... too often! Spent too long ... way too much time ... in front of the stupid windows! Let too many people see me! See me ... unclothed! So, on that night ... the night before, at ten-thirty or eleven o'clock ... he tied me back down! On my tummy! He was punishing me ... for my public display! For my immodesty!"

"He did that? Tied you down?"

"And that was not all! He ... like I said ... he punished me! Whipped me! With an actual whip! It wasn't a bullwhip! But, it was close! He practically killed me! All this ... on my bare fanny! Peeled away most of the flesh!

"Dear Lord!

"So, there I was," she continued. "When the Rahway cops broke in! I'm naked ... with a badly-welted, really-swollen, bottom! And this one stupid cop! He kept standing there! Just standing there!

Staring down, at me! At me ... and my war-torn fanny! Saying, 'Jesus, Lady! What happened? I ain't never seen nothin' like this before!' Finally, they untied me ... he and another cop! Then ... the both of 'em ... they hung around too long! Well, one of 'em had to run down to the squad car ... and get some kind of a bolt-cutter! To get rid of the damn padlock! So, that was a bit of relief! And ... finally ... they left! They did leave! And I was ... at long damn last ... able to, actually, put on my clothes! What an out and out relief that was!"

"Dear Lord! I've never heard of anything like that!"

"Neither had I! Not until I'd entered ... the holy sacrament of matrimony! I'd laid out, after that! For, about a-week-and-a-half! Before I came back to work. Needed to let my bum get back ... back to a reasonable size ... and shape! Figured that ... if it was still so damn swollen ... everybody would notice!"

"I guess I can understand that."

"Not only that, I really wasn't sure ... whether Gerard would even take me back, or not. He finally did, of course. I came back ... came back to work ... on the Monday, before the Friday! The Friday, you know ... when, in their infinite charity, they went ahead, and fired you!"

TWO

The conversation, in Janice's room -- which was still proceeding, taking place before my stunned eyes -- had been, completely and utterly, (well) stunning! I could never have guessed -- that her brief married life would've been so, obviously, tumultuous. From what very few, brief, occasions we'd ever spent together -- at the finance company -- she'd always appeared to be the out and out epitome, of stability. Of, even, placidity. Always-still -- calming -- waters. How she ever could've survived -- how anyone could've survived -- such a mind-twisting, seemingly-never-ending, series of unforgivable, unforgettable, outrages, was beyond comprehension! Absolutely beyond imagination!

She'd been, maybe, not absolutely calm -- while relating the clearly, highly-personal, undoubtedly-embarrassing, experiences, to me. But, she was close! The story -- of her, brief-but-violent, marriage -- had, seemingly, left me more shaken, than she'd been!

Of course, her life had gone on, since then. Much water had passed over the dam! Still, for her to have related those chilling (to say the least) actions to me -- and so calmly -- was, flat-out, phenomenal! And to have provided me with so <u>many</u> of such, highly-personal, details, was almost <u>beyond</u> reasonability! Yet there it <u>was</u>! There it <u>all</u> was! There it had <u>been</u>!

The whole, entire, <u>episode</u> was beyond <u>belief</u>! To <u>me</u>, anyway! A goodly portion of me -- was actually <u>grateful</u>! And I didn't know <u>why</u>! An, even-larger, part of me was (as you might imagine) greatly <u>troubled</u>! And, as you might also have guessed -- I'd not had the slightest <u>inkling</u>, as to why all (or <u>any</u>) of these emotions were, actually, <u>overwhelming</u> me! Totally bemusing me! I was extremely reluctant -- to even try and <u>guess</u>!

"You look rattled, Stephen," she'd, ultimately, observed -- after a few <u>smothering</u> moments, of weighty silence.

"That's only because I <u>am</u>, <u>Totally</u> rattled!" I finally acknowledged. "I can't <u>imagine</u> ..."

"Neither could I! <u>Imagine</u> it, I mean. Could <u>never</u> have ... <u>ever</u> ... conceived of such things! Especially ... when that crap was all <u>happening</u>! When it was all ... when everything was ... when it was all coming <u>down</u>! But, let me <u>tell</u> you: It <u>sure</u> ... the experience ... it sure changed my <u>outlook</u>! Those God-awful <u>hours</u>! Those God-awful <u>days</u>! Changed my outlook ... but, <u>good</u>! On <u>life</u> ... and on everything <u>else</u>! On <u>everything</u> else!"

"I can imagine. Or, at least, I <u>think</u> I can. On the other hand ... I probably <u>can't</u>! Can't, possibly, <u>imagine</u>!"

"I used to be," she went on, in a tone I'd never heard from her, "a damn Pollyanna! Everything, y'know, was beautiful! No one was out ... to do anyone ill! Just go ahead! Go ahead ... and trust everybody! I was completely dazzled ... by Borden! When we were still engaged! Especially then! He was such a ... such a go-getter! Living the 'American Dream' ... and all that! The epitome, he was ... of unmitigated success! What could go wrong? What could possibly go wrong?"

"Yeah. I guess I can understand ... where that thinking was coming from. Can, I guess, realize ... why you would've believed that. Listen, you ... you'd always seemed to be the perfect example, of ideal American Womanhood."

"Now? Now, I'm deathly afraid! I don't trust anyone! Not hardly, anyway! I've probably come off of it ... some of it, anyway ... over the past few months. Come off it ... a little. Have ... only recently ... gone back to wearing my 'normal' clothes. Stuff that shows me off. A little bit, anyway. Till then ... till that time ... I was wearing these really-frumpy clothes! Suits and dresses ... that some, sixty-year-old, woman would wear. Well, maybe they wouldn't! That was one reason I'd left the finance company."

"It was? That's why you left ... left good old Gerard?"

"Uh-huh. Like I'd told you, I'd waited to go back to work, there, till my fanny stopped being so ... well, so damn misshapen. Didn't want to start tongues wagging ... if I'd gotten away from my normal wardrobe. What I was wearing ... back then ... kind of showed off my rear end."

"I can attest to *that*! I'd *noticed*!"

"Well, *that* ... that whole *thing* ... got to be a real *hang*-up, for me. I'd felt ... that I could *never* make a major change! Not without a whole *lot* of questions! Which I really did *not* need to find answers to! So ... after a couple of weeks ... I decided to simply resign. Got me a job ... at an electrical engineering firm. In Newark. Started wearing those frumpy clothes. Went to all *manner* of interviews ... wearing these types of, dorky-looking, dresses. Well dresses ... and *suits*. Mostly, the latter. Big ... bulky ... woolen suits."

"*Sheeeee*! I never knew!"

"Over the past couple of years, I'd worked at three different places. It took me that long ... before, I guess, I ever came to my senses. Went to work ... about six months ago ... for this feminine design outfit. Interviewed ... in a *very*-tight dress! Emphasized my *fanny* ... which is *still*, apparently, pretty good-looking."

"I can vouch for *that*, too."

"Plus, I showed 'em ... at the interview ... a *generous* amount of leg! Got the *job*! So ... hopefully ... my *emotional* problem is over! *Hopefully*! To a *point*, anyway. *That* was the most important thing. Well, there *are* some nights, you know ... when I *still* have these God-awful *dreams*! But, for the most part, I seem to be ..."

"Are you doing all right? I mean ... at this present job? Your current employment?"

"Yeah. Actually, doing *really* well. Of course, *all* of my 'docileness' ... still *remains*, in the past. Not *nearly* as passive ... as I once was. *Au contraire*! In fact, I've even got two, boot-like, pairs of shoes ... and *both* of them have *spurs* on them! They're *decorative* spurs, of course! But, *spurs*, nevertheless! And, whenever I think I'm being taken advantage of ... or, if I think someone's trying to get too *close* ... I wear my damn *spurs*! *Seems* to convey the message. A bit of a *surprise* ... for me. In fact, the whole *thing* ... is a bit of a surprise. A *shock*, actually."

"That's *frightening*! That whole *thing*! *Frightening*! *Almost*, anyway!"

"Do you see me ... wearing *spurs* ... now?"

"Well, no. Should I be *thankful* ... for that?

I'd *not* been able to discern -- what those last remarks might've portended. Apparently, nothing. We went on to engage in a variety, of small talk -- for the remainder of the meal. Looking back, I have not the *faintest* idea -- as to what subjects we may have covered. Not after bone-rattling narrative -- expounding on her, short-lived-but-highly-adventurous, marriage to the, God-awful, monstrous, sadistic, Borden.

The dinner ended -- and I don't really know what I was *hoping* for. Maybe for the obvious. But, don't be too sure of that. I know that *I* wasn't. Ever since I'd *met* her -- "way back when" -- there had been something that had virtually *screamed*, that Janice was (*immensely*) "off limits"! Whether such a foreboding "spirit" would still have held true -- was *way* beyond me! I was deathly *afraid* of how I'd react -- or if I *could* react, at all -- if the evening was to give any "promise" of extending further.

But, as we'd adjourned from the restaurant, she indicated she was going to return to her "room". (Actually, she'd rented a two-room suite -- one of three in the building.)

I bade her "goodnight" -- and headed to my far-from-luxurious apartment. There, to spend an almost-sleepless night; rehashing her startling story. And dealing with the, out-of-the-blue, reuniting. Coping with the entire *experience*!

I got to work early -- a little past seven o'clock -- the following morning, *hoping* for an invite, to join her for breakfast. The call never came. She *did* smile, at me -- glowingly (or, at least, I'd interpreted it as such) -- as Evelyn had rented her the required Oldsmobile, at a little after eight.

I'd remained "on duty" -- till she'd returned, shortly before seven o'clock, that evening. (Had to withstand a multitude -- of "knowing smiles", from Maria.) Janice waved -- gaily -- at me, as she'd hurried past our counter!

A helluva day! A highly-disappointing one!

The following day -- was looking to turn out equally as unrewarding! She smiled at me -- as she'd brushed past me, in the morning! I did get to check her in -- at about four-thirty, that afternoon. (Maria was in the Ladies Room.) But -- fortunately -- things did pick up, at that point. She'd invited me to join her, in the restaurant -- "for din".

Whereas, our previous "dinner date" had been all about her -- and her, horrific-experience, marriage -- she went out of her way to draw me out. She seemed to almost "chew over" each experience, once I'd related it to her. I'd had no conception -- as to how serious (or sincere) this all might've been. I mean, how "intoxicating" can a-hundred-bucks-a-week-tour-in-a-hardware store be? But, she was devoting the meal -- to finding out what (and how) I'd been doing. since my unceremonious finance company firing. And I was very grateful -- for that.

We didn't delve -- too deeply -- into my marital problems. A disappointment -- and a relief -- at the same time.

Then -- once the "dining experience" had ended -- came the *strangest* episode of my *life*! She invited me up to her "room" -- at the rear, of the second floor. As mentioned, the venue was a two-room suite. A surprisingly-spacious one.

Once inside, she led me to the center of the "living room." Then, she pressed herself into me! *Relentlessly* (and with a goodly amount of *vigor*)! I *still* didn't know exactly what to expect. (And -- as it turned out -- for good reason!)

She *kissed* me -- deeply! And for an *extended* amount of time! Then -- as suddenly as all this had come about -- she pulled away from me.

As she put this regrettable amount of distance between us, she said (*very* huskily) "I want you to participate ... with me ... in a really *needful* experiment! Really *needful*! Really *important*! Really *critical*! To me, anyway!"

"Ex...experiment?" I rasped. "An *experiment*?"

"Experiment," she reiterated -- nodding, firmly. "Are you game?"

"I ... I guess so."

"Okay ... *fine*! *Wonderful*! Now, all I want *you* to do, is to sit there ... in the chair, over there. *I* am going to go into the bedroom. And ... when I come out ... I will have *removed* all my *clothes*! I will be stark *naked*! I will sit in this *other* chair! We can talk ... or watch television! Whatever you want! Till ten o'clock ... when the news comes on. But, I *will* expect you ... to stay in the chair! The whole time! For the entire time! I'll expect you to ... not put any kind, of a 'move', on me! Is that agreeable? Or am I out of my ever-lovin' mind?"

"No," I managed to murmur. "I think I can ..."

"Good!" she responded -- most emphatically. "This is most important for me! And it has to be ... be important ... with you!"

With that, she swept into the bedroom! And when -- two minutes later -- she reappeared, was wearing "not a drop" of clothing! Totally nude!

She was beautiful! Staggeringly -- breathtakingly, stunningly -- beautiful! Clothed -- or unclothed! I'd never beheld such out and out -- such classic -- beauty! Ever!

I watched -- intently -- as she turned on the TV set! Immediately, she seated herself, in the only other chair -- which was located, on the same side of the room, but was about 15 feet away.

I have not the foggiest idea -- as to what we'd watched, on the stupid tube! I do remember various snatches of conversation -- during the three--plus hours. But, virtually all of that escapes me, also. I remained in a stunned fog -- the entire period! I couldn't get my arms around what was happening -- or not happening -- let alone any kind of, fathomable reason for it!

But, I kept my promise! I don't think I hardly moved -- let alone, trying to make any sort of advance! I did my best -- to not even look at her! At first, anyway. But, her overwhelming beauty just simply overwhelmed me! And -- after the initial 10 or 15 minutes -- I couldn't pry my eyes away from her!

She didn't seem to mind! Sat -- for the most part -- with her legs crossed! But, it wasn't simply her exposed, to-die-for, bosom -- nor her dazzling facial beauty -- that had me simply entranced! It was the staggering, overall, gorgeousness -- of this, amazingly-statuesque, example of classic womanhood! Classic womanhood!

The time didn't exactly fly by! But, it went much more quickly -- than I ever could've imagined! It was almost like being in a state of suspended animation! It appeared that nothing had been accomplished -- except having spent an entire evening, of TV-watching! With a naked lady! A woman -- of immense, unimaginable, beauty.

And, when at 10:10PM, she thanked me -- for keeping my promise -- I knew that she was dismissing me! I arose! So did she! She came over -- and gave me a, non-hugging, "peck"! On my right cheek! It happened so quickly -- that I could not, possibly, have "returned fire"!

Hazily, I made my way to the door! Still in a daze! And my spiritless condition did not improve as I, more-or-less, stumbled down the hall -- toward the stupid elevator.

I was headed back to my, Alice-In-Wonderland, apartment! To do what? To relive my evening's experience? Or lack of same? To try and find some way -- some emotional way -- to deal with it? Who knew? Who the hell knew -- what was on my overheated mind?

I'd just pressed the button, for the elevator -- when I'd heard my name called! It echoed -- loudly -- throughout the hallway! It was Janice! She was standing, in her doorway! Still naked!

"Stephen! Stephen? Where the hell do you think you're going? Get back here!"

All of my fears -- all of them -- wound up being removed that night! Being gloriously removed! I guess that I must have had this fear -- this almost-subliminal fear -- for all of my life. That I'd be totally incapable of being able to perform -- with a woman who'd be nearly as beautiful, as my hostess!

There's all this talk, these days, about erectile dysfunction. There are commercials all over television -- advertising all sorts of products to "fight ED"! The malady is the subject of countless inane TV sitcoms. It's the frequent subject of conversations, at parties, social gatherings, water coolers -- and practically every place else.

But, in the seventies, such things were never mentioned! I'd never even known that such a problem even existed! Well, I guess I must've known it existed. I simply never knew that it had a name. I'd certainly never heard of it! Like, I'm sure, millions of other men, I'd thought that I'd been the only one -- in the entire universe -- who'd suffered from the malady!

Technically, I had been a virgin -- when Margaret and I had married. But, only because two previous encounters had failed! Miserably! The problem did not end (far from it) -- with our marriage. Four children notwithstanding!

But, on that magical night, in that magical room, in that magical hotel, in magical Houston -- with that magical woman -- I'd gotten myself all caught up (lost -- if you will); "swallowed up", by the "project at hand"! I performed! Apparently quite well! Janice seemed to think so! I was on another planet! Could never qualify, as a "disinterested observer"! I'd never been so completely overwhelmed -- nor as completely fulfilled -- in my life! The whole (ah) experience was absolutely incredible! Absolutely incredible!

Once the dense "fog" had -- at long last -- begun to clear, we wound up having an extremely interesting conversation! First of all, Janice advised me -- that I was only the second (after Borden) sexual partner she'd ever had. I was believing her!

The statement -- believable or not -- could properly be labeled "pillow talk". But, the verbal exchange became a good deal deeper than that. Much deeper!

"I ... I think I've always been wanting this to happen" I'd heard her, still-lust-filled, voice declare. As if by previous instruction, we'd both rolled over onto our sides -- facing one another. "I really mean that," she emphasized.

"You ... you can't mean that, Janice. You've only known me ... for just a little time, A very short time! You couldn't have ..."

"Well, I think that you're someone that ... well, someone that I've always been looking for. I really can't explain it. From, practically, the time you came aboard ... at the dear old finance company ... I'd always thought you were special. Especially the few times that our paths had crossed ... outside the office. Like, you know, at the lunch counter ... next to the office. Most guys ... well, they might not be all over me. That's one of the curses ... of all this so-called beauty. But, most all of 'em ... there was always a sexual element. To just about anything they'd have to say. Or the way they'd look! The way they'd leer! Even Gerard and Mitch."

Gerard, of course, was manager of the loan office. Mitch assisted him, out front. Closed loans. Handled most all of the out-of-the-ordinary business, out there. Stuff that the three "girls" couldn't/didn't/shouldn't handle.

"Mitch, especially," she went on. "He was always rubbing up against me. Well, not only me. But, the other two, also. I once asked him ... if he was ever rubbing against Alice. Negative. He always claimed ... that all the contact was absolutely accidental. 'Alice', he maintained, 'worked in the back room'. So, there was no chance ... none, whatever ... of his brushing up, against her."

"But, I was ... was different? Something ... someone ... different?"

"Yes. Well, I knew you were married. And that you had all those kids. I thought ... was sure ... you were happy. So, I never would've tried anything with you. Besides, I was all wrapped up, in Borden. The thing was: You never tried anything ... with me! To me ... well, that made you special. That thing ... tonight ... with me sitting there naked, for hours might've been awfully stupid. Would've seemed stupid, anyway. But, it proved ... in my own warped little mind ... that you were, what I'd always thought you were! Again, it was patently stupid! But, it was patently vital to me. That's why you're here ... even as we speak!"

"This has been ... well ... quite a revelation."

"Listen. In nineteen-fifty-three, or fifty-four, Gordon Jenkins ... who was a brilliant arranger/ conductor ... wrote a, kind-of-modern, operetta. I don't know if you've ever heard of it. It was called *Manhattan Tower*."

"Yes," I enthused. "I'm more than a little familiar with it. I've always loved that work. Gordon Jenkins was a pure genius!"

"Then, you know, that the man's tower ... that it was a hotel room. One that he'd rented ... for the short time, that he'd be in New York."

"Yeah. First thing he did, was ... he went to *Billie's Bar and Grill*. The lyric ... about the joint always amused me: *You can buy a glass of beer near here, clear beer ... or even near-beer ... here.*"

Then, you would know that his name was ... was 'Stephen'."

"Of course I knew that.. One of my favorite facets ... in the whole work."

"Well, from the time I'd first heard it, I'd always wished that ... someday ... I'd meet my 'Stephen'. The woman's name was 'Julie'. She was played ... on the album, by the way ... by Gordon Jenkins' wife, Beverly. And, I found myself wishing ... from time to time ... that I'd been named Julie. Had always looked to be able to find my 'Stephen'. I never did think that Borden had really ... uh ... qualified as a 'Stephen'. And now? And now, here I am ... with a bona fide, real-life, Stephen! That's pretty neat, I'd say!"

"I'd like to say one thing ... to you, Beautiful Lady."

"Whazzat?"

"E Griltch Ge Dunk Dunk!"

"E Griltch Ge Dunk? What the hell does that mean?"

"It's probably a tad before your time ... a few years before *Manhattan Tower* ... but, it's from an old TV show! *Kukla, Fran And Ollie*. Ollie, was Oliver J.

Dragon ... of Dragon Retreat, Vermont. He'd attended *Dragon Prep.* That glorious institution's colors ... were purple-and-chartreuse. And ... in dragon talk ... 'E Griltch Ge Dunk Dunk' means 'I love you'!"

"Oh! How romantic." Her voice was dripping -- with sarcasm. Then, it changed! For the better. "Wait a minute! Actually," she reflected, "that is romantic! Pretty damn romantic! And so like you! So like my image of what Stephen would do ... or say. Thank you!"

❖

Janice had left a wake-up call for five o'clock. Had a flight out -- at 6:20AM! That was back -- when you didn't have to be at the airport three-and-a-half days, before your flight (and have to remove everything, but your sanitary napkin)!

So, when the phone rang, she reached over, to the nightstand -- and turned on the lamp. Then, she picked up the receiver. She, apparently, was able to mutter something intelligent enough -- that the room clerk was satisfied that it had been an answer.

Then, she turned to me, and asked, "Are you up? Is every part of you up?"

Right then, we engaged in a, highly-satisfying replay of our previous "gathering of the clans" -- executed a mere few hours previously! Very rewarding. And -- if I do say so -- I'd performed (shockingly magnificently)!

Once the frenzied "activity" had come to a glorious conclusion, we'd simply lain there! Still "in the position"! Overcome -- completely saturated -- in total bliss!

The main thought -- one of "only" seven-trillion -- was, My God! This woman is so beautiful! And she doesn't have one drop of makeup on!

Well, she caught her flight (but, just barely). Me? I made my way back to my spectacularly-empty apartment. It was a good thing that I'd realized -- that, over the months, I'd come to know all of the hotel's room clerks. And they all knew me. Otherwise, I'd have had a problem -- with the lady, behind their counter, who was observing me! Watching me -- as I opened the safe, behind my own counter, and purloining a set of car keys, for the, heavily-drained, trip home.

On my lunch break, that same early-afternoon, I went to a *Hallmark* store -- in the, fairly-nearby, *Greenspoint Mall* -- and bought the most-flowery, most-decorative, most-schmaltz-riddled, greeting card I could find.

When I got back to the hotel, I sat down -- and wrote the most-sentimental, most-loving, most-flowery, message that my, gratefully-overwhelmed, heart (and still, highly-fevered, brain) was capable of generating. I -- lovingly -- placed it, in the hotel's outgoing mail-chute.

Six days later, I received an, obviously-expensive, white card -- about half the size of the one I'd sent to Janice. It was <u>from</u> Janice. All it said was a gold-embossed "Thank You" -- and was signed "With All My Love". I was <u>most</u> grateful for the missive. Even Scotch Taped it to the fridge, in my "posh" domicile.

Over the next three-plus months, we'd -- Janice and I -- developed a more or less routine. Nowadays, of course, a person can whip out their tiny cell phone, press a button -- and a phone'll ring in Cincinnati (or Rangoon) or someplace. Back in the seventies, it was a little more complicated. Half the phones (I think) were still rotary-dial. And there were the ever-changing, ever-expanding, area codes. So, it wound up -- that most people did a helluva lot less phoning. (I don't even <u>want</u> to get into texting -- and stuff like that.)

We <u>did</u>, though have a "Neanderthal" teletype, behind our counter. <u>She</u> had one in her office! And, for about three months, we were <u>typing</u> our daily greetings to one another. Always signing off -- with the classic "E Griltch Ge Dunk Dunk"!

But, that _changed_ -- too soon! Her company changed her assignment. And moved her down to Bordentown -- in South Jersey. She'd needed to be close by -- the Philadelphia market. And the Pennsylvania Turnpike. She would put an awful lot of miles -- on her new company Mercedes -- traveling to Central and Western Pennsylvania, as well as to numerous spots, in Ohio.

Sadly, she'd only be flying into Houston two or three times a year! The powers that be had wanted her to eliminate Texas, altogether -- as part of her itinerary. But, _that_ she'd refused. Had _insisted_ on keeping Houston -- and Albuquerque, New Mexico. (The inclusion, of the _latter_ city, had me _wondering_!)

So, that being the way things were going, I made arrangements to take _my_ vacation -- at Christmas time! She'd be unable to make it down to my Lone Star bailiwick before the holidays! And, by then, it had become _deathly_ important, for me to be _with_ her -- when that special time of year rolled around.

I was able to track down -- and, ultimately, speak to -- my owner! For only the third or fourth time -- in my glorious employment tenure, with his firm. (So, hopefully, he _had_ been satisfied -- with the job I'd been doing! A _most_-important consideration!)

And -- thankfully -- he _did_ sanctify the winter vacation! An even _more_-important consideration!

THREE

I probably (I undoubtedly) could've picked a better time, for a vacation. From a strict weather standpoint, anyway. I ran into a blizzard -- brief, but scary -- in Delaware. The temperature, though, seemed to hit (and remain at) Arctic levels -- from about halfway through Virginia.

On the other hand, the welcome I'd received -- at Janice's sixth-floor apartment, in Bordentown, New Jersey -- made it all worthwhile. I'd entered the building's smallish vestibule, rung her bell -- and, immediately, had gotten buzzed inside.

I'd hurried to the elevator! Hurried, even more, down to the end of the long (really long) corridor. Then, found her door slightly ajar! I knocked. But, the action pushed the portal even further open!

"Come in!" The throaty invitation came from the back portion, of the apartment!

I complied! And headed toward the source -- of that inviting voice! It turned out to be -- ta-DAH! -- the bedroom! And there she was! My hostess! Lying on the bed! She was "barefoot ... all over"! Totally -- without a stitch!

Of course, I'd -- hurriedly -- joined in the "clothing optional" environment! One thing, of course, proceeded to "lead to another"! Greetings don't get any better, more pronounced -- or more welcome -- than that!

Once the, rather-frenzied, highly-rewarding, dazzlingly-satisfying, renewing-of-acquaintances had been, so breathlessly, accomplished, we'd simply lain there. If a person were looking for a clear definition -- of the word "contentment" -- he/she might find a picture of Janice and me, in the dictionary. (Well, if they'd allowed such a thing.) We simply laid there -- consumed, by fatigue! By glorious fatigue!

Finally, I broke the esoteric silence -- after about 15 minutes -- with probably the most idiotic comment, on record: "For some reason, I'd expected your building to be higher. Be more ... than six-stories."

"There's a song, y'know ... in Rodger-and-Hammerstein's *Oklahoma*. This cowboy ... he's just back from a trip. He sings *Everything's Up To Date, In Kansas City*. He keeps singing, 'They've gone about as far, as they can go' ... about everything. In the song, he sings about staying in a hotel ... four stories tall. He says that's, 'about as tall as a building oughta be'. I've got two stories ... on that building. And this joint may not be the penthouse ... there ain't no such animal here ... I am on the top floor."

"How've you been?" It seemed like a logical comeback -- to that clarifying dissertation.

"You come in here ... come in and, first thing you do, is you screw me ... and now you wanna know how I'm doin'?"

"Well, there are such things ... as priorities! Besides, when I got here, you were ... what we, in the industry, call ... 'bare-assed naked'!"

"White man speak the truth! I'm fine ... now, that you asked. And you?"

"I'm fine! Now!"

"Really, Stephen, it's good to see you, again! And to see so much of you!"

"I could hardly wait to get here! I'm sure, though ... that they must've slipped another seven-thousand miles into the route, from Texas. About halfway through The Carolinas, I think."

"Well, I'm really glad you're here, Stephen. Really glad you're here. I've ... truly,,, truly missed you!"

"And ... hoo boy ... have I missed you! I still can't believe that, anyone ... any woman, as out and out beautiful, as you are ... would give me so much as a tumble!" I came up -- with a sweeping hand motion -- gesturing toward (and over) her entire, still-uncovered, to-die-for, body. "And yet," I continued, "here I am! Here we are! Lying here ... naked! After one of the most exciting ... most fulfilling ... interludes, that I've ever experienced. In my entire life!"

"Stephen? Stephen, you've got to get over that! How pretty I may ... or may not ... be, is of no importance. You are a most desirable man! And ... so far, anyway ... the nicest man I've ever met! Period! Para-giraffe!"

The size of my head could never have gotten any larger!

The first three days, of our wintertime get-together, were not spectacularly omnipotent. But, we did have a good time. Went up to New York City, on the second day. To a fency-schmency nightclub. Took in a nondescript, non-musical, Broadway show. (The only ones -- to which we could get tickets, at the time.)

On the third evening, we journeyed in to Philadelphia. Ate at a really nice restaurant -- wherein the food was much better than had been the case, at the stuffy joint, in "The Big Apple". Then, we took in a wonderful, professional, production -- of Frank Loesser's *The Most Happy Fella*. That had been -- till then -- the only opportunity I'd ever experienced, to witness this remarkable work.

I'd always loved virtually every song that had been written for the show. But, I'd especially worshipped the very beautiful *My Heart Is So Full Or You* -- which, some say, Mr. Loesser had always considered to be his most beautiful piece of music. I would have to agree. When "Tony" and "Rosabella" teamed up -- in a most-proficient duet, of the stirring song -- I wound up whispering the romantic lyric, in Janice's ear. I'd never heard a, more-languid, (nor long-lasting) sigh than the slow, soft, poignant, expelling of breath, that came from her -- in, highly-intimate, response!

It turned out to be a most satisfying evening! And -- as we'd headed back to New Jersey -- the night gave substantial promise of (ah) even more satisfaction! (Hee Hee!)

Then, a not-so-funny thing happened -- on our way to "Paradise"! We'd parked Janice's snooty Mercedes, in the basement/garage, of the building. As she'd pressed the "UP" button, at the elevator, the door began to creak open.

"That's unusual," she muttered.

It was awfully late, at night, for the cage to have been in the basement. It would've indicated that someone had recently left. Highly unusual -- for that hour!

In a matter of seconds, we found out why! Lurking inside the elevator -- were two huge black males! Each of these thugs, had a .45 caliber handgun -- both of which were even "huger"!

Janice saw the danger -- a second or two before (duh) I did -- and gasped! Loudly!

"Shut up, Lady!" hissed one of the gunman. Then, focusing his attention on me, he spat, "You too!".

I made the, what-I'd-thought-might-be-fatal, decision -- to grab at his gun! He quickly (and deftly) avoided the, patently-stupid, move! And cracked me with the .45 -- just above my left temple! Then, a second, vicious, blow -- which landed an inch-or-two above the initial smack -- sent me to the floor of the car! I lost consciousness -- for, probably, two or three or four seconds!

The next thing, of which I was aware, had Janice pleading, "Don't hit him again! What do you want? I've only got sixty-or-seventy dollars! You're welcome to it! Welcome to all of it! Here! Please ... take it!"

The fog was beginning to clear, for me! Just enough to see her extending her purse -- in the direction of the second assailant!

"Here," she urged. "Please ... take it, and go! Please! You've done enough! Enough damage! Just ... please ... take the money! Take it ... and leave! Please! Please ... go! Leave us alone!"

"Yeah, Baby," he rasped. "We'll take it! But ... hey! You some kind of looker! Let's have us ... some fun! Let's get ourselves ... up to your apartment!"

She started to protest! But, he pressed his gun -- firmly -- against her vagina, and asked "Do you want me to pull the trigger? This is awful-big firepower ... in this gun! It'll blow the snatch ... blow it right off-a you! Now, let's get our asses ... on up to your apartment!" Glaring down at me, he snarled, "You! Get your ass up, off-a the floor! We goin' upstairs!"

It took a goodly amount, of doing -- but, I managed to struggle, to my feet! With a significant pause -- on my knees! I'd obeyed orders -- but, I wasn't so sure that it had been the best move! That was due to the face that -- the one, who'd hit me, made as if to crack me again! But, thankfully, he did hold back!

"What floor's your apartment on, Sweetie?" growled the first thug -- pressing his weapon, even more harshly, into Janice's groin area.

"Six," doubled over slightly, she answered -- sighing deeply. "Sixth floor."

The gunman -- anxiously -- pressed the button, marked "6"! The car creaked into motion -- slowly (maddeningly slowly) -- rising to the top floor.

During the trip up, I felt the cold steel, of my attacker -- pressed (tightly) up against the flesh, of the side, of my neck! Close by the top of my coat collar! The other intruder was, by then, standing behind Janice -- his gun pressed (tightly) up, against the center of her, badly-quivering, bottom!

The door opened, and her gunman "urged" her, toward her apartment -- by nudging her buttocks! (Insistently!)

Surprisingly (although, I suppose, it undoubtedly *shouldn't* have been) her hand was as steady, as could be -- once she'd pulled her ring, of keys, from her bag! She unlocked the door -- and the four of us filed in!

We were "guided" back, to the bedroom. Once inside the boudoir, her personal gunman half-shouted, "Now you *two*! Get out of your *clothes*! *Both* of you! I want you fucking *naked*! Fucking *now*!"

"Out of our ... ?" It was the first thing -- that I'd been capable of uttering!"

"*Both* of you," he snarled! "*Both* of you! Bare-assed *naked*! *Now*!"

I glanced into Janice's eyes. The soft-brown, doe-like, coloring had seemed to disappear! To be replaced by a most *helpless* shading! A tinting -- that I'd never before seen! I'm sure that my own optics showed an even *higher* degree, of that same frightful element! The fact that I'd just discovered that I was *bleeding* -- (albeit slightly) from the two blows, to the head, that I'd taken, so recently -- was *not* helping!

But, what could we *say*? What could we *do*? Either *one* of us? We complied! My fellow prisoner found herself unclothed -- *well* before I did! It seemed, however, as though it took the pair of us *forever* -- to remove our clothing! And *that*, totally-mind-warping, period -- went all-too-quickly!

Once I'd wound up, in the buff, I was commanded to lie down, on the bed! On my stomach! I, of course, complied! (What else was I going to do?) As soon as I'd done so, though, my own assigned-terrorizer placed a pillow over the back of my head -- cutting off my sight of what was taking place (along with a goodly amount of my ability to even breathe)! Immediately, I felt the unmistakable pressure of the muzzle of that howitzer-called-a-handgun -- pushed, flush, against the other side of the pillow!

I was sure -- absolutely positive -- that, in a matter of seconds, I'd be dead!

I could still hear, though! And what I heard -- came from Janice's. steadier-than-I'd-thought-possible, voice!

"Please!" Her voice was pleading -- but, seemingly without panic! She seemed to be getting stronger -- as the, God-awful, ordeal continued to, sadistically, play out! "Please don't kill him! I'll do whatever you want! Whatever you want ... I'll do! Only please! Please ... let him live!"

"I'm gonna do whatever I want, anyway, Sweet-cheeks!" I could actually hear the evil smirk -- in the voice, of the interloper! The creep -- who'd assigned himself, to her. "Now," he hissed, "lay your ass down ... next to him! Only ... on your back!"

I could feel -- the fact that she'd obeyed! She was lying mere inches from my exposed right, face-down, side! Then, obviously, he'd climbed atop of her! In a matter of seconds I would know that the unthinkable was taking place! The mattress was vibrating -- violently!

And what could I do? The unmistakable pressure from that damnable gun! It was still pushing down -- upon the back, of my head!

It didn't take long for my friendly neighborhood rapist -- to "complete his rounds"! The "fulfillment" was accompanied by a loud screech! Then, I felt the mattress's load get lightened -- as the sub-human had, undoubtedly, arisen from the, obviously-terrorized, Janice!

"Now," suggested the vermin -- who'd just done the unspeakable deed -- to his fellow-traveler, "why don't you have at her!"

"NO!" My muffled scream was barely audible!

"Shut your hole," half-shouted the goon, who'd been holding the firearm to my head! "Shut your goddam hole ... and keep it shut!" I felt the gun -- that particular handgun -- being removed from the top part, of the pillow! Only to be replaced by a, jarringly-similar, pressure -- just slightly to the left, of the original, life-threatening, indentation!

"You've already used one hole," complained my personal attendant! "I'm gonna use the other one, now! Turn over, Baby! Turn yourself over! On your stomach! Lessee ... what that ass, of yours, looks like!"

I could feel the distressed woman's compliance! Then -- seconds later -- her loud, tormented gasp! He'd, obviously, entered her -- from behind!

Again, the entire mattress became the source of debauched, ultra-frenzied, activity! Janice was sobbing -- loudly, violently -- as the ruthless, vicious, penetration continued! I don't know how the mattress could've survived the frenetic assault! I almost didn't know how Janice could've survived! Except that I did know! She was, by then, half-moaning, and half-sobbing! Eventually, she just went to crying, softly!

I felt the subhuman sodomizor lift himself -- very slowly, excruciatingly slowly -- from the overheated bed! I'd scrunched my eyes closed! Expecting the inevitable bullet! The death slug -- to the back of the head!

I didn't expect Janice to stop crying! Not that quickly! But, she did! Incredible! She was incredible! The whole situation was incredible! And now, it would end! In a matter of seconds -- would be drawing my last breaths!

"Please," her tear-filled voice pleaded. "Won't you please go away, now? Please ... just go! Please! You've ... you've done enough!"

"I dunno," responded her first assailant. "I don't think we can just leave ya! The two of ya! To rat us out! Rat us out ... to the cops!" Obviously, that statement caused me -- to abandon all hope! What little -- that may have remained! "I mean," he continued, "we gotta be stupid sons-of-bitches ... to just go ahead, and to leave ya!"

"Look," she responded -- with less panic, in her voice, than I could've ever imagined. "I give you my word ... my sacred word ... that I won't go to the police! Or any other law-enforcement agency! I swear I won't! Look," she repeated, "I don't know what kind of records you guys might have! Either of you. But, if you're clean ... or even halfway clean ... you're not gonna want this, on your record! If the cops have you nailed ... for anything like this ... they're gonna come after you! Especially, if there's two dead bodies involved! So, you're gonna be up to your butts ... in problems."

She left them that tidbit to chew on! I couldn't believe the calmness, in her voice! In her entire demeanor! I was still trembling -- badly! But, Janice? She was a rock!

"And if you're clean," she continued, "or haven't ever been involved, in anything like this ... then, you're home free! I have no idea ... as to who you are! I think that ... if you were to go any further ... you will have 'bought the farm' Sealed your own doom!. Think on that!"

"Aw shit, Junior," grumbled that same assailant. "Let's just go ahead ... and get the hell out of here!"

And they got the hell -- out of there!

I'd still had that damnable pillow, covering my head! It weighed about 30 pounds! But, shortly before I heard the front door slam -- Janice removed the frightful, almost-smothering, thing, from me! I blinked -- and did my best, to look up at her! From her appearance -- and demeanor -- it was almost as though, none of this horrible nightmare had happened! (Almost!) Incredible! The whole thing -- was incredible! More than incredible! Truly, she was a rock! I couldn't imagine the sheer, out and out, hell -- that she'd just gone through! Or the unimaginable fortitude she was now displaying! What immense courage -- she had shown! Throughout the entire -- unspeakable -- episode! The God-awful series of episodes!

This remarkable woman! She looked down at me. I cannot begin -- to try and describe the expression, on her face. She'd probably tell you the same thing -- as pertains to what my, probably-contorted, countenance looked like!

"Janice," I finally managed to murmur. "I can't ..."

"Hush." It was not a command. It was not even a plea. I can't tell you what it was! It was -- simply -- Janice!

She pulled herself down -- and, sort of, "nestled" in, next to me. The word "nestled" doesn't really fit. But, I cannot think of another word -- to describe what we were doing! Well, in point of fact, there's no word -- that can really describe our situation! Suffice to say that we'd simply clung to one another! Clung desperately!

After a heavy, all-too-silent, period -- of I-cannot-tell-you-the-length (probably, 15 or 20 minutes; but, I really don't know) -- I, finally, said to her: "Janice, I really *must* leave! I have no *right* ... no right, at *all* ... to *stay* here! To *stay* ... in your *presence*! Given my *actions*! Or ... more *truthfully* ... my *lack* of actions! While all these God-*awful* things were taking place ... while they were *happening* to you ... I did *nothing*! Just *laid* there! Like a goddam piece of *cheese* ... or something! Like a piece of *shit*! I didn't do ... didn't do, a goddam *thing*! Not one damn *thing*! Not *one*!"

"What *could* you do?" she soothed, rubbing her, surprisingly-cool, palm across my chest. "What *could* you have done? I *shudder* to think," she continued (actually *shuddering*) "what they'd have *done* to you ... if you'd *tried* to do anything! Tried to do *anything*! Anything at *all*! *That* would've been worse ... than what the schmucks would've done to me! What those schmucks *did* to me! Anything you'd have tried ... would've gotten us *both* killed! *Both* of us! I thought we were both *dead* ... as it was!"

"Yeah," I groused. "The only reason we *weren't* both killed ... that we're *both* not dead ... was your *incredible* performance! The incredible *courage* you showed! I can't even *imagine* such grace-under-fire ... such out and out *courage* ... as you showed! *That's* why I have no right ... no right, whatever ... to *remain* here! To even *look* at you! To *see* your ... see your *nakedness*! To remain, in ... in your *company*! To remain ... in your courageous *presence*!"

"No, Stephen." Her voice was soft -- but rock-like. "I *need* you! Need you ... in my *presence*! If you were to get up ... get up, and leave ... I'd come apart! Just literally disintegrate! Go to pieces ... altogether! Go ... completely ... to hell!"

"That's not true! Anyone who could ..."

"That 'anyone'? She will go ... go completely ... go to pieces! If you don't stay here ... and hold her! Hold her tight! Hold her ... against you! Hold her close ... to shield her! Protect her ... shield her ... from just what happened! Otherwise, the horrible experience ... it will take over! It'll simply destroy me!"

I don't know exactly when it happened (can't even tell you approximately), but I'd begun to pat her on her bottom! It seemed like the right thing, to have done. And she seemed to have become -- at least, slightly -- more contented, as the, out-of-the-blue, "procedure" had gone on! And on and on!

There would be occasions -- in two- or three-minute intervals -- when she'd shake! Violently! Tremble -- from head to toe! But -- thankfully -- the length (and frequency) of these frenzied, frighteningly-spastic, outbursts would dwindle, over the next couple, or three, hours! (Yes -- hours!)

I was still caught up -- in a, mind-warping, whirling-dervish, of raw emotion! I knew -- in my heart -- that I'd had no business being there! Remaining there! Yet. she'd seemed content -- well, as much as was possible -- with my presence! What to do? Well, I continued doing -- exactly -- what I'd been doing!

Somewhere -- in amongst all the holding/shaking/ sobbing/patting -- we'd both (incredibly) fallen into deep, impenetrable sleep! Each of us! When I'd finally opened my eyes -- sunlight was flooding the room! I raised my head -- to look over the shoulder of Janice (who I'd been still holding closely) -- and saw that the clock, on the nightstand was announcing the time, as 10:43AM!

Dear Lord! We've slept the whole, entire, miserable, goddam, night away!

I didn't want to awaken Janice! For whatever reason! I did resume patting her behind, though. (For whatever reason. It just seemed to be, the right thing to do.) In any case, the fanny-patting routine did nothing to disturb her sleep. Clearly, it was a form of escape, for her! I didn't have to have been some sort of shrink -- to have figured that out!

It would be almost 11:30AM -- before this heroic woman would begin to stir. The, dreadfully-long, minutes in between had caused my troubled mind to erupt, once more, with the disconcerting question: What the hell am I doing here? In the presence ... of this remarkable woman?

When this remarkable woman opened her eyes, she (incredibly) smiled at me! Then, she clung onto me! Even more tightly! (Something I'd have thought physically impossible!)

"Oh, Stephen!" Her voice was a husky-sounding mass of sleep! (And who knew what else?) "Stephen," she repeated, "stay with me! Hold me! Hold me tight! Tight! Hold me ... against you! Tight ... against you!"

I held her! Tight -- against me!

It wasn't until mid-afternoon -- that we'd both struggled, out of bed! And -- in each of our cases -- managed to, eventually, regain our, virtually-hopelessly-unsteady, feet! This took place -- almost literally -- an eternity, after the unimaginable attack had occurred! In that, incredibly-lengthy, time span since, we'd simply clung together! Had -- desperately -- held on to one another!

Janice, once she'd convinced herself that she was steady enough of foot, padded off, into the bathroom -- and didn't close the door. I kept my distance -- till I heard the toilet flush. Seconds later, she'd turned on the faucets, in there -- and was filling the tub! Filling the enormous, sunken, erotic, facility -- with almost-broiling water, as it turned out!

I'd had no idea -- as to how she ever could've gotten into the, just-this-side-of-scalding, brew! I was able to determine the high-temperature, of the bathwater -- because I'd entered the bathing area, shortly after she'd submerged herself, into the lava-like liquid!

I picked up the large, natural, sponge -- which had rested on the far-rear corner of the immense tub -- and proceeded, during the next 35 or 40 minutes, to bathe her! Rub her -- caress her -- all over her, ruthlessly-ravaged, scarlet-by-then, body!

Twice during that -- should've been esoteric (but, was not) -- exercise, she'd used her toes, to flick on the hot-water tap! The excruciating, hot, mixture should not cool down! Heaven forefend!

I don't think we ate -- not one thing -- during the entire day! Once she'd stepped out of the tub (looking not unlike a broiled lobster) -- and I'd (gently) toweled her off -- she made her way (still awfully unsteadily) back to bed. She didn't "flop", on the surface. But, rather, she crawled up -- into a position, where she was lying, on her tummy.

I managed to locate a very-expensive container -- of soothing, creamy, highly-perfumed, body oil, on her rather-cluttered dressing table (vanity, as it was still called then). I wound up using practically the whole, entire, supply, to rub her down. To, tenderly, massage her -- in the least-erotic way, as possible!

It was not until I'd crawled up next to her -- that it occurred to me (for the first time -- in, literally, hours) that I, too, was naked! Didn't mean a thing! Well, not all that much, anyway! We wound up -- literally, for many additional hours -- lying on our sides! Facing one another! And <u>clinging</u> -- <u>tightly</u> -- to one another! <u>Ever</u> so tightly!

It was not -- literally -- till the following morning, that either Janice or I began to act even <u>remotely</u> "civilized: To "thaw out" -- as it were.. I really don't know, precisely, <u>how</u> we'd spent the entire previous afternoon, or evening. I <u>think</u> that we got up twice -- and even turned on the TV. But, after a few minutes, we were back in bed -- <u>holding</u> one another, once again! Tightly! Neither of us had even <u>thought</u> (I'm sure) of donning some item of clothing! We'd remained naked -- both of us --throughout! (Of <u>that</u>, I'm positive!)

On that "revival" morning, we managed to dress -- and wander, over to the *Denny's* restaurant, across the street! Don't <u>ask</u> me -- what we'd had for breakfast. Whatever it was, we finished it! But, we did <u>not</u> "wolf it down"!

After the "enriching" repast, we began to walk. I have no <u>idea</u> -- as to how far. Or whose idea, it might have been. But, we discovered a small park. (One she'd not known had existed.) We sat on a bench -- for, at least, an-hour-and-a-half. Actually, we'd wound up -- with my lying down, with my head, in her lap! I have no <u>idea</u> when, during the interlude, <u>that</u> would've occurred!

Somewhere in there, she leaned down -- and placed her face (and her lips) as close to mine, as she could. Her voice was a hushed whisper -- but, it was almost as though it was booming out through some kind of megaphone.

"Stephen," she emoted, "I *need* for you to stay by me. Stay *with* me. I realize that *girls* aren't supposed to be proposing to *boys*. And I'm *not*! Not proposing marriage. Not necessarily, anyway. But, I *do* need you! *Need* you ... by my side. Now ... and, quite possibly, forever."

"*Me*? *Me* ... the one who let you be *raped*, for God's sake? Who let you be *sodomized*?" I shuddered! *Violently*! "You want *me* ... by your side? *Me*?"

"Yes!" Her tone had gotten louder! And *firmer*! "Don't ask me to explain it ... because I *can*not! But, that *episode* ... that disgraceful *humiliation* ... for some reason, brought *home* to me the realization that, *yes*! I *do* need you! Whether in *marriage*! Or ... quote ... living in sin ... unquote."

«Oh, Janice! You can›t *mean* that."

"I was never more serious in my life. I *do* need you. Do you remember ... at the end of *Manhattan Tower*? 'Stephen' says to 'Julie', 'I can't *leave* you'? I'm hoping ... probably against hope ... that you'll say that to *me*! I'll even change my name ... legally ... to Julie, if that'd be what it takes."

"To be truthful," I replied, "I'd not really *thought* about leaving. Well, of course, I *did*! But, *that* was the night before last! Till then, I was just simply so hell-bent on *getting* here. Then, we had those first days ... filled to the brim, with all the *happiness*! All the happiness ... in the *world*! Then ... the other *night*! So I haven't really *had* all that much time to even *consider* leaving. *Especially* since you've wanted me to *stay*! I just ..."

"Well, consider it *now*! I *realize*, that you might have to go back down to Houston ... to clear up things, down there. But, *please* ... *please*, Stephen ... *please* come back to me! *Stay* with me! Stay *by* me! Now ... and *forever*! I *need* for you ... to be *with* me! Now ... and *always*!"

"I'd ... well, I'd *love* to! But, you *see*? It's really not that *easy*. Not all that *simple*! There'd be the two-weeks' notice ... that I'd really *have* to give to my employer. He *did* give me a break. Gave me a *chance* ... when he *really* had no business doing that. Have to gather up ... what few belongings I've got. Stuff like that."

"But, it's merely your *job*? And gathering up your *things*? That's *all*? No ... ah ... *relationships*, to end? No *woman* ... who'd be vying, with me, for your *affection*?"

"*No*! Not a *soul*!"

"Then ... is it *me*? Am *I* so ... ?

"*No*! Janice, I *love* you! I've never *permitted* myself to even *think* ... to even, for a minute, to *entertain* ... the foolish *thought*, that someone as *beautiful* as you, could possibly love me! And ... so far, anyway ... I don't remember hearing you say it! Say you love me!"

"Well, if I haven't, I should have! In my mind I've said it! Over and over! And over again! I do love you, Stephen! Maybe even ... probably even ... from our stupid finance company days! Definitely from the first time, that I'd laid eyes on you ... in Texas! I never would have invited you up ... shared my bed with you, shared anything, with you ... if I didn't, out and out, love you!"

"I believe you! And I suppose ... actually, I'm sure ... that I should have known that. Known it ... all along. But, Janice, I'm one of the most imperceptive human beings ... in the history, of the world. And I ..."

"Hush! You're one of the sweetest human beings ... in the history of the world."

"You ... you really believe that? Actually ... you believe that?"

"Of course! Go back to what I said ... about sharing my bed!"

"I've ... I've, I've, I've ..."

"You've got more time, than ... say ... the next thirty seconds to think about it! Like I said ... I'd like for you to, at least, consider the proposition".

That last word -- made us both laugh! Loudly! Almost non-stop! It was as though some kind of emotional dam had, at that very moment, just burst! It had been awhile!

"I've already considered," I was finally able to murmur -- once all the alleged "hilarity" had, at long last, played out! "I accept your 'proposition'!"

The, almost-deafening, avalanche of guffaws began anew!

It took a few more, side-splitting, minutes -- before she was able to respond, with a hoarse, "You do? You accept? You'll come live with me?"

"More than that! I want to marry you! Be your husband! If you'll have me! I didn't mean for that last part ... for it, to come out, as corny as it did."

"It came out ... just beautifully! But, I want the agreement sealed!"

"Sealed? How? By what?"

"I want you to turn your head ... inward!" I was still lying with the old gourd, in her lap. "I want you to turn your head! Turn your head ... to where your lips are as close to my vagina, as you can get them! Then, I want you to kiss me there! Over my clothes! That's fine! It's purely symbolic! Symbolic as hell! But, it closes the deal!"

So? So, I closed the deal! Three -- or four -- times!

FOUR

I really don't know what to tell you -- about my last three days, in New Jersey. My last three days -- of that one unforgettable trip! It all, pretty much runs together. There were no highs or lows. How could there be? And absolutely no sexual activity! There simply seemed to have been a silent -- unwritten, unspoken -- agreement, that called for a cessation, of all such intimacy.

However, all intimacy does not (necessarily) have to be sexual. Once or twice, each day, I bathed Janice. Once or twice a day, she'd insisted on bathing me. It didn't take a helluva lot of persuasion -- for me to have gone along with "the program". But, I'd never have suggested (nor "submitted) to it -- had she not called the shot!

Mostly, whenever we were alone, in her apartment, we were unclothed -- and engaged in many hours, of simply holding one another! On our way back from the park (and "The Agreement"), we'd stopped, at a small, neighborhood, drugstore. She bought a humongous container of, highly-scented, wonderful-feeling, body lotion! We went through -- almost the entire bottle, of the therapeutic stuff -- in just those few days!

There'd been literally no "schedule of events". Our existence was all pretty much nondescript. We'd always (both of us) seem to come up with the same idea -- whatever it might've turned out to be -- simultaneously.

There was one evening (the one after we'd reached "The Agreement", I think) when we drove into Philadelphia. I'd never driven a Mercedes before. We had filet mignons -- at a fency-schmency steakhouse. The bill came to about 92 bucks -- which, to me, was *astonishing*! *She* paid it! I'd had *less* than that staggering amount on me! (It was only *slightly* less! But, it *was* less!)

And that had been *it*! This was the only real, what-you-might-call, "red letter" event -- since the detested, God-awful, unspeakable, "encounter" with those two sub-humans! And -- while the "dinner date" had been *enjoyable* -- it didn't really set off any gigantic sorts of flares! I guess it didn't figure to.

It *was*, at the "steak joint", though, that we'd done the lion's share, of our, post-attack, discussions.

First off, I'd advised her that I was *far* from the richest man, in the world. And I opined that -- "moving up here, *naked* ... job-wise" was, undoubtedly, going to cause all kinds, of financial problems.

"Look," she'd admonished, "don't let money be a consideration. Not a *major* consideration, anyway. Borden had had a goodly amount of money ... in whatever banks, I was able to track down. I'd had to fight his parents ... to get my hands on it. On any of it! 'My grubby little hands' ... to hear them say it. They could.ve written me a check, for the amount, I finally got. Written it ... out of their petty cash drawer. So, I'm pretty flush! I'd imagine ... that you'll probably want to find a job ... once you're up here. I'm going to keep mine. So, finances should not be a hurdle, for you."

"Well, I will have to give notice ... at work."

"Understandable. But, as soon as you can discombobulate yourself ... get yourself turned loose from them ... please haul your fanny back up here. Please! I need you. I really do!"

So, it came to pass: I drove down to Houston -- almost non-stop. Phoned my illustrative owner -- and, verbally, gave two-week's notice! He was grossly upset -- but, he'd "reluctantly" accepted my termination/departure pronouncement. What choice did he have?

On the other hand, ten or eleven days went by -- before he ever showed up. I'd figured that he'd either forgotten about it -- or was going to let the current crew "just deal with it". As efficient as they were, I'm sure they could've handled it.

However, the guy showed up, ran an ad, and -- as he'd done with me -- hired the first man he'd interviewed. (Him, I was worried about. But, I really don't know, how he might've worked out. I can't say that I could care less -- but, I certainly wasn't going to hang around, to find out.)

I got back up to Bordentown two days later! And it never looked better! I'd had to coax (almost literally) a few hundred more miles -- out of my beloved old Plymouth. (Remember her? For what-ever reason, I'd never torn myself loose from her.)

I was, ultimately, welcomed -- back into the open arms, of Janice! An important note: Our "sexual abstention program" had (spectacularly) come to an auspicious end, upon my return! Right then, and there! Almost immediately! (Almost?)

Not only had this astounding woman rebounded -- noticeably, unmistaken ably -- from the unthinkable, intimate/sexual, aspect, of her horrible experience, she'd actually seemed to have returned, completely, to her normal, wonderful, self! Apparently, in all phases of her life! Each and every corner, of her life -- near as I could tell -- was, once again, "normal"! Incredible! I'd like to think that (ahem) my presence, had made a bit of a contribution -- to the, obviously-worthy, cause! No matter how insignificant, that "service" might've been!

The morning after I'd arrived, Janice made the "critical" decision -- to not go to work. That, of course, was great! We were so wrapped up in each other, at that point -- that very few of our actions were accomplished, outside of the, ever-inviting, bed. (Very few!)

It was the following morning -- while she was preparing, for her regrettable return, to her job -- that we'd finally gotten around, to some bona fide, legitimate, conversation. An interchange -- that was actually serious. We were both in the shower, at the time.

"Y'know?" I'd begun. "This might not be the time ... or the place ... but, we really ought to start talking, about setting a date. A date ... for us gettin' married-up. I still love you, y'know."

"Well, maybe we ought to cool it, a bit. For the littlest, of awhiles."

"I ... you what? I thought that we were ..."

"Listen, Stephen. If you'd not gone back, down south ... and I completely understood the fact, that you needed to go ... I'd have set the date, right then! Would've set it ... in stone! Right on the spot! But, you did! You did go ..."

"Well, I really had to."

"I told you ... that I understood! Told you that. Told you that ... right then! And I still do. Understand, that is. Still do! But, there's so much! So much ... that has come up ... since then! So much water, over the dam.

Wait till we get out. Get out of the shower! There's a picture ... a photo ... I want to show you! A picture I need to show you! A picture ... one that you need to see. You may not agree ... but, you do need to see it!"

"But ... but, you ... you ..."

"Hush," she soothed -- placing her forefinger, and middle finger, across my lips. Then, she kissed me -- deeply. "Just keep your shorts on! As if you were actually wearing shorts."

Then, she patted me, on my behind. I think that this, always-exciting, motion -- made me feel a little more reassured. More than I should have! Than I definitely should have!

Once we'd, erotically, toweled each other off, she (rather reluctantly) made her way -- still naked -- out, to the living room. Once she'd returned, she was holding two eight-by-ten, black-and-white, photos! Very clear -- concise depictions! She held them out -- then, handed them to me. Her hand was shaking -- trembling, noticeably -- as I'd, hesitantly, accepted them.

I almost vomited! They were photographs -- of those two black men! The same creatures! The schmucks -- who'd attacked us! (Well, they had -- in point of fact -- attacked her!) The sub-humans, who'd struck -- on that horrendous night! Both of these creeps -- were dead! Dead as hell! Both cretins -- each one of them -- had had his throat slit! Spectacularly sliced! From side to side! "Smiling" -- from ear to ear!

"But ... but, _how_?" I was -- finally -- able to summon the energy, to ask. "How did _they_ ... ? How did _you_ ... ? How could ... ?"

"I'd had ... well, I still _have_ ... a few contacts, in the Mafia, y'know. Alice's boyfriend ... for one."

(Alice, you'll remember, was the celebrated "Miss Drake -- of *The New Jersey Employment Commission*", at my erstwhile finance company connection! I was guessing, by then, that it had been common knowledge, throughout the office force -- that her "fiancé" had been a member of "The Mob".)

"That was the _reason_," Janice explained. "_He_ was the reason ... the reason, I didn't go, _shrieking_, to the police! Ranting to the _police_ ... once these bastards had finished with me. For one thing, I _knew_ that they'd just installed security cameras ... the building's management had! Just installed 'em ... in the elevator. Two or three weeks before."

I'm guessing that the introduction of such things was _not_ new -- in the seventies. But, _I'd_ been unaware of them. They were nowhere _close_ to being as universal -- not nearly, as widespread -- as they are now.

"I _knew_," my hostess explained, "that these Mafia guys would _see_ to it ... that they'd be able, to get their, vengeance-filled, little _hands_, on the elevator photos! And, I _knew_ ... that once they _did_ ... that they'd _act_! Well, it turns out ... that they'd actually _recognized_ these schmucks! Knew _exactly_ ... who they _were_! And *where* they were! And so ... they just went *ahead*! And ... they *acted*! Really *acted*! You're *holding* the evidence, of that ... in your hands!" (In my *spastic* hands!)

"But ... but ..."

"So you see? *That's* just one of the things, that have *happened* ... that have *changed* ... the lay of the land, since you *left*! I just *got* these ... just *received* these photos ... the day before you got back, up here! I was *staggered*! Well, at *first*, anyway! But, you know, there's a part of me ... a *sizeable* part of me ... that's *happy* with the result! That's *extremely* satisfied!"

"I ... I guess," I mumbled. "What *else* has changed?"

"Well ... for another ... I'm late, y'know! Late ... with my *period*! Four *days* late, actually! As of this morning! *Another* recent development!"

"*So*? If you're late, it's not as though ..."

"Listen! I'm the most *regular* person ... you'll ever *meet*! I haven't been to the doctor, of course. Not yet. But, I'm *sure* ... that I'm *pregnant*!"

"*Pregnant*? I can't ..."

"Listen, Stephen! I *want* to go ahead ... with this pregnancy! Go ahead ... and have the *baby*! I'm pretty *sure* ... that the baby is *yours*! Almost *positive*! But, it *might* ... just might *be*, it *could* be ... could be *his*!"

"I've never been *fond* of ... of abortion." I managed to reply. "But, you know ... in this *case* ... why don't you just go ahead? Go ahead ... and have it *removed*?

I mean ... we can always start again! Always, we can have another kid! I mean, it's not as though ... !"

"No! Who-ever-has-sired-this-baby ... it is a baby! A real ... living, breathing ... thing! A human being!"

"It can't be ... can't be ... that far along! Not that far!"

"I don't care! I don't care how far! I'm ... obviously ... not all that religious! Obviously! But ... and I believe this, deeply ... it's not in my hands! It's a real life! I'll not mess ... with something, that I'm not qualified to jack with! So ... if I am with child ... it's something else you're going to have to consider! Something else you'll have ... to contend with."

"My God! I never thought that ..."

"Plus, I'm sure you're going to want to get a job ... up here. I can, probably, line you up ... with a couple, or three, good interviews. But ... where-ever you wind up ... I want you to settle in! Settle in ... before we would ever take that big matrimonial step!'

"Listen, Janice! That's not something you'd have to ..."

"You are not all that experienced," she interrupted. "I don't care how old you are! Could care less, about what your age might be! You're like an innocent waif! You might be ... might be just imagining ... just imagining, that you love me! But, you're also kind of overwhelmed, by my ... by my. so-called, beauty! You just might find another lady. Some other lady ... one who's even more 'beautiful', than me. Or she may be ugly as hell ... but, you still might wind up totally enraptured with her! There's more to life ... than just beauty! That sounds moronic! Moronic as hell! But, it's true!"

"That's not ... that wouldn't ..."

"No." Her negative retort -- while not as vociferous, as before -- was firm. Unquestionably firm! As in cement! "No," she emphasized, once more, "it's just simply best ... best that we wait! That's the only way to do it!"

That seemed to end the conversation! Without saying another word, she, hurriedly, dressed -- and bolted out the door! Left for work!

The earthshaking exchange -- the, mind-boggling, evolvement of events -- had, obviously, left me with a lot to consider! A helluva lot -- upon which to chew! As I stood there -- stark naked! In more ways than one!

Janice returned home that evening -- much later than I'd expected. She didn't have much to say. Neither did I. We threw a couple of frozen dinners, into the, new-fangled, microwave -- and ate in silence.

We watched a couple insipid sitcoms, on her color television -- then went to bed. And, once "in the old sack-a-roo" -- though we were both, in the nude -- she'd stayed, on her side of the bed. And I'd stayed on mine!

❖

Morning broke -- and, not only was Janice not, in bed -- when I'd cracked my eyes open, she was not in the apartment! Something -- obviously -- was going to have to be done about this!

After a, terribly-restless, highly-disturbed, morning, I retreated to my old friend -- my venerable Plymouth -- and, at *Denny's*, I bought a newspaper, and forced down a moderate breakfast.

There had been a few "Rooms For Rent" ads, in the paper -- and I scouted out five of them. The only one -- in which I could see myself living (read "existing") had been rented, a few hours before.

I returned to Janice's apartment -- a little under an hour, before she got there. She suggested we go out for dinner. We wound up at a quiet little cafe, that she'd frequented, from time to time -- across town.

"I don't know, if you'd be interested," she noted -- once we'd ordered, "but. I set you up ... with an interview ... tomorrow. You can always just call ... and cancel. He won't mind. It's with Brent Foley ... of the wholesale car auction. They've got one ... here, in Bordentown ... every Tuesday. And one ... every Thursday ... in Manheim. Pennsylvania. That's about a hundred-and-twenty-five ... or, maybe, a hundred-and-fifty ... miles, west of here. Little town ... in the middle of Amish Country. Used car dealers ... from all over Jersey, New York, and Pennsylvania ... they flock, to both of these all-day auctions! More used car dealers ... than you ever knew existed. The auction is looking for someone to ... more or less ... keep track, of the units, at both sites. Not the money, necessarily. At least I don't think so. How many cars ... or station wagons, or pickup trucks ... go in and come out. You'd have to attend both auctions ... each week! I think the pay's pretty good. But, if you're not interested, that's okay. You can simply call Brent ... and cancel!"

"No, that sounds fine. That was nice of you. To go out of your way to ..."

"Naw. No big deal." She reached into her purse -- and pulled out a page, from a small *Spiral* notebook. She handed it to me -- and said, "I wish you good luck, with it."

I'd started to reply -- but, she'd held up her hand! We wound up eating our entire meal -- in abject, stultifying, silence!

We'd returned to her abode -- and watched "The Tube" for awhile. The bed scenario -- turned out to be a replay, of the previous night. I don't know why we'd even bothered -- to remove our clothes.

Dawn broke -- and I could barely make out the shadowy form of Janice -- as she was entering the bathroom. I'd heard the toilet flush -- and the shower start! Then, I woke up -- two hours later.

I phoned Brent Foley -- at the *Bordentown Wholesale Auto Auction* -- and set up an appointment, for two o'clock, in the afternoon. It was a Friday -- and he'd just gotten back to town. He'd spent the previous night, in Manheim -- having attended the auction, on Thursday.

Brent was one of the nicest people I'd ever met. As sketchy as the interview, in Houston, had been -- this one was the direct opposite.

He explained my duties -- to a tee -- "if it happens that we can get together. Janice speaks quite highly of you, y'know. Quite highly."

Mostly, I'd be responsible for checking units in, determining which ones would've been sold -- through the auction, and "off the block" -- and seeing to the accurate distribution of those vehicles sold.

"It's all, pretty much, third-grade math," he'd elaborated. "Just a hell of a lot of it! And there's always a constant flow ... of third-grade figures. It ... literally ... never stops. They never stop. There are secrets ... stuff that you'll pick up on, as time goes by."

"Secrets?"

"Yep. For instance, if some seller calls, and wants vehicle numbers, for ... say ... twenty-five vehicles. Don't give 'em twenty-five consecutive numbers. Whoever-it-is ... whoever that might be ... would never have been to an auction before. He or she would never be able to keep up ... with whatever units would've been sold, or not! If he or she has to jack, with twenty-five transactions ... or non-transactions ... in a row. He or she is ... what we call ...

screwed! We usually have two-hundred-and-twenty-five ... or, maybe, two-hundred-and-fifty ... units go through our auctions, on any given day. Both here ... and in Manheim. So, you'd want to give him ... or her ... eight sequence-of-three-or-four numbers. Like, six-through eight ... then, seventeen-through-nineteen, and three or four more, in the mid- or late-twenties, and so on! A helluva lot easier for the guy ... or gal ... to keep track, that way. Helluva lot! And ... eventually, anyway ... they'll be grateful."

"It sounds like a winner, Mister Foley. I believe I could handle it. And it sounds like a never-a-dull-moment situation ... which I'd enjoy."

"I guess that you, and Janice, go back ... quite a ways."

"Yeah. Used to work together."

"At *Bolen Finance*?"

"Yeah. She told you that?"

"She did. And, she let me in, on the circumstances ... that led to your leaving the company. She's spoken ... as I said ... quite highly, of you."

"Well, I appreciate that. Have you known her long?"

"We go back ... a few years before her days, at *Bolen*. Were college chums. But, that was all! I even knew Borden ... her husband ... a little bit! Well, apparently, no one really knew him. Let's just say that Janice and I go way back. When she was at *Bolen*, I was sales manager ... at the large Lincoln-Mercury dealership, in South Brunswick."

Brent agreed to *hire* me! I would start -- the following *Monday*! But, the interview wound up going a good deal *deeper* than that! It left me *wondering*! Wondering how *much* Janice would've told him -- about me!

He asked me, whether I'd be in need -- of a room to rent. *That* was a little frightening! How much *did* she tell him? When I'd advised him that I *would* be in need of living quarters -- he informed me that, a friend of his (named Mabel) was thinking, of renting out a room, in her private dwelling. The place was located six blocks from the Bordentown auction.

My employer-to-be set up a four o'clock appointment -- that same *day* -- for me, to look at the place. The room was *charming*! And *cheap*! Mabel -- who was *also* charming -- was a retired schoolteacher, in her mid-seventies, I'm guessing. The deal was made. I'd move in -- on Saturday. The very *next* day!

Before *that* important transaction took place, Brent had asked -- if I'd had dependable transportation. I would need to go to Manheim -- every week.

I really could *not* ask my glorious Plymouth to continue to give such valorous service -- and confessed that I did not.

He told me of one of his dealer friends -- who'd usually run 12 or 15 units through Bordentown, and (from time to time) would send a few, through

Manheim. This guy had left a "really nice" 1971 Mercury Comet -- on the Bordentown lot -- over the past two or three weeks. The Maverick-looking two-door was a low-mileage unit.

"He wants a little more ... than market-value ... for it. But, it's a premium unit! If you're interested, I'll pay him off. You can buy it from us! We'll just whack you twenty-five bucks a week ... for the payment! Interest-free!"

I could never have believed I could have accomplished so much -- in one busy day! In just a few hours!

Then -- upon honest reflection -- I was left to try and honestly assess, how much I, myself, had actually accomplished! The answer came back, "Not a helluva lot! Nothing much"!

That evening, Janice and I, finally, had another -- of our, all-too-rare, conversations. It all started up -- innocently enough, I guess -- with her asking, "Well, how did your day go?"

She'd just blown in -- from work. I'd been seated, in her living room -- trying to cope with the, overwhelmingly-heavy, silence! Without turning on the radio, or television.

"You don't know?" I'd replied, regretting (immediately) how sarcastic my flip response had come out. "I'm sorry," I hastened to add. "I just ..."

"Well, I did push a few buttons." She was smiling -- despite the fact, that her attitude could have been (probably should have been) completely the opposite. "I just never knew ... didn't know ... how anything might've come out. How did things come out, by the bye?"

"Well, Brent Foley ... he hired me! Starting Monday!" I felt as though I should have gotten up -- but, I'd remained seated. "Not only that," I'd gone on, "but, he also found me a room. In the home ... of a lady named Mabel. I don't know ... if you know her."

"No. Not really. I don't believe so, anyway. I'd have remembered the name."

"He ... this guy, Brent ... he is also going to finance a compact car for me. A Mercury Comet. Looks like a Ford Maverick. This one, I guess, is a low-mileage gem. Should last a long time. And the price ... was right! So, you see? I made quite a coup! All t hanks to you! Janice? Janice ... I'm most grateful! I'm afraid ... afraid that I haven't been very nice, lately! Not very nice ... at all! I'm sorry! I apologize!"

"Well, I did lay a lot ... a whole damn lot ... on you! All critical stuff! Really critical! A helluva lot ... for anyone to have to deal with! Ever! And it all came ... well, it came ... came thundering down, out of the blue, for you! Come blasting ... out of the blue ... directly at you! Directly at you!"

"Yeah, but still, I should have ..."

"Naw. Not so! You probably should have reacted ... exactly as you did! I had no right ... absolutely no right ... to have expected you, to act, in any other way! Any way ... other than exactly the way you did! Exactly as you have!"

"I don't know about that! I should have ..."

"Listen. Listen to me, Stephen. I felt that it was incumbent upon me ... absolutely incumbent upon me ... to offer as much assistance, as possible. Apparently, things turned out ... turned out, pretty well ... for you. Glad I was able to help. But, it was less ... than you think. Hardly any effort ... at all."

"To help? You were able ... to help? You did the whole damn thing!"

"Not really. Not all, anyway. Not the whole damn thing! You did have to show up, y'know. And you did have to impress him. He was under no obligation, to actually go ahead ... and to hire you. None whatever! That was ... completely, and totally ... up to him! Same goes for finding you a room. Although ... let me tell you ... if there's anyone, in town, who'd have a handle, on any available rooms-to-rent ... he'd be the one. In the whole durn town."

"And he'd be the one ... where it comes, to financing an automobile?" I queried -- knowing the answer. "Helping out a poor working stiff?"

"Of course! Who else would have his finger ... as far as the status, of so many automobiles, is concerned ...

have his finger, on top of such things? No one else. Not around here. None ... that I know of."

"Yeah, but ..."

"Listen, Stephen. Brent Foley is a good man! I've known him ... for years. I never would've expected him ... to act, in any other way, than exactly the way he did. The way he has. That's the way ... he has always acted."

"Still ..."

"Whatever little contribution, I may have made ... it's all up to you, now! From now on! As of this moment! It's up to you ... to go ahead, and keep this job. I'm sure that you can! I'm sure that you will! Otherwise, I'd have kept my big mouth shut. Listen to me, Stephen! I felt that I owed you ... owed you some little bit of help. So, now I can consider myself to be ... well, to be ... to be, off the hook, so to speak."

"As well as I know you ... I know that you don't' live your life, to simply be 'off the hook'; Have never lived your life ... to be 'off the stupid damn hook'."

She shed her coat -- and walked over to the couch! Where I'd remained seated.! She raised her skirt -- to where it was (substantially) above her, to-die-for, bottom! Then, she lowered her pantyhose -- and underpants -- to mid-thigh! This esoteric routine having been completed -- she plopped herself down upon my clothed lap!

She placed her arms around my neck -- and whispered (huskily) in my ear!

"Take down your pants!" I was almost <u>shocked</u> -- at the undiluted command, in her, suddenly-authoritative, voice. "We <u>can't</u> say goodbye ... so <u>stiffly</u>!"

"Yeah?" I'd rasped (even <u>more</u> huskily). "You wanna talk <u>stiffly</u>? You're making something <u>else</u> stiff!"

"That's ... as it <u>should</u> be!" She raised her behind -- a mere six or seven inches -- to allow me some <u>maneuvering</u> room! "Take your <u>pants</u> down," she repeated.

What else could I <u>do</u>? I <u>complied</u>!

FIVE

A new start! At a new company! New location! And a new -- completely foreign -- career! New routines (although they'd be hard to define, here)! New people!

Listen -- going in, anyway -- it was great! I learned a whole lot! A multitude -- of new things! Let me tell you: The auto auctions, themselves, were a form of -- a study in -- "controlled chaos"! Frantic! Frenetic! But, at the end, everything usually comes together! And -- somehow -- it all works out fine! A goodly portion, of my job, was to see that it, actually, did! To see that it -- for real -- does!

My main purpose -- in this wondrous new career -- was, more or less, to perform a "summing up", at the end, of the two weekly auctions. But, that outcome usually took place -- on the three non-auction days!

It was my job, to compile -- and to maintain -- statistics. Never-ending statistics: Number of units in! Number of units sold! Number of units remaining, on our lots -- specifying whether in Bordentown or Manheim! Just units! Other people kept track of the money -- pertaining to the myriad of operations, transactions, "deals", etc. etc. etc. And there was plenty of that! All of the time! Mind-staggering amounts -- of units and dollars -- in every far-reaching, complicated, phase, of "The Game"!

Something else -- that I never would've guessed: Many times, there would not be the two bidders -- that the auctioneer would have you believe existed. With the ever-expanding, ever-changing, crowd of bidders -- in front of the block -- it's possible that, if there was an actual, serious, bidder, located on one side of the crowd, the auctioneer will invent a second, nonexistent, one, who is (supposedly) located, on the other side, of the "audience". And, in that way, he would pit one against the "other".

When that happens, the auctioneer will tap the seller -- who is standing beside him, behind the large "counter", on the elevated platform. Tap him or her -- on the knee -- with his standard rubber hose. That way, the seller knows not to "accept" the "bid" -- from the ersatz bidder. Saves a good deal of embarrassment, if the seller is aware, of the scenario. Just one of the many intrigues -- that existed in that particular auto auction world.

In Bordentown, there were five lines -- all operating, at the same time. In Manheim, there were four. Truly -- it was controlled chaos!

Something else I'd discovered -- on my first visit (on that first Thursday) to Manheim, Pennsylvania: The vast difference! The glaring difference -- in the same exact people.

When I'd started, at the auction, we'd (especially the men) started getting away from that early-seventies trend -- of looking as dorky as possible. Not quite so many paisley shirts -- coupled with those "unforgettable" plaid bell-bottom slacks -- and/or "mutton chops". But, still, we remained fairly dorky.

On Tuesdays -- in Bordentown -- the guys were still semi-dorky. And the women wore dresses (or skirts and blouses) -- that began-and-ended, awfully near the center. On Thursday, however -- in Manheim, at the center of Amish Country -- the guys all wore tasteful clothing. Including a goodly number of three-piece suits. The gals wore, also-tasteful, feminine outfits -- that began near the throat, and ended well below the knee! Same people! Different setting -- entirely!

It even affected the auctioneers. In New Jersey, they seldom strayed from a, mostly-G-Rated, patter. But, every now and then, they'd drop a PG- or PG13-rated, remark. I'd never heard one, out and out, obscenity. But, in Amish country, the guys would never come close -- to uttering anything you'd not hear Mary Poppins say. They were all "Prince Charming". All of the time.

There were other differences: The facility, at Bordentown, featured a restaurant-of-sorts. Basically, your commonplace hamburger joint. There'd also been a plethora of coin-operated vending machines. From them, you got soft drinks, coffee, hot chocolate, potato chips, beef jerkies, and an assortment of (rather-plastic) pastries.

In Manheim, on the other hand, they'd operated a real-life -- honest-to-God -- restaurant. Freshly-cooked -- delicious, full-bodied, genuine -- meals! Real ones! Roast Beef! Meatloaf! Pork Chops! God-knows-how-many veggies! Three or four varieties of potatoes! Home-made apple, and/or lemon, pies! All prepared -- by the dedicated, wonderfully-efficient, Amish women. All of them remarkable -- in their food-preparation talents!

If there were any vending machines -- on the entire grounds -- I don't remember seeing any! Ever! An entirely different culture -- and environment! Entirely different! The stark contrast had been unimaginable, to me -- till I'd actually beheld it! Beheld the wonder -- of the Amish culture!

Those remarkable women -- the ones who'd operated the restaurant, in Pennsylvania -- were, mostly, rather-heavyset, ladies. Probably in their late-forties, or early-fifties. All were strictly business. There were three or four younger waitresses. They'd seemed to be not-quite-so-serious. But, looks are deceiving.

After six or eight weeks -- of making that, fairly-long, schlep (my Comet was proving to be a champion) -- I'd gotten to know a few, of the women. Well, a little bit, anyway. They were all -- as friendly as they could be. Just serious, is all. There was a definite limit to their "outgoing" ways.

The lone exception seemed to be a young lady -- named Mary Beth. She was -- easily -- 20 years my junior. I could see -- after three or four visits, to that glorious eatery -- that, in another (less reserved) surrounding, she'd had the potential, to be a bit of a real hell-raiser!

She'd stopped -- in front of my place, at the counter -- a few times; and we'd exchanged pleasantries. Nothing out of the ordinary, you understand. Certainly nothing the least bit off-color. I could just -- for some reason, or another -- tell that, given other circumstances, she'd be capable of "unbuttoning" a bit. Maybe "unbuttoning" more than just "a bit".

Then, after I'd been making the "Grand Tour" -- Bordentown-to-Manheim-and-back -- the Pennsylvania facility decided to hold a late-afternoon "flea market". It was glorious! Made up of much older cars. That classic auction was held -- out in the back portion, of the massive property! (How I'd wished I'd have had the funds -- to have bought that, simply-beautiful, 1936 Dodge! Or -- even more so -- that 1947 Cadillac! Or that "cherry" 1955 Ford Fairlane!)

Since I'd have to remain -- till early-evening -- Brent Foley sanctioned my remaining overnight, in Manheim. I was advised -- that there were many small, privately-run, rooming houses, in central Manheim. All charged "very reasonable" rates. So, there was no sense "in staying ... in luxury ... at one of the big-chain hotels".

So, at about 5:30PM, I was heading the valiant Comet -- in toward the central part, of town. And, about a half-mile from the auction grounds, I noted Mary Beth -- hiking in the same direction. She was walking, on "the wrong side", of the, not-at-all-busy, highway -- as she should've been. I stopped, across the road from her -- and rolled down my driver's door window! (Remember <u>those</u>?)

"Want a ride?" I half-shouted.

"No ... thanks," she'd replied -- in a tone that was much softer, than my own. "It's only another three-quarters, of a mile."

"Still, they say that 'The <u>worst</u> kind of riding,,, beats the <u>best</u> kind of walking'." (I <u>think</u> that might've been a line from "Manhattan Tower".)

She seemed to shrug -- slightly/ Then, she made her way -- across the, still-unbusy, thoroughfare. The pretty young lady climbed into the front seat -- and plopped her good-looking (I could <u>tell</u>) bottom right <u>next</u> to me! <u>Right</u> next to me! <u>Closer</u> -- on the old "bench seat" (remember <u>them</u>?) -- to me, than I'd have expected. <u>That</u> was nice.

"Look," she said -- before I was even able to get my little Mercury up to 30mph, "I assume that you're going to spend the night ... here, in town."

"Yeah. Can you recommend a good rooming house, or something?"

"Well, most of them ... and there are a lot of good ones ... will charge fifteen dollars. Maybe seventeen-fifty. You could stay at *our* place ... for ten."

"*Your* place?"

"Yes. I still live with my parents ... and an older sister. Oh, don't *worry*. We're Amish ... but, not orthodox. We've got that, new-fangled, electricity. Even a television set. Daddy even drives a car. It's an old Pontiac Bonneville ... but, it *is* a car. We don't ... any of us ... travel in horse-drawn carriages. Not any*more*, anyway. The thing is ... Daddy can always *use* an extra ten dollars, don't you see. *Always* use ... one of those."

"That'd be *great*! Uh ... I wouldn't be ... ah ... putting anybody out, would I?"

"No," she answered -- with one of the warmest smiles I'd ever seen. "We live, in a big, old, house ... on the other side of town. We have five bedrooms. And ... like I said ... we *do* have indecent electricity."

"Sounds like a deal."

On our way to her parents' home, Mary Beth filled me in -- on her life. Well, on her *professional* life, anyway. She was working -- full time -- at a drugstore, in the center of town. Worked the dayshift -- five days, a week. Fridays-through-Tuesdays. She had Wednesdays "off". And, of course, toiled -- on Thursdays -- at the auction. She'd, apparently, worked that schedule -- for three, or four, years. I was imagining this to be the effects -- of a typical, Spartan-Amish, upbringing.

On my journey -- from the auction to the home, of my passenger -- I'd passed three or four of the black, horse-drawn, carriages, all of which sported those *Department of Transportation*, florescent, triangles-for-safety, gismos, affixed to the back.

My knowledge of the Amish culture had been limited to, occasionally, seeing those vehicles -- with a quick glance at the occupants -- and, from interacting with those women, at the auction's restaurant. (I'd, long since decided that <u>this</u> was -- far and away -- the finest eatery I'd ever had the good fortune of attending. It was <u>that</u> good!)

Making the small-talk, with the lovely (and charming) Mary Beth, I was becoming, more and more, <u>impressed</u> -- with the philosophy (and dedication) of these basic, down-to-earth, remarkable, people.

My passenger was <u>far</u> from possessing the overwhelming -- almost <u>stupefying</u> -- beauty, of Janice. Well, maybe not <u>that</u> far. There seemed to be an, almost-indefinable, inner-beauty, to her. I know! That sounds as corny as hell! Well, it <u>is</u> corny as hell. But, it's <u>also</u> an accurate assessment. <u>Entirely</u> accurate.

And she possessed a <u>definite</u> charm. Also indefinable! And -- without doing, or saying, anything that would bedazzle me (or anyone else) -- she was "filling up" every corner, of my hokey little Comet. Amazing!

By the time we'd reached her parents' two-story, black-shingled, house, I'd become totally charmed -- by this amazing young woman.

Her parents were equally as authentic -- equally as genuine -- as their daughter. I gave her father a ten-spot -- plus two singles -- and he, immediately, invited me to "break bread" with them.

He was a rather tall -- really spindly -- man, in his mid-fifties. He worked -- six days a week -- at a local stables. His handshake -- while he'd not intended for it to be overwhelming -- was overwhelming. A man of great strength. Immense strength, physically -- and, I was sure, morally, ethically (and every other way).

Mary Beth's mother was a really heavyset woman, with a sincere, always-ready, smile. She was, at least, six or seven inches shorter than her husband. She seemed to embody the word "jolly'. (Santa Claus does not have a patent, on that designation.)

The couple's son -- Eric -- was still at work. He worked at a "mom-and-pop" grocery store -- a block-and-a-half, from the drugstore, that employed his sister.

What an incredible family. And -- I was convinced -- they were not the only such family, in the area. As you can, no doubt, ascertain -- I was completely taken, with these people. With this culture -- what I was able to discern, about it.

The dinner was overwhelming! (Have you noticed how much/how often I'm using that word?) It described -- to a tee -- how taken I'd become, with these people. And -- as the sumptuous meal was progressing -- I found my eyes positively riveted, on the daughter. Just watching her simply eat -- was the, heart-warming, embodiment, of all that had been happening around me, over the past few hours. It's the embodiment, of the old saw -- about, "if you were to look up the word 'charming', in the dictionary, you'd find a picture of Mary Beth".

She would look up at me -- every now and then -- while we were dining, and "catching" me gazing at her, she'd smile. That warm -- that, genuine-to-her-toenails, smile!

You may have discerned -- that I was, most definitely, bewitched, by this woman. On the other hand, any term -- that contained the word "witch" seemed, in that household, to be quite sinful! Still, it was the best I could come up with.

We'd watched a little bit of television, after dinner. Well, us three men did -- until Mary Beth, and her mother, finished cleaning up the "wreckage" we'd left behind, in the dining room -- and had done the, seemed-like-thousands, of dishes,

At about ten o'clock, the father -- Mr. Herald -- decreed that it was bedtime. The daughter showed me my room -- upstairs. I would nestle in (upon a real, bona fide, feather mattress) -- located at the far end, of what seemed like an, impossibly-long, hallway.

I did! Did nestle in -- on that unbelievable mattress. It must've taken -- all of ten minutes, for me to have fallen, into a deep sleep. I'd imagined myself lying there -- eyes wide open -- simply trying to deal with my, almost-out-of-this-world, surroundings! Wrong! Right off -- to La-La Land!

At about three o'clock, in the morning, nature called. I guess that I'd been so wrapped up in "My Amish Experience" -- that I'd forgotten to "go", before I'd turned in. So, I'd awakened -- with a definite need.

I'd been clad in my undershorts (boxers) and white tee shirt. (The top -- that Michael Jordan would become so enamored with -- years later.) I slipped into my trousers -- and headed down that, to-the-end-of-the-earth, hallway, to the john. The "necessary room" -- was located, at the far end.

I'd had no idea -- as to which, of the many rooms on the second floor, might have been Mary Beth's bedroom. Not until I was passing the second door, on my left. There, behind the opened door -- for whatever reason -- stood the daughter! She'd been standing in front of a sizeable chest-of-drawers. Looking into a large, oval-shaped, mirror, hanging on the wall -- above the chest.

She was wearing a Spartan, cotton, nightgown -- which covered her, from neck to toe. She looked at me -- as I'd stopped, in my tracks. Then, she smiled at me. It was a warm smile! But, also a seemingly-dismissive smile. (What else?) I continued my quest -- for the restroom.

Once I'd "taken care of business", I'd headed back -- to my quarters. Mary Beth's door was still open. Only, this time, she was naked! And she beckoned me!

I took two or three steps forward! Then, I stopped! There was something about this culture! About being in this house! Being among these people!

But then, she took two or three steps -- toward me! I would've thought -- that she'd have been a virgin! How, then, could she offer herself up? To me? There had never been one incident -- in all of my life -- where some woman would ever have made a motion, to invite me (lure me?) to their bed! Most especially -- a woman I scarcely knew! And how could she risk -- being discovered? In this house? With these people? How could any of this be taking place?

I can't do this!

But, there she was! Maybe three or four feet away! Her arms outstretched!

Something made me turn! And run! Well, I didn't actually run! But, I walked! Rather briskly! Fortunately -- really fortunately -- she did not follow me!

I got back to my room! (Also fortunately!) There was no way, however, to lock the door! I -- literally -- staggered to my bed!

I don't care how comfy the mattress was -- I could not get back to sleep! Nothing even close! I couldn't remember -- ever -- being so completely undone! So utterly rattled!

I was -- almost literally -- doing my best, to hide (to cower) beneath the stupid, home-made, blankets! My mind -- what was left of it -- was asunder, with an avalanche of disjointed thoughts, images, and God-knew-what-else!

Then, after ten or fifteen minutes of frantic -- of absolutely frenzied, mental, and emotional -- anguish, this image (this, imagination-generate, vision) came storming in! Adding, obviously, to all the other frenetic mish-mosh! The, wholly-unraveling, imagery was a, clear-cut, high-definition, picture -- of Janice! She looked -- in this vision -- to be about fourteen-and-a-half months pregnant!

I was sure that the woman was, actually, "with child". Mainly, because she was so absolutely positive, of that fact -- although we'd not "discussed" it, in such a long time.

It was -- in all probability -- my baby! Surely, I would have a goodly amount of responsibility, in the matter -- although Janice had never demanded anything, of me! Not emotionally! Not financially!

Not in any way! Ever! Still, the fact was -- that it was my baby! It had to be!

Well -- probably! But then, it could be -- could possibly be -- that black guy's kid! That was yet another image -- that I really didn't need, at that point! I suppose I shouldn't be admitting this -- even to myself -- but, the potential racial situation was rearing its ugly head! Something else I didn't need! What was I going to do -- what should I do -- if the baby comes out black?

Actually, I was trying to console myself! She could have "gotten rid" of it! That would -- most assuredly -- have left me, off the hook! Would it not? Well, that would've, undoubtedly, presented a "solution" -- where Janice's feelings were of no consideration! The whole "concept" (poor choice of words) was mind-broiling!

Janice was -- when all was said and done -- carrying the baby! And she'd gone through every conceivable aspect of pure -- unadulterated -- hell! She had been the subject -- the merciless target -- of a merciless, God-awful, degradation! Of incredible -- physical and emotional -- agony! Her pain and suffering -- would seem to be the basis, for the situation's final outcome!

Where was all this "mind-bending" leading me? Taking me? I'd been -- literally -- swept up, in a toxic whirlwind of, beyond-my-control, withering, emotion! And now -- was Mary Beth, on her way?

Or maybe -- lurking, outside my door? My unlocked door? Naked as could be? Naked as hell? It, all of a sudden, loomed -- that it was probably outrageous, to even think of the word "hell"! In that house! The one that was closing in on me!

The only logical answer was obvious: I'd had to get the hell out of there! True, it was the middle -- of the damn night! But, chances -- of my falling asleep, behind the wheel, between Manheim and Bordentown -- were, most positively, nil!

I got dressed, gathered up my stuff, "snuck up" to my bedroom door -- and peered out! No evidence of my personal *Circe*! So, bravely, I made my way down that, obscenely-long, hallway! Her door, by then, was closed! Thank God!

I successfully (so far, anyway) extricated myself from the house, skulked my way to my blessed Mercury Comet! It had never looked so "inviting"!

Climbing inside, I cursed the noise -- that the starter motor emitted! But, I was thrilled -- when the engine cranked to life! Leaving the headlights off -- till I was substantially down the, lightly-traveled, road! I'm sure that I set all manner -- of speed records -- for the first 12 or 15 miles, eastward, from that house!

But, as heavy as my proverbial foot, might have been -- I was unable (spectacularly, unable) to outrun the emotional tsunami that was filling up every square inch, of my glorious compact car!

I'd gotten back to my home base -- at about seven-thirty that morning! I stopped, at *Denny's* -- and (in addition, to a couple sweet-rolls) consumed a "barrel" of coffee. No help! My hands would simply not stop trembling!

And they were in far better shape -- than what is laughingly referred to, as my mental processes! (Far better!)

SIX

I'd gotten back, to Bordentown -- early enough, to get to work on time; which pleased Brent Foley. I was still -- far from being pleased! Hours would pass -- and my emotional freighter remained in a, most-precarious, taking-on-water, situation!

At about ten-thirty, I'd tried to get in touch, with Janice. Possibly have lunch with her. Since my little (or not so little) encounter, with Mary Beth, I'd had this gnawing, highly-troubled, need -- to see my fellow New Jersey resident. But, I was advised, by her secretary, that she was out of town. She'd been, in Houston -- all week! She was not scheduled to return -- till sometime, over the weekend.

I called the hotel, down there -- and learned that she'd checked out "a couple of hours ago". It was, after all, Friday. There would be no way to get in touch with her -- till "sometime over the weekend" -- in those pre-cell phone days. (Remember them?)

So, I was pretty well left to "stew in m own juice". And the flame was not lessening! Not in the least!

I was able to phone Janice -- on Saturday afternoon (after getting no-answers, twice, during the morning. She did agree to have late lunch/early dinner with me -- at a small cafe, just outside Trenton.

I picked her up, at three-thirty. It was her first expedition -- in my Comet. She approved, which -- after our, tragically-rather-stilted, greeting -- was a welcomed reaction. I couldn't understand why she'd want to go up to Trenton. It's a really beautiful town -- and not really that far away. But, really? Trenton? When there was a perfectly good *Denny's* available? As well as numerous other eateries -- in Bordentown?

When we got to the place she'd had in mind, though, I understood. It was a charming little restaurant -- that was a beef buffet. The roast beef and mashed potatoes -- flooded with brown gravy -- was out of this world. The place was well off the beaten path. Not all that many people knew of its existence. Including me. This exclusivity -- along with the attendant intimacy -- was quite expensive. But, well worth the few extra bucks.

We parked ourselves, in a rather large booth -- way in the far corner, of the cafe. It turned out to be the perfect venue. On the way up, neither of us had had much to say, to one another. Except for her exuberant approval of my little car. But, the environment -- in this charming little restaurant -- seemed meant to cause us to talk, to each other. Talk seriously! Talk frankly! I began:

"You're looking just as beautiful, as ever."

"That's nice of you to say. But, I've ... obviously ... put on a few pounds."

"Not so's you'd notice."

"Then, you're not noticing ... close enough."

"That's not true! It's never been true! I've always looked ... looked closely ... at you. Listen, you're as beautiful ... as you ever were."

"Again, that's nice of you to say. What's going on, Stephen? What's happening ... in your life? Why do you ... all of a sudden ... seem so hell-bent on seeing me? I popped back in ... yesterday afternoon ... at the hotel, in Houston. Vera told me that you'd called ... looking for me. She recognized your voice."

Vera was the main room clerk, at the hotel. The one where I used to work.

"Russ ... at the office." she continued, "told me, that you were trying to get hold of me, yesterday. He's the one who would've told you ... that I was in Texas. What was the emergency? The calamity? Am I getting the bum's rush ... or what?"

"With that bum of yours ... who wouldn't want to rush you?"

"Is that it? You've remarked, about my 'beauty' ... so called. Now, about how desirable my bum might possibly be. Is that ... what this is all about? You're horny? Simply looking for a roll, in the hay?"

"*No*! No. I was just ... I guess ... just groping for a line. Came up with one, just now ... that was in awfully poor taste. What I've *really* been meaning to say ... for some time now ... is that I've been a real horse's *ass*! Speaking of bums."

"A *horse's* ass? How so?"

"The way I *acted*. When we'd had that ... ah ... that *discussion*. About you being *pregnant*, and all. I just kind of ..."

"You just *kind* of ... kind of *acted* ... the way most guys *would've* reacted. I really had no *right*, to expect you to handle it ... handle it ... in any other manner, than the way you *did*. No right ... *whatsoever*!"

"No, it was ..."

"Look, Stephen. I laid a *lot* on you ... that morning! The reaction I got from you was ... was *exactly* ... exactly what I'd have *expected*! From *any* man! You ... or anybody *else*! Listen! I'd *really* had my mind made *up*! Already made *up*! I didn't cut you *any* slack! It was ... flat out ... a take-it-or-*leave*-it situation! Just as it still *is*! As it is ... right *now*! Even as we speak! You chose to *leave* it! *Perfectly* understandable! *Not* a problem! No problem at *all*!"

"Well, it *is* ... for *me*!"

"Then, that's *just* what it is! *Your* problem! But, it *shouldn't* be!"

"Look, Janice. Explain to me ... once again ... your reason, to carry the baby. Carry the baby ... to term. Even though he might be black! Be the product ... of someone who'd done you unspeakable harm! Unimaginable harm! If the baby's black ... then he's the result of the most God-awful experience, that a woman could ever endure! Ever possibly endure!"

"But, it's still a life! A person! A strong person! Let me tell you! Strong! Started ... not that long ago ... kicking! Kicking the hell out of me. Probably gonna wind up, as the place-kicker ... or maybe the punter ... for the Oakland Raiders! I can't just go ahead ... go ahead and ... and, you know, kill that little person! He ... or she ... deserves to live! I realize ... that practically no one, these days, agrees with me! Fine! I understand that! I just don't agree with it! I ... strongly ... disagree with it! Period! Paragraph! My argument isn't any stronger ... or any more complicated ... than that!"

"Janice? Janice, I think that ... if you'll allow me ... I'd like to get back, with you. Would like to renew our ... you know, our ... our relationship.

She responded -- with a soft laugh! Soft -- but, one that could be heard, it seemed, throughout the entire universe! One dripping -- with irony!

"You're just horny," she expanded. "You're just looking ... to take me to bed. Which ain't gonna happen, by the way. I'm not going to let you ... or anybody else ... see me with no clothes on. Not these days. I've put on too many pounds."

"I doubt that! You're just as beautiful ... as you ever were! But, I don't want to get back ... just to wind up, in the sack with you. Although, the *thought* of it is kinda ..."

"The *thought* of it is ... first and foremost ... in your oversexed little mind!"

"No ... it's *not*! I *promise*!"

"I don't *believe* you! Look, Stephen. Let's just stay as we *are*. *Friends*! But, not especially *close* friends! I'll break bread with you ... from time to time. But, I *ain't* gonna break out my, getting-pudgier-by-the-second *body*, with you. Or *for* you."

That was where she'd left it! Plainly, the subject was *over*! The result left me -- out in the *cold*!

I was almost afraid to journey to Manheim, the following Thursday. (Almost?) I'd spent all Wednesday night (all *sleepless* Wednesday night) trying to come up with some non-cockamamie excuse -- to get out of the trip. But, the results -- were all too cockamamie! So, I wound up going!

I'd packed down an extra round of toast and pork sausage -- at *Denny's* -- that morning; hoping to stay away from that remarkable restaurant, out in Amish Country. I was absolutely *petrified* -- at the thought of crossing paths, once again, with Mary Beth. (My old back problem! This yellow streak!)

The heavy breakfast was no help! At about one-thirty, after having fought my way through all those delicious odors -- wafting out of that stellar dining room -- I could, no longer, resist! *Matters Even Worse Department*: Going in so late, I found that the place -- had pretty well emptied out.

I seated myself at the far end of the counter -- contriving to locate myself as far from the kitchen (the nerve center, of the place) as possible. That proved to be counterproductive, as well. Mary Beth spotted me -- and, forthwith, descended upon me. And there'd be no one, at the counter, to interrupt us! (Wonderful!)

"Stephen," she approached me. The tone was far too loud! For my liking, anyway! "Stephen!" This second time, her voice was pitched much lower. (Denks God!)

"Look, Mary Beth. I just ..."

"You just have to listen! Listen ... while I apologize! Listen! I don't know what possessed me, last week! I really don't! I doubt that you'll ever believe me ... after what happened, last week ... but, I've never been, with a man! Never! Not before! Not after! Certainly not during! I don't even know why I was up ... at that hour. I'd slept well, till then! I'll go to my grave ... believing that something told me, that you'd be passing by. Be coming down the hall ... at that particular moment! And that was why ... or I think it was why ... I'd gone ahead, and opened my door! Opened it ... probably two or three minutes, before you actually came by."

"Look, Mary Beth."

"Please! Let me finish! Please!"

I sighed -- deeply -- and nodded, my assent.

"Listen, Stephen. I love you! I think I've loved you ... ever since you set foot, in this place! That was the dumbest ... the absolute stupidest ... way, of trying to ... well, trying to snare you! Trying to trap you? Well, to try and get you to ... to come my way! If I didn't love you ... I never would've accepted the ride, from you. I'd dreamed of such a scenario. Just such a happening. For a long time. Thought it was ... well, that it was ... was fate! And ... when I woke up, in the middle of the night, and there you were ... I was simply lead-pipe certain that it was Kismet!"

"Oh, Mary Beth. You can't ..."

"When you'd continued ... had gone on by ... I went ahead, and resorted to that disgusting ..."

"It wasn't disgusting! I just wasn't prepared for ..."

"Stephen! Stephen, listen! Listen to me! Oh, Stephen ... I'd make you such a good wife! I'd devote my life to you! My entire life! To nothing ... but, making you happy! Don't you see?"

"Mary Beth? Look! This isn't getting us anywhere! I couldn't ... ! I mean, I'm honored! But, I simply can't ..."

"Yes you can! Or, at least, you could! If you really wanted to! Stephen? Stephen ... I'd be such a blessing to you! Every day! Day in ... and day out! I'd be such a ... :

"Mary Beth ... you can't! I mean, I can't! I mean ..."

"All right," she half-sobbed.

All of the "fight" -- all of the life -- went out of her! Poof! The pent-up energy didn't merely drain! It was gone! One moment -- it was there! Next moment -- it was gone! Just like that!

And -- just like that -- she slunk back to the kitchen!

Wonderful! Now you've broken someone *else's* heart!

I, obviously, had been completely devastated -- by the, emotion-wrought, episode, with Mary Beth. To the point -- that I didn't go to work, on Friday. There wasn't, usually, all that much to do, on Friday. I don't know if that would've been any sort of difference-maker. As you will have surmised, I was, flat-out, "hiding out" -- under my "security blanket" -- until sometime, in mid-afternoon.

What was I going to do? I'd felt as though I'd reached the end, of my rope! Looking back, I realize that I wound up being -- far too emotional! But, there were thoughts -- of suicide! Visions of "ending it all" -- dancing through my little head!

I suppose that -- in the present day's climate -- one could go looking, on the internet for some kind of "psychological emergency medical practice" (or something), on the internet. But, Al Gore had not invented it, as yet!

I, *frankly*, didn't know *what* I was going to do! I was having a bad *problem*! Just trying to face up to -- to *deal* with -- the next *hour*! Hell, the next *minute*!

I was becoming more and more certain -- that I was badly in need of a real-life psychiatrist! But, where do you find one? Well, I was *convinced* -- that you *don't*! Not with the weekend -- merely hours away!

But -- even during the week -- how do you go about trying to find a *shrink*? Do you *dare* ask your boss -- for instance -- about locating one? What would -- what *could* -- he or she think? "I've got some kind of basket case ... working for me"?

Finally -- sometime during Saturday afternoon -- I *found* a Yellow Pages, from the phone company. (Remember them?) *They* had a listing of, at least, a *few* shrinks! (*Thank* you, Ma Bell.)

On Monday, I closed the door, to my office -- and began dialing for head doctors! The first five or six advised me -- well, their *staffs* did -- that I'd need to be *referred*! By a *medical* doctor! That was the only way that they did business!

I got a, not-all-that-prevalent-for-the-times, answering-machine reply -- asking me to leave my number, and "a brief message" -- from a female doctor's office. This came after that initial plethora of discouraging inquiries. I, of course, left a, possibly-longer-than-brief, message.

I dialed through three or four additional, highly-frustrating, numbers -- then, gave the hell up! Gotta know when you're licked -- and all that.

Late that afternoon -- just as I was fixing to leave the office ("girding my loins" -- for Tuesday's auction) -- Dr. Brenda Braniff returned my call. She didn't seem all that interested -- in my going in, to all of my problems. Not on the phone, anyway But, she would see me -- after hours. The flood, of business -- vis-a-vis the following day's auction -- ruled out Tuesday. So, I made an appointment -- for Wednesday evening, at seven-thirty. (The "eve" -- of another, projected, trip to Manheim.)

I was glad to get the chance to, at least, discuss my travail -- with someone! (With anyone!)

Her office was set, in the front part of her, rather-opulent, home -- just east, of Trenton. The, moderate-sized, room was, most probably, originally "scheduled" as a den. Dr. Braniff answered the door -- after the loud, "articulate" Westminster Chimes doorbell had rung once, Answered it -- in person. She was wearing a, rather-loose-fitting, black sweater -- and a Kelly-green mini-skirt. Actually, the skirt was a micro-mini! And that was giving the frock, all-the-best, of it -- modesty-wise!

She even had a couch -- which, I guess, is now considered gauche. A throw-back to a bygone day. She bade me lie down -- on said icon -- while she pulled up a, plain-Jane, chair, right next to the couch. The latter looked like a fugitive -- from someone's dining room. The purpose of all this -- I became convinced (shortly, after the session had begun) -- was to assess the amount of energy I'd expend, in an effort to look up her skit! The green item of clothing was located far up the, ever-so-generous, expanse -- that her cross-legged position was, flagrantly, exposing!

She took no notes -- but crossed (and re-crossed) her legs, countless times! (Yes -- she was wearing underpants!) Still, it was therapeutic -- to "unload", all of my troubling concerns on her! But, that would've held true -- relief-wise -- had I been able to "dump" the whole, mind-numbing, diatribe, on anyone! Or anything!

This whole, sad-story, encounter -- took, probably, 20 minutes. The good doctor had a few questions, during my lengthy discourse. Mostly, though, they pertained to specific clarification of such things -- as time references and precise locations.

At the end, of my having poured out my heart -- and soul (what was left of it) -- she made a, one-size-fits-all, recommendation: I don't remember her exact wording -- but, it was the equivalent of, "I think we all should do the best we can",

Then, she wrote me a prescription! She said, as she'd handed it to me, "Here! Get this filled, at the drugstore. This'll calm you down."

I was quite upset! For one thing, I believed that I was going to be charged eighty -- or ninety -- dollars! And -- for what? A generous look, at admittedly, good-looking legs -- and a prescription for goofballs?

By the time that she was handing me the piece of drugstore paper, I'd assumed a sitting position -- at the center of the couch.

"And," I pressed, "what about tomorrow? I gotta go ... to Manheim, y'know. How'm I gonna deal ... with that? With her? With Mary Beth?"

"Well, you're just going to have to deal with it ... as best you can! She's had a week ... to cool down. Or recover ... or whatever. There might be no problem, at all! We'll just have to wait and see ... won't we."

"Oh ... you've been a big help!"

I thought that she'd be -- at least -- somewhat upset! But, she was not. I guess I was upset enough -- for the both of us!

"Get up!" She may not have been upset -- but, she'd barked out the command! Full bore! "Get up," she repeated. "And bend over the desk!"

I complied! Much more quickly -- than I'd have supposed. For some reason -- that was beyond me.

"Now," she announced, "I'm going to give you another prescription. This one's a little stronger ... than the other one. Don't ... for heaven's sake ... take one of these, before you drive to Manheim! Or just before you start back! But, once you're there, you might want to take one ... or two! Depending on what you find! Depending ... on what may be awaiting you."

Having said that, she grabbed hold of my right buttock -- and squeeze! Hard! I didn't, of course, know how to react! She kept hold, back there! I tried to remain as stoic -- as "unconcerned" -- as I could! After one or two, anguish-producing, minutes, she switched her, surprisingly-vise-grip, clutch -- to my other cheek! I think I gasped -- slightly -- but, renewed my effort to "retain my dignity".

Then, she began to slap me, back there! This was becoming very troubling, for me! Extremely troubling!

After about 10 or 12 smacks, she stopped! Finally!

"How'd that feel?" she asked.

"It hurt! And it was stupid! What was that all about?"

"Just testing."

"Testing? For what?"

"Never mind. You wouldn't understand."

She allowed me to straighten up! And handed me her bill! It was for only $25.00! I didn't understand it! Any of it! All of it! But, I did have my prescription!

Two of them, actually! I "dog-earred" the one that was -- presumably -- the stronger of the pair.

I'd had my prescription! But, could find no place -- to get it filled! Any drugstore -- that was open, at that hour -- was no help! Their pharmacy had -- in most cases -- closed at six o'clock! A couple had remained open till nine. But, I was still too late!

I finally made my way to my room. But, I could not sleep! Spectacularly, I could not sleep! Not only was I highly-troubled -- by what might await me, on Thursday, in Manheim -- but, I was having a problem coming to grips with the conduct, of Dr. Braniff! An exceptionally difficult time -- trying to figure that out!

Things couldn't have been more confusing! Nor weighed more heavily, on me! All of these things were totally foreign -- virtually unheard of -- for me!

- I'd not seen my kids -- in such a tragically long time.
- I'd never thought that I'd -- ever -- "get to first base, with a woman anywhere nearly as beautiful, as Janice.
- And now, she was pregnant! With what might be my baby. Or, what also might be the child, of a black man. A subhuman -- who'd actually raped her! Merely the racial portion -- involved

in that situation -- <u>bothered</u> me. More than I'd wanted to <u>admit</u>! Even to <u>myself</u>!

- Obviously, the fact that the possible father (the <u>late</u> possible father) had assaulted Janice -- in the <u>worst</u>, most <u>humiliating</u>, most <u>degrading</u> way -- <u>should</u> have been the <u>one</u> disconcerting factor! But, there <u>was</u> the racial element! The old "600-pound gorilla, in the room".
- An Amish woman (of all people) had -- literally -- thrown herself at me!
- That same Amish woman <u>wants</u> me to marry her! In the worst <u>way</u>!
- And I'd just been "turned loose" from the strangest <u>session</u> -- with the absolutely-strangest psychiatrist -- that <u>anyone</u> could've imagined!

So, there were <u>more</u> than a few items, on my, wish-it-was-numbed, mind! A <u>multitude</u> of highly-troubling things, on which to ponder! Which to try and <u>avoid</u> -- at all costs!

The next day -- in Manheim -- presented a <u>new</u> problem. One on which I'd not counted. (Well, I <u>really</u> hadn't foreseen -- <u>any</u> of these "quirks of life".)

I'd run through a whole <u>list</u> of mental, to-myself, arguments -- as to whether I should go into the restaurant, or not! Finally, the spellbinding aroma took over -- as you probably knew it would. Well, that -- and a hunger pang or six. But, this time I was going to be "smarter". I'd not wait -- till the joint would've cleared out. Less chance of a one-on-one -- with Mary Beth -- don't you see.

As it turned out, there was no "confrontation" -- of any sort. After about ten minutes -- when I'd not spied the woman, at all -- one of the older women approached me. She took my order -- then, went on to explain that Mary Beth had called in sick, that morning.

"First time I remember her doing that ... ever," remarked the lady, sighing deeply -- as she'd walked away.

Hmmmm!

Then, exactly one week later -- in the same venue -- I'd had the same woman advise me, that she'd not seen Mary Beth "in a week". "No one has," she'd added. Then -- when my response must have been a shocked expression -- she shrugged (which didn't help) then said, "No one knows! Nobody!"

That gave me a good deal more to "chew on". I'd gotten my prescription filled -- but, hadn't taken one of those "horse pills", until the previous night. (It hadn't helped -- at least, as near as I could tell.)

After things had quieted down, at the auction, I drove to Mary Beth's house -- hoping to find her there (but not having the faintest idea -- as to what I was going to actually say to her)!

Her father answered the door! Strange, I thought. I'd believed that it was far too early -- in the afternoon/evening -- for him to have been home.

Before I could get a word out of my mouth, he proclaimed -- in a low-pitched (but, filled with cement) voice -- "I have nothing to say to you, Sir! Please leave! And do not come back! Ever!"

DOUBLE hmmmm!

On the drive back to Bordentown, I had a whole lot of time! Too much time! To do a whole lot of thinking! Never a good prospect!

- They'd not seen Mary Beth, at the restaurant, in eight days!
- Her father was -- obviously -- grossly upset! Obviously! Presumably, that would've gone for the rest of the family.
- Mary Beth, herself, had been nowhere to be seen. But, that was not to say -- that she wasn't somewhere, in the background.
- Still, why would the woman, at the restaurant, not know anything -- about her whereabouts? And appeared so -- well, so concerned? One would think that -- as close-knit as that community is reputed to be -- that someone

> would've had some sort of glimmering, as to her location. And/or her well-being. (Would they not?)

❖

The following day, I asked Brent, my boss -- if there'd be any way that he could find out what happened to Mary Beth. He was very dismissive! Literally waved it off!

"Waitresses come and go," he philosophized. "Even out there."

I was really afraid to pursue it any further. I didn't need to begin having to answer a whole bunch of troubling questions -- about a possible "romantic alliance" with (somewhat of) a "business associate".

I even made an appointment to see Dr. Brenda Braniff, once again. On Saturday afternoon! It was a yet another "do the best we can" session -- sans all the fanny-grabbing. She offered absolutely no help! But, I came away -- with another prescription! (It proved to be of no more help -- than the previous ones.)

Finally, I called Janice! We journeyed -- on Sunday afternoon -- to that cozy little roast beef joint, outside of Trenton.

Against my better judgment, I explained (confessed?) the whole, entire, situation -- vis-a-vis Mary Beth. Throughout my, extremely-labored, diatribe, Janice continued to lay the warmest, most-understanding, of smiles upon me. Far and *away* -- the most comfortable I'd felt, in *weeks*! (Which, I guess, isn't saying *all* that much. Since that one night -- in that Amish home -- there hadn't been all that much peace and contentment, for "The *Kid*", here!)

"Listen," she finally said -- once I'd run (completely) down. "I can *certainly* understand your feeling ... for this woman. Understand it *completely*! But, Stephen, you *have* to realize, that you accepted her *hospitality*! That ... of her entire *family*! Maybe you should take better care ... in those situations ... to see to it, that you relieve yourself, before turning in. But, all that night *involved* ... was your getting up, to *pee*. *She* was the one ... who'd opened her door! *She* was the one ... who'd removed her *clothing*! *She* was the one ... who'd extended her *arms*! Who'd invited you *in* ... so to speak!"

"Yes. But, if you could've *seen* her father! Her *father*, for heaven's sake! That poor *man*! I know, damn well, that ... if it were *my* daughter ..."

"Well, I can *understand* that! But, it *isn't* your daughter. I've always *believed* that there's something special ... something very *special* ... between daddies and daughters. And, if something has happened to this girl ... to this woman ... it's *sad*! *Horribly* sad! *Extremely* sad! But, it's *not* anything ... over which you could *possibly* have had any *control*! What this girl ... this woman ... may have decided to *do*, is beyond your *control*! Or what she may have decided *not* to do. All out of your *reach*! So ... unless you're madly in *love* with her ... you've *got* to do your best to turn *loose* of it! Let it *go*! Easier *said* ... than *done*! I *realize* that!" She paused -- for what was no longer than four or five eternities -- then, fixed her eyes on me, and asked, "*Are* you in love with her? *Madly* ... or otherwise?"

"*NO*! Of *course* not!"

"Well, for being so ... so *definitely* ... *not* in love, with her," you're sure *unraveling* more than I would've expected."

"No." My outrage had flown -- quickly. "It's just that ..."

"Look, Stephen. It's only *natural* that, if you've become *close* to someone ... man *or* woman ... that you'd be *concerned*, about that person! But, you've *got* to determine ... got to *realize* ... where your responsibility begins. And where it *ends*! Now, if you're in *love* ... with Mary Beth ... that's *one* thing! If you're *not* ... then, we're talking something *else*!"

"Yeah," I responded -- exhaling a sigh, that should've blown out every window, in the joint. "It's just that ... ! Listen, Janice. I can't *tell* you what a *comfort* you are to me. What a comfort you've always *been* to me! We're back, now, to where I'm proclaiming what a *horse's* ass I've been. What a horse's ass ... I've *always* been."

She laughed. "Are we also back ... to someone I know being *horny*?"

❖

Dr. Braniff should have been present. Taking notes. Lying in bed, that night, I found myself wondering -- actually pondering -- whether the "Good Doctor" had an actual license, to (legally) practice the stuff she was pedaling. Well, she was pedaling prescription drugs. Legal prescription drugs! So, she must have had a license! On the other hand, given the well-known (and well-documented) corruption, in The Garden State's political situation -- both inside, and outside, of government, "One never knows ... do one?"

On the other hand, I did realize -- anew -- how Janice had been (seemed like forever) the most calming influence, in my life! On my life!

The point had been driven home (once again -- and even more definitively) on that Sunday afternoon! In that roast beef joint! Outside of Trenton!

SEVEN

It was August 17, 1977 -- and a phone was ringing! Somewhere! It was the middle of the night! Who makes phone calls -- at that ungodly hour? Oh! It's my phone! Right!

I managed to clamor my way out of my, never-as-comfortable-as-now, bed -- and staggered to the dresser -- which is where the phone had been implanted.

"H'lo?"

«Are you interested ... in taking me to the hospital?» It was Janice. «My water just broke!»

"Of course! Now?"

"Right now! My water's done broke!"

"I'll be right there!"

"I don't want to offend you ... but, let's take my car. I love your little Mercury ... but, getting in and out of it, would be a bear! Especially in my condition!"

I was ready to leave -- right then! That's how excited I was! But, reason caught up with me -- just as I was headed toward the door! It wouldn't be "politically correct" -- to go flitting about the outside world -- stark naked!

❖

On our way to the hospital, you'd have thought that Janice and I would've been wrapped up -- conversation-wise -- in the imminent arrival, of the upcoming "bundle of joy". And that was what I was intending -- with my first remark, after the mother-to-be and I had settled into her Mercedes.

"Janice," I'd begun (hoarsely), "I've been doing a lot of thinking. A helluva lot of thinking. I want to be married to you! To have this baby ... be our baby! To be our child!"

"It's kind of our child ... anyway. Why all this talk ... about being married?"

"Well ... for one thing ... it's not brand new. I have brought it up before. You didn't want to know ... from such things."

It was true! A couple months previously, we'd journeyed to San Antonio. Had flown down there. And the trip seemed to have taken too much of a toll, on her. It would be the last excursion -- of any significant distance -- she'd make, pre-maternity.

There had been a few lesser drives. Like those -- to that charming little roast beef joint, near Trenton. Each time, I'd -- more or less -- proposed marriage (in varying degrees, of poetic, romantic, language) to her. Each time, she'd refused to let me really pursue the idea -- past a few, not-well-chosen, words.

I don't know what caused me to revisit the subject -- on our way to the hospital. I guess I must've been talking "off the seat of my pants". It just seemed like (only) the most-important priority, in the world. In my world, anyway.

"I guess," she responded, "that I still don't want to know, from such things! There are a load (she was rubbing her tummy) of other things ... that are on my, admittedly-preoccupied, mind. I thought that some of those things ... as opposed to the sanctified state, of marriage ... might be a part of your thinking."

"Probably should be. But, Janice? Ever since that night, in San Antonio ... that wonderful dinner, at the 'Space Needle'-type restaurant ... marrying you has been, at the forefront. The forefront ... of all my thinking! All my thinking! Seeing you there ... rotating around, with that beautiful city behind you ... it all cleared away! I wanted ... more than anything ... to be your husband! Did then ... do now!"

"I have to admit: I was touched ... by your proposal ... that night. That was the only reason ... that I didn't stop you, immediately. Like all the other times."

"Well, it was pretty close to immediately."

"Not really. The only reason I didn't cut you off ... after only a few words ... was that I was, pretty well, taken with the scene. Wonderful dinner! That landscape ... rotating around ... so many stories beneath us! I'd always wanted to go there. Go to that restaurant. Ever since The *HemisFair* opened. On the other hand, I didn't want the whole *experience* ... to allow us to get carried away."

"Look, Janice! This may ... or may not ... be the time to be asking to *marry* you! But, I *do* ... do *desperately* ... want to be your husband! More so *now* ... than any other time!"

"I think we'd better *wait*! Wait, until we *see* ... till we're able to actually *see* ... what this baby *looks* like."

"I don't *care* what it looks like! It's my *kid*! And I want to be ..."

"You say that *now*! But, let's wait and *see*! If your feeling ... your *commitment* ... is *that* strong now, it'll *continue* to be that strong. In a few days ... or in a few weeks."

"Listen, Janice. We can almost ..."

"We're almost *there*," she interrupted -- as I, almost-unknowing, was pulling into the Emergency Room's parking lot!

She'd called ahead! Wouldn't you *know*? The hospital personnel already had the make, description, and license number of her car! The technicians were out, in force -- opening the passenger-side's door! *That* had concluded the conversation!

Janice's term of labor -- lasted almost *eleven* hours! I have no idea -- as to what they might've been doing, to make her as comfortable as possible, but it *had* to have been a long, pain-filled, slog! I guess that it was about that time period -- when hospitals, thankfully, started relaxing their rigid visiting hours schedules. But, this hospital was not one of them! I could not see the valiant patient -- till almost evening, of the following day! ORG!

In fact, I got to visualize the baby -- about 20 minutes, before they'd finally allowed me in to see Janice!

The baby? Oh yes -- the baby! A beautiful little girl! She was black! Well, kind of a Milk-Chocolate Brown. But, she was -- definitely -- the biological spawn, of that hideous black guy! (The late black guy!) And -- to these eyes, anyway -- she was, out and out, gorgeous! Simply gorgeous! I don't remember her birth weight! That was so overshadowed -- by the sheer beauty, of this little girl!

When I -- finally -- got a chance to see the "New Mommy", the first thing, out of her mouth was, "Well ... what do you think?"

"About what?"

"About what?" she mimicked -- in a discordant, nasal, voice. "You know damn well ... about what! The baby! That's what!"

"You mean ... my daughter?"

"You ... your daughter? Have you seen her? Seen your daughter?"

"Of course! Of course I have! And she's beautiful!"

"You really ... really *mean* that? Your *daughter*? She's *beautiful*? You're not giving me a line ... a line, of total *bullshit* ... are you? Because, if you *are* ..."

"One doesn't lie ... doesn't bullshit ... about one's *daughter*!"

"Stephen? Stephen, I'm having a *terrible* ... a *horrible* ... time! A God-awful time ... trying to *decide*! Trying to, out and out, *decide* what to do. I mean, I'm just ..."

"What's to *decide*? You'll marry *me*, of course! Decision *made*! And we'll ride on off, into the sunset ... and live happily ever after. No big, earthshaking, decision *necessary*!"

"Are you *sure*? Listen, Stephen ..."

:*No*! *You* listen! We've beaten this dog ... long *enough*! You and *me*! We may not be the *perfect* pair. *No* one is perfect. Well, there's very few of us *left*. But, I *defy* you ... to name a better couple than *us*. And *now* ... we'll have a beautiful *daughter*! A beautiful *daughter* ... to complete the *set*! To fill out the *picture*! To round out the *portrait*!"

"I *wish* I could be as ... well, as ... as upbeat as you."

"Well, you *did* just finish going through about fourteen-and-a-half years ... of hard labor. And twenty-six years ... of pregnancy! You're ... just now ... coming up for air! Me? I've been moldering away ... downstairs, in that, damnable, God-forsaken, waiting room ... *my* only calling, being, to smoke *cigarettes*, and ..."

"You don't smoke cigarettes! Do you?"

"No ... but, it would've been keeping, with the image I'm trying to project. Besides, I probably still would've smoked 'em ... if I'd had 'em."

"But, you really want to ... want to marry me? Despite the baby?"

"Despite the baby? Hell no! It's almost because ... of the baby! Almost! Like I said ... she just completes the set! The big red bow ... on top of the package! The maraschino cherry ... on top of the sundae!"

"I ... this is a bit of a surprise! Well, a pretty sizeable surprise! I mean ..."

"Well, don't you worry yore kind little hort, M'Dear! We'll take on the world! We might get our fannies kicked ... from time to time. The world can be pretty damn formidable. Every now and then, anyway. But ... with our gorgeous daughter, by our side ... we'll do all right. Do better than all right!"

Janice spent three days, in the hospital. She did fine -- but, having a baby, at her age (even though there were, apparently, no complications) is not an easy task. (Speaking as a man, I can't imagine any child birth situation as being "an easy task". I'm convinced -- that, if men had to be relied on, to bring babies into the world -- civilization would've died out centuries ago!)

Brent granted me a two-week vacation. That was nice of him. I pretty well moved into Janice's apartment -- the better to assume the role, of "Susie Homemaker". And to tend to my daughter.

Speaking of the latter, her mother and I did not discuss a name for her -- till we were on our way home from "The Horse Pistol" (as she'd called it).

"Have you decided on a name for the kid?" I'd asked.

"Yeah. I've given it plenty of thought. Do you have any ideas?"

"Nothing real specific. I'd like for you to pick out a handle, for her."

"How about Julie? We haven't discussed *Manhattan Tower* ... one of my all-time favorite albums ... in ages. You remember that I'd talked about liking your name. Because the guy's name ... in 'Tower' ... 'was 'Stephen'. Well, I don't know if you remember ... but, her name was 'Julie'. So, if we name her Julie ... then, I will have the complete set! I'll have a Stephen ... and a Julie! Doesn't get much better than that!"

"Does that mean you'll marry me?"

"Of course! Why would I want to break up a set? Besides, I've been so ... well, so ... so touched, by the way you actually love the baby! That took a lot ... a hell of a lot ... of convincing, for me. But, you made the sale! Right from the start! The very start! So ... Julie it is, Dad?"

"Julie it is!"

Julie was just three months old -- and doing well! Even more beautiful than before! It was then -- that her, also-beautiful, mother and I (eventually) got hitched! (I "made an honest woman", of her!)

Brent Foley "gave the bride away". (He kept threatening to not give her away. "But," he'd advised me, "she is for sale.")

We were married by Justice of The Peace, Bonnie Braniff -- in a rather nondescript ceremony. (Yes, the good JP -- was/is bona fide sister, to a psychologist! Doctor You-Know-Who.)

Brent -- and his nifty wife -- "took custody" of Julie, for a week. That way, Janice and I could journey -- up to a scenic lodge in Vermont, for a really laid-back honeymoon. There was a pronounced lack of emphasis, on the word "laid"! I'd -- conscientiously -- continued a "program", whereby I spent a goodly amount of time, rubbing her down. Especially her legs -- which had been bothering her, since the final month-or-so, of her pregnancy. (Well, there were a few "stray trips" -- to her elegant bottom! Truth in advertising: More than a few!)

Once we'd gotten back to South Jersey, things seemed to assume a sort of "normalcy" -- which lasted for, not-quite-six, months. First of all, there'd been my weekly trips -- to Manheim. Although I'd not seen Mary Beth -- in what had seemed like forever -- my assigned duties, out there, continued to trouble my wife. At that point, I'd still had no idea -- as to the Amish woman's wellbeing! Or her whereabouts!

I guess that the final "nail in that coffin" -- was Janice's first (and only) trip, back down to Houston. She missed Julie (and, hopefully, me -- at least a little bit) -- to such an extent, that she felt she could no longer continue at her present employment. This, despite the fact that her bosses had been extremely cooperative -- in giving her sufficient time off. (As had Brent -- in, I'm sure, deference to the fact that he and my spouse "went back ... a long way".)

It was decided -- that we would go into business, for ourselves. I became "Susie Homemaker" -- while my, better-head-for-business, wife made all the arrangements. Set everything up.

We became owners -- of *The Nook*! A 'hamburger joint"! The previous owner was pushing 75-years-of-age -- and the enterprise was becoming too burdensome for him. Over the years, he'd "branched off" -- into some rather esoteric foods. Exotic -- for the times, anyway. These had been -- for the most part -- ideas fostered by his two, mid-forties sons. Neither of them, however, had been "motivated" enough to, actually, aid in putting any effort, into seeing that these new gastric entrees would become successful.

The old man confided to Janice, "If I'd had it to do over again, I'd have stuck with just the basic 'Burger and Fries' thing."

So? So, that's what we decided to do!

I was not without some contribution -- of "brainpower"! I'd decided -- that we should make up two batches, of hamburger meat, every morning! My wife and I agreed that our product consist of -- only -- the finest, of Grade-A ground beef! And -- this was (to me) vital -- we'd offer hamburgers, with large pieces, of chopped onion, fried right inside the thick patty. The chunks, of onions, were far from being of uniform size. And the number of them -- in each patty -- varied. (But, hopefully, not too greatly.)

There was another important factor: The patties were really thick! Four or five times the girth, of one of *McDonald's* saintly offerings! And none were to be perfectly round! We stayed away from the (to-me-dreaded) look, of uniformity! Each one, of our specialty items, had "jagged edges". Nothing perfectly round -- or square! Plus, our "classic" -- sold for about four times the prices, that the fast-food giants were charging!

We were even "making a wad", on French fries -- although, there was nothing particularly exotic, about them. Then, Janice came up with the idea -- of "Home Fries"! "Real-life" potatoes! Peeled! ("From scratch", of course!) Sliced (a study, in irregularity), and fried, in a "vat of margarine". Not only that, but actually fried -- in an actual, true-to-life< frying pan. A giant one! The "delicacy" sold for three times, what the competition was offering -- potato-wise! Then, four times! Then, five times! We finally "quit, while we were ahead" -- price-wise!

Janice even managed to contact some dopey, world-famous, French chef. This was well before "The Net" -- made such connections so easy. From this guy, we managed to get a "secret formula" -- for a delicious chicken noodle soup! The ingredients, of this wondrous product? I still don't know! Janice always "whomped it up". She made the dough, for the noodles -- every night, at home -- and, the next day, she rolled it out, on a table we'd had, in the back room of the eatery. She was really talented -- with that old-fashioned rolling pin. Then, she'd, quickly, slice up the result -- forming them, into the least uniform batch of noodles, that one could ever imagine! While in the huge "soup pot" -- some of them curled up. Some did not. Another "unique" product, which we also sold -- for an "obscene" amount of money! Fortunately, everyone loved the stuff!

And -- when it, finally, came down to how our corny little enterprise went over -- we were successful! Blatantly successful! Successful -- as hell!

The place was located, in an advantageous part of town -- which was a giant help. About three-and-a-half blocks, from the sainted auction grounds. A goodly portion -- of our "steadies" came from "my old stomping grounds". I'm sure Brent played a significant part in our success. In the first few weeks, anyway.

We were only open -- from 9:00AM-till-6:00PM. We were closed, altogether, on Sunday. That "compressed" schedule provided us with a goodly amount of "quality family time" -- during the evening hours. The vast amount of -- the overwhelming bulk of -- our business, came, from our steady, reliable, ever-blossoming, lunch crowd. We'll always be grateful!

Every now and then, we'd get a few, "roll-and-coffee", late-breakfast, patrons. (And Janice had, thoughtfully, established a source -- for procuring excellent sweet rolls.) Still, for the most part, it was our bountiful, hamburger-mad, luncheon crowd!

We'd set up an immense -- custom-made -- playpen, in the back room. And furnished it with a plethora of toys -- for my, fast-growing, most-beautiful, daughter. Janice "worked her magic" -- with the soup, and peeling/slicing potatoes -- back there! During the, fortunately-numerous, times of high traffic, she'd "help out" -- in front! Especially manning that monster, of a frying pan!

Well, we'd had six booths -- located at the far wall, of our long, rather-narrow, facility. And my industrious wife did 90% of the "waitress work".

(She was a wonder!) I did a little, of that, always-vital, operation. But, it was surprising -- almost shocking -- the number of customers, who would journey, the few feet, over to the counter, and pick up their own order. Another portion of our hokey little operation -- which was most satisfying!

As "time-and-a-half went on" (quoth Victor Borge), the strain was becoming "a bit much" -- for "the mere two of us" (quoth Janice). So, we hired an experienced fry-cook, from one of the local hotel restaurants. Charlie was a great help! To me -- especially! (Janice continued to manipulate the glorious contents -- of that glorious, "magic", frying pan. And, of course -- to make glorious, "magic", soup!)

Oh yeah! On Sundays, my highly-energetic, dedicated, wife usually made up four or five apple pies -- for the restaurant. And they were usually gone -- by Tuesday or Wednesday. (On Sundays, I was "too pooped to participate" -- and took advantage, of my "day of rest". Janice, on the other hand, was indefatigable!)

In addition, to all this other stuff, she'd, also, roll out flat little round discs of pie crust. A dozen or so, of them. These small dandies measured about seven or eight inches, in diameter. She'd spritz her own "secret" mixture, of cinnamon and sugar, on top of each one. We got 85- or 90-cents, for each one of those flavorful dandies!

❖

We stayed with *The Nook* -- owned it, and made a healthy profit -- for a-little-over-25-years. (Would you believe? A quarter-of-a-century!)

During that time, my daughter -- Little Julie -- got to a point, where she wasn't "little" anymore. But, during the all-too-few years, when she was little -- she was wonderful! Remarkable! And -- in the ensuing years -- she remained so! (Improvement being impossible!)

When she was three or four, she'd assumed her "waitress duty". Her mother had always dressed her in totally-feminine, frippery. The trend -- from whatever-little-I've-been-able-to-know-from-trends -- seemed to be dressing girls (little and big) in more "serviceable" garb. Not for Janice.

When things got a little slow -- at the eatery -- and Julie was completely ambulatory, her mother would direct her to bring this hamburger, or that piece of pie, to a certain booth. The little girl also had her own waitress "uniform" -- which consisted of a lacey apron, and a gigantic bow, in her hair. She did this -- for years -- until she was twelve or thirteen, when she became totally capable, of full-time waitressing. (When "this kind of stuff" didn't conflict, with her "school-housin'", of course.)

Before then, though -- back to when she was just a little girl (back to three or four) -- at home, she used to crawl up, into my lap, make a copious number of "spit curls", and secure them, with bobby-pins. The purpose: "To make me look sexy". (Of course!)

Sundays -- especially -- were wonderful, in those days. It didn't occur to me -- until well after it should have -- that, while I was being made to "look sexy", Janice was, continually, slaving away, in the kitchen. Making pies, etc. etc. etc. Virtually every weekday evening, she was creating noodles! Plus, an abundance of other stuff -- most of which, I'd not had a clue!

Julie, meanwhile, graduated from high school -- and turned out to be Class Valedictorian! She won herself a scholarship -- to *Princeton University*. I was always so proud of her -- that I was "popping my buttons"! On a daily (if not hourly) basis!

Along about 2003, I finally began to realize -- that the backbreaking pace was taking a God-awful toll, on my wife. We'd accumulated "a fist-full of dollars", by then -- and it was time to retire! It took a real heap of arguing (and a copious amount of cajoling) -- to convince Janice, of this fact. I think that the convincing argument -- the one that "made the sale" -- came from our beautiful daughter. She backed my position -- to the hilt.

Once "retired", we were going to do a whole lot of traveling! It didn't work! About six weeks -- after the sale of the restaurant closed -- Janice died! The pace -- indeed -- had done her in! (Stupid me! I never saw it coming!)

Her doctor advised me -- weeks after her demise -- that this wonderful woman had fought internal "female problems"! For years! It took me long enough to figure this out: But, it finally became obvious to me -- that my Janice was convinced that she'd be incapable of ever becoming pregnant again. That had to be the major reason -- why she'd decided to carry our magnificent daughter, to term!

I'll be eternally grateful -- that she did! Eternally grateful!

BOOK OF BOB

ONE

The year was 1971 -- and I was Jack Benny. (i.e. the old 39-years-old trick.) My, kind-of-out-of-kilter, career had found me (at long last) in a niche, that I was completely enjoying.

For virtually all my life, I'd been lurching -- into all kinds of vastly different occupations. Vastly different! Such as: a four-year hitch, in the Navy; tending bar, at two different saloons, in northwest Detroit; working as a gas station attendant, in Birmingham, Michigan; selling (or trying to sell) overpriced waterless cookware, overpriced encyclopedias, overpriced vacuum cleaners, and expensive *Fuller Brush* products, in Detroit. Also, a unique situation, wherein I was "carrying a book", on a, very-strange, "debit insurance" route, in River Rouge.

Then (for a glorious change) I'd enjoyed a fairly successful career, in the rent-a-car business, in "Beautiful Downtown Detroit". The old saw -- about "And Master Of None"? Over my life, that was me! (Except, possibly, for my, fairly-happy, satisfying, five-year whirl -- at *Clovis Car Rental*.)

Happily, in 1971, I'd (at long last) found my true, 42-year-old, "personality"! I was playing ("tickling the ivories") -- on an immense, highly-polished, finest-quality, piano/bar instrument. These satisfying sessions -- took place, at *The Past-Time Lounge*, on Cass Avenue, located in the northern end, of Detroit's, then-still-vibrant, downtown district. The place was really quite charming -- although spectacularly out of place, in that bustling, business/somewhat residential, locale.

I think that -- what made most of us employees a little uncomfortable -- was the presence, of fairly-large number of hookers, just outside! They sold their wares -- up and down the street. Fairly large contingent. However, Cass Avenue was not the primary stomping grounds -- of The Motor City's massive collection of "sidewalk stewardesses. Nor even the second largest conglomeration, of those worthies. Those venues -- would've been two concurrent side streets. Both ran east from Woodward Avenue -- across from the historic *Fox Theater.* (Where the splendorous *Comerica Park* -- home of the, present day, *Detroit* Tigers -- now resides.)

Still, the "overflow" onto Cass Avenue -- always caused more than a raised eyebrow, or six. By more than a few people. We were successful, though.

I'd like to think that my "dulcet tones" -- emanating from the trusty old piano/bar -- was a small part, of our thriving enterprise.

The bar's "Main Attraction", though, was beauteous Vi -- our owner. She was a very shapely blonde (from a bottle, so they said) -- who'd tended bar, virtually every night. She'd always worn a clinging, velvet-like, dress! Without fail -- one that began, and ended, awfully near the middle! She had a red one, a light-blue one, a dark-blue one, a kelly-green one, and a canary-yellow one! But, the one that, unquestionably, drew the most attention -- was her, much-applauded/much-anticipated, "Saturday Night Special"! Her black dazzler!

In addition to being so spectacularly constructed, Vi was an excellent "mixologist", as they call them nowadays. Plus, she was an excellent conversationalist! (And equally adept -- at listening! She would discuss anything, that you'd wish. From politics (local and/or presidential) -- to the Tigers, Lions, Red Wings, and Pistons. An added quality: She'd never shy away -- from a highly-sexual discussion! Ever! It could be said that she'd encouraged them! Aggressively encouraged them -- for the most part, At least, that's what some, of our sainted clientele, claimed.

Things, in the early-autumn of 1971 had been going pretty well for me. I'd never married. Hadn't really had all that many girlfriends. No really-close girlfriends. Which, I guess, would explain my unmarried status -- and more than a few (fortunately-whispered) questions, pertaining to my (ah) "sexual orientation".

There had, most always, been (to my way of thinking) a whole lot of females -- of every age, and physical description -- who'd while away an evening, singing along with me, at the good ol' piano/bar. Some were (ahem) a little more aggressive than others. Those were the ones that I usually wound up dating. There was not one "shrinking violet" in that crowd. Yes, I slept -- with a few of them (NYAHHH!)! But, nothing ever really took! I doubt that I'd ever expected anything to "blossom"!

Still, I was -- unquestioningly -- happier, (and on a steady basis) than ever before, in my "young life". I guess that it didn't take much.

So, why -- in 1971 -- was I not still gainfully employed, in the, till-then-moderately-successful, rent-a-car game? Especially since my first boss, in that field (a wonderful woman, named Mary Jane) had told me -- on numerous occasions -- "Bob, not only are you good ... but, you're damn good"! She'd been the first -- and only -- person, who'd ever said that to me. Till then, anyway. I can still hear her saying it! (Rest In Peace, Beautiful Mary Jane!)

She and I ran an exceedingly difficult operation -- on busy Washington Blvd. In the very heart, of downtown! This was, in the late-fifties and early-sixties -- when most of the airlines were still operating, out of Willow Run Airport (35 miles northwest of The Motor City). And virtually all the many sales reps were staying -- at the four or five huge hotels, downtown.

We were required -- to park (and, if need be, wash and refuel) the cars, of the airport's customers, overnight. It was also up to us -- to deliver those folks to their particular hotel, in the evening. Then, we, faithfully, delivered their car, back to them -- the following morning.

In addition, we ran the Travel Desk -- at *The Statler Hotel,* two blocks to the north. And we manned a small, car-rental, desk, each weekday morning, at *The Sheraton Cadillac,* which was located a block, in the opposite direction. Not the easiest -- of entities to make run smoothly.

Listen! We were <u>great</u>! Mary Jane and I worked <u>wonderfully</u> together! Purred -- like the most-efficient motor, you could ever imagine! Each one of us <u>always</u> knew -- knew <u>precisely</u> -- what the other was thinking and doing! And what <u>projects</u> each of us might be involved in! On a minute-to-minute basis!

It was <u>classic</u> "chemistry"! (I'd overheard one of our afternoon rental agents ask our sales rep, "Are Mary Jane and Bob ... a <u>thing</u>?" And Joan, our rep, had replied, "Naw. That'd be <u>incest</u>!")

Unfortunately, in 1961, Mary Jane became pregnant. Kind of late in life, for her. Fortunately, I was promoted to manager. But, it was <u>never</u> the same. I'd hired three different ladies -- over the three or four months, after Mary Jane had "deserted" me. But, the pace was too frantic -- for each of them! Which was understandable. (You'd have to have been Mary Jane -- or me,)

Then, magically, Mary Jane phoned me -- at home! She was -- denks God -- ready to come back! She asked, if I'd hire her -- to assist me! I answered with something like, "Oh, I dunno. Submit your resume ... and we'll see." Then, of course, I half-shouted that I'd be thrilled -- to work with her, once again! (Who wouldn't? Who the hell would not?)

But, just a mere week -- before she was to return -- she found out, that she was "with child" once again! Org! (Mary JANE!) That actually ended her rent-a-car career. We had remained close friends -- over the years.

After yet another futile hire, I managed to actually find a woman -- a couple years my junior -- who'd come as close, to "being Mary Jane", as anyone could reasonably expect! (I'd despaired that such an animal even existed!)

The new employee's name was Ruth. Ruthie Peters. I knew -- when I'd hired her -- that she'd been a few months pregnant. That was fine, with me! I'd worry about replacing her -- when the time came.

But, she'd impressed me -- right from the git-go. I knew that she'd be able to catch on -- to that, very-complicated, highly-unique, situation. And -- for the nonce, anyway -- that was good enough for me!

I'd needed the dedication -- and the, unquestioned, beyond-a-doubt, efficiency! Badly!

Ruthie developed -- even more quickly, than I'd had any reason to expect. And, as time went along, we became quite close. Drawing ever more close -- as I was finding out, more and more, about her.

She was, at that point, in an "unfortunate" (and, I was to learn, a very difficult) marriage. Beset by the fact that Rudy, her (constantly unemployed) husband -- was what is commonly known, as a total schmuck!

And there had been many other problems -- primarily financial! But, not all! For one thing, she'd given birth -- about a year-and-a-half earlier -- to twins! Both had been inflicted -- with RH-Negative blood! I haven't the foggiest idea, as to what that same condition would entail -- in this much more modern, and sophisticated, medical world! But, back then, they'd had to -- completely -- replace the blood, in the babies! All of it! In both of them! I also have no idea -- as to what that procedure would've required, back then! (Probably just as well.) But, I do know -- that it was terribly expensive!

"Expensive as hell," as Ruthie had explained. Costing "a couple thousand dollars" -- for each offspring. And these were early-1960s dollars. I never did find out how they'd managed to contend with that overwhelming situation! After a certain point -- in all of our discussions -- Ruthie would, inevitably, simply clam up! Every time! Every time! Most frustrating!

Rudy -- her, still-non-working husband, would pick her up. Promptly, at 3:30PM. Each and every day. In their fancy, bright-red, 1952 Cadillac convertible. (He'd always required that they own a Caddy convertible -- no matter how old, the "classic". And, maintenance-wise, this one was beginning to cost 'em "more than a few bucks".)

In the, still-really-pretty, car, they'd possessed some kind of (sophisticated-for-the-times) double-car-seat -- for the babies. The device was securely anchored -- permanently -- to the passenger's front seat. Of course, as soon as her dedicated spouse would pull up, in front of the office, he'd climb into the backseat -- and spread out! Poor baby! The drive in must have exhausted him! Ruthie would, then, have to drive them out -- to their "bare-threads" apartment, in suburban Romulus. Where the brand new Detroit Metro Airport would soon be located.

As the months had passed, of course, she was plainly feeling the effects -- of what was becoming (well, what had become) a, fast-deteriorating, physical, situation! This meant -- that her patience was beginning to wear thin. Even at the office! She was just as efficient as ever -- but, her mode of toleration (mostly toward our customers) was starting to cause me more than just a little concern!

A couple of months -- before her pregnancy would come to term (and the prospect of yet another RH-Negative birth situation had positively haunted her) -- she really exploded! At a Willow Run Airport customer!

The guy was impossible! He'd called for his car -- at about 8:15AM! This was at the height -- of our frenetic rush hour! He'd ordered his unit -- to be sent, to him, at *The Sheraton Cadillac*. We'd, of course, complied! After this clown had waited -- what he'd considered "an outrageous amount of time" -- he'd walked, up the block! To our office!

Of course, by that time, his car had been dispatched -- to the hotel. I'd had to get one of our other porters (as our service agents were known, in those pre-historic times) to run over, to the hotel -- and to advise his fellow-porter to bring the stupid car, to the stupid office! I could not spare having one man "stranded" -- at the hotel. I most certainly could not afford to spare another -- to go and fetch him!

And this guy kept bitching -- about how "piss-poor" our service was. He was going to be late for an appointment! And (of course) it was all our fault!

About that time, Ruthie had had enough! It had been a fairly-troubling morning, anyway! She turned to him -- and, at the top of her lungs, had bellowed, "Well, if you'd have gotten off your ass ... when you should have ... you wouldn't have the problem!"

Then, she burst out -- <u>sobbing</u> intensely! I got her back -- behind the peg-board partition, where my desk was! It separated my personal space -- from the customers' retail space. I sat my friend down, in my chair -- and hurried back out, to the public area! About that time, the porter pulled up -- with his damn car!

"<u>There</u>." I hissed. "There's your goddam <u>car</u>!"

He'd stormed out -- but, that would <u>not</u> be the last, that we'd hear of him!

Roland Yates -- at that same time -- had become the company wunderkind! He'd been operating -- in the "back office" (our, barely-tolerable, record-keeping, administrative entity), located on the other side, of the building. It was almost <u>spooky</u>! You see, Roland had had <u>eyes</u> -- on running the Washington Boulevard station, himself!

He'd even had the audacity -- to have given Mary Jane a hard time! <u>Many</u> times! Totally <u>outrageous</u>! I'd witnessed some of the huffy interchanges -- in the first few months, that I'd been employed. At one point, Mary Jane had told our sainted city manager -- Marvin (Flash) Hollett -- that, "If Roland Yates wants this goddam office, so <u>bad</u> ... he can damn well <u>have</u> it!"

Mr. Hollett -- who'd gotten his nickname, after a former Red Wing defenseman (Flash Hollett -- who'd played for the Detroit hockey team, from 1943-to-1946) -- was <u>not</u> stupid! He <u>knew</u> that he could not afford to lose Mary Jane. This was before I'd had a chance to show what potential I may've possessed.

Once the Willow Run manager's slot had opened, the sainted Roland Yates was given the berth! At least, he was 35 miles away. We wouldn't have to deal with him -- on a daily basis.

Roland proceeded to dazzle <u>everyone</u> -- including, I think, Dear Old Flash! He wound up -- setting all kinds of revenue records, out there. He <u>was</u> very good -- at what he did. He just didn't need to be a total bastard -- while doing it!

After four or five months, our main competition <u>hired</u> ol' Roland away -- at what was <u>purported</u> to be a "monumental" salary! Apparently, it wasn't all <u>that</u> stupendous! Either that -- or there had been a number of promises broken, along the way! He didn't <u>stay</u> there -- all that long!

In the meantime, I'd been offered the Willow Run managership -- when he'd left. But, I'd turned it down. The airport <u>was</u>, after all, 35 miles away. Besides, Washington Boulevard <u>was</u> my "home". I <u>loved</u> it there!

A man named Willard Kaleta -- who'd always worn a clip-on bow tie (and had replaced Roland, in the back office) -- ultimately took the airport job. And <u>failed</u>! <u>Miserably</u>! The poor guy was in -- <u>horribly</u> -- over his head!

So, "Flash" went out -- and hired Yates back! The task was, apparently, much easier accomplished -- than he'd feared. God was back, in His heaven -- and Roland was back, at Willow Run! All was well, with the world! Life, I guess, was wonderful, for Mr. Hollett -- once again.

Then, the Corporate Office, in Boston, interfered! They promoted "Flash" Hollett! He became a vice president -- and a regional manager. To replace him, they hired our competition's up-and-coming young "star". (Their version, of Roland Yates!)

Our new city manager's name -- was Franklin Turley! (Got all that?) Turley and Yates had become close buddies -- when they'd both toiled in the, high-pressured, vineyard, of *Brand X Rent-a-Car.*

That, it turned out, was at the center -- of all Ruthie's (and, eventually, my) troubles!

The customer -- the schmuck, who'd been told, by Ruthie, to "get off his ass" -- was still upset, when he'd checked his car in, that evening, at the airport! Roland happened to be nearby -- and, the following day, he got together, with his good friend, Turley. Anything Yates could do to harm me -- corporate-wise -- as a "descendant" of Mary Jane's, he was more than willing to engage in!

So, the two of them wound up descending on Washington Boulevard -- and pinned Ruthie! Ganged up on her -- back behind the pegboard partition! During this inquisition, she finally broke down again! Informed them -- of her many physical difficulties. (Most of which I'd been unaware.) She, ultimately, admitted -- that she was, currently, suffering from vaginal bleeding! They'd, of course, fired her -- immediately!

I realize that -- given such a serious medical condition, like the one, which was plaguing poor Ruthie -- she should not be working! At anything! Anywhere! At all! Ever!

Sadly, I found out -- three or four weeks later (and, from whom, I don't remember; but, I'd considered the information to be reliable) -- that Ruthie was, at that, critical, point, washing walls, and cleaning toilets, in her seedy apartment complex! To pay the rent! Can you imagine? I don't know what dear Rudy, her husband, was doing! But, I can guess! (What is zero times zero?)

That was the last I was to hear of Ruthie! Or of Rudy! Or of the kids!

I'd gone ahead, and hired a lady -- from Back-Bay Bah-ston -- to replace Ruthie. She turned out to be "adequate". But, no one could really replace her predecessor. Just as it had been impossible -- for Ruthie to have filled Mary Jane's slot. Filled it completely, anyway. But, Martha was a nice lady -- and I loved to hear her talk. Given the accent, and all.

In the meantime, there were other troubles -- lurking, in Paradise! Apparently, God was no longer in His heaven. When Roland Yates made his "grand" return (I'm sure people cheered) he was no longer contented -- with "merely" running the massive operation, out at Willow Run Airport!

As previously indicated, he'd always had his jaundiced eye -- leveled, squarely, on the Washington Boulevard operation. I'd long been filled with overwhelming doubts -- as to whether he'd actually be capable, of running "my enterprise".

Admittedly, he'd done well, at the airdrome. Both times. But, he'd had the benefit of three or four times the personnel -- that manned our sanctified downtown location. And he didn't have to park anyone's car -- overnight. Or wash, refuel -- and deliver -- those units, the next morning. Plus, if one of his customers broke down -- it was not going to be in neighboring Ypsilanti. It would be in Detroit! Or one of the suburbs! Which meant we (or the people, in our northwest station) would have to resolve the situation!

I firmly believed that only Mary Jane -- or I -- could've actually run the Washington Boulevard office. (Well, maybe Ruthie could have -- eventually. But, we'll never know, will we? She'd never be given the opportunity.)

So, Roland Yates -- with absolutely no concept, of what would be involved, in such a move -- decided to add the downtown operation jewel, to his "dazzling" repertoire! This would be his "Crown Jewel" -- as it were!

He now had an ally! The, newly-commissioned, city manager! He and Franklin Turley had, as mentioned, been ever so "tight" -- since they'd both toiled in the fields, of our exalted competition. So, whatever Roland wanted -- Roland was, fare-thee-well, going to get!

So, they'd created a "special niche" -- for me! My very own slot! Yeah! For "Good Ol' Bob Conacher"! The grandiose plan took some real doing -- and required a goodly amount of time! (Not to mention a considerable ration of, hard-to-come-by, corporate dollars!)

The corporation's office -- in New Orleans, for heaven's sake -- had bought way too many 1963 Ford Galaxies! Way too many! And had paid too much for them! Way too much! And had bought them too late -- in the model year! Way too late!

Consequently, they were listed on the corporate books -- at way too high, in value. Too expensive -- for the city manager, down there, to sell. It was verboten -- company policy-wise -- to sell our units, at a (gasp!) loss! And so, these "white elephants" were simply sitting around, down there! Throwing the operation's P&L Statement -- onto the rocks! Big time! The corporation had, of course, cut loose the sinning city manager!

Well, Roland Yates and Franklin Turley -- to the rescue! They decided to have the Louisiana cars transferred! Brought up to Detroit! All virtually new -- top-of-the-line -- beauties!

At the same time, Turley convinced the, head-up-their-fanny, National Office -- to allow him to create a wholly new program, in Detroit! Brand spanking new concept! And this wondrous, "pioneering", program was to be "administered" -- by, newly-important, old moi! I say "administered" -- as opposed to the word "run"! The only thing running -- as it turned out -- was "Good Ol' Bob Conacher"!

The Head Office sent out three high-powered guys -- from Massachusetts! These tigers -- fanned out, all across Detroit's northern suburbs! They signed up (would you believe?) 11 gas stations -- to act as our substations, in the, far-flung, metropolitan area!

Basically, these, newly-commissioned, operations -- would rent out our cars, and check them in. (The latter -- at least, in those days -- required merely third-grade math, and not much more.)

The gas station would receive a seventeen-and-a-half percentage portion, of the rental's "time-and-mileage" revenue. And, of course, they'd get to charge us, for gasoline -- when the cars checked in. And to sell us the occasional headlight, or fan belt, or windshield wiper. It was -- basically -- a really good deal, for these guys! Fairly lucrative! And an easy sell -- for the guys from Mass!

So, once these corporate hawks had left town, we'd had, newly-formed, substations -- in Pontiac, Mount Clemons, Birmingham, Royal Oak (two of them, there) Oak Park, and Ferndale! How they'd ever found a brother of one of my uncles -- who'd just opened a large *Standard Oil* station, adjacent to the then-giant *Northland Shopping Mall* -- at 8 Mile Road and Greenfield -- I'll never know! But, they did! And he became part, of the grand scheme! "My kingdom"!

And, as indicated, "Good Ol Bob'" would be the one -- to head up this "revolutionary-concept" program!

Oh! And Washington Boulevard (under the "guidance" of Guess-Who) -- as well as Willow Run -- would keep all those shiny, new, New Orleans cars! "Good Ol Bob'" got the older -- sometimes showing signs of rust -- units! Some were pretty shabby-looking!

I told Turley that I didn't want this "Golden Opportunity"!

"It makes no sense," I'd protested -- in front of a "shocked" (shocked, I tell you) Roland Yates. "Look, Mister Turley," I'd pleaded, "I'm the only one! The only one, you've got ... who can run Washington Boulevard. Roland doesn't have the foggiest idea ... as to what the hell's involved down here."

Yates, of course, continued to be grossly upset -- that anyone would dare to question his messianic abilities! (Well, in point of fact, no one ever had! Not in -- forever!)

"I can damn well run that station, Bob," he'd hissed. "Run it ... in my sleep! Probably a helluva lot better ... than you ever could! Damn well ... better than you ever have!"

I think my rejoinder was something like, "Roland? Roland ... you've got your head, up your ass! Firmly ... and squarely ... up your ass! You're gonna be in way over your head ... at Washington Boulevard! Completely in ... way over your head! You don't have the slightest idea ... what it takes, to run the joint! Part of that is ... because your head is filling your rectal cavity! Filling it ... to damn well overflowing! And part is ... because you, jolly well, don't pack the gear, to manage it!"

Plainly, I was not endearing myself -- to this sainted, benevolent, pair!

"I was going to authorize a ten-dollar-a-week raise for you, Bob," snarled Turley. "Now, I'm not so sure!"

"You cut out my goddam feet ... cut me off, at the knees ... and I'm supposed to be grateful, for a, pissy-assed, raise? A raise ... of ten pissy-assed dollars? Yates has had a hard-on for that job ... managing Washington Boulevard ... from way back! Since Mary Jane's heyday! He did his best ... to undermine her, to Mister Hollett! But, ol' Flash ... he was smart enough to know who was capable, of running the joint! And Roland, here, wouldn't make a good wart ... on Mary Jane's bottom! Nor on mine!"

"That's e-fucking-nuff!" screamed our, "sent-from-heaven" city manager. "Now, you're going to take this Substation Program, Bob! And you're gonna fucking run it! Otherwise, you're fucking gone! Outta fucking here! I don't wanna hear another fucking word! Not from your fucking mouth!"

So, instantly, I was heading up the new operation -- sans the ten-dollar raise!

To be sure -- to be absolutely certain -- that I "knew my place", I was assigned a "new" company car! This one had a tow-bar! A big, iron thing! It was welded, solidly, to the frame! In front!

The idea was, as follows: Whenever I would arrive at one of our sanctified substations -- and could tell that they'd had too many cars, on hand -- I was to hook my glorious car, onto one of their full-sized automobiles, and drive the rental car (towing mine), until I would get to a substation that needed a unit or two. I would, then, unhook my marvelous car -- and leave the Ford or Chevy or Plymouth, at the deserving station.

They could've bought me a new Falcon -- or a Valiant, or a Corvair! Instead, they dug up this old, tired, 1958 English Ford! One with no radio! This

Prefect was pretty well -- on its way to, full-scale, rusted out, status! No matter! They gave it a cheap, green, paint job, welded the tow-bar to the thing's frame -- then, slapped a *Clovis Rent-a-Car* logo sticker, on the outside, of each front door. (A four-leaf clover -- natch!) So, "The Jitney" was it! For "Good Ol' Bob"!

The substations, themselves, turned out -- to be a mess! These high-shooters -- from Boston -- had left it up to me, to train the gas station's personnel! In each case. Train all of their employees!

The Northwood station -- at Woodward Avenue and 12-mile Road, in Royal Oak -- was a 24-hour operation. Training three shifts -- was a million laughs! The other stations -- each had "only" two shifts. And -- with one or two exceptions -- those situations weren't much better!

But, eventually -- in about two weeks -- we were "up and running"! (In a manner of speaking!)

- The *Standard Oil* station -- in Birmingham -- was (far and away) the best of these tenuous dealers. No competition! (My actual "Crown Jewel"!)
- The two old geezers -- who'd owned the *Texaco* station, in Mount Clemens -- were way out of their element. They were, in fact, fixing

to dissolve the partnership. The one -- who might've caused the station to survive -- was opening a lawnmower-repair shop. The other guy -- who was as nice, as he could be -- was doomed! And he "retired"! (I lied to ya! They'd only had one shift -- consisting of the two old coots -- and were only opened, from 8:00AM-till-6:00PM!)

- How they'd ever found the guy, in Ferndale, I'll never know! Seldom was he ever there! And *Marathon OIL* -- which had taken over all of the many *Speedway 79* stations, in town -- was in the process, of tearing down this old building, and constructing a new one! "To *Marathon* standards"!
- The guy who owned the *Sunoco* station -- in Royal Oak proper -- was nice enough, and helpful. But, he'd employed the laziest staff known to man.
- The *Mobil* dealer -- in Pontiac -- had so many things going (like running a bookie operation, delving in the "Numbers Game", and operating a call-girl syndicate) that operating a rent-a-car gig (even part-time) was far down, on his priority list! (Even selling a few gallons of gas -- and the oil change/lube job -- elements were not that all-fired important.)
- The owner of the *Standard Oil* station -- in Oak Park -- was pretty good. So were his employees.

But, somehow or another, they'd <u>never</u> had more than six or eight cars, out on rental, at one time. To this day, I don't know why!

- Uncle Clete's brother did pretty well. He was -- without a doubt -- the second best, of the substations. Next two the two mid-thirties partners, in Birmingham.
- Northwood -- the 24-hou4 operation -- gave me the most <u>revenue</u>! And, of course, the most problems! "Steve-o", the owner, ran the place -- like a Russian Czar! But, he couldn't be there 24/7! And "when the <u>cat</u> was away" -- well, you can <u>guess</u> what the "kittens" (and <u>raucous</u> "kittens", they were) were doing!

<u>This</u> was to be my life's <u>calling</u>! My life's <u>work</u>!

I <u>did</u> labor -- in this unwieldy situation -- for a little longer than three months. But, it was just too much!

Physically, I'd spent most of my time coupling -- and uncoupling -- that stupid Jitney! Running cars from here to there! I was, though, able to stay, pretty much, in my area.

Well, once each week, my duties <u>did</u> call for me to make up a weekly revenue report, for each entity/ And, of course, collect the monies taken in (less the substation's commission, and gas and maintenance charges).

Then, I'd been required to meet with Franklin Turley -- downtown -- and turn in (and explain/ justify) those figures (and each one, of those funds) to him. (Another million laughs!)

His former assistant, Willard -- the guy, with the bowtie -- had been dispatched, once again, to "manage" the operation, at Willow Run. (He'd done so well before, don't you see.) So -- due to Willard's absence -- it was with "The Great Man", himself, that I'd had to meet. Two or three times, Roland Yates decided to sit in on these sessions. To grace us -- with his presence. Those always wound up, being more like third-degree grillings -- than meetings.

I'd moved! Out to Birmingham -- which was, pretty much, the geographic center, of my, newly-formed, work area. My beloved territory. I'd managed to find a really neat two-room apartment -- just three-and-a-half blocks, from the substation, there. I'd had to sleep, on a Murphy bed -- one which swiveled out of a huge closet. But, surprisingly, it was very comfortable.

No matter where I might've been living, the job was untenable! About three weeks, into the program, the thing, in Mount Clemons finally blew up! They ultimately closed the *Texaco* station. They'd had 14 cars -- out on rental. The contracts were, woefully, incomplete -- and, extremely, difficult to read.

I'd had to track each customer down, find out when he/she was going to be finished with the car -- and make an appointment, to check him/her in. Then engage in the unmitigated joy -- of using The Jitney's trunk-surface, as a makeshift counter.

Twice, I'd had to track down overdue cash rentals, in Pontiac -- and once, in Ferndale. (The latter was a major deal! The renter was fixing to head south, with the car! South -- like to Alabama! And I'd had to confront him, at a neighborhood bar! Another "million-laughs" situation!)

I was, obviously, running myself ragged!

The final straw -- came, on a Friday morning, when I was, busily, trying to transfer cars, among my substations! I was preparing for a, fairly-busy, weekend. At the height, of my efforts, I was ordered -- by our sanctified city manager -- to "Get your ass down here! Now! Fucking now!"

I got to "Beautiful Downtown Detroit" -- about 45 minutes later. After waiting outside, of Turley's office, -- for the better part, of an hour (till Roland Yates finally showed up) -- I was, eventually, allowed entry, to the Inner Sanctum!

Turley threw a rental contract -- across his desk -- at me. It was from the Northwood substation!

It had been time-stamped at 3:15AM, on a Tuesday morning -- from the previous week. And it sported a brown ring -- right in the center -- where someone had, obviously, set down a coffee cup! And I was catching all *kinds* of hell, for it!

I finally submitted my *resignation*! In *suppository* form! In the middle -- of my, top-or-my-lungs, diatribe -- I "advised" the pair, that "I could *not* be at Woodward-and-Twelve-Mile Road ... to *tell* some, stupid-assed, mechanic to *not* set the fucking coffee cup, on the fucking rental agreement!"

I also advised them -- that they could pick up The Jitney, at the Birmingham substation! Whenever they damn *pleased*! And I was -- *POOF*! -- *out of there*!

TWO

Things, immediately, assumed a whirlwind pace -- from my, more-than-unsettling, (to me, anyway) resignation. from *Clovis Car Rental*! A dizzying series, of events! (Well, dizzying -- in my hokey little world!)

First of all, I'd immediately returned -- to my former substation, in Birmingham. That was the business location -- nearest to my modest apartment. I dropped off The Jitney, and filled in, the partners (John and Gene) -- who'd owned, and operated, the *Standard Oil* station -- as to what had just taken place downtown! Word-by-word -- without "cleaning up" the description! I was -- obviously -- still quite upset!

"I really don't know ... how you'd always put up with all the bullshit," observed Gene. "All the bullshit! As much as you did! As long as you went along with it!"

"Yeah," agreed John. "We weren't involved in a tenth of it ... but, neither of us could understand how you'd put up with the way they always shit all over you. Look! Take one of the stupid-assed rent-a-cars. Take it, on home. Keep it ... for the weekend. Those assholes ... downtown ... they'll never be able to figure something like that out. To track anything down. And then, on Monday, come and see us. Come on in ... about midmorning. I think Gene and I might have something ... something concrete ... to offer you. Let my partner, and I ... let us get together. Talk some things over. And, maybe, we'll be able to come up with something ... on Monday ... to, maybe, help you out, a little bitty!"

I took one of the Galaxies! Somehow, not being without wheels made me feel better! *Much* better! It was almost critical to me -- to not be tied *down*. At least, for the weekend. Not being *stranded*! Even temporarily! And what John had had to say -- about making me some kind of an offer -- gave me a goodly amount, of additional succor! Then -- once I *was* able to "calm down" (which came surprisingly *quickly*) -- I'd begun to feel downright *good*! Better than I'd felt -- since Turley and Yates had "cut me off ... at the knees" -- Washington Boulevard-wise! (This, although I'd had no earthly idea -- as to what John and Gene might have up their, hopefully-corporate, sleeves!)

As noted previously, Birmingham had been -- far and away -- the most successful, and most productive, of *all* the substations. If one would exclude the figures, of the Northwood Station -- the lone 24-hour location -- Birmingham was fast reaching the point, where they were doing virtually *twice* the revenue, of *all* the *other* substations *combined*!

John and Gene were the most, on-top-of-it -- most competent -- of all, of the substation operators. Rodger -- who'd owned the *Sunoco* station, in Royal Oak proper -- was pretty astute. "Steve-o" (aka "Attila The Hun") was also very sharp. But, his employees were <u>definitely</u> out of control! The guy, in Oak Park, was kind of a nonentity -- as his minimal rental utility being so <u>very</u> low, would attest. The rest -- especially the pair of owners, in Ferndale and Pontiac -- were (to put it charitably) absolutely no bargain!

I <u>was</u> a little disappointed -- with my uncle's brother. But, I'd halfway convinced myself -- that he was <u>not</u>, in a real-advantageous location. If he'd have been located -- directly on the other side, of that massive complex -- then, I'm positive that he'd have been much better off. In all phases, of his business.

In any case, this was to be a weekend -- for me. to "unbutton a little" -- and relax! Which -- surprisingly -- is exactly what I <u>did</u>! More than I could've <u>imagined</u>!

On Monday, John, Gene, and I repaired to a, rather-large, combination coffee shop/drive in -- on Woodward Avenue, a few miles north of town. A <u>really</u> neat place! We'd convened, in the further-most booth, at the rear of the bustling joint.

"We'd like to take you on ... to employ you ... in a, more-or-less, hybrid position," began Gene. "A 'kind-of-bastard' position, if you will."

"I don't understand," confused ol' me responded. "Me? A bastard?"

"Well," explained John, "we think there's a definite future for us ... in the rent-a-car game. But ... we figure ... that'll have to come, somewhere down the road. Soon, we hope."

"Yeah," agreed his partner. "We're not big enough ... yet ... to be able to afford a full-time person. One to actually devote all his time, and energy, to running such an operation. <u>Exclusively</u> running a car-rental entity."

"Somewhere down the <u>road</u>, though?" offered John. "We <u>hope</u> so. We hope <u>to</u>."

"In the meantime," expanded Gene, "we'd like you to work ... exclusively on the drive. Easy enough. Pump the gas. Always check the <u>oil</u>. <u>Always</u> check the oil. <u>Always</u>!"

"And <u>always</u> wash the windshield," added John. "That way, the guys working, in the bays ... oil changes and lube jobs, and the like ... they won't have to drop what they're doing. And rush out, y'know ... and service the drive. <u>That</u> can be a bit of a bear, Frequently is!"

"Yeah," explained Gene, "the <u>drive</u> is the most <u>important</u> part! Those people ... they can just drive on <u>off</u>. There's a *Marathon* station ... right here, on Maple

Road. Just across Woodward. And a *Mobil* Station ... and a *Shell* station ... just a couple of blocks, further east. We don't need our customers ... going to one of those. To one of them."

"But, when the car rental thing does rear its ugly head," advised John, "that will be your primary interest! Your first duty! If the drive gets busy, we'll handle it, from the bays."

"We always have," laughed Gene. "How's that sound? Whatcha think?"

It sounded great! Especially since the salary they were offering was $5.00-a-week, more -- than I'd been "hauling down" at, generous-to-a-fault, ol' *Clovis.*

It was further pointed out, to me -- that I'd not have to jack with The Jitney. (Who knew when my former employer would -- ever -- pick up the stupid Prefect?) They were pretty close friends, with Rodger -- in Royal Oak. We could get extra cars from him -- when he'd not need them -- and would give him cars, not required, in Birmingham. I'd run the car one way, or the other, and either John and Gene or, perhaps, Rodger would get me back to the station. An ideal situation!

Also, they'd want me to "suavely appropriate" additional cars -- over an "appropriate amount of time". "Slick 'em" -- from Ferndale and Oak Park and Pontiac. Build up our "fleet"! If I could even con Uncle Clete's brother -- out of the "occasional" auto ... that would be "not frowned upon".

Eventually -- if things were to "break properly" -- the partners would look in to buying enough units, to own and operate their own, permanent, profitable, rental entity.

"Who knows where *Clovis* will be ... or what they may be thinking ... down the road?" mused John. "They don't appear to be the steadiest of ships, in the harbor

I'd not thought of that! That, herc-to-fore, unpleasant, possibility gave me a surprising degree -- of unrest! That ended up, an absolutely wonderful --most-rewarding -- get together! Truly -- a God-send!

❖

A week-and-a-half later, *Clovis* sent someone -- to pick up The Jitney! It was Willard -- the bow-tie guy! He'd been "liberated" -- once more -- from Willow Run! He would be "administering" the substation program -- ever hence!

A lot had happened -- since I'd recently extinguished my employment there: For one thing, Franklin Turley -- our beloved city manager -- had, as noted, sent Willard back out, to manage the Willow Run Airport operation (again). And, as also noted, he'd duplicated his past record -- of failure. (Again.)

Turley then had, finally, hired one of his other "close friends" (beside Roland Yates) from the competition -- to run Willow Run. Willard was, at that point, brought back, to the glorious administrative office -- which was his "natural habitat". It was to prove, however, to be a temporary move..

As indicated, Willard was named -- to take my spot, administering the wondrous substation program. And -- once again -- he was, totally, out of his element. I'd assured him -- that I'd help him "as much as I could". But, it was, more-than-evident, that he was in -- well over his head.

Also, he'd advised me, that Yates was having his problems -- at dear old Washington Boulevard! "It's too soon ... to know for sure," he'd announced, "but, he's really getting his ass kicked!" The continuing revenue figures, from downtown -- were "not encouraging", according to Willard. And he'd been in a position to know -- how-ever-temporarily!

I was doing my best -- to control my grief! No black armband for me!

As time wore on, so many things happened -- although none were, of truly earthshaking importance:

Most importantly -- to me, anyway -- I'd settled in -- at John's and Gene's *Standard Oil* station. For my entire life, I'd always been overwhelmed, by anything mechanical -- or electrical! No expertise -- whatever! To me, a rubber band -- is a machine!

But, I did master the "art" of pumping gas. (I realize that this requires absolutely no special talent.

Nowadays, everyone pumps his/her own petrol.) On the other hand, I found I was able to read an engine-oil dipstick -- and even install a quart of oil, into the engine block. (Huzzah!) And to even operate that sponge/squeegee stick -- permitting me to, capably, clean off a windshield. Any windshield! These were no small accomplishments -- given how busy the driveway traffic was, for that station. Consistently busy! Especially early, in the morning.

Detroit was 15 miles away -- to the south. Indeed, Maple Road was also known as 15-Mile Road. And a, seemingly-overwhelming, number of our customers, back then, actually worked -- in The Motor City! And virtually all of them filled up -- on their way in, to work. I pretty much worked from 7:00AM-till-6:00PM. I was on straight salary -- so, my two bosses were happy with the, extra-hours, "dedication to duty". I was thrilled! These guys were (far and away) the best -- the absolute finest -- employers, I'd ever had.

My expenses, understandably, were minimal. My little apartment's monthly obligation (utilities included, in the rent) -- and a little food, here and there. And that was it! I could use any of the rental cars -- for my own personal needs! Didn't even have to pay for gas! Was that great -- or what?

Strangely (or, perhaps, not) I was actually beginning to come closer -- to Willard (he, of the bowtie brigade). He really wasn't running his fanny off -- as I'd been required to do. Mainly, he appreciated the fact that I'd gotten to where I would do all his paperwork, for him -- vis-a-vis the Birmingham operation. We were, by then, his biggest substation -- and were increasing our lead, each and every month. (Probably each and every hour.) Northwood's 24-hour operation notwithstanding.

Plus, I'd spoken to the station owners -- in Ferndale and Oak Park -- and "put 'em to sleep"! Seduced them long enough (and often enough) -- that they'd both decided to give up the *Clovis* program.

Willard was thrilled -- to not have to go to those stops, every week. He and I "transferred" the 15 or 20 cars, from those entities -- out to dear ol' Birmingham. Why the downtown administrative office let us get away with those maneuvers -- is beyond me. Well, for one thing, they'd never replaced the bearer of bowties, down there. That office must have resembled the proverbial "Chinese Fire Drill", by then!

And, I guess, the estimable Mr. Turley had, by then, a good many other worries! For one thing, Washington Boulevard's revenue was "falling off the cliff"! In addition, there had been no one to keep track -- of who-had-how-many-cars! Mine -- or anyone else's! Or where -- any of them might be! Laughingly referred to -- as "Car Control"! Didn't exist!

Another happening -- of more than passing interest: The guy in Pontiac wound up under arrest -- and was, physically, ensconced in Oakland County's jail. He would be, eventually, facing more city, county, state -- and federal -- charges, than there are degrees, on your thermometer.

I managed to work my way through the governmental authority (which-ever-one-it-was) that was running the *Mobil* station -- till whatever they were going to do, to dispose of the operation. The result was -- that we increased our fleet! Boosted it up -- another 10 or 12 cars -- which Willard and I picked up, and delivered to our favorite *Standard Oil* station. The "bowtie guy" had had to sit, at the barely-operating station, out there, till all the cars had, finally, checked in! Fortunately, none had turned up missing! Or even badly-overdue!

I even talked Uncle Clete's brother -- into relinquishing his few cars, and also dropping out, of the glorious program.

That left Royal Oak -- and Northwood! We'd worked up a really good working arrangement -- with Rodger. In fact, his accountant started doing all of their paperwork -- for Willard (who was fast becoming quite a "gentleman of leisure").

His lone problem -- was "Steve-o", at Northwood. And, by then, I'd reached a point -- where I'd always stood clear of "Old Attila". Willard had advised me -- from time to time -- that the station was "doing pretty well". And he'd been required to get them a car or two, every now and then. (Virtually all of those -- came, from Washington Boulevard. Hee Hee!)

They finally fired Franklin Turley! "Flash" Hollett returned -- "temporarily" -- to straighten everything out! He closed down Washington Boulevard. He offered Roland Yates the managership, of the downtown Philadelphia operation -- "take it ... or leave it". He took it!

That proved to have been -- a bit of irony! About three months -- previous to Yates' exit, heading east -- "Flash" had called me! And had offered me that same Pennsylvania billet! But, I'd turned it down! There'd been a good deal more money -- salary-wise -- involved. But, I was "too comfortable" -- where I was! And, besides, I'd gotten to where I was up-to-here -- with big corporations, in general. And *Clovis*, in particular! And my bosses appeared more credible, than ever -- when they'd questioned the steadiness of *Clovis*!

A month or so -- after "Flash's" return -- all hell broke loose. Willow Run was becoming "past tense"! There'd been that all-new, opulent-for-the-time, air terminal -- that came into being, in suburban Romulus. *Clovis* opened a, rather-lavish, operation there! And that was it! No other Detroit facilities! (How about that, sports fans?)

It has to be understood -- that, in the long span of time, since I'd lost the Washington Boulevard entity, not <u>that</u> many sales reps were staying, at the big downtown hotels. Not any longer. *Howard Johnson's* and the *Holiday Inns* -- along with a surprising number of smaller, individual, companies -- were setting up a multitude, of new-fangled <u>motels</u>! <u>Everywhere</u>! So, the "heyday" -- of an office, like Washington Boulevard -- was fast becoming extinct. (A <u>reality</u>! But, it broke my <u>heart</u>!)

And -- eventually -- Mr. Hollett turned his attention to the, long-moribund, substation program! He <u>cancelled</u> it! Brought "The Bowtie Kid" back downtown -- to assist him. A brilliant move. I'd long since developed a new respect for Willard. And he <u>was</u> back in his element!

Rodger -- in Royal Oak -- was ready to "throw in the towel", anyway. So, he simply let *Clovis* pick up his cars. I'd <u>thought</u> that "Steve-o" -- at Northwood -- would/could work out some kind of deal! But, he and "Flash" couldn't <u>stand</u> one another -- and almost came to fisticuffs, at their only meeting!

Mr. Hollett had to get some kind, of court order -- and actual <u>police</u> enforcement -- to finally "repo" the *Clovis* cars, out there!

John and Gene? They worked out a <u>deal</u>! (Denks God!) They <u>bought</u> all 67 cars, from "Flash"! (At a <u>much</u>-reduced price-per-unit, I'm sure!) Then, they set up their <u>own</u> DBA. I was <u>still</u> in business. Not only <u>that</u>, I did <u>not</u> have to work the drive, any longer. (Well, I hadn't! Not in months! Not all that often, anyway!)

The years went on! We, ultimately, got up to 85 units -- and *Colonial Car Rental* turned out to be eminently successful! Eminently successful! And the generous raises in pay -- were more than gratifying!

I'd never been so comfortable in my life! I even indulged -- in taking piano lessons, for heaven's sakes. Piano lessons! Something I'd always lusted for! Ever since I was a little boy! And -- over the following almost-two-years -- I became quite proficient at it! (If I do say so, myself!) It had been a lifelong "vocation" (almost, anyway) for me. I was known -- since I was, maybe, seven or eight -- to be a "music nut". Just never had realized any means of really satisfying this "basic need". Or this helluva want, anyway.

In late 1970, Gene fell ill! Massive heart attack! The medical setback was devastating -- not only physically, but emotionally. The affliction was felt -- throughout the gas station employees, and clientele -- where he was dearly loved! Dearly loved!

Most of us visited him -- usually during the evening hours -- once he'd been allowed to return home. I was a caller, probably as often, as most.

And I got to know his wife, Audrey, quite well. She and I had, of course, made acquaintances a few years before. But, I'd never really gotten to know her -- or her teenage daughter, Vernadine -- till Gene's unfortunate attack.

In their, rather-expansive, home -- in the eastern end of Birmingham -- they'd, for years, sported a beautiful concert grand piano! I'd never had the cherished opportunity to ever have played on one of those. My instructor had always come the half-mile -- to my apartment. (Which must have "pleased" my fellow tenants. Those first, dozen-or-so, lessons had been pretty grim.) So, the only instrument -- on which I'd ever played -- was my own, 35- or 40-year-old, *Kimball* upright (which had badly needed tuning, at the beginning). An old, out-to-lunch-fashion-wise, blond-wood, number. And here, I was beholding a bona fide concert grand!

I'd asked my hostess -- if it would be all right, if I "tickled the ivories ... a little bit". Being the kindly woman that she was, she'd invited me to "knock myself out"! Which I did!

I'd built a fairly substantial "repertoire" -- of mostly "schmaltzy" old songs -- by then. It had taken some doing -- in those pre-internet days -- but, I'd found an old book, of Rodgers & Hart music. Then, another one! This new treasure, containing a multitude of songs, by Jerome Kern -- and by Irving Berlin. Added to them, were smaller books -- containing the memorable scores from *My Fair Lady, Oklahoma, Carousel* and *The Most Happy Fella*. (All schmaltz! The interest had never "took" -- when it had come, to rock and roll. It was schmaltz -- or nothing!)

In any case, the tune I was most adept at playing -- at that point -- had been Rodgers & Hart's *Lover*! And I'd wound up dazzling Audrey! Not only my hostess -- but, her daughter! Even Gene hollered -- from the back bedroom -- to "play it again, Sam"! (The worst Bogart impression -- I'd ever heard.)

I'd finally wound up -- giving a, more-or-less, "concert", on that magic night! And -- I don't know what possessed me -- but, I sang (rather softly) the lyric to *My Heart Stood Still* (another R&H ballad). Can you imagine? They wanted me -- honestly -- to sing something else! I was able to muddle through *My Heart Is So Full Of You* -- one of my all-time favorites, from Frank Loesser's *Most Happy Fella*. Then, I "trilled" Irving Berlin's *Always*.

Audrey reached into the piano bench "cavern" -- after asking me to rise, of course -- and withdrew the sheet music, to her all-time favorite ballad, *September Song*. I'd never seen the, black-and-white, musical scoring, of the very-beautiful song before -- although I was more than a little familiar with it.

It took me no less than five times through -- but, the fifth rendition was the charm! I "did all right", with the tune! Then, Vernadine asked me to sing the, emotionally-gripping, lyric. I did that well enough -- that Audrey presented me, with the actual sheet music. But, I was admonished -- by the daughter -- to bring it back, with me, whenever I was coming to visit.

I was so moved by the "command", that -- at home, over the next two or three weeks -- I'd wound up practicing the poignant work often enough, that I'd actually mastered it! Had even committed it -- to memory!

These "performances" became a three-or-four-times-a-week staple! I was, absolutely -- in "Seventh Heaven". These hokey gatherings -- gave me a, really-out-of-the-blue, opportunity to "hone" my musical "skills"! Not only my "pianistic" talents -- but, my soft "vocal stylings". (I'd never forgotten that Nat Cole had once proclaimed that he was not a singer. He was a "song stylist". In a manner of speaking, I was trying to emulate him.)

Significantly, Gene seemed to enjoy the "cornball" sessions! He'd even reached an encouraging point -- where he'd ask to be wheeled out, to the living room. Eventually, he was able -- to walk out, unaided! (YAY!)

The two partners finally decided -- at that point -- to sell the station! "It has been a good run" -- both of them would say, at various times. Had said -- quite often!

John and Gene found a buyer -- almost immediately! The new owner did not want to keep me on. He'd wanted his "own personnel" to run "the rent-a-car gig". That turned out to be his wife -- who proved to be very proficient, in the position. So, there went the old job -- for moi! But, I was not panicking! I felt that something good -- would work out for me. (It always had!)

The really wonderful pair -- for whom I'd worked so long -- "sold" me (they practically gave it to me) a low-mileage, 1969, Chrysler two-door sedan. They'd always known -- ever since that, almost-retro-looking, model had come out -- that I'd loved the body style.

The new owner was smart enough -- to have retained John's and Gene's mechanics, and their service attendants! So, the whole, entire, adventure had turned out well. (Except for Gene's heart attack, of course. And he appeared to be "doing not bad", denks God!)

And what was I -- your humble correspondent -- going to do for "gainful employment"? More good fortune!

Audrey's sister -- a, well-put-together, lady named Vi -- had just bought a bar! On Cass Street! In "Beautiful Downtown Detroit"! Audrey, then, convinced her to install a piano/bar! Which she did!

And she hired ME!!!!!

THREE

That brings us up to 1971 -- where we were at, at the beginning of this scholarly diatribe. I was working -- plying, by then, my wares, at the piano/bar, in Vi's saloon! The joint was located, as stated, on Cass Avenue -- bordering northern downtown Detroit. An area, where -- as also stated -- a substantial number of "hostesses of horizontal pleasure" were plying their, substantially-different, wares.

This was a, surprisingly-large, residential section -- albeit generously interspersed, with a fairly-large number of commercial sites. I worked six nights each week -- from 9:00PM-till-2:00AM (closing time). We were closed on Sundays. Vi had an efficient, nightly, crew -- to clean up -- so, we were usually "out of there", once we could chase the last customer, into the night. I wasn't making anywhere near -- what John and Gene had been paying me. But, still, I was happy. Vi was so neat to work for. And -- most importantly -- I was enjoying what I was doing! Immensely! It was not "work"!

One evening -- after about three months, on the job -- I was making my way down Cass -- strolling the two blocks, from the lot, where I'd always parked my, elongated-looking, Chrysler -- when it happened!

There -- amidst the usual number of hookers -- I spied her! It was Ruthie! It was! My old "cohort" -- from those blessed Washington Boulevard days! It had been a decade -- more or less -- since I'd last heard of her!

She'd been oh-so-pregnant, then! And, tragically, bleeding from her vagina! Washing walls and floors and toilets (to pay her rent)! Grappling with twins (who'd been born with an RH-Negative blood disorders)! And having to deal -- with a deadbeat husband! (Other than that, she'd been in pretty good shape.)

On this 1971 evening, she was wearing a "something I'd just sprayed on", (i.e. very-tight) dark-green, dress -- which featured a devastatingly-short skirt. The, seen-better-days, frock pulled flush -- against her, still-to-die-for, bottom. The top, though, of this, probably-at-one-time-expensive, number was even more eye-catching. Surprisingly, it was a high-neckline fashion -- with an exceptionally interesting "slit". The "opening" was very narrow, where it began -- just below her right shoulder. But, it widened -- noticeably -- as it swept across her firm, jutting, breasts! It was patently obvious -- that she was not wearing a bra. And she'd still possessed the body -- that could "get away" with lack of such an, otherwise-necessary, accoutrement!

This was my Ruthie? My Ruthie? All of a sudden, she was a "lady of easy virtue"? Well, maybe not so all-of-a-sudden? Could this, possibly, be?

"Ruthie!" I hollered!

There was -- for the slightest instant -- the, unmistakable, sign of total recognition! It had shown -- ever so briefly -- on her, still-lovely, face! But, only for the swiftest, of seconds! She turned to face me! And I beheld the damndest facial expression! Unlike anything I'd ever seen before!

"You've got the wrong person, Mister," she'd rasped.

Her voice was a strange blend, of unidentifiable ingredients -- none of which were the least bit familiar to me. Yet, I knew that it was the voice of Ruthie. Of that, I was certain! Positive!

"I don't know you, Mister," she'd added -- a tired dimension, now rounding out her tone. "Never saw you before ... in my whole life!"

"Ruthie," I responded -- albeit much weaker than I could've imagined. "Ruthie? Ruthie ... I know it's you! This is you! I know it's you! It's so good ... so great ... to see you again! After all these years!"

"I don't know what you're talking about, Mister. Have no idea!"

Obviously, I was getting nowhere! And I'd not the faintest idea -- as to what to do! What to say! How do you handle such a situation? I -- most assuredly -- was not doing well! Most assuredly!

"Look," I finally managed to explain, "I work at this bar, here. Play the piano. Big piano/bar. Please! I'd love to be able ... to talk to you! Talk with you! I've really missed you! I have, Ruthie! Missed you ... ever since our days at *Clovis*! Our wonderful days ... downtown! At Washington Boulevard! Please! Please come in ... and see me! At the bar! Anytime! Any time! Please!"

"I still don't know ... what the hell you're talking about, Mister. My name's not Ruthie, for God's sake! I'm ... I'm 'Fascination'. That's my name! So, give it up!"

"Aw c'mon, Ruthie! 'Fascination'? You can do better ... than that! Please ... try and feel comfortable! Comfortable enough ... to come in, and see me! I'll even play *My Funny Valentine*, for you! Would love to play it, for you!"

That put just the slightest bit -- of a, rather-startled, expression -- on her lovely face! But then, I'd figured -- that it was probably best, that I "quit, while I'm ahead". (Or, at least, not quite so far behind.) So, I continued on -- into my place of employment. For whatever good that might prove to be.

For virtually the entire shift, that night, I'd continued to (constantly) watch the door -- hoping that the next patron in, would be Ruthie! T'was not to be!

And, over the next three or four days -- well, three or four nights -- I'd looked through the "ready line", of hookers, on my way in. No <u>Ruthie</u>! (I really don't know what I would've done -- or said -- <u>had</u> I been able to encounter her.)

Each time -- once I'd settled in, at the piano/ bar -- there'd been a certain amount of, inexplicable, <u>relief</u>; at the absence, of yet <u>another</u> confrontation, with her. But -- in each case -- a sense of, undeniable, frustration would also build, and <u>overtake</u> the stupid relief! <u>Obliterate</u> it!.

I'd <u>refrained</u>, on those nights, from playing/ singing *My Funny Valentine* -- one of my many, many "standards". One of our "regulars" -- Marilyn -- a, presumably-single, woman, in her late-fifties -- asked me about it. <u>Twice</u>! So, on the third night, I "broke down" -- and did the tune. From the <u>heart</u>! <u>That</u> rendition moved Marilyn! <u>Noticeably</u>!

Then -- after the better part of a week (I <u>believe</u> it was the following Monday) -- there she <u>was</u>! It was a few minutes past 10:45PM -- when she'd, unsteadily, found her way in, to the bar! <u>Finally</u>! At long <u>last</u>!

<u>Now what do I do</u>?

What I <u>did</u> -- was to stop playing, whatever song I'd been halfway through! And to start playing -- *My Funny Valentine*! I'd begun to "stylize" my best -- on Lorenz Hart's poignant lyric -- as she'd, unsteadily, seated herself, immediately to my left!

The crowd, at that point, was on the sparse side. I looked over at Vi -- behind the bar. She was aware, of course, as to who (or, really, what) Ruthie was. I'd thought that I'd get a disapproving glare! Instead, it was a quizzical grin! Actually, a look -- of pure puzzlement! I didn't know what to make of that! It was, of course, the least of my concerns!

There were only four people -- a rather-elderly couple, Marilyn, and a thirty-something lady, I'd never seen before -- seated at my hokey little site. And none of them seemed upset -- with the fact that I'd surprised myself, by launching into a, quite-extended, version of "Funny Valentine"! Virtually all of these efforts, though -- were turning out to be strictly instrumental.

The reason was -- that Ruthie's first, hushed, raspy, words to me were, "Why did you start to play that?"

"You once told me that it was your favorite song," I'd answered -- not missing a note. "Remember? You said that your father called you 'his funny valentine'. Don't you remember? Remember that I'd had a couple of versions ... on my old, reel-to-reel, tape recorder, at the office, on Washington Boulevard? Remember? I'd always liked Eydie Gorme's recording best. But, you ... you'd always preferred Gordon Jenkins' version ... from the forties. The singer, on that rendition, wasn't even a professional vocalist. It was Charles LaVere ... Jenkins' piano-player, for heaven's sake. We used to talk about that."

"Yes," she answered -- almost tearfully. "And you must remember, that there was something ... a certain something ... in his voice, on that recording. In Charlie's voice. Something ... that would always touch me. Touch me ... deeply. I dunno."

"Ruthie? Ruthie ... it's so good ... good to see you again! I've missed you! Really missed you! And, hell ... I've worried about you! Really worried about you! Still had! Still have! Even ... after all these years!"

"Well, it's a long story. I'll have to tell you about it ... sometime."

"You'll tell me about it ... tonight! I get a break ... a 'pause for the cause', don'tcha know. And I'm fixin' to take it ... right now! I want you ... to get to that back booth, over there! And then, I'm going to want you ... to fill me in! And I'm damn well ... not gonna let you get away from me! Not this time!"

More obediently than I would've expected, she'd grabbed up her beaded handbag -- and headed, for the designated booth. Immediately, I brought my first session, of the night, to a quick, abrupt, end -- and joined her.

"Now," I began -- more forcefully than I could ever have imagined, "tell me all about yourself. Is that original ... or what? Last I'd heard, you were pregnant as hell, bleeding from the unmentionable spot, cleaning latrines, scrubbing floors ... and, in general, living it up! Then your shapely fanny disappeared! Why? Where? Where did you go? And *when*? Fill ol' Bob *in*! And don't leave *anything* ... not one damn *thing* ... leave it out! *Go*!"

"Well, you know, you're asking a *lot*! A *hell* of a lot! First of all, I managed to deal ... to deal successfully ... with the bleeding. Hadda go on welfare ... to get it taken *care* of! And the lady, that got assigned to me ... *she* was *wonderful*. An OB-GYN! One who was just starting out ... on her practice."

"She *solved* that? *Solved* it ... for you? Made you all *well*? *Cured* you?"

"Well not *completely*! She didn't solve *all* my problems! But, she *did* do wonders for me. Brought all the *worst* stuff ... the really *bad* stuff ... brought it under control! There were *other* things, though! *Other* things, y'know ... mostly emotional ... that she got in to, with me! And kind of guided me through. For instance, I gave up the *baby*! Gave her up ... after I'd *had* her! *Healthy* baby! No RH-Negative problems! *Nothing* like that! *Beautiful* little girl! Simply *beautiful*! But, I went ahead ... and put her *up*! Up for ... you know ... up, for *adoption*!"

"*Really*? You gave her *up*?"

"Yep! *Look*, Bob! I *had* to! The good doctor absolutely *convinced* me ... that it was the only *answer*! And she got me to throw Rudy's ... my *husband's* ... throw *his* ass ... throw it *out*! Hadda get the sheriff ... to come! Come ... and do the deed! Get his ass ... get it the hell ... out of there! *Physically*!"

"Holy *mackerel*! I never *knew*!"

"I'm sure! Rudy was really pissed! Really pissed off! That I'd given the baby up! He could care less ... about having kids, under foot! It was that I'd made the decision! Which meant that he ... automatically ... didn't approve! And you really can't cross him! You don't cross him! Not Rudy! Not without ... all hell breaking loose! So, I left! Took off! In that stupid-assed Cadillac convertible! The one ... that he'd so deeply loved! Took the twins ... and the Caddy ... and I, damn well, split!"

"Really? Well, that's what I'd heard. But, I didn't ... I never ..."

"Went ... drove to ... drove out to California! Los Angeles area. Didn't know anyone, out there. But, neither did Rudy ... thank God! Figured it would be easy for me to 'get lost' ... fall through the cracks ... out there, in L.A.! Couldn't get a job, though! Not right away, anyway."

"Yeah. I don't imagine you could."

I didn't have hardly any money! So, I made my debut! As a ... ta-DAH! ... whore! Became a goddam streetwalker! A frigging hooker! Did pretty well, though! Really well ... in a few instances! And so, I 'hung in there' ... with 'The Profession'! Of course, I was a good deal younger ... and a helluva lot better lookin' ... back then!

"You're still a beautiful woman!"

"Don't shit the troops, Bob! Everything's going to hell ... looks-wise! I'm sagging! All over the place!

Anyway, I got me a nice apartment, out there. Got to where I could even afford a, live-in, nanny ... for the twins. Before that, I'd left 'em alone! Had to! For ... like .... hours, at a time! Totally irresponsible, of me! But, there wasn't much else I could do! Still, I'm really not proud of it! Proud of anything! Far from it!"

"Well," I sighed, "I guess there wasn't much you could do. Things, apparently, did work out, for you. Eventually."

"Not really! I lost the twins! Somehow, Rudy managed ... to track me down! Tracked them down! The twins, I mean! He snatched 'em ... from me! Actually ... from the nanny! To this day ... to this very night ... I still don't know where they are! Where the hell they might be! Haven't the foggiest damn idea!"

"How'd that happen? How could all that happen?"

"Well, my hands were pretty much tied! You'd be surprised ... or maybe you wouldn't ... at how many, of my customers were interested, in stuff that was not straight sex! Mostly stuff ... that their wives, or girlfriends, couldn't do! Or wouldn't do. Mostly, refused to do! Wouldn't give it to 'em!"

"I know that I'm leading ... with my chin. But, like what? What were ... ?"

"You may find this tough to believe ... but, many of them wanted me to simply spank them! Well, some ... to actually beat them!"

"I'd heard of such things, y'know. But ..."

"So ... after I got me a pretty good fund built up ... I rented me, a fancy townhouse! A rather *opulent* one! Three floors! And I'd set up a, 'for-real', *dungeon* ... a real-life *dungeon* ... on the ground floor! Had even a *jail* cell ... eventually ... built right in! *Lots* of whips and chains ... and restraints! *Shackles*! Stuff like *that*! Some of the 'toys' were ... well, were pretty *exotic*! And *expensive* as hell!"

"*Really*? What about the *kids*? The *twins*?"

"*They* were restricted ... from the first floor. Living room, dining room ... and kitchen ... *they* were, all on the second floor. *That* was our *home*! Three bedrooms ... all up, on the third floor. Including one ... for the nanny. I *think* that the kids had reached a *bit* of knowledge ... as to what was going *on*! Things, that were taking place ... down, on the ground *floor*. The *nanny* ... for *sure* ... did! *She* knew! For *sure*!"

"How did *Rudy* ... how did he *ever* ... ?"

"Well, I got a little too *cute*! Too cute ... for my *pants*! Too cute ... for my *panties*! For my own *good*! They'd had a *lot* of *underground* publications, out there, back then! Still *do*, I guess! And I was running a really big *ad* ... in a couple of 'em! Advertised myself ... as 'Madam *Xaviera*! Or, maybe it was *Mistress* Xaviera! Don't remember which! *Somehow*, Rudy ... the son of a bitch ... he was able to identify me! From the goddam *ad*! I have *no* idea *how* he was able to put that together! Have idea ... as to where he was! Or where he is ... now! Where he could be ... now! With my kids!"

"How did he kidnap 'em? I mean, the nanny must have ..."

"At gunpoint! That's how! Real damn gun! Big one! Threatened her! The nanny! Threatened ... to shoot her! And then ... he herded the kids out! Out ... and away! Last any of us ever saw ... or heard from ... them! Any of them!"

"Dear Lord! I can't even imagine ..."

"That wasn't the worst of it! Well, yes it was! The worst of it, I mean! But, he'd turned me ... turned me in! Reported me! To the goddam authorities! The place was crawling ... with Los Angeles police! Cops! All kinds ... of cops! Sheriff's deputies! Plainclothes men! The whole damn works! The nanny? She turned on me! Turned State's Evidence! I wound up in jail! Almost three goddam years! Three goddam years! Locked up!"

"I can't believe this! Any of this!"

"You would ... if it happened to you! Believe me ... you would! When I got out ... no one would touch me! Not even any ... of the carload, of pimps, out there! Couldn't even go back to my old profession ... of being a damn streetwalker. Under threat ... of physical mutilation! Physical harm ... threatened by everyone! Everyone ... in the whole goddam world!"

"Dear Lord!"

"So, I left! Left the damn state! Came back here! And you've seen ... the wholesome way, that I've been operating!"

"Well, you've got to stop! Gotta stop ... operating that way! This very night! No more!"

"You talk mighty big, Sheriff!"

"Well, I was never more serious ... in my entire life! Where do you live, these days?"

"I don't live ... anywhere. I stay ... I exist ... in a, flea-bitten, rooming house. About three-and-a-half blocks from here. Share a cramped room ... with two other whores! One of whom ... never seems to bathe! Or to even use a damn tampon!"

"Well, them days are over! You're coming home! Coming home ... with me!"

"Well, I'm not gonna lay you! Not gonna let you screw me! That'd be too close to home ... if you get my drift! Screw up ... literally ... all that I think I feel for you!"

"If you even try ... try to lay me ... you're the one who's gonna get spanked!"

"I might even enjoy that! Listen! You get so tired ... so sick of ... being the one, who's always in authority! The one ... who always gives the orders! The outrageous orders! The one ... whose word absolutely goes! No matter ... how much, stupid-assed, playacting is involved, in the game! And that's what it always is! A stupid-assed game! A silly scenario!"

"No playacting involved," I responded. "As of right now, you're out of the whoring business!"

We'd, eventually, repaired -- to the piano/bar. I'd finished out my shift -- singing/playing, mostly, the familiar, schmaltzy, ballads. Including *My Funny Valentine,* three or four times. The bar had been scantly occupied, when two o'clock rolled by. Ruthie and I left -- at about 15 minutes, after closing.

There was a newly-opened *7-11* store -- open 24 hours -- on Maple, just across Woodward from where I lived. I stopped there -- and bought a big container of the most-erotic body-rub lotion, that they'd stocked. (I also bought her an ice cream-on-a-stick -- to enjoy, on the way to my apartment.)

Once there -- without so much as one spoken word -- we'd both removed our clothes, and had, immediately, enjoyed (immensely) a, very-hot-water, shower! Together! I'd soaped her down -- regretting the fact that I'd not even looked for a, more-esoteric, bar of soap. Other than the slab, of *Ivory,* that had been my "normal" stock in trade. My guest seemed quite appreciative -- for the attention, that I was "lavishing" upon her. The unexpected attention.

Then, using one of my, too-stiff, towels, I dried her off! Again, much gratefulness -- for my "devotion to duty".

Once the Murphy bed was engaged, I'd had her lie, on her tummy -- and I took the better part, of an hour, massaging her! She'd always been a very attractive woman! But, lying there -- naked -- she was absolutely, stunningly, beautiful! None of that unclothed splendor was -- surprisingly, or not -- sexually stimulating, to/for me! Not at that point!

I was solely devoted -- to her complete comfort! And it had worked! For, after awhile, Ruthie was totally -- and completely -- asleep! Seemingly, almost beyond being awakened! For a good while, anyway!

Things, at that point -- in the "therapy" -- became quite foggy. For me, anyway. We both woke up -- at shortly before noon, the following morning. Neither of us had any clothes on. I'd not really intended to remove my own "rags". Don't really remember -- doing so.

But, there we were! Both naked! Each of us lying on our left side -- in a sort of fetal position! The back of her body -- pressed, firmly, against the front of mine! Or vice-versa! I felt her stir! She was facing my large-faced alarm clock, on the bedside stand.

"Holy crap!" she exclaimed. "Do you realize what time it is?"

I'd answered -- with something like, "Fmmmmph?"

"It's almost noon! I can't imagine ... could never imagine ... sleeping this long! What happened last night? The last thing I remember ... was you rubbing me down! Rubbing me up? Did ... ah ... anything else happen? You know what I'm talking about!"

"Nope. Not a thing! We both remain ... as virtuous, as angels. I kind of pooped myself out ... during the operation. Don't even remember ... getting myself naked!"

"Well, I probably shouldn't say this ... but, I'm glad you did. Helluva way to wake up! Quite a sensation, y'know! Hasn't happened to me ... haven't felt such a thing, like this ... in, actually, years! Decades, maybe! Decades probably!"

"All part of the soivice. How're you feeling?"

"Great! Are you sure ... that nothing happened?"

"Couldn't be more positive! Didn't think that we were ready ... either one of us ... for such things. Hell, we may never be ready ... for such things."

"Well, I don't know about that! But ... for the nonce ... you're probably right."

I moved backward -- and away from her. Then, I slapped her, on her shapely bottom, and asked, "Are we ready to get up?"

"Ow! That hurt! But ... since you're being so insistent ... it probably is time, for us to roll on out."

We "rolled on out" -- and headed for the bathroom. While I began to run the shower, she sat, on the commode -- and relieved herself; which was a bit of a surprise. Maybe it shouldn't have been! But, it was!

As had happened, the night before, I lathered her up -- generously -- and, wishing the washcloth would've been eons softer, I did my best to bathe my guest. After about 15 minutes, of such an operation, we discovered that the supply, of hot water, had not been as inexhaustible -- as had been the indication, in the wee-small hours. So, we exited. And I dried her off. Gently! She seemed to accept the "service"! Accept it -- gratefully!

We dressed! Seeing her don that confounding dress -- was giving me a bit of a problem. She could tell. She didn't have to be particularly perceptive.

"It's been my uniform-of-the-day, now. For far too long." Her voice was almost deserting her. Far too long. But, listen. It was the only decent thing I'd had ... to wear. Although, it's far ... from being altogether decent."

«Well, before we go out to eat breakfast ..."

"Can't we eat here?"

"We could, I suppose. But, it's kinda important, to me ... to buy you a nice breck-breck. Is that all right?"

"I'd love to break my fast ... with you. No matter where!"

"But, first ... I would like to take you to *K-Mart*! Is that class ... or what? Get you some serviceable stuff ... to wear. Knock-around clothing! Get rid of that damnable abortion ... of a dress! I hate that damn dress!"

"Well, it was a ... necessary ... 'tool of the trade', y'know."

"Except that ... now you're out of that particular trade! And I'd love to burn that, shit-assed, frock!"

"Now? Burn it ... here and now? You may have noticed ... but, I'm not wearing anything, under this 'shit-assed frock'."

"Well, you can continue to wear nothing ... under the 'shit-assed frock'. But, how about ... temporarily ... wearing one, of my shirts? And, maybe, a pair of my slacks? You can roll up the pant legs. I'll take you over to *K-Mart*. Again, I ask: Is that class ... or what? And we'll get you some casual stuff. You pick it out. But, I hope you'll select a few dresses ... and/or some skirts and blouses. I hate that women are ... more and more ... wearing, stupid-assed, slacks. And even jeans. I've seen some ... wearing jeans and high-heels, together. Org!"

"Yes. I've noticed. Even the jeans and heels."

"We'll get you something feminine ... hopefully feminine, anyway ... to wear. Then, there's a really neat restaurant ... on Woodward, on up toward Pontiac ... that I'd like to introduce you to. Then, once we've packed away a few groceries, for breakfast, we can go to this really nice ladies clothing store ... and get you a frock, or three. Something ... that you can really be proud of. In the meantime, put that stupid dress ... in the bathtub. And ... when we get back ... we'll set fire, to the ridiculous thing. I hate it!"

"Tell me," she laughed, "what do you really think ... of the dress?"

❖

I'd had no idea -- when I'd suggested that Ruthie don a shirt and pair of slacks, of mine -- how completely feminine she would wind up looking. But, she wound up "abusing the privilege"! She'd tied the shirt's tail. Knotted it, in front. As loose as it was, the converted top accentuated her breasts! And, though the pants were a little baggy, around the seat, the "back flap", of the shirt's tail, covered that particular expanse. Left a good bit -- to the imagination. (Especially a warped one -- like mine.)

As advertised, we'd headed to *K-Mart*. Ruthie was like the proverbial kid -- in the proverbial candy store. We came out -- loaded down with three or four sets of skirts and blouses, a sweater or two, two shirtwaist dresses, an assortment of bras and panties. (Some, of those "unmentionables" were "disgustingly serviceable", and very Spartan. But, a few were located -- on the [hoo HAH!] risqué side!) Those items -- along with numerous pairs of pantyhose. Even a rather wide-reaching selection, of cosmetics (which I'd not thought of -- till she'd, quite-apologetically, brought up the subject).

Then, on to the drive-in/coffee shop! That sanctified site -- where John and Gene and I had originated our employment deal, that long ago. I'd pretty well established nifty relationships -- with virtually all of the "worker bees" there, over the years.

Ruthie fell in love with the place! Most especially with their strawberry whipped-cream pie!

After packing away more calories -- than either one of us would care to acknowledge -- we'd headed for an exclusive, ladies fashion, outlet. We spent a little more than I'd, initially, cared to fund -- for two dresses. But, refer to the, kid-in-a-candy store remark, shown above -- vis-a-vis Ruthie! It turned out to be a <u>most</u> rewarding expedition! I didn't regret <u>one</u> moment! (Or one <u>dollar</u>!)

It was, as indicated, an expensive -- but, rewarding -- shopping excursion. And, on the way back to the apartment, I'd gotten a container, of charcoal lighter!

And we <u>did</u> burn that stupid dress -- in the bathtub! First thing!

❖

Thus began a, rather-stilted, "feel your way", relationship -- with Ruthie. Never known -- for my sense, of "being on top of things" ("downright imperceptive", so many people have opined) I still sensed, that our personal interrelations would be very precarious. For who-knew-how-long? Not unlike walking on those proverbial eggs. So, I did my best -- to try and "think things through", before doing (or saying) anything! (So unlike me.)

Although we'd would wind up sleeping together -- and in the nude -- our situation took all of four-days-plus, before it ever became sexual! On the other hand, when it did "bloom", it became ultra-sexual -- in spades!

During that critical fourth night -- at along about four-thirty, in the morning -- she'd awakened me (from a, rather-troubled, sleep).

"Bob?" The voice, at first, seemed to be coming from Saturn, or someplace. "Bob?" she repeated. "Do you, maybe, think I'm ... that I'm ... I'm unattractive?"

"Unattractive?" I came out of my stupor -- immediately! "Unattractive? You? Of course not!"

"Then, why have you ... ah ... stayed, on your side, of the bed? In short, why have you not screwed me? Never screwed me! I may not be a raving beauty. But, I really thought that ..."

"You're wrong! Wrong, Ruthie! You are a raving beauty! Definitely are!"

"Then, why do I remain so ... ah ... so unscrewable?"

"You're not! You're certainly not ... not unscrewable!"

"Then, why am I not properly screwed? Why have I not been thoroughly screwed? It's been four damn days, now ... and I ..."

"I just thought that, given your ... given your experiences ... over the past number of years ... I just simply thought, that you'd kind of welcome a ..."

"A holiday? Some relief? A respite? From my ... troubled ... former life? From my 'heart-rending-experiences'?"

"Well ... uh ... yeah. I guess."

"Look ... Bob. Did it ever occur to you? Occur to you ... that, maybe, I have feelings? Feelings ... for you? I don't know as they're feelings of love, exactly. Don't rightly know what they are. Feelings of affection, maybe? Possibly feelings of admiration? I just don't damn know! But, there's something ... something that I really feel, for you! And it ain't platonic! Not purely, anyway! Otherwise, I really would never have slept with you! Sexually ... or non-sexually! Hell, I wouldn't even have let you see me ... see me naked! I never ... really ... never would've come, into the bar. Gonne into that bar ... on that night. God knows ... I sure as hell didn't intend to! Not until ..."

"Yeah, but Ruthie ..."

"I appreciate the fact that ... am grateful for the fact that ... you wanted to give me a respite. A 'time off' ... from my former life! Grateful as hell, I am! But, I do have these ... these feelings. These feelings ... for you, What ever, in hell, they might be! And, I'd like for you ... hell, I'd love for you ... to screw me! Screw me good ... as we say!"

Now, who could possibly refuse -- to honor that modest request?

❖

As the weeks seemed to, quickly, roll by, Ruthie and I had, pretty much, settled in. Fallen in -- to a, fairly-comfortable, non-threatening, unexciting, routine. Nothing outstanding (let alone spectacular) appeared to be happening. Or in the immediate offing.

We'd developed a, really-nifty, practice (a ritual, if you will) -- of doing "brunch" -- most late mornings. At the glorious eatery -- just north of Birmingham. These enjoyable practices -- usually wound up lasting almost-two-hour, sessions, up there. Almost always, they were capped off with generous slices -- of that, highly-decadent, strawberry/whipped-cream pie. Ruthie loved it up there -- and the staff, up there, got to where they loved her. (Hence, the "always-generous" slices!)

Afternoons were, most often, spent -- with the two of us listening to boodles of schmaltzy music, on my stereo. Sometimes in the nude! Sometimes not! No matter our state of dress, she seemed completely overwhelmed, by the number -- and variety -- of the many LP records I'd accumulated, over the years. And the many different recordings -- of *Mt Funny*

Valentine, in the sizeable collection. Plus, some of the other -- even more-sentimental -- lyrics would move her to tears! Literally!

On most nights, I'd take her into the bar with me. I'm not sure whether Vi was thrilled, by the arrangement. She was (I could tell) happy -- that my "new squeeze" was always dressed far more tastefully, than on her initial visit.

There were times -- when toiling over the piano/bar -- that my feelings toward Ruthie (whatever they might've been) would, positively, come to the surface. In almost-overwhelming quantities! On those, rarified, nights, I'd always wind up playing -- and singing -- *My Funny Valentine,* five or six times. Those occasions, most always, prompted an unmistakable fisheye from Vi. But, those, visual, "daggers" -- always seemed to have been, of the non-lethal variety. (Thank God! I didn't really need any further complications!)

Eventually, as our time together rolled on, I'd begun to notice that Ruthie's sleep was becoming more and more fitful! More labored! Trouble in paradise? Listen, her tossing and turning was proving to be much more troubling -- to me! Virtually every morning, I would attempt to draw her out. (But, never over "brunch". I was loath to louse up

<u>those</u> "enchanted", strawberry-and-whipped-cream, experiences.)

As far as I could ever get her to level with me -- was the fact that she was having "simply horrible" dreams. But -- without exception -- she could <u>not</u> remember any <u>portion</u>, of the content, of these staggering nocturnal illusions! She <u>swore</u> to that! And I <u>believed</u> her! The God-awful contortions, that her pretty face would take on -- as she'd endeavor, to recall what she'd just envisioned -- solidified the fact, that she <u>was</u> being truthful!

At long last, she'd finally owned up, to the fact -- that not knowing the fate, of her twins, was beginning to "get to her". And were -- undoubtedly -- the cause, of her nightly torment! Not so <u>mysterious</u>, I guess. Where might her children might be? And/or whether they were with her sainted ex-husband (thriving or not)! Hence the, God-awful, <u>dreams</u>! The <u>unrelenting</u> nightmares! The, mind-twisting, tumult -- that this, ever-increasing, anxiety was producing! Each -- and every -- <u>night</u>! The, constantly-roiling, condition was, obviously, becoming less and less easy to deal with!

Gene's wife suggested -- a psychiatrist. Dr. Groom was a "dear friend" of hers. (What else?)

After a few sessions, with the good doctor (at what, I was convinced, were at a "substantially-discounted" rate) the "shrink" suggested -- that there were a number, of significant issues, "hidden ... deeply ... in the vast depths, of her, highly-troubled, subconscious"! Items that remained, substantially, "under the surface"! Were hidden there -- buried there -- until she was asleep. Then, upon her awakening, they simply -- "just disappeared"! "Went back underground!"

Dr. Groom suggested a novel treatment! A really novel treatment! A session -- in which the doctor would use *Sodium Pentothal* (aka "Truth Serum"). The good doctor, himself, had referred to it -- as "Flack Juice".

He'd warned that such sessions were "potentially very dangerous". They could result in "permanent ... irreparable ... damage, to the psyche". But, he was absolutely convinced -- that this type of "therapy" was the only way to "get to the bottom", of what was afflicting Ruthie, so badly! Was dragging her down -- measurably -- day by day! So, she agreed to undergo the "therapy"! Submit -- to a joust, with the "Flack Juice"!

I was not allowed "anywhere: near the office -- when the actual session would take place! Gene's wife took her to the doctor -- and then, she sat in on the entire examination! (Which I'd thought was highly unusual!)

The hour-long, "really unusual", session did result -- in a number of surprising (to me, anyway) "revelations! "Stuff," Dr. Groom seemed to have established, "that she'd heard her husband mention, from time to time ... whether he'd been asleep, or awake". Mostly the former, I'd gathered. They were, all of them, things that -- "for whatever reason" -- Ruthie's conscious mind refused to deal with. Or even recognize.

Seemingly, most significant -- of these many revelations -- was a name, "Hazel Whitcomb"! Her name -- and a small town, in Nebraska! Grand Island! That, apparently, had been mentioned -- often!

Upon review, Ruthie'd had no idea as to where the name -- or persona -- of Hazel Whitcomb would've come from. Totally unfamiliar with the name! But, she'd thought that Rudy -- her ex -- might have grown up, in Grand Island. ("It was somewhere ... some little town, in Nebraska," she'd acknowledged, once the effects, of the "Flack Juice" had, slowly, worn off.)

Gene had a "dear friend" (also, what else?) -- who was a detective, on the Birmingham Police Force. My former employer's wife turned over "every possibly significant item" from Ruthie's bout, with the "Truth Serum" -- to the officer.

The latter gave his "sacred pledge" -- that he'd track down "anything and everything" that he could possibly dig up!

FOUR

The Birmingham detective -- about a week-and-a-half later -- announced that he'd found nothing on a Hazel Whitcomb. "Not one thing!" There were, he'd discovered, only four Whitcombs -- in the Grand Island phone book. None had a name -- remotely similar to Hazel. Three were males. But, to be absolutely certain, he'd phoned each of them! None even knew, of a Hazel. The detective was positively convinced -- that none of these people could, possibly, have been connected with Rudy. Or anyone else -- in Ruthie's life.

He did uncover a fascinating aspect, though: There was a Rudolph Mortimer -- with whom the Grand Island Police Department was slightly familiar.

The sergeant -- with whom the detective had spoken -- said that the eminent Mr. Mortimer had wound up, with four recorded arrests. In each case, the "beef" was for DWI. They didn't "seem" to know all that much more about him, out there. Three of the cases had resulted -- in nominal fines. The most recent (eight months previous) had been "significant". The term went unexplained. That fourth charge had also resulted, in a "warning", which, seemingly -- "off the record" -- had proven to be ineffective.

There had been a dearth of official information -- regarding that last remark. Or the significance -- of the word "significant". The Grand Island contact had simply refused -- to comment any further. Despite the Birmingham detective's unrelenting efforts -- to draw him out.

When advised, of this little "Mortimer" nugget, Ruthie had turned "Casper Ghost White". Rudy's middle name, it turned out, was Mortimer. Another notable factor: While he'd been married, to my partner, he'd had more than a few, law-enforcement, encounters! Mostly run-ins -- with the Inkster, Michigan, police! All for drunk driving!

I arranged -- with Vi -- to take a couple of weeks' leave-of-absence! Of course, off we went to Nebraska. The Birmingham detective had given us the Mortimer's residence -- as listed, by the Grand Island police. Obviously, that would be the first location -- to which we'd be headed! The only logical starting-off point! The only imaginable starting-off point!

The place turned out to be a, well-kept, middle-sized, single-story, brick, bungalow -- located, in a middle-class neighborhood. There were no cars parked outside -- either in the street, or in the driveway -- when we'd arrived.

It was at that point -- that it occurred to both of us, that neither one of us knew what the hell we were going to do! Should we approach the joint? Ring the bell? Knock softly? Beg-your-pardon style? Knock loudly? Authoritatively? Right then? Wait awhile? How long?

Probably no one would be home, at present -- from all appearances! But, what if there was? What if someone was there? And he or she answered the door? Then, what? What do either of us say? What the hell do we do -- either of us -- for heaven's sake?

I know, what you're going to answer: It all depends! Everything pivots -- upon who might open the door! But, let me tell you: Logic isn't much help. Not in a situation like this one. So? So, we decided to do the "intelligent" (read "coward-like") thing. We'd wait! Indefinitely! Maybe infinitely! Put the joint "under observation", as we say.

We must've sat there -- for the better part of three whole, unending, hours. Looking -- stupidly -- at one another. It was getting close to five o'clock, in the evening. And the "novelty" -- had long since worn off. In addition, it seemed as though a multitude, of neighbors, must've been staring out their windows -- at suspicious old us! I'm sure that some of it -- maybe most of it -- was our own jittery imaginations, playing their outrageous games, with our heads. But -- most assuredly -- not all of it could be attributed, to this sort, of spookiness.

Finally -- at long last -- a six-year-old, shiny, bright-red, Cadillac convertible pulled into their driveway. That fact alone -- the inevitable Caddy convertible -- proved to be a warning! A soul-jarring event! For both of us!

The people inside the car -- had had the top up. When they began to disembark, it was the woman -- who climbed out first. From the driver's seat. Ruthie did not recognize her. Still, apparently, not much had changed -- driver-wise -- if, indeed, this was Rudy, and company.

It was! It was Rudy! He'd, finally, gotten out -- on the passenger's side!

"It's him!" gushed my distraught partner. "It's fucking him!"

But, that was not the complete passengers' manifest! I don't know how truly shocked Ruthie might've been! On the other hand, it (sure enough) rattled me! Head to toe! This was an added -- probably-unneeded -- dimension: A little girl -- who'd looked to be barely preteen -- appeared! She'd exited -- from the back seat!

We'd just sat there, Ruthie and I! In the front seat, of my Chrysler! And we simply stared, at one another! Then, back at the trio! What do we do now? What the hell -- do we do now? We were both shaking! Almost from head-to-toe! Literally! (Almost?)

We certainly couldn't go to the police! At least, we didn't think so. We'd had a nice story to tell them! Juicy, in fact! Erotic, even! But, nothing -- nada -- with which, to back anything up! We'd probably get laughed -- right out, of the place!

Still, on the other hand, we couldn't just simply *sit* there! Do *nothing*, more than -- to just shake our stupid heads, at one another! And mutter, "How *about* that?"!

"I'm going *in*!" That was Ruthie -- after about three mind-warping, interminable, minutes, during which our prey had disappeared, inside the house. "*Damn* the results," she'd snarled. "I'm going *in*! I don't know *what* I'm gonna *do* ... if I *get* in! *When* I get in! But ... I'm, fare-thee-well, going *in*! After all this *time* ... after all these goddam *miles* ... I'm going, fucking, *in*! Right *now*!"

Before old, tongue-tied, Bob, here, could say a word, she was up -- and *out* of the car! And headed across the street! I managed to, breathlessly, catch up with her -- as she'd gotten, to the front lawn! But, I'd not the foggiest idea -- as to what I was going to *do*! Or *say*! I *certainly* was not going to *stop* her!

She swept up the three steps -- onto the porch -- and mashed the button, to the doorbell! *Leaned* on it -- as a matter of fact! Four or five times! I'm sure that my conception of this particular time span is *way* off beam! But, it *seemed* as though I'd barely gotten both feet planted (in a manner of speaking) onto the porch -- when the door opened!

The *woman* had answered! Ruthie, immediately, pushed past her -- and confronted her former husband! He'd been standing -- in the middle, of the smallish living room! With his mouth -- *literally* -- hanging open! The little girl was seated on the circular stool -- in front of the old-looking upright piano! She was facing us! And frightened -- as she could be!

"Ruth ... Ruthie?" the man finally managed to croak out -- after what seemed like an eternity..

"You bet your sweet ass ... it's Ruthie!" answered the, obviously-uninvited, guest! "You can just bet your sweet ass ... that it is!"

"Rudy!" It was the woman -- still standing, incredulously, holding the inside handle, to the front door! "Rudy ... what is ... who is ... what's ... ?"

At the same time, the little girl screamed! That was the most jarring effect, of all! (So far, anyway!)

"Take it easy, Honey," counseled Ruthie, in the direction of our, obviously-tattled, hostess. She was still a foot or two -- from Rudy! And ignoring the child! That seemed strange! Hell, everything seemed incredible! Was incredible! "It's all right," repeated Ruthie, in the general direction, of our dismayed hostess.

So saying, she hauled off and conked her ex -- with a frightening, roundhouse, closed-fist blow! A punch -- that would've made George Foreman proud! Or would've buckled his knees! How our reluctant host ever withstood the force of the clobber, I'll never know! He was, however, not able to survive -- the well-aimed knee! Ruthie's right knee landed -- with "great prejudice" -- to a very vulnerable spot, of his, fast-crumpling, body!

He wound up, of course, on the *floor*! *Instantly*! Writhing about -- *relentlessly*! Clutching -- *fiercely* -- at his, undoubtedly-shattered, private parts!

Happily, the little girl didn't go "off the deep end"! Not *completely*! She simply sat -- like a marble statue -- on the piano stool! The look -- of out and out horror -- remained, however! From top to bottom! Blossomed -- to an even *sharper* degree!

Ruthie placed what *should've* been a lethal kick -- which landed, on our unappreciative host's right ribcage! I could hear *bones* -- being shattered! He was all *through*! (Well, he'd *been* all through -- for quite *awhile*!) He was *moaning* -- an indescribable animal sound -- still cringing, on the floor! *Writhing*! Big time! By then, the God-awful moaning was fast-turning -- to out and out *crying*! (To actual, bona fide, *bawling*!)

His distaff antagonist readied one more kick -- then, thought better of it! She turned to (finally) confront our, still-semi-dazed, hostess -- who'd remained clinging, tightly, to that sturdy handle, on the front door!

"Do you *know*?" my fellow interloper asked, in a husky whisper. "Do you *know* ... have any *idea* ... who this son of a bitch is? Who he fucking *is*?"

"My ... my *husband*?"

"Can you send the little girl ... to her room? Or someplace? She doesn't need to ..."

"Trinity?" said the woman -- weakly. She'd finally turned loose, of the stupid front door. Then, she'd locked it -- with an accentuated, "ShowTime", exaggeratedly-deliberate, motion. "Trinity?" she repeated. "Don't worry, Baby. This'll all work out all right, Everything's going to be all right. Don't worry, Sweetheart. But, right now, I need for you, to go back there ... back to your room! Don't come out, Baby! Not till I come ... and get you! And don't worry! It's all over! And it's all ... it's all right"

Obediently, the girl arose! And looked, in desperation, toward her mother -- who'd, valiantly, tried to shoehorn as much encouragement, into her, badly-shaken, smile, as was possible.

The girl's look, of desperation, disappeared! To be replaced -- by some sort of indescribable, almost-enigmatic, expression! This -- as she gazed down, at her, in-definite-pain, father! After what seemed like an eon or two, she made her, highly-unsteady, way, to the rear -- of the one-story domicile.

The lady of the house then approached Ruthie -- while totally ignoring, the still-pain-wracked, form, of the floored Rudy. She, in fact, almost had to step over him!

"Now," she inquired -- in a tone, more emotion-free than I could've imagined -- "Can you ... please ... tell me what this is all about? Please?"

"Yeah," answered Ruthie -- in an, equally-emotion-free, tone. "I was his wife. Or did he ever mention That? Ever mention ... Ruth Peters?"

The question brought an even more emphatic, sob-laden groan -- from the floored, still agony-wracked, Rudy! But, no one was paying attention!

"No," answered the woman. "He never did. I'm Beverly Mortimer ... Beverly O'Neil Mortimer. We've been married ... Rudy and I ... for almost eleven years. Ever since we found out ... that I was pregnant, you know. Pregnant, with Trinity."

"And he's never mentioned ... being married before? Father of twins? And father of yet another child? A little girl? One who'd be fairly close ... to Trinity's age? He never mentioned that? Never mentioned those? None of them? None of those? None of this?"

"No! Never! Nothing! Not at all!"

"Well, he was! He did! And he saw to it ... that I lost the kids! My twins!"

"Because she was a fucking whore! That's why!" Rudy had summoned enough strength -- to have made that labored, very-hoarse, observation. "A fucking whore!" he labored on. "That's what she was! That's what she is!" He was running on empty, by then! "Just ask her," he managed to wheeze.

Then, the life seemed to go out of him. The only way to tell -- that he was still alive -- was his continued, loud, labored, attempts, at breathing! And the continued writhing!

"But," asked Beverly, disregarding the agony, in which her husband was immersed, "you did?" She stared down, at the beleaguered man! "You did father three kids? Three kids? By this woman?"

"With that ... with that ... that bitch", he managed to respond -- experiencing even more difficulty.

"He's right," affirmed Ruthie. "This bitch! But, let me tell you: He was so damn cruel to me! Beat me! Lots of times! To say nothing ... of his never getting off his worthless ass. Could never be bothered ... getting a damn job! And ... like I said ... he beat the hell out of me! On three separate occasions. At least three times!"

"You had it coming, Bitch," was Rudy's, still-strained, reply. "You fucking had it coming!" The last five words -- seemed to really drain whatever energy that had remained -- from his, badly-battered, frame!

"He's also right," affirmed Ruthie. "I did become a whore! I was out in California! I ran away from him! In Detroit! Couldn't put up with him! Not anymore! And he wouldn't hear of such things ... as a goddam divorce! Religious soul ... that he is! I gave our baby ... our new baby ... up for adoption! Rather than subject her ... to life with this bastard! That really pissed him off! He beat the shit out of me! Kicked me ... like this!"

She unleashed another, even-more-vicious, kick -- at our fallen host! His same, belabored, ribcage! The result caused him even more agony! Just when he'd thought that to be impossible!

"So," Ruthie explained, "I had to run! Had to split! Had no other choice!"

"I guess ... I guess, that I can see that," responded Beverly.

"But, you see?" continued Ruthie. "He tracked me down! Found me! Turned me in! To the authorities! I lost the kids! My twins! And I wound up ... in fucking jail! For a good, long, fucking, period of time! Never could find up what happened to my kids ... who I've always loved! Loved ... dearly! But, I couldn't find 'em! Either of 'em!"

"Good Lord," gushed our hostess. "There's no ..."

"They ... the authorities ... they weren't going to give me that information," lamented Ruthie. "Not to a documented whore! One lady ... at Child Protective Services, though ... she did assure me! Did assure me ... that the twins, had been adopted. She said that they were in a good home! Good environment! Told me that!" She looked down at the, seemingly-to-improve-slightly, Rudy. "Damn you," she hissed. "Damn you ... to hell! God damn you! You son of a bitch! You no-good bastard!"

She kicked him again! Mercilessly! This time -- in his other ribcage!

"I don't know how he ever found his way ... to Grand Island," continued Ruthie. "But, he ..."

"I was fucking born here," wheezed the fallen man. "Fucking born here!"

"He was always cheating on me, too," furnished Beverly. "Tried to divorce him, I did! But, you're right. Religious bastard that he is ... he wouldn't give me one, either. I've been saving up, you know ... a dollar here, a dollar there ... to hire me a lawyer! Hopefully, a real son of a bitch shyster lawyer! One who'd come down on him! With both feet! Listen! He's always kept me ... on a really tight leash! Especially, whenever it came to finances! And ... once ... he also beat the crap out of me, too! I told him ... warned him, then ... that, if he ever tried that again, he'd better damn well kill me! Kill me dead! Because I would ... for sure ... kill him! Kill his ass!"

"How about your little girl?" I asked -- finally entering the conversation. "Your little Trinity! How much does she know? About all of this? Any of this?"

"Well, you know kids," came the reply. "You can't hardly put anything past 'em! Past kids ... nowadays! Especially something this serious! This pervasive! This long-lasting!"

"You're just ... you're just ... !" Rudy was trying to speak, once again! Obviously, not with a great amount of success!

"Help me drag him downstairs," Beverly pleaded. Not to me! But, to Ruthie! "Give me a hand! Help me ... in dragging his no-good ass! Dragging it ... down! Down ... into the basement"

Surprisingly -- at least to my shocked psyche -- my partner agreed! Readily! Each woman grabbed a foot -- and yanked Rudy, in labored fits and starts! They pulled him -- through the dinette! Then, through the kitchen! Eventually, I could hear three bumps! Loud ones! Presumably his head, bouncing, off the steps -- down, to the landing, by the side door! After that, a whole bunch of, almost-deafening, clobbers -- altogether different sounds -- as he was, mercilessly, yanked, down the wooden steps, and into the basement!

Then, two or three minutes later, Beverly -- alone -- reappeared, in the living room! Ignoring me she grabbed her purse -- from atop the marble coffee table -- and headed, once again, for the lower level!

The next sounds I heard were totally unexpected! Totally! There were two of them! Both were, kind-of-hollow-sounding, "pops"! Almost like a couple of firecrackers going off! But, I knew that they could've been nothing else -- other than actual gun shots! Yeah! Gun shots! Bullets!

Let me introduce you to my new "sister": Beverly Conacher Gibson. And to my new "niece": Trinity Gibson.

"The Girls" -- Ruthie and Beverly -- came up with that "adopted" last name. I guess Beverly was a bit, of a baseball fan. And Bob Gibson -- the nonparallel

St. Louis Cardinals pitcher -- was still fairly near the top, of his game. So -- why <u>not</u>? Why not <u>Gibson</u>?

The whole ensuing series of scenarios were all products -- of the, incredibly-devious, minds, of "The Girls"! Guys -- <u>never</u> try and match wits (or come up with devious plans) against women. Especially when they are, obviously, hell-bent on some kind of (ah) <u>cover</u> up!

First of all, these ladies conducted a thorough, painstakingly-long, search -- of the entire house! They packed away anything (and everything) that could <u>possibly</u> tie them, to the identity -- of the, freshly-minted, corpse, in the, blood-splattered, cellar. A couple of giant garbage bags -- filled, to the brim, with incriminating stuff -- wound up, in the trunk of my Chrysler.

Following that, obviously-necessary, operation, they packed up virtually all the clothing -- and personal effects -- of Beverly and Trinity. Filled three, full-sized, suitcases -- plus a smaller "overnighter", and (yet) another garbage bag. All <u>that</u> gear also wound up, in the Chrysler'! In the back seat!

"The Girls", then, descended back into the morgue/basement -- leaving my new "niece" and me, to cringe, in the living room. (A form of "bonding", I guess it was.) Bev and Ruthie emptied the unfortunate Rudy's wallet -- relieving him, of upward of $700! (The amount was a <u>shock</u> to me. But, not to either of "The Girls".) They'd -- ever so carefully -- replaced the decrepit billfold, leaving a ten, a five, and four ones, therein. (Was that generous -- or what?)

Then, off we all went!

Our first stop: A small, family-run, motel -- on the outskirts of town. They'd had a suite, consisting of living room, kitchen, and two bedrooms available. Ruthie checked us in -- under her own name. Surprisingly (to me, anyway) she'd still retained a Michigan driver's license. One with her old -- really old -- Romulus, address listed. If someone's address had to be recorded -- that was (obviously) the one to be shown.

Then, both of "The Girls" changed -- into shorter skirts. (Flagrantly shorter -- in Beverly's case.)

Ruthie and Trinity piled, into the Chrysler -- and Bev and I, into the Caddy. We drove to the nearest Cadillac dealership -- and "we" sold the nifty convertible, to the used car manager. He'd wanted to steal the car from us -- as always. But, showing a shameless helping of shapely leg, Beverly (who -- for the scenario -- was my "wife") "talked him" into throwing an additional $350, into the mix. The poor guy was pretty "withered" -- by the time we'd vacated the lot.

I'd signed the title over -- as the sainted Rudolph Mortimer! Then, we all squeezed, into the Chrysler --- and headed back to the hotel. One down!

The following morning -- after a, somehow-rewarding, breakfast at *Denny's* -- we all made our way, to a Chevrolet dealership, on the far side of town.

Dealers didn't ask all those many questions -- in those "unsophisticated" days. At least, not in that part of Nebraska. My "sister" bought a, stylish, three-year-old, Monte Carlo. Again -- aided, and abetted, by a generous display of leg. She bought it, in the name of Beverly C. Gibson. She probably paid a couple hundred dollars too much, for the vehicle. "Point of least resistance" -- and all that! Two down!

About halfway back to the hotel, we stopped -- at a payphone -- and Bev phoned Police Headquarters, "alerting" them to the "possibility" of a dead body, in the basement, of her former residence.

Then, hurriedly, we returned to the hotel!

Why, you may ask, did we bother -- to remain, in Grand Island? As opposed to simply "running like hell"? To the hinterlands?

Again, a part of the, well-thought-out, grand plan -- as formulated, in the evil brains of "The Girls". They were of a mind -- to follow local news reports! Bulletins -- latest reports -- covering the demise, of my new "sister's" once-spouse! (Hard to follow those things -- in Detroit.)

FIVE

Six days later, a Chrysler, and a Monte Carlo, made their way -- eastward. Taking care -- to observe all speed limits.

Why did we wait almost a week -- before abandoning the "scene of the crime"? Well, for one thing, we were all -- as previously indicated -- more than just a tad interested, in the local media's coverage, of the fate of one Rudolph Mortimer. But, additionally, there was the, more-than-trifling, matter, of a car title! The paperwork -- pertaining to Beverly's Monte Carlo.

"The Girls" had decided to list the street address, of the hotel -- in which we'd remained ensconced -- as the "residence" address, in applying for the new title. The hope was that -- whoever would issue the paperwork, in Lincoln, the State Capital -- would not be aware, of the fact that the location was <u>not</u> anything, other than a private residence. <u>Success</u>! It took five days -- for the cherished document to arrive. But, it <u>did</u> get there! And everything, shown, on the official certificate, was "in order"!

Surprisingly -- or not -- there had not been much news coverage, of the murder itself. Nothing close -- to the volume, that we'd all expected. (Maybe even looked forward to?) Even during the first two, or three, days. By the time we were all ready to depart "This Vale of Tears" (quoth Beverly), news of "the crime" had seemed to have dried up -- completely.

Knowing her late husband, as well as she did, Beverly was lead-pipe certain -- that there would never have been any insurance money, to collect. Apparently, the presumption was accurate. But, we didn't want to risk our, rather-precarious, positions -- in an attempt, to find out "for sure".

"He never thought of anyone ... but, himself," observed his secret widow. "Ever! He'd never 'squander' ... which, in his mind, is what he'd be doing ... wouldn't 'waste' a penny ... and go ahead, and actually leave something, for anyone else! Not in a million years!"

As far as finances were concerned, my new "sister" and "niece" came out, pretty much, ahead of the game. But, only slightly. The fortunate "Rudy's wallet windfall" -- was, probably, the difference. They'd possibly given away a few bucks -- vis-a-vis the sale of the Cadillac. But, the well-kept, well-maintained, model had proved to be a good deal more valuable -- than the price, of the Monte Carlo. Which allowed them to pay a little over the normal market value, for the Chevrolet. About as well as they could've hoped to have come away with. Especially given the, filled-with-intrigue, circumstances, looming behind the scenes. This -- from a pure dollars-and-cents standpoint.

So? So, it was off to Birmingham, Michigan!

John and Gene -- my two former employers, and continuing benefactors -- were, of course, magnificent, in their concern. A monumental help -- as always -- in the massive amount of critical assistance they'd offered! And the, from-the-heart, encouragement!

I'd. of course, leveled with them -- completely. All the way down the line -- when it came to the town's newest pair of citizens.

Gene was able to speak -- off the record -- to the detective, who'd brought the existence of Rudolph Mortimer, to our attention. Apparently, someone from the Grand Island Police Department had made a perfunctory call -- "very perfunctory" -- to determine whether his inquiry might've had anything to do with the demise, of their esteemed citizen. According to Gene, it didn't take much, for the Birmingham cop to convince the caller -- that the inquiry had been totally unrelated, to the "untimely" fate, of Mr. Rudolph.

"I think," advised my friend/benefactor, "that the son of a bitch may have had a bit of a reputation, out there. It didn't seem like they were all that interested ... not at all anxious ... in moving heaven and earth, to find the 'fiend' who did him in."

Fortunately, my landlady was expecting a new vacancy -- "in the next week, or so". Ergo, we'd all "squeezed in" -- into my modest "diggings" -- for eight, wholly-crammed, days. There were a few, understandable, breeches of modesty/privacy -- as the duration had worn on. But, nothing serious. Thankfully, none involved Trinity.

Eventually, the "Gibsons" found themselves set up -- in their "glorious" (quoth Trinity) new residence.

John›s wife had a close friend (what else?) -- who›d owned a thriving bookkeeping/tax accounting service. It happened that he›d needed a junior clerk -- and he hired Beverly, on the spot. The salary was anything, but staggering -- but, fortunately, sufficient enough, to allow my newest "relatives" to exist; in their, rent-reasonable, apartment. And to buy an adequate amount of groceries, for the nonce.

We -- Ruthie and I -- got to babysit Trinity. ("Sit on me" -- according to the young lady, herself.) She was a positive joy! Almost "The Daughter I Never Had". And she "adopted" me -- as her surrogate father! Almost immediately! I can't tell you how rewarding that was!

Another stroke of good fortune: There was an ice cream parlor -- located a-block-and-a-half away. Trinity and I spent a goodly amount -- of our "quality time" -- there! The two waitresses there loved her. (They were not the only ones!)

Of course, there was the matter -- of getting "The Young 'Un" enrolled, in school. I felt that -- if anything -- this would be our weak link. If the Birmingham School System started nosing around Grand Island's School System -- the absolute best we would be able to hope for, would have them finding no record, of a "Trinity Gibson". And, simply, returning the inquiry. Anything more serious? Well, we'd have to handle that factor -- if/as/when it ever reared its ugly head!

Obviously, the biggest danger was the child's first name! How many Trinitys -- could there be? In the whole -- of Grand Island, Nebraska? And -- should they turn up a Trinity Mortimer -- the name of the daughter, of the man who'd, so recently, "assumed room temperature" -- would that little nugget not raise, an eyebrow or two, out west? Despite the police force, out there, apparently not being all that determined, to bring Rudy's killer to justice?

Again, my good fortune: John's wife had had three close friends (what else?) -- whose, most-cooperative, fannies were all seated, on the Birmingham School Board. She was able to convince each of them -- that they should simply "work around" the girl's previous record.

Admittedly, in these "more sophisticated", "advanced", days, everything is listed -- in some computer! Somewhere! Today, you cannot scratch your bottom -- without it appearing, in a multitude, of someone's software! Somewhere! (Listing, undoubtedly, which cheek -- and how many strokes!)

But -- denks God -- those seventies, "Neanderthal", days were, fortunately, in full-flower! That was over 40 years ago! Things, back then, were not quite that efficiently "structured"! (Not even close! Again -- our good fortunate!)

So, it came to pass -- that the newly-minted "Gibson Family" was able to settle in! And, for the next few years, live what could be considered a fairly-normal existence. Quite a change -- for them!

During the ensuing years, little changed -- between Ruthie, and myself. I'd pressed -- often -- for her hand, in marriage. "You'd have to take all of me," was her, ever-constant, reply. But, then she'd always turn me down! Always!

"I'm not worthy of you," she'd continually remark.

"Not worthy of me? That's patently ridiculous!"

However, no matter how impassioned -- or how "logical" -- my argument might've been, she'd always rejected it. I'd never abandoned the pursuit, though! Still, each heart-felt foray -- into the subject -- met with the same, frustrating, response! Always!

I continued to man the piano/bar, at Vi's little bastion of social civility, on Cass Avenue. Two or three times a month, Ruthie would journey down there with me. She'd accumulated the opinion that Vi was never overwhelmingly happy to see her -- but, I don't think that was the actual fact. (Well, close -- maybe.)

The police (finally) cleaned up the "Sidewalk Stewardess" situation, in the bar's immediate environs -- and, fortunately, that allowed the number of attendees, patronizing the bar, to increase. And improve. Both in size -- and in character. Vi opined that the new state of affairs was, undoubtedly, "just as well". She'd allowed as how she was getting "too old to be throwing people the hell out".

Beverly was proceeding well, in her job. Had, in fact, received two promotions -- and had, over her first year there, attained the "rank", of "Number Three", in the office; positioned just below the owner, and the lady who'd "managed the joint". The raises in pay -- most assuredly -- helped!

Ruthie and I continued to -- more or less -- babysit Trinity, although she was growing like the proverbial "weed". I was still able, however, to treasure those, ice cream-laden, sessions with her -- on most afternoons.

I was particularly thrilled -- that she'd, long since, begun, to actually call me "Dad"! Thrilled -- down to my toenails! Me! A "dad"! Can you imagine? It doesn't get any better -- than that!

As 1975 was drawing to an end, I was beginning to notice "little things" -- having to do with Ruthie. She was becoming, slightly, more and more forgetful. Not senile, mind you -- although she did mistake December 24th for Christmas Day, that particular year. I'd thought that -- on the few occasions, when she'd not donned her panties -- that she was simply trying to "send a subliminal, suggestive, message" to me. But, the fact that she was sans underpants -- meant that she'd just "plain-assed forgot" to step into them. (I'd always "forgiven" her!)

Then, on the sixth of January -- 1976 -- Vi fielded a call, at about 11:15PM. It was from a, semi-hysterical, Beverly! Ruthie had been rushed to the hospital!

I, of course, dropped everything -- and headed, for the medical unit! At speeds -- far in excess of the legal limit! My, newly-added, family awaited me there!

The doctor advised me (along with Beverly, and Trinity) that Ruth had suffered "a sort of seizure"! One about which very little was known -- at least, in the mid-seventies. The medical team -- three doctors devoted to her care -- were "quite frankly, stumped". They'd even called in a specialist -- from *Henry Ford Hospital*, in Detroit! But, as of the time, of the consultation, he'd not yet arrived!

Before he was able to get there -- my true love died! I was, obviously, devastated!

But, I'd have been more destroyed -- had she not performed one last, valiant, heroic, act:

It was, patently, painfully, plain -- that she was struggling to speak! In her labored voice, she asked that the three of us stand before her. Which, of course, we did.

"Bob and Beverly," she rasped, "I want the two of you to get together! At least, I want you to ... to think about it! Consider it! You two ... you go together! Like toast and butter! And Trinity ... she needs a father! Not one who just babysits her ... or even takes her, for forbidden amounts of ice cream. But, a real ... live-in, bona fide ... dad! Bob? Bob, you're as close as they come! Now I want you to go ... go all the way! I want the two of you to ... seriously ... consider it! Consider marriage! Getting married ... the two of you! Consider ..."

With that, she "left us"!

Both Bev and I had been weeping -- more or less silently! But, we both burst out -- crying loudly! It was at that point -- that I was touched more deeply than, I think, at any time in my life: Trinity took each of our larger hands -- into her, substantially-smaller, right one! It was at that point that the two of us -- the adults, in the room -- stopped the bawling! Ceased! Cold!

Beverly and I recently celebrated our <u>thirtieth</u> wedding anniversary! Almost immediately, after Ruthie's death, we'd <u>moved</u>! Physically changed addresses! We'd had to get away from that, once-enchanted, building. It could never be the <u>same</u>! Not without <u>Ruthie</u>!

We bought a huge, 25-year-old, two-story, Tudor, house -- a few miles north of Birmingham. Near that fabled, storied, strawberry-and-whipped-cream, restaurant.

Trinity seemed to understand (and accept) the fact that we weren't (yet) married. She <u>was</u> able to remain, in her "old" school -- which was a bigger help than we could ever have imagined. It meant a few-mile drive every day -- to deliver her, and to retrieve her. Small price to pay.

Bev had -- eventually -- moved up, at work. To where she was named assistant -- to the owner, of the tax business. Then, about ten years ago -- when <u>he'd</u> retired -- she <u>bought</u> the firm. That first-mentioned, long-ago, promotion had turned out -- to be a genuine Godsend. Back then, we were becoming -- more and more -- afraid, that she'd bitten off a little more than she could've chewed, from a financial point of view. Since then, though, everything had always gone exceptionally <u>well</u>!

Vi -- also eventually -- gave up the bar. This was, in the late-eighties. Gene had passed away a year before -- and John would die, about a year later.

❖

I was able to open my own bar -- a half-block (across Woodward Avenue) from where that sainted, original, *Standard Oil* gas station had been located. I hired a very talented man -- to manage the joint. He and another man -- that he'd hired -- served as our primary bartenders.

Carl -- the manager -- had a small stage installed. He went on -- to book-in various instrumental groups (trios or quartets, for the most part), as well as the occasional singer. All proved to be extremely-talented musicians.

As soon as she became "of age" (well, actually, she was nineteen-and-a-half) one of those singers turned out to be one (and there was only one) Trinity Conacher.

In an age, where rock had become king, "Miss Trinity" truly wowed 'em -- by doing schmaltzy, "cornball", songs! Tunes that her father (i.e. me) had made his livelihood performing. Of course, our night-in/night-out clientele was substantially "more mature", than your "normal" rock-concert crowd. And that helped. Immensely!

But, my wondrous daughter did possess an enormous amount of pure talent!

After not-quite-seven years, of my having acquired the bar, "The Wife" and I retired. The pair of us. We've both gotten ourselves involved -- in "a little bit of writing". Bev authors a weekly column -- on finances -- for *The Detroit News*. And I've written a novel or six -- all of which have sold reasonably well.

Our glorious daughter? She went on, to be a TV talk-show hostess -- on Channel 4, in "The Motor City". A top-rated show!

They say there's no such thing -- as "living happily ever after". But, by golly, we've come close! As near to that glorious goal -- as is possible!

THE END